THE HELIOS CONSPIRACY

A SPECTRE THRILLER

C.W. LEMOINE

This book is a work of fiction. Names, characters, places, and incidents are either products of the author's imagination or used fictitiously. Any resemblance to actual events or locales or persons living or dead is entirely coincidental. The views in this book do not represent those of the United States Air Force Reserve or United States Navy Reserve. All units, descriptions, and details related to the military are used solely to enhance the realism and credibility of the story.

Cover artwork by Joseph Duncan

This book is dedicated to you, the reader. Thank you for making this amazing journey possible.

THE *SPECTRE* SERIES:

"Victory is reserved for those who are willing to pay its price."

— Sun Tzu

PROLOGUE

Louis Armstrong New Orleans International Airport

G ulfJet Ten Fifteen, climb and maintain one-two thousand, turn left heading two-seven-zero, cleared for takeoff Runway Two," the First Officer heard the female controller say over his David Clark Pro-X noise cancelling headset.

"GulfJet Ten Fifteen, climbing to one-two thousand, left turn two-seventy, cleared for takeoff," replied Captain Mark Heck before turning to his First Officer. "You're cleared for takeoff, PA is complete, lights are on, your airplane."

"My airplane," came the reply as the First Officer pushed the 737's throttles forward. He paused momentarily as the digital N1 readout on the engine display read 40% and then clicked the Take-

Off/Go Around (TOGA) button. His left hand rode the throttles forward as the autothrottles engaged, stopping as it reached the pre-determined takeoff thrust.

"Thrust set, ninety-point-five N1," Captain Heck announced. He looked down and saw that his First Officer's hand was still gripping the throttles and slapped the hand away. "Thrust is set, my throttles."

"Sorry."

First Officer Cal "Spectre" Martin resisted the urge to respond with a knifehand to the throat. It was only his second flight out of training and he was still on probation. The skills he had acquired from his previous life as an F-16 pilot were no longer useful in his transition to the civilian world. As ridiculous as he thought it was that he couldn't control his own throttles, he withdrew his hand, focusing on guiding the 737-800 down the dark runway.

"80 knots," Captain Heck called out.

"Check."

The 737 smoothly accelerated as the runway lights zipped by. "V1," was the call from the aircraft annunciator.

"Rotate," Captain Heck directed

Spectre gently pulled back on the yoke and the nose of the aircraft lifted off the runway. Moments later they were airborne.

"Positive rate," Captain Heck called.

"Gear up, please," Spectre said. It was still weird to him to have someone else in the cockpit. After spending much of his career flying solo, it was a major adjustment. "Flaps up," he added as they accelerated.

"GulfJet Ten Fifteen, contact departure. So long," the controller said.

Captain Heck contacted the New Orleans departure controller as Spectre climbed and started his turn to the west.

"Whoa whoa, where are you going?" Heck asked with a bewildered look.

"We were given two-seven-zero on climbout," Spectre replied. He was confused by his Captain's surprise and worried that he may have missed a new clearance. "Weren't we?"

"Yes," Captain Heck replied sharply. "But I didn't spin your heading bug."

"What?"

"FM Part One specifically states that the Pilot Flying shall not make any turns without the Flight Director either in LNAV or in Heading Select Mode with the heading bug set to the appropriate heading," Heck said, reaching up and spinning the Heading Select knob on the Mode Control Panel until Spectre's heading bug sat atop 270 on his heading display.

"You're kidding, right?" Spectre asked as he resumed his turn.

"Excuse me?" Captain Heck asked gruffly. "The Flight Manual is your Bible, son. There's nothing to joke about."

"Copy," Spectre said, engaging the autopilot. He was starting to regret his life choices.

In the last five years he had gone from a combat F-16 pilot, to a light attack pilot for a covert paramilitary organization, to a Senator's Veterans Outreach Rep, to an A-10 pilot. After realizing that the bureaucracy of the military wasn't for him anymore, he had looked to the airlines as the next logical step. With mandatory retirements and a looming pilot shortage, they were hiring in droves.

But despite Spectre's combat experience, he didn't have the requisite flight time to get hired by one of the majors. So he settled for an Ultra-Low Cost Carrier startup based in New Orleans – GulfJet Airlines. It was merely a stepping stone to something he hoped would one day provide for his infant son, but for the time being, Spectre wasn't too thrilled with it. He felt like a glorified bus driver.

Captain Heck ran through the climb and cruise checklists as Spectre focused on flying. It was a quiet night on the radio, one of the benefits of flying for an airline that tried to take advantage of "after hours" flying to take business from the other budget airlines. Their flight to San Antonio would be pretty short, and with a quick turnaround planned, he'd be back in New Orleans before two A.M.

Spectre leveled off at their final cruise altitude of thirty-two thousand feet and slid his seat back. He looked out the window at the swamp below as the Captain started ranting about something in their contract.

The light from the full moon clearly illuminated the Gulf of Mexico and Louisiana coast. It reminded him of his mission with Kruger and his team to take down Jun Zhang on the Chinese oil platform. It had been such dangerous times, but in hindsight, a lot more fun than droning around on autopilot listening to a guy who probably should've retired five years ago complain about whatever it was he was bitching about.

"Calvin, did you hear me?" Captain Heck asked gruffly as Spectre continued to stare out the window.

"Huh?"

"The latest email from the company. Can you believe they want us to clean up the cabin between flights? That's embarrassing for the profession! Do I look like a janitor?" Captain Heck asked angrily.

"No, sir."

"Exactly! What if the passengers see that? They'll have no confidence in us. It's bad enough that we have to wear these stupid green shirts and tacky ties. Whatever happened to the traditional white shirt and black tie uniforms? I mean, I know the company has only been around for a couple of years, but this is ridiculous. It's not in the contract!"

Spectre shrugged. "I'm just the new guy," he offered.

"Yeah, but by the time you're off probation, we'll probably have a Tentative Agreement. And you'll be voting on it. Where did you fly before?"

"This is my first airline."

"Well, where were you before?"

"Military."

"Well, sport, you're in the big leagues now. You need to know what the company can and *can't* do. I am personally going to vote *no* regardless of what they put on the table. They need to know who's running this show."

"Right," Spectre said as he looked back out the window. He thought about his wife and son back home. As much as he hated adjusting to his new mission in life, their happiness was more important than anything else in the world. The job would one day provide a stable future for little Calvin and allow him to have more time off at home. He knew he just had to pay his dues to get there first.

But it wasn't like he hadn't paid his dues before. He had lost a kidney in the defense of his country, and nearly lost the love of his life several times as he rooted out corruption at the highest levels and even saved the President. He had paid his dues for his country, but now he was paying for the opportunity to have a normal life with Michelle and Calvin. It was a trade he would gladly make any day of the week.

The rest of the flight was quiet as Captain Heck finally took the hint that Spectre didn't want to bitch about the contract, work rules, pay, or the company. They set up for the approach into San Antonio. It was a clear night, so they planned to use the Instrument Landing System (ILS) to back-up the visual approach. Spectre briefed the approach and then focused on managing the autopilot as they descended toward the city.

As they set up on final, Spectre confirmed that the gear was down and that the flaps were set appropriately as Captain Heck ran through the Before Landing checklist. The 737 wasn't quite as nimble as the fighters he had flown before, but it was a fun challenge to land.

Reaching the last five hundred feet, the winds were somewhat gusty. He felt something binding the controls. Fighting through it, he looked over to see the Captain's hands on the controls with him.

"Are you flying or am I flying?" Spectre asked angrily.

"You're flying. I'm just helping."

"Please don't," Spectre snapped.

Spectre continued down toward the runway as the resistance subsided. As the Ground Proximity Warning System called out thirty, Spectre began to flare. He pulled the yoke back, once again encountering resistance as he retarded the throttle to idle. Suspecting that the Captain was once again on the controls with him, Spectre quickly looked over, only this time, the Captain's hands were on his knees.

I can't fucking believe it, he thought as he continued fighting the resistance, and turned his attention back to the runway. The yoke was being impeded by the Captain's gut. The last inch of travel needed to make a smooth landing wasn't going to happen, and the aircraft hit the runway with a shudder before the nosewheel slammed down.

"Were you a Navy guy?" the Captain quipped. "This ain't an aircraft carrier, sport. Anyway, speedbrakes deployed."

Spectre slowed the aircraft and the Captain took over taxiing duties. It was just after midnight, and the airport seemed dead. They taxied to the gate, and completed the Parking Checklist as the engines spooled down.

"Alright sailor, go say bye to the folks," Captain Heck said with a cheesy grin. "He who lands, stands."

As Spectre stood, he pulled out his phone and turned it on. After it finished powering up, he noticed that he had a voicemail. He listened to it as he opened the cockpit door and put on his hat.

"Cal, it's me. Call me as soon as you get this. It's an emergency." It was Michelle's voice. Spectre's stomach turned.

"God, please let my family be ok," he said under his breath as he pushed past the standing customers waiting for the gate agent to open the door.

He hurried off the aircraft as the cabin door was opened. He dialed Michelle's cell phone and ran up the jetbridge.

"Cal, can you talk?" Michelle answered.

"Are you ok? Is Calvin ok?" Spectre asked frantically as he stepped into the empty terminal and tried to get away from the passengers waiting to board.

"We're fine, but there's something else. It's not good."

"What is it? Is Bear ok?" Spectre asked. His childhood mentor "Bear" Jennings was the only other person in the area that he considered to be family.

"Bear is fine. He's here now. It's not any of us. It's Kruger."

"Kruger?" Spectre asked, trying to catch his breath. His heart felt like it was about to pound through his chest. "Mack?"

"I just got a call from Director Chapman," Decker said and then hesitated. Chapman was the director of the Central Intelligence Agency.

"Cal, Kruger is dead."

"What?" Spectre yelped as he sat down near an empty gate. "No way. When? How?"

"This morning. There was a gas explosion at their office in Falls Church. Jeffrey Lyons was killed too. Julio Meeks is missing," Decker said with a sniffle as she choked back tears.

"No way," Spectre said softly. He was in shock. "What about the others?"

"The CIA doesn't exactly keep tabs on the team, but Director Chapman told me they were on a mission for the Agency and lost comms. Everyone's gone, Cal. Odin is gone," Decker said with a sob.

"Do you trust Chapman?" Spectre asked.

"He has no reason to lie to us, Cal. He knows we're out of the game. He said he wanted to call me when he saw the names on the report. He knows we were still friends with them. Cal, it's awful. They're all dead!"

As Spectre struggled to find the words, he looked up to see Captain Heck huffing and puffing as he waddled up to where Spectre was sitting.

"This is no time for personal calls, champ. We've got thirty minutes until pushback!" Captain Heck barked.

"I'll be home in a few hours. We'll figure it out in the morning. Try to get some rest, sweetie," Spectre said, ignoring the Captain.

"We have to go, *now*," Captain Heck said, tapping his watch.

"I love you baby. Kiss Calvin for me. See you in the morning," Spectre said, holding up a finger to Heck.

"I love you too. Be careful. I'll be up when you get home," Decker said.

Spectre said goodbye and hung up.

"You're on probation and personal calls are not allowed on duty," Heck barked.

"Sorry. A friend of the family died," Spectre said, looking up at the captain with glassy eyes.

"Well, suck it up. We've got to stay on schedule!"

Spectre stood, towering over the portly captain as the two went toe to toe. Captain Heck cowered slightly as Spectre leaned in.

"If you don't show some respect, the schedule will be the least of your worries, bub," Spectre growled, channeling his fallen friend. "Got it?"

Captain Heck nodded slowly as his shoulders slumped in defeat.

"Good. Now, let's go," Spectre said as he stuffed his phone in his pocket and walked back to their gate.

CHAPTER ONE

Rome, Italy
Two Months Earlier

Nicholas Stone stared at his three fingers of whiskey as the reflection of the flames from the fireplace danced across the glass. He had retired to his villa's study to enjoy a nightcap in peace after a dinner with friends that could only be described as tense.

"Sir, Mr. Lyons is here to see you," his faithful assistant Charles said, poking his head past the study's large wooden door.

The large leather chair squeaked as Stone turned and placed the whiskey on a nearby coffee table. He frowned as he nodded to Charles. "Send him in," he said with a soft sigh.

Charles opened the door further, ushering in a man with a shaved head, wearing a polo shirt and tactical pants. Jeffrey Lyons was much younger than the elder Stone, whose thinning white hair barely clung to the sides of his wrinkled forehead.

"You wanted to see me?" Lyons asked tersely as he walked in. He walked with a swagger indicative of the arrogance he had displayed earlier at dinner, which had culminated in a heated debate with the other partners.

"Please, sit," Stone said with a grandfatherly tone. "Would you like a drink?"

"I'll pass," Lyons said as he sat down on the leather couch across from Stone.

"Very well," Stone said, retrieving his own drink and taking a sip as he eyed Lyons.

Lyons shifted uneasily in his seat before breaking the silence, "Look, if this is about earlier, I—"

Stone held up his hand to silence Lyons. He had always treated the younger member like a son or grandson. It pained him to be forced to have this conversation, but he knew it was the only hope of righting the ship and saving the young man.

"You are a very passionate person, Jeff," Stone said. "You remind me a lot of myself when I was your age."

Lyons said nothing as Stone paused for effect.

"But your passion lacks discretion, and the others are very worried about the path you have chosen."

"And what path is that?" Lyons asked.

"Look in the mirror, my boy," Stone said, gesturing to Lyons' attire. "You present yourself as a soldier. This is not the look of a man with your family's prestige."

"I have been busy cleaning up the mess you made," Lyons said with a scowl. "Or have you forgotten already?"

Stone laughed. "Oh, I remember. And I also recall that it wasn't a mess for you to clean up."

"It almost started a World War!" Lyons protested.

"Indeed," Stone said. "And that was something we discussed beforehand."

"You can't seriously think what you're doing is good for America."

Stone shrugged. "In the long run, it will be."

"How do you figure?"

"Globalization is good for everyone," Stone explained. "No one country should hold absolute power."

"So you'd rather let countries like China or Russia rise to power?" Lyons asked angrily.

"There must be balance, Jeff," Stone said calmly. "Look at where you're standing right now. The Roman Empire could not last forever. The British Empire did not last forever. And until the 1990s, even the Americans were balanced by the Soviets. Since then, we've seen America emerge as a sole superpower. And look what that lack of balance has brought us – perpetual war, greed, excess, and a world financial structure on the brink of collapse. How is that good?"

"You speak of the United States like it's another country. You *are* American, or have you forgotten?" Lyons asked.

"I have five homes, and none of them are in the United States," Stone said. "I haven't been an American since 1992, when I moved here."

"So, what is your point?" Lyons asked.

"The world is bigger than just one country. Your father saw that, and now it is time for you to see it too. You have been running around the world with your team, intervening to help a corrupt, bloated, and dysfunctional government. You can't keep bailing them out, or they will never learn," Stone replied.

"How is that any different from what you're planning with Helios? Is that not intervening?"

Stone smiled. "It is, but it is an attempt to restore the balance."

"I am still an American first," Lyons said. "I will never sign off on it."

Stone frowned, shaking his head as he stared into the fire. "This is not what your father would have wanted."

"I don't care," Lyons said defiantly. "Helios is not the answer. Even Mr. Stevens agrees with me."

"Oscar Stevens is eighty-five years old and has chosen no heirs. When he dies, it will just be the three of us. I do not want to see you on the wrong side of history, my boy. That's why I'm begging you to please reconsider," Stone said.

As Lyons began to respond, he felt his phone vibrate in his pocket and pulled it out. He looked at the caller ID and excused himself. He answered as he stepped out into the hallway. A few minutes later, he returned and walked up to Stone.

"Something has come up, and I need to go," Lyons said as he held out his hand to Stone.

Stone slowly stood, accepting the young man's firm grip. "This is what I am talking about. You cannot be flying all over the world with this team of yours, fixing the problems of the American government."

"My team is what makes Odin," Lyons replied.

"Odin is a myth," Stone shot back. "It's a fantasy that died years ago. You are the only one who plays these silly games anymore."

"I'm sorry, but I have to go," Lyons repeated.

"Very well," Stone said. "But please, at least give it some thought. We all want the same thing here."

"And what's that?" Lyons asked.

"What's best for humanity, of course," Stone said.

Lyons turned and hurried out of the room. Moments after he left, Charles walked in.

"How did it go, sir?" he asked.

"Not well," Stone said, shaking his head. "Do you know where Mr. Cruz is right now?"

"I believe he's enjoying a cigar by the pool, sir," Charles replied.

Stone picked up his drink and walked out of his study. He headed down the wide hallway toward the pool area where he found Walter Cruz smoking a Cuban cigar as he enjoyed the crisp night air.

"Did you talk some sense into the boy?" Cruz asked without turning around.

"He's just as defiant as he was at dinner," Stone said as he stepped out onto the patio with Cruz.

Cruz offered him a cigar. Stone accepted, lighting up and taking a long pull.

"His team just called him," Stone said.

Cruz looked at Stone and smiled. "Trouble in the desert?" he asked with a raised eyebrow.

"I don't think it will work," Stone said. "Even if you take his team away from him, I think he'll just keep finding more men."

"His father was just as stubborn," Cruz said. "Always favoring the chainsaw instead of the scalpel."

"Well, his father never talked about running for President either," Stone said.

Cruz belted a hearty laugh. "That kid will never be President."

"President Clifton is not seeking reelection," Stone said. "It's possible."

"I won't let it happen," Cruz said ominously.

"Maybe it's not such a bad idea," Stone replied. "I never agreed with how the Johnson situation played out, but maybe if we can talk some sense into Jeff, it could be exactly what we need."

"He seemed to lack every bit of sense at dinner this evening," Cruz said. "Quite the outburst."

"He's a flag waving American," Stone said. "Maybe we can use that to our advantage."

Cruz turned to face Stone and lowered his voice. "We need to start thinking about the future."

"The future?"

"I sincerely hope that losing his team will take him down a few notches, but if it doesn't...."

"If it doesn't?"

"Then we need to talk about his continued participation with our group," Cruz said.

"You mean..."

"Yes," Cruz said flatly.

Stone shook his head. "I've known that kid since he was a baby. We can't—"

"Helios is bigger than any one man," Cruz reminded Stone.

Stone stared out into the darkness, pondering the implications of Cruz's threat. Although Lyons had shown his willingness to buck their system, Stone hadn't lost hope that the young billionaire would come around and see the greater good.

"Let me work on him some more," Stone said softly. "Maybe what's happening in Iraq will be enough to humble him."

Cruz laughed. "You are nothing if not optimistic."

"Give me three months. That's all I'm asking for," Stone said.

"Fine," Cruz said, flicking the ashes from his cigar. "But if, in three months, he is not singing our tune..."

"Then I will personally take care of it," Stone replied.

CHAPTER TWO

The bagpipes playing in the distance created a mournful soundtrack for the dreary afternoon. It was cold and wet. The light mist had just turned to rain as the two men watched the funeral proceedings conclude from their isolated vantage point.

"And then there were three," Nicholas Stone said, watching the casket being lowered into the freshly dug grave. "We're a dying breed, Walter."

"Yet it's just the two of us here," Cruz said as he opened his umbrella. "Where is young Mr. Lyons anyway?"

"You of all people should know," Stone said, turning to his old friend.

"His team's performance in Iraq was much better than I expected."

Stone let out a derisive laugh. "Delta, British SAS, a Filipino Commando, Russian Spetznaz...you didn't even look at their personnel records, did you?"

"It was simply a miscalculation," Cruz replied. "Do I need to remind you that it was *your* idea to neutralize his team in the first place?"

Stone's tone suddenly turned fatherly. "Jeff is a good kid. He's just very passionate and very hard headed."

"It's been two weeks since Rome, and he's still running around the Middle East playing soldier. I don't think your talks have worked."

"What did you expect? He won't just change his mind overnight, Walter."

Cruz turned and waved his crooked finger at Stone. "We don't have time for this. Everything needs to be in place before the meeting with our new partners. At that point, he is either with us or against us."

"Then I will handle it," Stone said, taking a step back.

Cruz shook his head. "It's too late. I have already made arrangements."

Stone's eyes widened as he gripped his umbrella tightly. "The Israeli?"

Cruz nodded.

"What about his team?" Stone asked.

"What about them?"

"The one running the team— Lyons calls him Kruger – isn't going to be an easy target. If you'd read his file, you'd know he was Army Delta and then part of Project Archangel before Jeff recruited him," Stone said.

"Project Archangel? That group Johnson ran when he was Secretary of Defense?"

Stone nodded. "Kruger was injured in Iraq, but he's still not someone to be underestimated."

"Does he have any value to our operation?" Cruz asked.

"I think the whole team does," Stone replied. "Which is why I'm asking you to give me more time to sway Lyons. Now that Stevens is dead, Helios has a much better shot if we're all in this together."

Cruz considered Stone's offer for a moment and then said, "One month."

Stone frowned and leaned in. "Give me three months. Lyons and what's left of his team are still trying to chase ghosts in the desert. I think he'll come around once that settles down. Let me work on him."

"You asked for three months two weeks ago."

"Fine, two more months."

"And if you can't?"

"Then I will personally oversee his removal," Stone replied coldly.

* * *

After the funeral, Cruz took his private jet to Newark, New Jersey, from which his private helicopter then flew him to his office in Manhattan. It was just after 9PM when his pilot gently set the helicopter down on the roof and his personal assistant, Mara, rushed out to meet him.

"Sir, Mr. Jäger is here to see you," she said as she turned to walk with him.

"Very well, my dear," Cruz replied. The Israeli was a man of precision. There was no doubt that he would be punctual for their meeting.

Mara accompanied Cruz through the roof access door and down a flight of stairs to his private elevator. It took him to his corner office on the 75th floor, which had an impressive view of World Trade Center One and the Hudson River. He sat down in his large leather chair next to the fireplace and nodded for Mara to see Jäger in.

A few moments later, Mara entered with a tall, dark haired man in a three-piece suit. He moved smoothly across the room with the poise of an athlete. His clean-shaven face showed no emotion as he scanned the room on his way to meet Cruz. It was as if every movement he made was part of a cold, ruthless calculation.

"Thank you for joining me," Cruz said as he stood to greet the man. "I'm sorry I'm late. We were held up at Newark."

"I am at your service," Jäger said graciously with a slight Hebrew accent.

Cruz smiled. It was something he had always appreciated about the man before him. There was never a question of loyalty or morality, just a severe focus on mission success. Jäger had been Shayetet 13, the Israeli equivalent of the British SAS and U.S. Navy Seals, and later Mossad, before going to work for Cruz. He had served as Cruz's most trusted security adviser and "fixer" for nearly a decade. In Cruz's mind, there was no one more qualified, and no one more dangerous.

"What have you learned?" Cruz asked.

"Lyons is still in Iraq. Two members of his team are flying back to Virginia tomorrow for medical care, along with the bodies of four others. The rest of the team is staying behind, operating with the CIA," Jäger replied.

"Do they know what we did?"

"That is not possible. Unless you give them the device we used, there is no way they will learn that we gave the ISIS commander the mission plan," Jäger said confidently.

"When the time comes, I want you to personally oversee this mission," Cruz said.

"As you wish," Jäger replied.

CHAPTER THREE

Falls Church, VA
One month later

Two armored Yukon Denali XLs pulled into the parking garage and stopped near the building's service elevator. Four serious looking men in dark suits emerged, quickly sweeping the area for threats as they escorted Nicholas Stone into the elevator.

Stone punched in his six-digit security code and the elevator ascended to Jeffrey Lyons's office. As the doors opened, Lyons stood from behind his desk and approached Stone, greeting him as the security detail spread out into the office.

"Did I get my dates mixed up? I thought we were going to do a conference call tomorrow," Lyons said as he shook Stone's hand.

"We need to talk, Jeff," Stone said with a stern look.

"Of course," Lyons replied, stepping aside and offering Stone the leather chair across from his desk. "Can I get you a drink?"

"I'm quite alright," Stone answered, before taking his seat across from Lyons.

"You ok?" Lyons asked, studying his mentor's face. "You're not going to quit on me too, are you?"

"Quit?"

Lyons chuckled softly. "Remember Kruger?"

Stone nodded. "The guy you put in charge of your team even though you barely knew him?"

"Yeah, well I guess you were right. He just walked away. Said he wanted to become a nurse," Lyons replied. "A nurse!"

Stone frowned, leaning forward as he sat on the edge of his chair and rested his elbows on the desk in front of him. "Jeffrey, I want you to listen to me very carefully."

"What is it? What's happened?"

"Son, you would be wise to do the same thing," Stone continued. "Walk away. Go back to running your businesses. Forget about Odin. Forget about the Presidency."

"I already told you I'm not going to give up like that," Lyons replied. "This team has done a lot of good for this country…for the world. As much as I hate to lose Kruger, he can be replaced. We can still make a difference."

Stone shook his head frantically. "You're not listening to me!"

"What has changed?" Lyons asked calmly. "What's going on?"

"Helios," Stone mumbled. He looked around the room, making sure no one heard him.

"Walter's fantasy?" Lyons asked with a derisive laugh. "It will never work."

"Maybe not, but if he feels like you're getting in his way…"

Lyons suddenly turned serious. "Then what? He'll lecture me? Tell me how disappointed my father would be? Well, guess what? I'm not my father, and I won't vote for something that amounts to high treason."

"It's not a vote," Stone said softly.

"The hell it isn't!" Lyons shot back. "With Stevens gone, it's just the three of us now and I'm the swing vote."

"You weren't even at the funeral."

"No," Lyons snapped. "Because I was out doing what you two don't have the balls to do anymore."

"Calm down, son," Stone said. "I'm only here with your best interests in mind."

"My best interests? How do you figure?"

"If you don't cooperate, I'm afraid Walter may try to do something foolish."

Lyons laughed. "Yeah? Him and what army? I don't know if you've noticed, but I'm the only one playing 'war games' as you called it. Don't threaten me with a good time!"

"Jeff, you can't let your ego take over here," Stone warned.

"Ego? No, this is not ego. You're not going to come here to *my* office and threaten me just because Walter is acting like a petulant child!" Lyons yelled as he stood.

"We all want what's best for society," Stone replied calmly. "Walter is just passionate about this project."

"Thousands…*Millions* will die if he has his way," Lyons said. "It's a half-cocked attempt at social engineering. I won't sign off on it, and if it he tries it, I *will* stop him."

Stone let out an exaggerated sigh as he stood. "Sometimes I wish you were less like your father."

"First, he wouldn't approve and now I'm too much like him?" Lyons asked, still angry from the thinly veiled threat earlier. "Just like Walter's plan, you're not making any sense."

"I'm sorry, Jeff. I truly am. You're like a son to me."

"Then you should know that what we're doing here is good and righteous. Do you know how many lives we've saved? How many attacks we've stopped?"

"I'm not arguing that," Stone replied. "But there comes a time when you need to look at the bigger picture and move on. What would even happen if you *did* win the Presidency? Are you going to continue running around the world with your own death squad, doing the work you don't want people to know about?"

"I'll cross that bridge when and if I get to it. In the meantime, I'm going to let my team keep hacking the mission. Neither you nor Walter will stand in our way. And if he wants to try, well, *Molon Labe*," Lyons said as he showed Stone back to the elevator.

Stone stopped and studied his protégé. "I hope you know what you're doing."

Lyons squared up with his mentor. "I will do what's best for my team and this country."

"Very well, then," Stone said dejectedly. "Thank you for taking the time to meet with me."

Lyons watched as Stone entered the elevator and his men piled in behind him. When the door closed, he returned to his desk and picked up the phone, dialing Walter's direct line.

Walter's secretary picked up on the fourth ring. "I'm sorry, Mr. Cruz is not in at the moment."

"This is important," Lyons said.

"I can take a message," the woman answered.

"No, just have him call me as soon as he gets in. We need to talk," Lyons said.

"Yes, sir, I will pass the message as soon as I see him."

Before Lyons could hang up the receiver, there was a loud buzzing sound followed by a massive explosion. Jeff Lyons looked up in time to see a massive ball of fire racing toward him.

CHAPTER FOUR

Alex "Wolf" Shepherd heard a volley of gunshots behind him as he sprinted through the narrow alleyway. The walls of the nearby buildings splintered as rounds ricocheted off and zipped past his head.

His lungs burned and his legs felt as though they would give out at any moment. Pure adrenaline propelled him through the dark, dusty streets. He was down to his Ka-bar knife to defend himself as he fled the half dozen armed men pursuing him. He had exhausted his ammunition early in the firefight.

Shepherd wasn't exactly sure who his pursuers were, but mercenary seemed to be the best description he could come up with. They appeared to be Westerners dressed in civilian clothes, but wearing tactical gear and carrying modern American weapons.

He had noticed the brand new Trijicon ACOG optics on one of their rifles shortly before the shootout began.

He exited the alley into a marketplace. It was well after midnight and there was a mandatory curfew in effect. He used the carts as cover as he zig-zagged his way to the other side.

"We know who you are, Alex Shepherd!" one of his pursuers yelled. "There's nowhere to run!"

Shepherd kept running despite the sudden urge to stop and face his attackers. He had seen them near the CIA compound in Benghazi, a place his teammate "Cowboy" had instructed him to go when they found that their safe house in Tobruk, Libya, had been compromised after their latest mission.

It had taken him nearly three days to get there. He had hoped to find Cowboy waiting for him there with a cold beer and an explanation of what the fuck was going on, and where the rest of his teammates in Tobruk were. Instead, he was greeted by a hail of bullets as soon as the Libyan militiamen guarding the CIA compound saw him, and then the mercenaries started their pursuit.

Shepherd continued through the marketplace into another alleyway. With what appeared to be a hostile CIA pursuing him, he really didn't have a backup plan. It just wasn't a contingency they had planned and briefed for. He kept running, pushing through the pain and weakness as his attackers took random shots at him.

He exited the alley onto the street. He could hear vehicles in the distance and yelling. Shepherd was out of options, but he knew he couldn't surrender. Whoever was chasing him didn't seem interested in taking him prisoner. They wanted blood.

Shepherd ducked as he heard gunfire behind him. He looked back to see headlights fast approaching. Ducking behind a parked car, he heard more gunfire, although this time it didn't seem to be aimed in his direction. He looked up to see a pickup skidding toward him as the driver fired out the window at the mercenaries.

"Get in, mate!" the driver yelled. *Cowboy!*

Without hesitation, Shepherd darted for the passenger door and jumped in. The truck sped off as the former British Special Air Service Sniper turned and tossed an AK-47 to Shepherd. "I can't bloody shoot and drive. Get to work!"

"Where the hell have you been?" Shepherd asked as he leaned out the window. He fired at the pursuing mercenaries, dropping one as they stopped their foot pursuit. They returned fire, hitting the tailgate of the pickup before Cowboy swerved onto a side street and lost them.

"Watching you piss off the whole world," Cowboy said with a grin.

"You told me to get to the CIA compound!"

"I didn't tell you to aimlessly wander up to them."

"Who the hell are those guys and why are they shooting at us?"

Cowboy shrugged as he made another hard left and pushed the accelerator to the floor. The Toyota pickup's engine roared as they started to pick up speed.

"I don't know, but I've been watching them since yesterday. I would have done the same thing you did, but I saw them moving Jenny and decided to wait and see if you'd show up. They started shooting before I could get to you," Cowboy explained.

"Jenny…that's the pilot chick, right?" Shepherd asked.

Cowboy nodded. "They had her in Flexcuffs and were moving her from another building."

"What about Tuna and the others?"

"I only saw Jenny," Cowboy said.

"We need to get her out of there and find out what the fuck is going on," Shepherd replied.

"We need to establish comms with Kruger and Coolio first," Cowboy said.

"Yeah, the radios they gave me are still tits up. Just a high pitched squeal every time I key up."

"Bad encryption," Cowboy said.

"You think they abandoned us out here? Turned off the lights and went home?"

"No idea, mate," Cowboy replied flatly. "First order of business is to attempt to reestablish comms per the SOP."

"And if we can't? It's not like we have a lot of allies out here. Those dickheads back there looked like Americans to me and they came from the CIA compound. Which means the fucking CIA is trying to kill us!"

"We don't know that yet," Cowboy replied calmly.

"They knew my name! My fucking real name. Not 'Wolf' or whatever, but Alex Shepherd!"

"Are you serious?"

"Yeah. Right before he fired off a few rounds in my direction, he yelled my name. I'm telling you, we're on our own out here. We need to get Jenny and anybody else out of there and get the fuck out of this country."

"We'll go to the airport," Cowboy said. "If I remember correctly, the CIA has a hangar with comms equipment, weapons, and extra gear. If we can get in, we can try to get in touch with Kruger and the others for an evac mission."

"Don't you think they'll be guarding something like that pretty heavily in a country like this?"

"Oh, I have no doubt, mate," Cowboy said with a sly grin.

"And we have a ka-bar and an AK-47 between us?"

"Looks like it," Cowboy replied.

"Great!"

"Don't be such a wanker! I thought you Yanks were all about having the odds stacked against you!" Cowboy said with a laugh.

"Good point," Shepherd replied, tossing the knife onto the seat next to Cowboy. "I'll keep the rifle since you Brits are afraid of them."

"Fine by me. It's more personal that way."

CHAPTER FIVE

A lright, cleared to shut'em down and parking checklist when you're ready," the captain said as the 737 rolled to a stop.

Spectre stood as the captain reached up and flicked the FASTEN BELTS switch off as the first officer rattled through the parking checklist while the engines spooled down. He turned around and raised the jumpseat, sliding it back into its storage location before carefully opening the flight deck door.

"Thanks for the ride, fellas," Spectre said.

"Anytime!" the captain replied before returning to his postflight duties.

Spectre stepped out of the cockpit and stood next to an attractive young flight attendant as she thanked the deplaning passengers. He thanked her for allowing him to ride with them and then exploited a break in the flow of people to grab his bag from the coat closet. He quickly extended the handle and then made his way up the jetbridge and into the terminal.

Entering the busy terminal, Spectre found the signs pointing to the baggage claim area and quickly navigated through the sea of travelers. He nodded to the police officer working the terminal exit and then headed for Baggage Claim Door #5 where he was to meet his ride.

As he exited the terminal, he spotted a tall brunette woman with aviator sunglasses and a dark pantsuit standing next to a black Chevrolet Tahoe. Aside from her demeanor and punctuality, the badge on her hip gave her away as the FBI agent that had been sent to escort him.

"Special Agent Tanner?" Spectre asked as he approached her.

"Good morning, Mr. Martin. Special Agent Madison Tanner," she replied, holding out her hand.

"But you can call me Maddie," she added as Spectre shook her hand.

"Thank you for meeting me, Maddie," Spectre said with a warm smile. "You can call me Cal if you'd like."

"Here, let me help you with that," she said, leaning down to take Spectre's bag.

Spectre smiled graciously as he refused Maddie's offer and wheeled his bag to the rear of the vehicle. He tossed it into the cargo area of the Tahoe and then took shotgun.

"Ok, I don't mean to come off as a fangirl or anything, but I'm a huge fan of you and your wife," Maddie said as they headed for the airport exit.

"You are?" Spectre asked with a laugh. "Are you sure you picked up the right guy?"

"I was in the academy when the Midway Island attack happened," Maddie explained. "They stopped all training and we watched it on the news in real time. It's one of the scariest things we've faced as a nation in a long time."

"Definitely wasn't much fun," Spectre said, looking out the window at passing traffic as he thought back to the attempt on the President's life.

"But Special Agent Michelle Decker! The hero of Midway. She saved the President's life. Against all odds, she persevered with the Bureau's motto of fidelity, bravery, and integrity," Maddie explained.

"I remember," Spectre replied.

"Oh, right. And you were there too, of course. But Agent Decker is a hero in the agency. I told myself right then and there I wanted to be like her one day. I was sad when she left the agency. I always wanted to work with her," Maddie continued. "I guess she had a kid or something."

"Our son," Spectre said.

"I'm so sorry!" Maddie said, finally realizing her faux pas. "Here I am going on and on about her with you right here. I'm sure you're tired of hearing about it by now."

Spectre laughed. "Not really. It's why I married her. But she's not just a national hero. She's an awesome mother, wife, and my best friend. Her heroics didn't end at Midway."

"You received a medal for being there too, didn't you?" Maddie asked.

"Participation trophy," Spectre replied with a wink. "So anyway, what can you tell me about the explosion at Jeffrey Lyons's office?"

"Yes, of course," Maddie said, suddenly turning serious. "I must say, I was surprised when my boss assigned me to pick you up for that reason. The FBI currently has no interest in the case. It's a local matter being handled by the Fire Marshal."

"An act of terror doesn't raise any eyebrows at the Bureau anymore?"

"So far, there's no evidence to suggest that it was. The Fire Marshal's preliminary report stated that they found evidence that it was a gas explosion," Maddie said. "No one suspects foul play."

"So a billionaire that has been targeted before mysteriously dies in a gas explosion, and no one thought to question it?"

"The Fire Marshal is still investigating," Maddie replied.

"What about Julio Meeks and Fred Mack?"

"Who?"

"The other victims in the attack!" Spectre growled, growing impatient that the young agent had no idea what was going on.

"I'm sorry, Mr. Martin. I really don't know any specifics beyond what I read in the summary," Maddie replied sheepishly. "Lieutenant Drake from the Fire Marshal's office and Detective Windsor from Falls Church PD will be meeting us at the scene. They should be able to answer your questions."

"No, I'm sorry," Spectre said. "I shouldn't have snapped at you."

"It's ok. Were they friends of yours?"

"They saved our lives on more than one occasion. They both have done more for this country than Michelle or I could have ever imagined," Spectre said with a soft sigh. "I can't believe they're gone."

"Wow," Maddie replied softly. "I had no idea. I thought all the victims just worked in the office for Jeffrey Lyons and his billionaire empire."

"Just promise me one thing."

"What's that?" Maddie asked.

"No matter what happens, or what you find out, stick to your core values. Don't let the bureaucracy get in the way. Find the truth and get justice for these heroes," Spectre said solemnly.

"I can almost hear Special Agent Decker saying something like that."

"It's exactly what she said to me before I left," Spectre replied.

"Then consider it done. I'm happy to help, sir."

CHAPTER SIX

The once modern office building at the edge of downtown Falls Church, Virginia, had been reduced to rubble and ash. Emergency vehicles filled a nearby parking lot and a command center had been set up next to the heavily damaged parking garage.

Spectre saw investigators and rescue workers still working their way through the debris as they drove past. Maddie parked next to a white RV labeled COMMAND CENTER and motioned for Spectre to follow.

She knocked on the Command Center door. Moments later, an older gentleman wearing a pressed white shirt with a gold badge emerged. Maddie flashed her credentials and introduced herself. The man identified himself as Lieutenant Drake and then invited them in. He introduced them to Detective Windsor, a middle-aged man wearing tactical pants and a polo shirt, and the four sat down at the rear of the RV.

"So what's your interest in this, Mr. Martin?" Lieutenant Drake asked as they sat down. Maddie had simply introduced him as Cal Martin without any further explanation.

"The victims were friends of mine."

Lieutenant Drake frowned and looked at Maddie. "This is an ongoing investigation. I was told the FBI's interest was strictly advisory, Agent Tanner."

"That's correct, Lieutenant. I've been assigned to assist in whatever way I can," Maddie replied. "Mr. Martin is here on a not-to-interfere basis."

Detective Windsor studied Spectre, sizing up the former fighter pilot. "Are you law enforcement?"

Spectre shook his head. "Just an airline pilot."

"Military?"

"In a former life."

"Mr. Martin may be able to assist with identifying the victims," Maddie interjected, trying to get things back on track.

"Already been done," Lieutenant Drake replied. "In fact, it's a pretty clean case. Gas explosion with a clearly defined electrical ignition source. I'll be filing my final report in the next few days. You can read it then."

Just as Spectre was about to speak, Detective Windsor turned to Spectre and asked, "Unless you can tell us what's in the basement, perhaps?"

"The basement?" Spectre asked.

"We found what appears to be a structure underneath the first floor of the building. It's a mix of steel and titanium. The access we found had a pretty thick vault door. We couldn't get in or cut through it. Thermal picks up nothing. We have no way to get in and assess if there are any survivors, although at this stage of the game it would likely be a recovery effort," Lieutenant Drake answered.

Spectre thought about it for a moment. Although he had never been in Odin's headquarters, he had often heard Kruger and Coolio refer to the "basement" as where the secret operations of Odin were conducted. It housed their servers, equipment, and served as their operations center. He wasn't sure what their plan was in the event of such an attack, but he was almost certain they had a fallback plan of some kind to avoid discovery.

"No idea," Spectre replied. "How many victims did you say there were?"

"I didn't, but there were six."

"What were their names?"

Detective Windsor flipped through one of the files in front of him. "Jeffrey Lyons, Lindsey Taylor, Frederick Mack, Sheila Stewart, Mark Wilson, and Julio Meeks."

Lyons, Coolio, and Kruger. Decker had mentioned that they had been victims, but Spectre didn't want to believe it. As far as he was concerned, Kruger was ten feet tall and bulletproof. There was no way the former Delta operator and warrior had been killed in a simple gas explosion. It just didn't make sense.

But the list also brought up another question. *Where was the rest of the team?* Spectre guessed that they were probably still in the field somewhere, but if that were true, surely they would have a representative on site to deal with the fallout of the attack and preserve the secrecy of their organization.

"Where are the bodies?" Spectre asked.

"In the county morgue," Lieutenant Drake replied.

"May I see them?"

Spectre saw Lieutenant Drake and Detective Windsor exchange a look before Lieutenant Drake answered. "I'm sure that can be arranged."

"Is there a problem?" Spectre asked.

"Some of the bodies were pretty severely burned, Mr. Martin," Detective Windsor answered. "We had to identify several of them using dental records."

"That's fine," Spectre replied. "When can we go?"

"You can go there now if you'd like," Lieutenant Drake replied.

Spectre stood and looked at Maddie. "Perfect. Let's go."

"Thank you for your time, gentlemen," Maddie said as she turned to follow Spectre out of the Command Center.

CHAPTER SEVEN

They had a plan, but Shepherd didn't like it. No matter how they tried to justify it, they would be killing Americans – likely current and former American servicemen. There was no way around it. He would have to kill friendlies.

Friendlies. That word was starting to have less meaning in the last few days. They were the same friendlies that had nearly killed him. The same friendlies that had taken Jenny, Tuna, and the others prisoner. He was beginning to look fondly back on his time fighting with the Kurds when at least he knew not to trust anyone.

They were perched atop an abandoned apartment building overlooking the airport, and had taken turns surveilling the hangar all day and into the night. It was heavily guarded by trained operators much like the ones that had tried to kill them the day before. There would be no easy way to secure the equipment and get out.

After a cursory sweep of some of the empty apartments, they had found an extra AK-47 and spare magazines. It wasn't quite the arsenal they needed, but it was better than what they had started with.

Cowboy's plan was simple – create a diversion, use stealth, and get in and out before anyone noticed. They would strike right in the middle of the window of circadian low at 3 AM, taking advantage of the body's natural tendency to rest. It would hopefully keep the body count to a minimum. But they would still be killing Americans, Shepherd had pointed out.

"This is survival, mate," Cowboy replied. "We don't have the luxury of tiptoeing through the tulips and talking about feelings with these blokes. Kill or be killed."

After all he had been through, Shepherd refused to die in Libya. Because the odds were stacked relatively high against them, kill was the only option. He intended to get his new friends home alive. He owed them that much.

The sound of an approaching diesel engine woke Shepherd before Cowboy nudged him. Shepherd rolled onto his knees to see a convoy of armored SUVs approaching from the direction of the CIA compound.

"What's going on?" Shepherd asked.

"I'm not sure."

Cowboy counted three SUVs as they passed their observation position and entered the airfield. The cheap pair of binoculars were ok for basic surveillance, but a set of night vision or thermal optics would have been useful. The blacked out SUVs made a hard turn toward the hangar as the large hangar doors opened.

"Looks like they're going somewhere," Cowboy whispered.

A group of operators emerged from the SUVs. They looked like carbon copies of the men guarding the facility. They opened the rear door of the last SUV and removed three prisoners wearing burlap sacks over their heads.

"It's them. Fucking hell! They're moving them!"

Cowboy handed the binoculars to Shepherd as he started to gather up his gear. Shepherd watched as a sleek business jet was pulled out of the hangar. A man in a suit exited the lead SUV and approached the prisoners. His appearance was a stark contrast to the others. He was well-groomed and had no facial hair. He approached the tallest prisoner and removed the burlap sack from his head before ordering the guards to force the prisoners to their knees.

"Cowboy…" Shepherd mumbled as he watched the scene unfold.

The man in the suit drew a handgun from a shoulder holster. He appeared to order the guards to remove the burlap sacks from the other prisoners, revealing a female and another male. The man in the suit appeared to be making a speech as he casually waved the handgun in front of them.

"What is it?" Cowboy asked.

"We need to get down there. I think I see Tuna, Waldo, and Jenny. This guy is about to execute them."

Shepherd had only been with the team a short while and the binocular zoom wasn't that great. He couldn't tell who was who, but he was almost certain the prisoners were Tuna, Waldo, and Jenny. They were all wearing orange jumpsuits.

"Hold on, mate."

Shepherd watched as the man pointed the handgun at Jenny and then suddenly turned it on one of the other prisoners. He saw the handgun recoil and then a lifeless body crumpled to the ground as the register of the shot echoed in the still night.

"Goddammit!" Shepherd yelled before tossing the binoculars aside and running toward the stairs.

"Bloody hell!" Cowboy said, sprinting toward the stairs to catch up with Shepherd.

Reaching the ground level, Shepherd ran for the pickup truck and started its engine. Cowboy reached in and killed the engine. "You can't, mate."

"What the fuck do you mean I can't? We have to save them!"

Cowboy shook his head. "Stand down."

"He just executed one of them! I think it was Tuna."

"We're not running in there without a plan."

"We have to get to them before they kill Jenny and Waldo."

"Won't do any good."

"What the fuck do you mean?"

"I mean you need to calm down and *think*, mate."

"What?"

"If we go in guns blazing right now, they're dead and we're dead."

"And if we don't, they're dead."

"They're already dead, mate."

Shepherd stared at Cowboy, not sure what to think. His chest was heaving and adrenaline coursing through his veins.

"You hear that?" Cowboy asked. "That jet is already running. They'll be long gone before we get there."

"There's nothing we can do for them now," Cowboy added. "I fucking hate it, but that's how it is."

"Goddammit!" Shepherd yelled angrily. "What the fuck is going on here?"

Cowboy put his hand on Shepherd's shoulder. "It's just you and me. We have each other's back and we get out alive. That's what we need to focus on now."

CHAPTER EIGHT

The body was charred and horribly disfigured, but Spectre came to the gut-wrenching realization that he was staring at the body of the former billionaire leader of Odin. Although he had faked his death in the past, this time there was no getting around it. Jeffrey Lyons was dead.

Maddie had stayed outside to check in with her office back in D.C. while the coroner showed Spectre the bodies. Doctor Harper had started with Lyons, warning Spectre of the gruesomeness before sliding the body out of the cooler and unzipping the body bag. He stood silently by as Spectre paid his respects.

"Where's Kruger?" Spectre asked.

"Who?"

"Freddie Mack. He was one of the victims."

Dr. Harper walked across the room and picked up a clipboard from one of his exam tables. He studied it briefly and then searched for the storage unit. When he found it, he opened it, sliding out another body bag. He motioned for Spectre to take a look after he unzipped it.

Spectre winced as he saw what remained of his old friend. Kruger's body was heavily charred and completely unrecognizable. He had obviously been very close to the explosion that took down the building. It was a horrible thing to see. After all Kruger had done for Spectre and his wife – to die like this. It was heartbreaking.

"Goodbye, old friend," Spectre said. He turned away as the coroner zipped the bag shut and slid it back into the locker.

"Would you like to see the others?"

Spectre shook his head. He had seen enough. He had gone there because he didn't believe it could be real. With everything he had been through with Kruger and his team, he didn't think it possible that such a skilled operator could die like that. He had wanted to see for himself.

"Thank you for your time," Spectre said.

Spectre walked out of the morgue and found Maddie sitting in her Tahoe still on the phone. She finished her phone call as he took shotgun. He sat in stunned silence, not sure what to do next. He just couldn't believe it.

"Are you ok?" Maddie asked.

"Those people saved my life more times than I care to remember. Kruger was always ten feet tall and bulletproof. How the hell does something like this happen?"

"Sometimes bad things just happen. There's no rhyme or reason," Maddie replied.

Spectre felt his phone vibrating in his pocket. He pulled it out and saw that Michelle was calling. He excused himself and stepped out, answering as he stepped away from the Tahoe.

"Hey, babe."

"How's it going over there?" Michelle asked.

"It's not good."

"You saw them?"

Spectre let out a long sigh. "Yeah. They're dead. I can't believe it."

"Oh, sweetheart," Michelle replied. "I'm so sorry."

"They're treating it as an accident. Open and closed case."

"Bear will be here in a few minutes to take Calvin. I should still be able to make the late flight out there to be with you. We'll figure it out, Cal," Decker said. She had stayed behind with their son, Calvin, until their family friend "Bear" Jennings returned from a fishing trip to watch Calvin.

"Don't bother," Spectre replied. His voice trembled.

"Cal…"

"There's nothing left to do, Michelle," Spectre replied. "I saw the bodies. I saw the building. They showed me the report and the gas valve they found. It's over."

"What about the others?"

"I don't know. Gone? Moved on? They're not exactly a public group."

"That's my point," Michelle said. "Tuna and Kruger were best friends. Don't you think he'd be around somewhere? And who's going to take over for them? Weren't there other billionaires involved?"

"I don't know."

"Kruger was my friend too," Michelle said. "I'm coming."

Spectre knew there was no point in arguing with her. She was determined to find out the truth for herself, and there would be no stopping her until she was satisfied that the case was closed. It was what had made her a great Special Agent with the FBI, and one of the things he loved most about her.

"Give Calvin a hug for me then, and tell Bear he still owes me twenty bucks from the bet we made on the last Saints game," Spectre said.

"I will. You be careful up there, Cal. I don't like any of this."

"I'll be fine," Spectre replied. "Have a safe trip up here. I love you."

"Love you too. Bye, babe," Decker said as she disconnected the call.

Spectre smiled briefly, thinking about his family as he turned back toward the Tahoe. As he drew near, the smile suddenly vanished as he saw Maddie slumped over in the driver's seat. He sprinted around the front of the vehicle, opened the driver's door and caught her as she fell into him.

She was breathing, but unconscious. Spectre lowered her to the ground to try to assess her injuries.

He heard a pop just as he turned to check his surroundings. The Taser darts buried into his back and the electricity surged through his body. It caused him to lock up and he fell forward, hitting his head on the front quarter panel of the Tahoe.

Spectre faded out of consciousness as he collapsed onto the concrete.

CHAPTER NINE

M ichelle Decker Martin unbuckled her seatbelt as the aircraft came to a stop at the gate. She waited patiently as the passengers of the low cost carrier deplaned. As a non-revenue customer utilizing her husband's travel privileges, she had grown used to getting on and off the plane last to accommodate the paying passengers.

With the last few passengers trickling down the aisle, Decker stood and retrieved her rollaboard from the overhead. She thanked the crew as she exited and extended the handle to roll her luggage up the jetbridge.

As she reached the gate, she was greeted by two uniformed officers and two men in plain clothes with FBI shields clipped to their belt. "Michelle Martin?" one of the plain clothes asked.

"Yes?" Decker asked. She wasn't expecting an escort. She had arranged for Spectre to be escorted to the crime scene with the local FBI field office, a favor from the Director. But she had told no one that she was traveling to D.C. to meet Spectre. She planned to rent a car and catch up with him at the hotel in Falls Church.

"We need you to come with us, ma'am," the agent said.

As a former Special Agent with the FBI, Decker knew there was no point in making a scene or demanding answers on the spot. She nodded and quietly walked with them to a secure area where they offered her coffee and secured her luggage. She was then taken to a small interrogation room with the two plainclothes agents.

"Mrs. Martin, my name is Special Agent Dillon Wells and this is Special Agent Steve Nickerson," the agent sitting across from her said. "I apologize for interrupting your travel like this, but there's been an incident with your husband."

Decker's heart sank. "What kind of incident?"

"As you know, Mr. Martin was escorted by Special Agent Tanner this morning to Falls Church per the request of the Director," Wells explained.

"What happened?" Decker demanded. "Cut the bullshit."

"Mr. Martin is missing and Special Agent Tanner was found in the morgue parking lot. She was unconscious with minor injuries and her government issued vehicle had been stolen," Agent Nickerson interjected.

"What?" Decker yelped as she turned to face the burly agent standing behind her. "Where?"

"They had gone to view the bodies of the building fire victims at the county morgue," Agent Wells said. "The coroner said Mr. Martin seemed very disturbed when he left. Irate even."

"Did Agent Tanner say what happened? Does she know who took him?"

"Special Agent Tanner is at the hospital being treated for her injuries and we have agents currently working the scene, but we wanted to speak to you as soon as possible."

"What are you doing to find my husband?" Decker asked, leaning forward with her elbows on the table.

Wells shifted uneasily in his chair. Nickerson walked out from behind Decker and tossed a piece of paper onto the table in front of him. "These are your husband's call logs. You were the last person he called."

"You subpoenaed his phone records?" Decker asked angrily. "You seriously think he's a suspect?"

"Your husband has a history of—"

Decker slammed her hand on the table, cutting Wells off. "Absolutely not!"

"Ma'am—"

"Is this what they're teaching at Quantico these days? Investigate the victim? Are you kidding me?"

"We're doing everything possible to locate your husband, ma'am. Obviously this is something that hits very close to home in our office," Nickerson said.

"As a suspect..."

"All possibilities are being investigated at this point, ma'am."

"We'll see what the Director and Attorney General have to say about this," Decker said angrily. "Where did you put my luggage?"

Wells frowned. "Ma'am, Director Schultz ordered it."

"Ordered what exactly?"

"That your husband be considered a person of interest in this case," Wells answered.

"Why? Why would the Director get personally involved?"

"Because he knows your husband's history, Mrs. Martin. We all do," Nickerson answered.

Decker leaned back and folded her arms, doing her best to contain her growing anger. "And what history is that, pray tell?"

"Mr. Martin spent some time in prison for the murder of Senator Wilson and has a history of battery against law enforcement officers. It's not a big leap to —"

Decker held up her hand, cutting him off. "First of all, you know as well as I do that he was cleared of those charges. In fact, his last position with the A-10 squadron in New Orleans was a direct favor by President Clifton."

"A job from which he resigned and came home early from a deployment due to insubordination. Yes, ma'am, we read his file. And while he may have been cleared in the battery of the Florida Highway Patrolman, the dashcam of that incident tells a very different story. It's not a stretch that he would be a person of interest," Nickerson said.

"Ok, so what's the motive? Why would he hurt Agent Tanner and take off?"

"That's what we're trying to ascertain, ma'am," Wells answered. "We were hoping to talk to you about that. You were the last person to talk to him. Have you spoken to him since?"

"I spoke to him shortly before I left my house, and I have been traveling ever since. Cal is innocent and you should be looking for him instead of trying to ascertain anything," Decker snapped. "Am I being detained?"

"We just have a few questions for you and then you can be on your way, Mrs. Martin. Finding Mr. Martin is in everyone's best interest," Wells said.

"Ok, what do you want to know?"

"What was Mr. Martin's interest in the death of Jeff Lyons?" Nickerson asked.

"He was a friend of ours."

Wells turned to his yellow legal pad, flipping over a page as he read from his notes. "That's right, you were involved with his faking his own death two years ago, weren't you?"

"I was on the manifest for the aircraft that crashed, yes. He did not fake his own death."

"How did you meet him?"

"Through a mutual friend who worked for him."

"And you believed the gas explosion in his office building wasn't an accident?"

"It seemed suspicious. The victims were friends of ours. Cal and I both have an interest in the case."

"So you called in a favor."

"I wanted to ensure Cal had access to the site."

"Why?" Wells asked.

"Why?" Decker repeated. "What do you mean?"

"You were a Special Agent and a prosecutor in a former life, weren't you? And your husband was neither, is that correct?"

"Correct."

"So why did you send him?"

"I don't know if you have children, Agent Wells, but it's not that easy to just pick up and leave when you have a small child. Cal works for an airline and was already on a trip. It was much easier for him to get here first."

"To do what?"

Decker glared at the middle-aged agent. "To see for himself."

"The Coroner said Mr. Martin was visibly angry and nearly pushed him out of the way upon seeing the body of Frederick Mack. Do you know why that is?" Nickerson asked.

"He was a friend of ours."

Wells flipped through his notes once again. "That's right, former Army SFOD-D, also known as 'Delta.' He had quite the service record and was employed as a security consultant for Mr. Lyons."

"Sounds right."

"Did your husband have a history with Mr. Mack?"

Decker looked down at the notes Wells was eyeing. The two had more than just a history. Spectre and Kruger had fought side by side, taking down a corrupt Vice President and his Chinese co-conspirators. Kruger had saved both Cal's and her lives on countless occasions, and more recently, Spectre had repaid the favor in Iraq while flying an A-10. It made sense that Spectre would be angry at the sight of Kruger's body. The man was a national hero – a warrior.

"They were friends," Decker said finally.

Decker looked up at Wells, who was still pretending to read his notes. "What's your point?" she asked.

"You know the routine, ma'am. We're just trying to see what his motive could have been and where he might have gone."

"There was no motive, you idiot!" Decker barked.

Nickerson pulled out his phone and placed it on the table. He opened an audio file and hit play, watching Decker as the recording began.

"Shortly after his phone call to you, your husband placed a second call to a man we have been tracking on the terror watch list. He's an American named Nidal Abu Hissan," Nickerson said.

"Oh, bullsh—"

"Just listen," Nickerson said, pointing to the device.

"It's me. You did it. They are dead."

Decker's stomach turned as he heard Spectre's voice. *How?* It made no sense.

"Thank you for the tip, my friend. When will we meet?" the voice on the other end asked.

"Soon. I need to get rid of someone first."

The recording ended. Decker sat speechless, staring at the phone.

"Perhaps you know less about your husband than you thought, Mrs. Martin," Wells said softly.

CHAPTER TEN

W e're fucked," Shepherd said, breaking a three hour silence. They were driving to Tripoli in hopes of linking up with an MI-6 agent he assumed Cowboy knew from his time with the SAS. Short of rowing a boat to Europe or stealing a plane, it was their last hope of escaping war-torn Libya.

Cowboy looked over at Shepherd as he maneuvered the beat-up truck down the desolate road. The sun was starting to rise and they were both exhausted, running on pure survival instinct. "We're not fucked."

"That guy fucking executed Tuna," Shepherd said. "Right there. On his fucking knees!"

"Are you sure it was Tuna?"

"He had a beard."

"Well, gee, mate, that narrows it right down in this part of the world," Cowboy said, stroking his scraggly beard.

"Two males, one female," Shepherd replied. "I don't think it's a coincidence. Jenny, Waldo, and Tuna."

"Then I guess we'll see him in Valhalla," Cowboy said dryly. "But in the meantime, we need to focus on delaying that meeting as long as possible. We get to Tripoli. We find the MI-6 safe house, and hope whatever caused the Yanks to turn on us hasn't gotten to them too."

"You think it was Odin?"

"What I think doesn't matter right now."

"I mean you've been with this group longer than I have. It just seems sketchy. A billionaire runs this super-secret special ops group, killing terrorists all over the world and the CIA knows about it. Yet when the shit hits the fan, they hunt us and execute everyone without a second thought. That's fucked up."

"You were a cop, weren't you?" Cowboy asked.

Shepherd nodded.

"Did you always jump to conclusions like this without all the evidence?"

"I don't think getting shot at is that big of a jump."

"Focus, mate," Cowboy said. "We get out of here together. We go home alive. That's all that matters right now. You can't worry about the others or Odin or anything else. There's nothing we can do for them. Got it?"

"Got it," Shepherd replied dejectedly.

"Good, now keep your eyes open. We're on the main roads for speed, but there are about fifteen different factions between ISIS, anti-government rebels, and the Libyan Army that would love to chop our heads off."

Shepherd checked his weapon. They each had an AK-47 and two spare magazines – enough for self-defense but terrible for anything beyond that. They needed to get out of this shithole and to a place where they might be able to get answers. But as much as he hated to admit it, Shepherd knew the Brit was right. Survival was the priority.

Driving down the desolate highway brought back memories of his time in Iraq and Syria. It was less than a year since his family had been killed and he had been recruited to fight with the Kurdish YPG, an elite militia that had taken a stand to keep ISIS out of their own back yard. He had served as a sniper, experiencing firsthand the atrocities that ISIS was capable of.

Their pickup truck bounced along the deteriorating road as the hum of the engine served as the soundtrack for their impromptu road trip. Shepherd scanned the highway ahead, fighting off sleep as he looked for any signs of movement or activity. He had been trained by the Kurds to look for signs of improvised explosive devices and ambushes as part of their convoy training.

Cresting a hill, a flash of light to their left suddenly caught Shepherd's eye. It was followed by a thunderous explosion and black smoke billowing a few hundred meters away from their position. Cowboy slammed on the brakes, pulling off to the side of the road as he grabbed his rifle.

The two men exited the pickup. "Look!" Shepherd yelled as they maneuvered for cover. He pointed out a drone that was in a sharp left hand turn away from the explosion.

Cowboy opened the passenger door and grabbed the binoculars. The drone continued its climbing turn away from the explosion, flying right over their heads as it turned east into the sunrise.

The road they were on snaked down into the valley. Cowboy saw a group of vehicles behind a burning truck. Two of them sported the ISIS black flag. There were fighters using the truck bed as cover and shooting at a position off the highway. Cowboy scanned right and found a disabled vehicle with a group of four to six men attempting to hold the position.

"If I had to guess, that drone is trying to protect a group of operators," Cowboy said, handing the binoculars to Shepherd.

"Friendlies? Americans?" Shepherd asked. He never thought he would have to make such a distinction, but the events of the last twenty-four hours made it difficult for him to know who was, or wasn't, his friend anymore. Not trying to kill him would be a good starting position though.

"Can't tell," Cowboy replied.

Shepherd viewed the firefight through the binoculars. The drone turned back inbound, causing them both to duck as it fired another hellfire into the fray.

"Looks like they're fighting it out right in the way of our drive to Tripoli," Shepherd said as he stood back up and handed the binoculars to Cowboy. "Is there another route we can take?"

"Not in this area," Cowboy replied, studying the men. "We'd have to double back at least twenty clicks."

"So now what? This shit could take days. We don't have that kind of time."

"Then I guess we'll have to give them a hand," Cowboy said with a grin.

"What?" Shepherd yelped. "You want us to get into the shit with a couple hundred rounds between the two of us? And help people that will probably start shooting at us when it's all over?"

"They won't start shooting at us, mate, I promise," Cowboy said confidently.

"How the hell can you possibly know that? Did you forget what happened in Benghazi?"

"Because they're not Americans."

"They're not?"

Cowboy shook his head, still looking out through the binoculars. "They're British SAS."

CHAPTER ELEVEN

It took Shepherd and Cowboy an hour to flank the scene of the firefight. They had to leave their pickup truck on the side of the road, fearing a drone strike if the friendlies mistook it for another ISIS vehicle joining the fight. They moved slowly and methodically as the battle continued.

The British SAS team had dug in and established a defensive position, taking advantage of the high ground near their disabled vehicle. They were holding their own against the poorly trained ISIS fighters. The fighting had slowed to a few sporadic potshots from the cowardly terrorists, as a British sniper proceeded to pick them off one by one.

The tangos were oblivious as Shepherd and Cowboy moved in behind them. It was almost comical to Shepherd watching them blindly fire over the hoods of their pickups every so often as they tried to figure out how to capture the SAS team. Shepherd estimated that they were down to six or seven fighters after starting with a dozen or more. He was surprised they hadn't fled in terror. But judging by the positions of some of the bodies, a few had done just that.

They approached with their weapons raised, moving as a two-man team through the desert. One of the tangos caught their movement out of the corner of his eye and turned to face them. Cowboy fired three rounds, hitting the man in the chest and throat. Shepherd followed up, dropping two others that were standing nearby, debating their next course of action.

The sudden gunfire behind them caused confusion and panic among the remaining Daesh fighters. The men turned and raised their rifles as Shepherd and Cowboy closed the distance, but with the help of the SAS sniper, the tangos were dispatched.

"Over there!" Shepherd yelled, pointing out the last fighter running down the highway.

Before Cowboy could respond, they heard the crack of a round and the fighter tumbled face first onto the asphalt. Unsure if their roles as friendlies had been established, Cowboy and Shepherd took cover behind one of the trucks.

Cowboy pulled his knife and crouched over one of the fresh terrorist bodies. He cut the man's white shirt, careful to avoid the blood-soaked portions and attached it to the end of his rifle. He held it up above the truck like a makeshift white flag as he motioned for Shepherd to follow.

The two slowly approached the SAS position. As they neared the disabled SAS vehicle, Shepherd saw that it appeared to have been disabled by a roadside IED. Cowboy stopped next to it, slinging his rifle across his back as he held his hands up.

"He who dares, wins," he said in his thick British accent.

Two men wearing desert camo descended from the hilltop pointing their rifles at Shepherd and Cowboy. "We're all friends here," he added as they closed the distance.

"Who the hell are you?" one of the men asked.

"Special projects team, mate," Cowboy replied.

"Bullshit," the man replied.

"I used to be, at least," Cowboy said. He had served with the elite counterterrorism unit of the Special Air Service before getting out and joining Odin.

"Who the fuck is he?" the other man asked, pointing to Shepherd.

"Me? I used to be a cop," Shepherd said. "And we just saved your asses, so the least you could do is say thanks."

"Yeah, right," the lead operator said. He covered Shepherd and Cowboy while the other disarmed them. Cowboy and Shepherd made no effort to resist, instead holding their hands up to show that they were friendlies. "What are you two blokes doing out here?"

"Trying to get to Tripoli to see an old friend. Do you know Diana?" Cowboy asked. Diana was the codename used by the MI-6 operative running Tripoli operations at any given time.

"She sent us out here," the operator replied.

"We need her help," Cowboy said.

"You guys are fucking ballsy," the operator answered. "You're lucky we didn't shoot you."

"Again, a little gratitude would be nice," Shepherd said.

"Let's go," the lead operator said.

They walked Shepherd and Cowboy up the hill to where the rest of the team had holed up. One of the men appeared to be heavily injured with field dressings covering various wounds. Shepherd saw a sniper/spotter team perched a few meters away.

"Captain Rogers," the operator said, addressing the man standing near the wounded soldier. "We have guests."

"Thanks, Trimble," Rogers replied as he approached Cowboy and Shepherd. "Who are you gentlemen with?"

"We're contractors," Cowboy said. "But I used to wear the beret."

"What unit?"

"The 22nd Alpha Squadron and then special projects."

"I see," Rogers said, studying Cowboy before turning to Shepherd. "And you?"

"I used to play Call of Duty online if that counts," Shepherd replied with a shit-eating grin.

"A Yank," Rogers said with a forced smile. "Well, I appreciate what you did to help, but as you can see, we're a bit busy at the moment."

"I noticed your ride is tits up," Shepherd said. "We have one a few miles up the road."

"That's quite alright," Rogers replied. "Our helicopter extract should be here in the next twenty minutes."

"We need your help, sir," Cowboy said.

"I'm not sure I can be of any assistance out here."

"We carried out a mission to stop a chemical weapons transfer between al-Maqdis and the Youth Shura. When we got back to our safehouse, we found that our team had been captured or killed, and we were pursued by the Libyan army. We made it to the CIA compound in Benghazi, but weren't exactly given the friendliest of greetings."

"They fucking shot at us," Shepherd clarified.

"You're going to have to be more specific than that," Rogers said. "Why would the CIA shoot at contractors?"

Cowboy hesitated for a moment and then said, "We're part of Odin."

Rogers laughed. "Odin?"

Cowboy nodded.

"My friend, you must have me mistaken for someone a bit less experienced. I have spent many years in Africa and the Middle

East and heard the tales of such a team, but we all know that, like its namesake, Odin is simply mythology. A battlefield wives tale young soldiers tell around campfires," Rogers said dismissively. "Now what contractor do you work for?"

Cowboy pulled down the collar of his shirt slightly, revealing the skull and valknut tattooed on his chest.

Rogers's eyes widened as he recognized the symbol he had seen on the battlefield many times before. "We'll make room on the chopper."

CHAPTER TWELVE

S pectre's head was throbbing as he slowly opened his eyes. He felt disoriented, groggy, and had the world's worst hangover. As he started to regain his senses, he realized he was in a very comfortable bed staring at a white ceiling. He was naked and felt the cool sheets against his body as he rolled to his side.

At first, the face full of hair seemed like any other wake up at home. He tried to make sense of his surroundings. The last thing he remembered was seeing the FBI Special Agent slumped over the steering wheel of her Tahoe. He had no idea how he had ended up in bed with Decker, or where he was. He didn't typically sleep in the nude, but that wasn't the biggest problem.

As Spectre's eyes adjusted and his mind started to clear, he suddenly realized that the hair in his face wasn't Decker's golden blonde hair. Startled, he lunged backward, rolling out of bed and falling onto the floor before leaping to his feet. "Who are you?" he demanded.

The woman rolled over and stretched as she sat up in bed, exposing her bare breasts. The attractive young brunette tilted her head at Spectre as he grabbed a pillow to cover himself. "What is wrong, my love?" she asked with an accent Spectre didn't quite have the brain power to pinpoint. Eastern European? Russian?

Spectre stepped back, trying to figure out what the hell was going on. He was in a hotel suite of some sort. He noticed a bottle of champagne chilling in a bucket of ice near the nightstand. "What the hell is going on?"

"What do you mean?" the girl asked as she lazily got out of bed. Her long hair now covered her breasts, but her tight body was still very exposed. Spectre did his best to look away, instead turning to the window behind him to try to figure out where he was.

He saw an airport and a river. As his eyes adjusted to the daylight, he recognized the Washington Monument on the other side of the Potomac River and the Capitol Building. A 737 flew by on final approach, barely audible behind the suite's soundproof glass.

"What the fuck is going on here?" Spectre demanded again, turning back to search for his clothes. "Who are you?"

"My love," she said as she walked around the foot of the bed to approach him. "Don't you remember the night we had together?"

Spectre's heart was racing. Nothing made sense. He found his pants balled up on the floor and rushed to put them on. The woman continued walking toward him, making no effort to cover up.

"Get back," Spectre warned, fastening the buckle on his belt. "I'm not kidding."

"Calvin, my love—"

"And put some damned clothes on!" Spectre yelled, looking away.

The woman refused to stop, still approaching with a look of concern. As Spectre retreated toward the window, the door to the luxury suite suddenly flew open and two large men in suits entered followed by a much older man. Spectre grabbed the nearest weapon he could find, a knife from a nearby room service tray. He spun the knife around in his hand, blade down as he assumed a fighting stance.

"That won't be necessary, Mr. Martin," the older man said before turning to the woman. "Nadia, would you please give us a moment alone?"

Nadia nodded and grabbed a bathrobe off the bathroom door, covering herself as she exited with one of the guards. The man nodded to the other guard and he followed behind the first guard, leaving Spectre and the man alone in the room.

"Who are you?" Spectre demanded, still in his bladed fighting stance.

Ignoring Spectre's question and the threat of the knife, the man pulled a chair from the nearby desk. He was wearing a dark blazer with khaki pants and white boat shoes. He casually unbuttoned the blazer and sat, crossing his right leg over his left as he sat back in the chair.

Spectre stepped menacingly forward, keeping his left foot in front of his right and balancing his weight on the balls of his feet. He calculated his potential escape options as the man stared casually up at him.

"Please, have a seat," the man said calmly as he pointed to the foot of the bed. "Let's talk, Cal."

"I don't know what the fuck is going on here, but I think I'll be going now," Spectre said. He didn't move, still not sure what his exit strategy would be.

"The first part is readily apparent," the man said, "and the second… Well, I don't see you moving. Of course, you're free to leave at any time, but why don't you have a seat instead?"

"Who are you?"

"Put the knife down and let's talk as civilized men, Mr. Martin. Or would you prefer I call you Spectre?"

Spectre hesitated and then slowly approached, keeping the knife firmly in his right hand with his other hand guarding his face.

"Calvin William Martin. Thirty-six years old. Six feet tall, one hundred and eighty five pounds. Brown hair. Blue eyes. You live in Belle Chasse, Louisiana," the man said.

"So you have my driver's license?" Spectre said, still advancing slowly toward the man.

"Son of Linda and Wayne Martin. Your mother was a bookkeeper and your father an Air Force Lieutenant Colonel. He flew AC-130s in Vietnam. They were both killed by a drunk driver on the way home from a Christmas party. And you were adopted by Mr. Charlie Jennings. I believe you call him, Bear, is that right?" the man asked.

Spectre stopped and stared at the man.

"You went to Louisiana State University and then joined the Air Force Reserve. You struggled in Officer Training School. Your superiors said you had a problem with authority, but excelled in leading others. You graduated number one in your class in Air Force Undergraduate Pilot Training, Introduction to Fighter Fundamentals, and your F-16 B-Course. You were nearly washed out of Survival School at Fairchild for actually managing to escape."

"Are you writing my biography?" Spectre muttered, still standing a few feet from the man.

"You were a shining star at the 39th Fighter Squadron and on track to be the youngest Air Force Reserve F-22 pilot, until you met Chloe Moss. Your relationship with Ms. Moss strained your standing in the squadron. Your professional development took a downturn, and after strafing during an Emergency Close Air Support Scenario in Iraq against the rules of engagement, you were permanently grounded."

Spectre's grip loosened on the knife. "Go on."

"You took a job at Anderson Police Supply, taking over marketing. You became an NRA Firearms instructor, learned Krav Maga, and proposed to Ms. Moss. But unfortunately, she was into someone else – a Cuban Intelligence Agent named Victor Alvarez."

Spectre's eyes widened. It was a name he hadn't heard or thought of in many years. *Victor Alvarez.* Spectre dropped onto the bed with a slight bounce as the man continued.

"Victor convinced Ms. Moss to steal an F-16, faking her own death and flying it to Cuba. Of course, you didn't believe it. You assembled a team and launched a rescue mission. You recovered Chloe and the aircraft, but were told that she succumbed to her injuries in the hospital."

"She didn't?"

"A Russian assassin named Svetlana killed her, actually," the man said. "But anyway, at the funeral, you were recruited by a man named Charles Steele for a group called Project Archangel. You flew with them for several months before bad luck seemed to find its way back to you again and you were shot down over Syria."

"Who the fuck are you? How do you know all of this?"

"I suppose that's a fair question, now that I have your attention."

Spectre sat on the edge of the bed as the man seemed to enjoy Spectre's anxiousness.

"My name is Walter Cruz, Mr. Martin," he said finally.

The name meant nothing to Spectre. "And? How do you know all of this? Who do you work for? And what do you want from me?"

"I work for no one, Mr. Martin. In fact, I'm here to ask for your cooperation."

"Cooperation?" Spectre scoffed. "Is this how you think you get people on board? Tase them, drug them, and put them in bed with strange foreign women? Whatever happened to e-mail?"

"I prefer a sure thing."

"And what about Special Agent Tanner? Did you do that too?" Spectre said as the image of Special Agent Tanner in the Tahoe suddenly came rushing back.

"No, Mr. Martin, I'm afraid you did."

"Sure thing, pal," Spectre said. "I guess you didn't study my file thoroughly enough. If you did, you'd know that shit has been tried before. It doesn't work, and to be honest, it's getting a little old."

Spectre saw his shirt on the floor. He grabbed it and stood, heading for the door. "I'll see myself out."

"You're a wanted man, Mr. Martin," Cruz said. "And I'm sure your wife won't be too happy to see that you shared a bed with young Nadia last night."

Spectre laughed as he pulled the polo over his head. "Michelle knows better. I'm an acquired taste. One night stands aren't really in the cards for me. Besides, I prefer blondes."

Cruz stood and turned to face Spectre. "Very well, Mr. Martin. But there's one more thing you should know before your walk out that door."

"Make it good," Spectre said without looking back at Cruz.

"I know who killed your friends, Kruger, Coolio, and Jeff Lyons."

Spectre froze, then slowly turned back to face Cruz. "What kind of cooperation are you looking for, exactly?"

CHAPTER THIRTEEN

Shepherd, Cowboy, and the SAS team were picked up by contractors flying a Russian Mi-8 Hip helicopter and taken to Tripoli. Upon arrival, Shepherd and Cowboy found that Sierra Carter, the MI-6 Agent he knew, had flown back to London. She wanted them to meet her there for a full debrief.

They were shown to private rooms in the safe house, given fresh clothes, and allowed to shower, eat, and sleep. They both felt like they hadn't slept in months and enjoyed the much needed rest. The next morning, Captain Rogers escorted them to the airport, where a Royal Air Force Bae 146 transport aircraft waited to take them to London.

"Good luck, gents," he said. "I don't know what you're involved in, but if Miss Carter is interested, you'll need it."

They found cots in the cargo hold and both tried to sleep on the direct flight to London. Shepherd was less successful than Cowboy. The captain's words resonated with him for some reason. His life had changed so much in the last year. It was hard to believe that luck of any kind was even possible.

He had been a shift corporal with the St Tammany Parish Sheriff's Office, a devoted father, and husband. He had been a SWAT sniper/countersniper and a man that loved his life. But when a group of radical Islamic terrorists hijacked the school bus his wife and daughter were on, all that changed. Everything changed.

After watching his family brutally murdered, Shepherd set out on a path of vengeance. He started in Jackson, Mississippi where he interrogated and executed a fat little imam that had funded, harbored, and coordinated the terrorist cell. Then he drove to Atlanta where he kidnapped and killed a Saudi royal that had financed the Imam. It was there that he had found the Kurdish YPG movement.

He found a local recruiter in Atlanta, a man who was looking for fighters to help the Kurds in their fight to defend Kurdistan from ISIS. With nothing left to live for, Shepherd joined, flying to Iraq where his skills as a SWAT operator soon made him stand above and beyond the other recruits. He met a man named Zirek who had been equally affected by the horrors of ISIS. Zirek took him directly to the frontlines in Syria.

Shepherd found vengeance there, quickly earning the nickname "The Wolf" as a deadly sniper. He grew close to Zirek and later a YPJ fighter named Asmin. He thought he had found a new family there.

But, as with everything else, that reprieve was short-lived. Zirek and Asmin were both brutally executed by ISIS propaganda ministers. Shepherd watched Zirek's crucifixion and burning alive, while he awaited his own looming execution. It was the second most horrific thing he had ever seen, behind the deaths of his wife and daughter.

He had nearly given up the will to live when a commando team, led by Kruger, rescued him. Kruger had introduced himself and told him about his team. They were Odin, a secret group of operators funded by a billionaire named Jeff Lyons. They went where no military would go, to do things to bad people that no one else would. Shepherd jumped at the opportunity to join and avenge his friends.

Vengeance never quite came, however. In the last year, Shepherd had learned that vengeance begets vengeance. It was a never-ending cycle of violence. No matter what happened, he would still have to live with the deaths of his family and friends. No matter how much he killed, nothing would make that pain go away. But he pushed forward anyway.

And now, here he was. His new team had seemingly abandoned him. They were being hunted by unknown forces, presumably Americans, for unknown reasons. The only person he truly trusted was Cowboy, but even then he wasn't completely sure.

Cowboy seemed to trust the SAS operators and this Sierra Carter lady. He trusted her enough to essentially turn themselves in, and risk walking right into the hands of the people trying to kill them. Shepherd hoped Cowboy was right, although it didn't really matter anymore. They had already run out of options anyway.

Shepherd finally dozed off and slept for the last two hours of the flight. He woke up just as the plane touched down and the thrust reversers roared to life. The four-engine, high wing aircraft taxied into a secure area at RAF Northolt and shut down. As they grabbed their bags with their old clothes, Shepherd and Cowboy were greeted by an entourage as they exited the aircraft.

Cowboy took the lead. An attractive young brunette woman stepped forward and hugged him. She was wearing aviator sunglasses, khaki tactical pants, and a polo shirt. Cowboy turned to introduce Shepherd.

"This is Sierra Carter," he said. "Sierra, this is Wolf."

"Alex Shepherd," he said, extending his hand. Her hands were soft, but her handshake was firm.

"Pleased to meet you. Shall we talk?" Her accent was intoxicating. Shepherd wondered what her history was with Cowboy.

Carter led them through a nearby hangar and into a building. They passed through a series of vault doors into a secure area where signs warned that cell phones and other electronic devices were prohibited. The rest of the people with her had all gone their separate ways, leaving Sierra with the two Odin operators in a small briefing room.

"Would you like anything to drink? Tea? Water? Coffee?" she asked as she ushered them into the room.

They both asked for coffee. She disappeared for a few minutes and then returned with two cups and a handful of creamer packets and sugar.

"I forgot to ask your order, Mr. Shepherd," she said, handing him the Styrofoam cup and the packets.

Cowboy winked as he accepted his cup, apparently made to his specifications. Shepherd made a mental note to ask him later what their deal was.

"So, you boys have been awfully busy," Carter began as she sat down across from them. "Where would you like to start?"

Shepherd looked nervously at Cowboy. He wasn't sure how much she knew about Odin and their mission in Libya. Their cover story had been that they were working as contractors, but with the way things had completely fallen apart, he wasn't sure what the best course of action would be.

"We've been burned," Cowboy said bluntly.

Carter smiled. "I'll say. You boys have a capture or kill order on your heads. You're lucky it hadn't reached us before Captain Rogers found you."

"I'm sorry. I'm new here," Shepherd said, leaning forward onto his elbows. "Can someone please tell me what's going on here? Why would our own governments want to kill us?"

"We're classified as a COD Team, mate."

"COD?"

"Contract On Demand," Carter answered. "It means a government can use you to do their dirty work, but if you're accused of something illegal, you can be reclassified as an enemy of the state without due process."

"Plausible deniability and all that," Cowboy added.

"It's how Odin typically operates when contracted by NATO governments," Carter said.

"You know?" Shepherd asked.

"I've employed such services before," Carter replied with a knowing grin. "But of course that's classified."

"Is that how you two know each other?" Shepherd asked.

Carter and Cowboy exchanged a knowing look. "Reginald and I have known each other for all our lives."

"She actually connected me with Odin when I left the SAS," Cowboy said.

Sierra rolled her eyes. "You didn't tell him you're my brother?"

"Oh, yeah. That too."

"You're such a bloody muppet," Sierra said with an exasperated sigh before she turned back to Spectre. "Unfortunately, yes, we are related by birth."

"Wait a minute. Didn't you tell me your name was Sullivan Winchester or something when we first met?" Shepherd asked, thinking back to the day Cowboy picked him up from the hospital in Incirlik and introduced him to the Odin team.

"It was a cover name, mate. Couldn't give you my real name before you were even on the team" Cowboy said nonchalantly before turning back to Carter. "So did you try to contact Kruger?"

Carter frowned. "I've got some bad news."

"Bloody hell," Cowboy said, seeing the look on her face. "What happened?"

"An explosion took down the office building. Killed everyone," Carter said with a pained expression. "I'm sorry."

"Fuck!" Cowboy yelled, slamming his fists down on the table.

"So who put the order out for us to be burned or whatever?" Shepherd asked.

"That's where it gets a bit more confusing. The notice came from the CIA servers, but no one at Langley has any information on it. Seems to have gotten lost in the bureaucracy. And they consider you boys Tier One terror threats."

"Do we look like ISIS?" Shepherd asked, pushing up his sleeve to reveal his pale skin.

"In today's world, there's no way to tell on appearance alone. We've seen plenty of Westerners travel to the Middle East to fight on both sides. You of all people should know that, Mr. Shepherd."

"Good point. So now what? What about the others?"

Carter shrugged. "I've put feelers out, but no one seems to know. We have a liaison with the CIA in Benghazi who said they had three high-value prisoners for a short time, but an Israeli picked them up. Listed as part of a joint CIA-Mossad venture. That's all she knew."

"And he executed them!" Shepherd yelled.

"We're working on trying to figure out who he was, but so far snake eyes."

"So basically, we're fucked," Cowboy said.

"For now, yes," Carter said. "But I've never known my big brother to let that stop him."

Cowboy forced a smile. "Any ideas?"

"I've managed to remove you both from the burn list. I can keep you both here while we figure it out. My bosses are allowing me to work this case, but for the time being they don't know we're related. I suggest we keep it that way. I've listed you as Reginald Jones."

"Brother and sister. I never would have guessed," Shepherd said. "But anyway, I think we need to start by figuring out who the man in the suit was. My gut tells me he's not who they say he is. Do you have a list of all aircraft with flight plans out of Benghazi in the last few days?"

Carter nodded. "I'll have my analysts work on that this afternoon. I see your law enforcement background hasn't left you, Mr. Shepherd."

"Speaking of, I'm hungry. Got any doughnuts?" Shepherd replied with a wink.

CHAPTER FOURTEEN

Piórkowo, Poland

The Bombardier Challenger 650 luxury business jet touched down gently onto the moonlit runway. There were no runway lights, but the crew did a good job of navigating using their night vision goggles. The aircraft rolled to a stop just short of the former CIA black site's main building.

The stairs lowered and two armed men emerged escorting three prisoners in orange jumpsuits with hoods over their heads. Still sporting his expensive, tailored suit, Jäger followed them down the stairs. He instructed his men to secure the prisoners, noting that one was still dripping blood from his ear and needed to be tended to, then he walked to the nearby communications shack.

The small, secure building had served as a satellite communications station for the CIA to transmit information back to Langley during the Cold War. The site had seen many KGB and Eastern Bloc spies pass through its doors as prisoners, but now it was the private property of billionaire Nicholas Stone.

Jäger placed his thumb on the fingerprint scanner and then punched in his six digit code on the door. The lock clicked open, and Jäger entered, revealing the renovated server room. He closed the door behind him and turned the light on, walking straight to the safe in the corner of the room.

He extracted the secure hard drive and server crypto key, installing them both in the computer at the workstation. He removed his coat and draped it carefully on the back of the chair as the computer booted.

Jäger sat down as the system requested his login information. It first prompted him for facial recognition, followed by his thumbprint, and finally his sixteen character password. When he was finally logged in, the system attempted to ring Stone's webcam.

Moments later, the old billionaire appeared wearing a robe and t-shirt. He was in his villa in Rome. What was left of his white hair seemed to stick up in different directions as if he had been sleeping just minutes earlier.

"Do you have them?" he asked as he put on his glasses.

"We have managed to secure three. They are being delivered as we speak."

"Three?" Stone asked angrily. "What of the others?"

Jäger did not react to Stone's tone, instead remaining emotionless as he stared at the camera. "Two were able to escape."

"No shit, Sherlock. How?"

"Local assets can often be less than reliable. I will see to their capture personally. I am told that they are under the care of MI-6."

"Fuck!" Stone yelled. "We can use the system to gain access, can't we?"

"My credentials as Mossad worked in transferring the prisoners to Benghazi, but I believe this MI-6 agent may pose a challenge in that regard."

"How is that?"

"Agent Sierra Carter's brother is Reginald Carter, one of the men in question. She has been assigned to this case."

"Make it happen. Remove her from the equation if you have to."

"Of course, sir," Jäger replied coldly.

"Helios phase one begins in a week. We cannot afford any of Lyons's team getting in the way."

"Should I terminate them?"

Stone shook his head. "No. They may still be useful when the time comes. Were you able to gain allegiance from any of them so far?"

"One," Jäger replied. "A pilot, although his hearing may be permanently damaged in his right ear."

"I don't care about the pilots. What about the operators?"

"The one we captured in Libya – Turner – is still defiant. Although I discovered his weakness when I shot the pilot's ear in Tripoli. I think he may come around soon. I am confident they will all be compliant soon."

"Let them sit for now. I want you to personally oversee the capture of the remaining team members. You can work on turning them after there are no more loose ends."

"Of course, sir. Will there be anything else?"

Stone shifted in his chair as he considered the question. Finally, he let out an exhausted sigh. "One more thing."

"Do you have a team in place in Virginia?" Stone asked.

"Arrangements can be made, sir."

Stone looked away, as if nervous that someone might hear him. "There's a woman. Her name is Michelle Decker Martin. She needs to be removed from the board."

"As you wish," Jäger said without hesitation. "I will make the necessary arrangements."

"I just… I mean I know that Cruz has a plan, but I also know what she did with Johnson. She's way too much of a wild card. We can't take that risk. I don't think he realizes that," Stone said, as if trying to justify his decision to the Israeli assassin.

"Very well, sir," Jäger replied.

"Put your best people on it. Make it look like an accident if you can," Stone said.

"Do you wish for me to handle it personally?"

Stone considered the question for a moment. He knew how dangerous the woman had been in the past. She had thwarted an assassination attempt on the President, escaped the custody of a Chinese assassin, and taken down the Vice President of the United States. It was risky to send anyone but Jäger to take her down, but it was even riskier to have Odin operators talking to MI-6. That was the most pressing issue.

"No," Stone said finally. "Make other arrangements. I need you to take care of the loose ends with Odin first."

"All of my men are the best," Jäger said. "It will be done."

"Cruz can't find out."

"Yes, sir," Jäger said. "Will there be anything else?"

"No," Stone said. "Just get those loose ends tied up as soon as possible."

"Of course."

The video chat ended. Jäger powered down the computer and then removed the hard drive and crypto key, replacing them in the safe before putting his coat back on and exiting. He walked to the building next door. One of his men had taken up a post guarding the front door. Jäger nodded and the man punched in his code and opened the door for the Israeli assassin.

He walked through the narrow hallway, stopping at each cell to check on his prisoners. Their hoods had been removed and they had been given fresh jumpsuits. He stopped at the first cell where the pilot that he had grazed in Tripoli was asleep on the cot. His ear was freshly bandaged. He had been the first to turn, but Jäger questioned his future usefulness.

The second cell housed the female pilot. She sat Indian style on the floor, apparently meditating. Jäger also found no use for her, but figured she would serve as sufficient motivation for the others when he returned.

Jäger moved on to the last cell. The bearded former Army Ranger was pacing in his cell. He turned and walked to the door when he saw Jäger stop and watch him.

"You should save your energy, Mr. Turner. You will need it," Jäger said ominously.

"Let me out of here and I'll show you how much energy I have left, motherfucker," Tuna replied angrily.

Jäger smiled. It was always fun to break someone with such bravado and defiance. He would enjoy watching the man crumble. It was only a matter of time.

"Soon enough, Mr. Turner," Jäger replied before continuing down the hall.

"Fuck you! Be a man and face me, you pussy!" Tuna yelled in rage as the Israeli walked off.

Jäger walked through another series of doors with cipher locks before heading down a set of metal stairs to the basement. It had been used in the past for the most gruesome and brutal interrogations of Russian spies.

At the base of the stairs, Jäger punched in his code on a steel door. When it unlocked, he opened it slowly, revealing a naked man with his arms attached to chains hanging from the ceiling. The man had a hood on over his head and his body hung limply, the balls of his feet barely supporting his weight on the floor.

Jäger walked up to the man, stopping a few feet from him. Jäger's men had done a good job in repositioning the high-value prisoner to the site in Poland and preparing him. Jäger was looking forward to watching the man break down, but unfortunately he would have to wait until his mission with the two stragglers was over.

"How the mighty have fallen," Jäger said as he ripped the hood from the man's head. "Look at what has become of you."

There was no response. The man was still limp. Jäger bent down, looking to see if the man would open his eyes. "The stories are almost mythical. I have heard so much about you, but this…this is disappointing. You are no god."

The man slowly looked up at the Israeli, blood dripping from his lip from an earlier encounter with Jäger's men. Jäger flashed a wicked smile as the two men made eye contact. "Nothing?"

"You'd better pray to your god to have mercy on your soul now, bub," the prisoner growled through his red beard, "because when I get to you, *I won't*."

CHAPTER FIFTEEN

Decker's first stop, after being released by the airport police, was the hospital where Special Agent Tanner was being treated. She hoped the young FBI agent would give her a good starting point in her search for her missing husband, although Decker was aware of the possibility that all of the agents involved were complicit in another setup of Cal Martin.

After the interrogation, the agents had been clear that she was not a suspect but should be contactable. She gave them her cell phone number and reiterated that they should be looking for her husband as a victim and not as a suspect. She knew it didn't really matter, though. As she had driven her rental car from the airport to the hospital, she had seen them following her. They weren't even trying to hide the fact that she was under surveillance.

Decker walked up to the information desk and flashed the badge the Jefferson Parish Sheriff's Department in Louisiana had given her. Although she had retired from the FBI, she was a consultant for the sheriff, and spent her time balancing a small private practice and assisting as a legal adviser on cases. She had been given a commission and qualified annually with her Glock 17 duty weapon just to stay current.

"I'm looking for Madison Tanner's room, please," Decker said as the woman looked up from playing a game on her phone.

The woman didn't bother to inspect Decker's credentials, instead turning to her computer to look up the information. "You said Tanner, right?"

"Yes, ma'am," Decker replied as she stuffed the badge wallet back into the front pocket of her jeans.

"Room three-forty-seven," the woman said and then pointed down the hall. "You'll want to take those elevators."

Decker thanked the woman who ignored her and returned to the game she was playing on the phone. She found the elevators and made her way up to the third floor. As she exited the elevator, she passed a couple of uniformed officers that had been waiting for the elevator. They eyed her, but said nothing as they entered the elevator and the doors closed.

The floor was quiet as nurses made their rounds. Decker walked past the nurses' station and found the room number that the woman at the reception desk had given her. She knocked twice and a weak female voice responded, "Come in please."

"Special Agent Tanner?" Decker asked as she slowly opened the room's large wooden door.

Decker walked into the room to see a young brunette sitting up in a hospital bed. She was wearing a gray t-shirt with her legs tucked under the white blankets. As Decker got closer, she noticed bruising around Tanner's neck and on her arms.

"Do you have a moment to chat?" Decker asked as she approached the foot of the agent's bed.

Tanner hesitated for a moment and then her eyes widened as she recognized her visitor. "Michelle Decker!" she said with a squeal as she realized her idol was standing in front of her. She started to swing her legs off the bed as the IV stretched against her arm. "I need to get dressed!"

Decker stopped the young agent, trying to calm her as she walked to the side of the bed. "Please. It's ok. I just have a few questions."

"I can't believe I'm finally meeting you! And like this! I look like a wreck!"

"Believe me, I've been there," Decker said, trying to calm her. "Please, try to relax. Are you ok?"

"I can't believe you're standing in front of me! I'm a huge fan. I've read so much about you!"

Decker smiled graciously. "That's nice. But are you ok?"

Tanner blushed. "Yes. Yes, I'm fine. I'm just here for observation for the night. Mild concussion and a few bruises. I'm sure you've seen worse."

"Do you remember what happened?"

"Oh my gosh, they're looking for your husband, aren't they?" Tanner asked nervously. "I told them I didn't think he did it, but they said he's done this before. They said the Director himself ordered that he be considered a suspect. I'm so sorry."

"Madison, focus!"

"My friends call me Maddie, but you can call me whatever—"

"Ok, *Maddie*, I need you to focus. Can you tell me what you remember?"

"Ok, well," Tanner said as she adjusted herself on the bed. "I met your husband at the airport early this morning as I was assigned. He was very nice, but I'm not surprised you would land a guy like that. Anyway, I brought him to the scene of the building collapse in Falls Church and we talked to the investigators."

"What did they say?"

Tanner shrugged. "Nothing, really. Gas explosion. All signs point to an accident. Your husband didn't seem to like that. He was pretty upset. The victims were your friends, weren't they?"

Decker nodded. "And then what happened?"

"We went to the morgue. Mr. Martin wanted to see the bodies of the victims. He didn't say much on the drive over, just that he couldn't believe it had happened. Were they your friends too?"

"Yes," Decker said sharply. "What happened at the morgue?"

"I walked in with Mr. Martin and introduced him to the coroner. The coroner took him to the back and I walked back outside to check in with the office to see what they wanted me to do when we were done. After I finished the phone call, I saw Mr. Martin walk out of the morgue. He looked pretty upset and didn't say much when he came back. That's when it happened."

Decker nodded for Tanner to continue.

"Mr. Martin got out of the Tahoe to take a phone call. I didn't think much of it, but the next thing I knew, someone opened my door and grabbed my arm. I was in a chokehold and couldn't breathe before I realized what was happening. I didn't even get a look at whoever it was, it happened so fast," Tanner said, shaking her head as she rubbed the bruised area around her neck.

"The next thing I knew, I was in an ambulance on the way to the hospital. They told me your husband had done it," Tanner said and then added, "but I didn't believe it. He didn't seem capable of doing something like that. He was very sweet."

"Cal has been through a lot," Decker said, leaning forward in her chair. "I don't want anything bad to happen to him again. I really need to find him, sweetie, so if there's anything you're not telling me, please, please tell me."

"I wouldn't hide anything from you, you're my—"

"Try to think, Maddie," Decker said, cutting her off. "Did anything else happen? Did anyone say anything that seemed off? Anything about the scene at the office building or the morgue?"

Tanner considered it for a minute, looking away from her idol as she did. "Well, and please don't be mad at me for saying this, but I noticed your husband lying when we were talking to the Fire Marshall and Falls Church detective."

"Lying?"

"Yeah, I'm pretty sure at least," Tanner said shyly. "I don't think it makes him bad, but—"

"Explain," Decker snapped, once again cutting her off.

"In the Academy, they taught us about micro expressions and 'tells' to gauge whether a person is lying. It's where your face makes subtle changes—"

"I am not that old. I remember. Go on."

"Well, Detective Windsor asked Mr. Martin if he knew how to access a basement at the site of the explosion. It's a structure made of steel and titanium, and Detective Windsor said it had a solid vault door. I don't think he was seriously asking, but your husband's reaction caught my attention. He hesitated for a second and looked away. I saw the micro expression in his face before he said he had no idea, and then he quickly changed the subject," Tanner explained.

"Did they ask him about it?"

Tanner shook her head. "No, I don't think either of them picked up on it, but I'm almost certain there was more to it."

"Is the office building scene secure?"

Tanner shrugged. "They're not considering it a crime scene, so other than a few barricades, I doubt there's any police presence."

Decker stood and extended her hand. "Thank you for your help, Agent Tanner. I really appreciate it."

Tanner reluctantly shook Decker's hand. "I'm really sorry about what happened."

"It happens," Decker said. "Now, get some rest."

Decker turned to walk out. As she reached the door, she heard "Wait!" and saw Tanner pulling the IV out of her arm and jumping out of the bed. The young agent bolted to the closet and grabbed her pants.

"Let me help you!" Tanner said.

Decker turned back as the young agent hurried to get dressed. "I don't think that's a good idea."

"It's my fault your husband is missing. I let you down. Let me make it up to you. I'll help you find him."

"Maddie, I don't think you—"

"It's what you would do, isn't it?" Tanner asked, cutting off Decker. "It's the right thing to do. I can help you find him."

"You could get into a lot of trouble," Decker said. "You really should just rest."

Tanner buttoned her pants and grabbed her shoes. "I want to help," she insisted. "Please."

"Alright then," Decker relented. "Let's go."

CHAPTER SIXTEEN

The blue and white Bell 429WLG helicopter lowered its landing gear as it started to slow. Spectre was glued to the window as the pilot raised the nose and descended on the luxury high-rise in Manhattan. The sun had just set, leaving an orange glow on the horizon that reflected beautifully on the skyscrapers.

The sense of euphoria Spectre had felt since eating at the hotel in Arlington further enhanced his awe of the view. The feeling had started after eating at the hotel, and although he had slept on the short flight from D.C. to New York, it still hadn't worn off. It made the city seem all the more surreal.

The helicopter gently touched down on the roof helipad and a man from Cruz's security detail opened Spectre's door. He stepped out first, shielding his eyes from the rotor wash as Cruz followed behind, chatting with his assistant.

Once clear of the helipad, Spectre turned and allowed Cruz and his young female assistant to take the lead. He followed them through a set of doors and onto an elevator that took them to Cruz's private office.

"Have a seat," Cruz said as he motioned toward the leather chairs near the window.

"Can I get you something to drink?" Cruz's assistant asked.

"Water, please," Spectre said, still trying to shake the haze. "In a bottle."

The woman retrieved a bottle of water from a nearby mini-fridge as Spectre took a seat in one of the chairs. The view was spectacular. He could see the World Trade Center Freedom Tower out in the distance. It was a testament to American resolve and resiliency.

Spectre graciously accepted the bottle of water and inspected the cap as he opened it, looking for signs of tampering as Cruz returned carrying a tattered folder.

"You drugged me, didn't you?" Spectre asked as Cruz sat down and placed the folder on the coffee table.

"I wanted to make your flight more comfortable," Cruz said. "The effects should be wearing off shortly."

"What the fuck is going on here?" Spectre asked. "Why did you need to drag me all the way to New York to tell me what happened?"

"Because I needed to show you, Mr. Martin," Cruz said as he picked up the folder and handed it to him.

"What is this?" Spectre asked as he looked at the weathered brown folder.

"Open it."

Spectre slowly opened the folder. On the inside cover, someone had drawn a skull with Odin's trademark Valknut symbol on the forehead. He turned to the first page, a copy of what appeared to be part of the passenger manifest of the Lusitania on May 1, 1915 on its voyage from New York to Britain.

There were two sets of names circled in red – Witherbee and Stone. They occupied first class accommodations. "Who were they?" Spectre asked, pointing to the marks.

"Keep going," Cruz said.

Behind the partial manifest, Spectre found a newspaper clipping dated May 8, 1915 from the New York Herald. The headlined declared that the Lusitania had been sunk and over a thousand souls had been lost. Attached to the back was another clipping of a smaller article stating that the family of hotel proprietor Charles Witherbee had been among those that had died. Next to it, a similar article stated that wealthy banker Alfred Stone had also lost his family.

After the articles, Spectre found what appeared to be U.S. Army personnel files. Spectre casually flipped through them. They were hard-looking men of a much different era. They had all served in either the Spanish-American War or Philippine-American War. There was a vague contract signed and attached to each that said, "For exceptional services rendered" and listed a fee of one dollar per day.

The final page had the same skull and valknut as a letterhead for a typed manifesto. Spectre picked it up from the file and began reading it out loud.

"When, in the course of human events, it becomes clear that the will of the government is insufficient to seek justice on behalf of the people and to stand against the evils of the world. That noble statesmanship yields to gamesmanship. That honor yields to pomp and circumstance. That justice cannot be done. It is in these times that ordinary men must take extraordinary measures. That vengeance must be dealt swiftly and without process," Spectre read, looking up to see Cruz hanging on his words.

"We find that the governments of the United States and other world powers are inadequate to sufficiently deal with such inequities, and we must therefore proceed without further counsel. We have chartered these men to see justice served. To deliver vengeance in honor of our colleagues, our friends, and our families.

"We enact this charter with three basic rules. First, only those who pick up arms may be considered combatants. Great care shall be exercised to prevent harm to women and children. Second, spoils of war shall not be stolen from the battlefield. Third, each man's greatest responsibility is to the man fighting next to him. Each man will fight to the death, if necessary, in defense of his fellow man," Spectre said, pausing as he looked up at Cruz.

"Fight with honor. Fight with courage. Avenge the fallen. Stamus Contra Malum. Signed, Charles Witherbee and Alfred stone," Spectre finished. "Odin charter?"

Cruz nodded. "They killed the U-Boat commander and then used guerilla warfare in the Balkans to help degrade confidence in the Kaiser. They were very successful."

"So that's how Odin got its start, huh? Why are you showing me this? What does this have to do with the deaths of Lyons and my friends?"

"Odin has changed a lot over the years," Cruz replied. "It has been passed down from generation to generation. Starting with two men, it has had as many as six and until recently had four. But now, sadly, we are once again down to two. I am one of them, of course. The other is a direct descendant of Alfred Stone. Jeff was from the Witherbee line. He was very passionate about Odin."

"Ok," Spectre said slowly, still not sure where Cruz was going with this.

"It started much like what you probably saw with Lyons and his group. Direct action. Kill bad guys and do what weak governments would not. Standing against evil in the most literal sense of the word, you see. But as the world changed, we saw that bullets and bombs weren't the answer. Spilling blood isn't always the best way to effect change," Cruz said.

Spectre stared blankly at the old billionaire, waiting for him to get to a point.

"At one time, each member of the council had his own group for direct action. It was complicated, but we worked together and sometimes worked with governments to get things done. I was the first to disband my team. I didn't feel like bloodshed was the way to go anymore. There were other means at our disposal."

"Like what?" Spectre asked.

"Media, politics, and societal influence," Cruz said. "In 1915, news traveled as fast as the printing press. Today? Milliseconds. We're no longer just an isolated country. We're a planet of connected people."

"Globalism."

"Precisely, but don't say it like it's such a bad word. A unified world is a wonderful thing, Cal. You don't need teams to kill people when you can eliminate the bad guys through social change, and even more importantly, when you're not creating your own enemies."

"I take it Lyons didn't believe that crap?" Spectre asked.

"Jeff was a very opinionated person, much like yourself. Although he was young, he believed that the only way to stop evil was to fight fire with fire. But as you saw in your military career, that hasn't exactly worked. It has only caused unnecessary deaths and spent treasure while giving rise to even more enemies. I had hoped he would eventually outgrow it and see the futility of it all."

"So you killed him?"

Cruz seemed taken aback by the question. "Of course not! Ever since his parents died, Jeff was like a second son to me. I would have gladly traded my life for his."

"Ok," Spectre said. "You said you know what happened. Who killed them?"

"I don't know if you're aware, but Jeff was contemplating a run for the Presidency. He believed he could cut through the bureaucracy and rid Washington of the corruption and incompetence. He planned to finance his own campaign, which made people very nervous. People, especially people of our influence, get nervous when men talk change and are beholden to no one, you see," Cruz said, leaning back in his chair as he crossed his legs.

"Who killed them?" Spectre asked angrily.

"You might want to calm down. There isn't much you can do about it, son."

"Who. Killed. Them?"

"I have it on good authority that President Clifton ordered a team to remove my poor boy from the board," Cruz said, hanging his head.

"Bullshit!"

"I wish it were a lie, but my sources are solid. How do you think I knew so much about your time with Project Archangel? I have many resources that allow me access to incredible amounts of information."

Spectre considered it for a moment. He wasn't sure if he was still feeling the effects of being drugged, but Cruz's explanation made perfect sense. Spectre never trusted Clifton, and had no trouble believing that she was just as corrupt as every other politician in Washington.

Seeing Spectre consider the possibility, Cruz pulled out his phone and put it on the table. He unlocked the device and then opened an audio playback app before hitting PLAY.

"Lyons and his team are leaving a trail of bodies in the Middle East. Complete destabilization," a male voice said.

"I am aware," a woman replied. Spectre recognized President Madeline Clifton's voice.

"You know he's considering running for President, right?" the man asked.

"I already told you I'm done after this term. He can do whatever he wants."

"But ma'am, what about Johnson? Lyons was very vocal about the corruption and bringing down the house of cards. He's going to throw you under the bus."

"We survived Johnson and a nuclear explosion. I'll survive Lyons in retirement," Clifton said confidently.

"You may survive, but the party won't. He knows everything," the man said.

"What do you propose?" Clifton asked.

"He has a team of operators and enough money to fund a hundred campaigns by himself. We have to stop him or he'll destroy this country."

"How?"

"Let me worry about that, ma'am.

The President sighed. "Do what you need to do."

"Yes, ma'am."

Cruz picked up the phone as the recording ended. "See what I mean? Even the people that seem the purest can turn ugly when their empire is threatened. Lyons tried to fly too high, too fast."

"So why are you telling me this? Why did you bring me here? What do you want from me?"

Cruz smiled. "Like Odin's forefathers, I seek justice. Justice for my friends. Justice for your friends. Justice for a country that is run by untouchable bureaucrats. Although I disbanded my team, I believe the time for direct action is once again upon us. I know your background. I know your history. I want you on my team."

"To do what exactly?" Spectre asked suspiciously.

"I know you killed Vice President Johnson. The problem is the corruption didn't end with him. I know you think Clifton was innocent, but she was just as guilty as Johnson. They're all part of a corrupt establishment. You didn't finish the job, and now your friends are dead, Cal," Cruz said. "My son is dead."

"You want me to kill the President of the United States?" Spectre asked, feeling numb once again as he thought back to Kerry Johnson and the misery he caused.

"I want you to seek justice, Cal. Stamus Contra Malum. You're the only one left to stand against evil."

CHAPTER SEVENTEEN

Tanner was starting to grow on Decker. Not as a friend or colleague, but she was starting to feel like the kid sister Decker never wanted. Her overly enthusiastic fangirling of Decker aside, Tanner seemed to be an intelligent and competent agent.

After leaving the hospital, they had taken Decker's rental car to get food and then headed toward the scene in Falls Church. Decker used the time to get to know the young special agent – in part to keep the topic of conversation off of Decker's past, but also because Decker wanted to get to know the agent risking her career.

Madison Tanner had just turned twenty six in August. She had a Masters in accounting and finance and had graduated from the University of Texas just three years earlier. She had grown up as an Army brat, following her father around the world while he served as an Army Intelligence officer. She had joined the FBI after a recruiting event on campus caught her eye and hadn't looked back since.

Although she had previously never considered a career in law enforcement, Tanner explained, she excelled at it. She had taken home nearly every award during the academy and received the highest marks during her initial field evaluations during her first assignment. Although she was too shy to talk about it, Decker could tell that Tanner was a rising star in the FBI, much like she had been early in her career.

"Was it hard giving it all up?" Tanner asked, breaking a short silence as they continued to the scene of the collapse.

"Giving what up?"

"You know," Tanner said sheepishly. "Your career. Everything you worked for. I mean, I'm sure you could have done absolutely anything after saving the President."

"Not at all," Decker replied.

"Really? You didn't like it?"

Decker shook her head. "No, I loved the job. Of course there were things I didn't like, but it was a great experience for me."

"So why stop? I'm sure you could have gone wherever you wanted."

"I could have, but it was time to move on. I found the life I wanted to live. I wouldn't change anything for the world."

"Your husband seems like a very sweet guy," Tanner said.

A slight grin flashed across Decker's face before suddenly turning serious as she remembered that he was still missing. "That's why I will do everything in my power to find him."

"Do you think he really called a terrorist?" Tanner asked.

Decker glared at the young agent. "Of course not. Cal is not that kind of guy."

"But he has been in trouble before."

"He has done what he needed to do to survive," Decker said. "And to save other people."

"You really love him, don't you?" Tanner asked.

"With all my heart and soul," Decker said. "We've been through a lot together, and he is the best thing that has ever happened to me."

"That's so sweet. You're so lucky."

"Am I?" Decker asked, giving the young agent another look. "This doesn't feel lucky."

"I'm so sorry! I meant to have a guy like Cal. I wasn't saying—"

"Relax. It's ok," Decker said. "Let's just find him and figure out what's going on."

"Of course," Tanner replied. "Again, I'm so sorry."

There wasn't much left to say as they drove the remaining distance to the building. Decker parked in what had once been the parking lot and grabbed her flashlight out of her bag. She immediately recognized Kruger's pickup and decided to start there.

"Do you know if anyone checked these vehicles?" Decker asked.

"I'm sorry, ma'am, but I don't know much about the investigation. It doesn't look like they've been touched."

Decker tossed Agent Tanner a flashlight from her bag. "I'll check this out, you go see if you can find the entrance to that basement."

"Yes, ma'am," Tanner replied as she flicked the light on and headed for the building wreckage.

Decker turned, shining her light into the cab of the four-door Dodge Ram pickup. She noticed that the driver's door was unlocked and tried the handle. It opened, sending up a cloud of dust, causing Decker to cover her nose and mouth. The dome light turned on, illuminating the front bench seat.

A cursory search of the front seat revealed nothing of interest. There were a few Gatorade bottles that had been used as spit receptacles and a half-empty water bottle. Decker looked under the bench seat and found a holstered Glock 19 with a spare magazine. She looked up to make sure the spunky young agent didn't see her, then tucked the handgun into her waistband at the small of her back and stuffed the spare magazine into her pocket.

With the front seat clear, Decker stepped to the rear of the truck and opened the door. She saw an open box sitting on the bench seat. It appeared to be a box of personal items from Kruger's office. As she shined the light on it, she found a coffee mug and various effects. She picked up a Russian Spetsnaz patch, turning it over under the light to see if anything of interest was written on the back.

Moving on, she continued riffling through the box. He had items from other members of the team – a 160th Special Operations Aviation Regiment "Nightstalkers" patch from Shorty, one of Axe's dogtags, a picture of him with Axe and Tuna in Afghanistan, and the nametag patches of Rocky and Elvis. She found the newspaper clipping he had saved of the school bus massacre declaring TERROR IN SUBURBIA.

She remembered the attack all too well. Kruger had quit the team as a result, angry at himself for letting it happen. A school bus full of small children had been burned alive at the hands of terrorists. It was one of the most gruesome things she had ever seen. But yet, somehow, Kruger had managed to bounce back. Or at least, Spectre had convinced Kruger to bounce back and get back in the fight as they worked together to find one of Spectre's missing coworkers in New Orleans.

Decker continued looking through Kruger's things. She found a course catalog from a community college in Florida with several pages folded and a GI Bill pamphlet. "A nursing program?" she said to herself as she flipped through the pages.

She continued digging through the box and came across a small notebook. She opened it and found handwritten notes as well as usernames and passwords for various systems. As she flipped through the pages, she heard footsteps behind her and turned to see Tanner jogging toward her. She shoved the notebook into her back pocket and closed the door of the truck.

"I found it," Tanner said as she approached. "It's barely accessible with all the debris, but I think we can get in if we can figure out a way past the security."

"What kind of security?"

"Keypad of some sort with a handprint scanner," Tanner replied.

"Let's take a look," Decker said as she pointed for Tanner to lead the way.

Decker followed Tanner through the parking lot and past the barricades. They carefully traversed the rubble, heading toward the partially collapsed parking garage. They reached the entrance to the basement where the digital security system appeared to still be powered.

"Any ideas?" Tanner asked.

Decker inspected the access panel. As Tanner had reported, there was a hand scanner next to a keypad. Out of curiosity, Decker placed her hand on the scanner. Seconds later, the cracked display flashed red and reported that access had been denied.

"I can see if we can get someone from the crime lab to crack the safe, but no one is around at this hour," Tanner said.

Decker pulled out the notepad from her back pocket and then put the flashlight under her chin. She started flipping through the pages, hoping Kruger had been careless enough to write down some type of override or access code in his notebook.

"Where'd you find that?" Tanner asked, shining the light on the pages.

"My friend's truck," Decker said.

The effort appeared fruitless. Kruger had used the book to store his email and computer passwords, but there was nothing to indicate anything more complex than that. As she flipped through the pages, she found a list of six-digit combos and decided to try it.

"Here, read these numbers to me," Decker said, handing the book to Tanner.

"Three one six two two four," Tanner said. Decker followed along, typing them in as Tanner read them. The keypad once again flashed red and denied access.

They went through two more combinations, both ending in the same result. "Are you sure these are access codes?" Tanner asked.

"Just keep going. What's the next one?" Decker asked.

Tanner read the fourth set of numbers. As Decker entered the fifth number, the screen suddenly flashed green and read ACCESS GRANTED.

Startled, Decker and Tanner stepped back as the lock clicked open and the door started to swing outward toward them. Decker instinctively drew her handgun, crossing her shooting hand over her flashlight as the door opened, revealing a shadowy figure approaching. Surprised that Decker was armed, Tanner hesitated and then followed suit, drawing her weapon and pointing it downrange.

"Hello ladies," a male voice said.

The man approached, his face coming into view as Decker's flashlight illuminated him. Decker gasped as the man stopped and put his hands up.

"Don't shoot," he said casually. "It's good to see you again, Michelle."

CHAPTER EIGHTEEN

A frontal assault on a British military installation was conceivable, but not desirable. Even a snatch and grab operation was possible; he certainly had the men and assets available to pull either off. But Jäger knew that the only way to guarantee the survival of the two high value targets being sheltered by the British MI-6 was to get them to willingly hand the two men over.

It had worked brilliantly in Benghazi, but that was slightly easier. The group Jäger had arranged to take down the Odin team was already being used by both the CIA and Israeli Mossad. It was easy to forge the mission order and direct the transfer to Benghazi and subsequent release to Jäger and his men posing as Mossad. No one even raised an eyebrow.

But the two men that Stone wanted alive were different. They had managed to evade capture. MI-6 was keeping them safe, and worse yet, the agent handling them was the sister of one of the men. It would take a lot more than forged electronic orders to convince them to hand the two men over.

Jäger adjusted his hat as his driver stopped and presented his credentials to the base sentry. The soldier inspected the documents and then peered into the back. "Good morning, Colonel," he said before returning the credentials and saluting.

The gate opened and the BMW proceeded through. Jäger was accompanied by two of his British contractors. Jäger's driver was Tom Wellington, a former intelligence officer of the Royal Navy. Former Royal Marine David Simmons rode shotgun. All three were wearing British military fatigues.

Jäger and his small team were posing as members of Britain's MI-5 Section G counterintelligence service. Jäger had assumed the identity of Colonel Jonathon Lander, a mid-level manager specializing in section G9 dealing in Islamic extremists. His credentials and base visit request were both authentic, having been sent from the actual MI-5 server in London. It would be impossible for anyone to discover his true identity without physically visiting the paper archives, and by then it would be too late. Jäger didn't intend to stick around long enough for anyone to fully vet him.

Wellington stayed with the vehicle while Simmons accompanied Jäger to the front door of the building. Jäger pressed the intercom button, looking directly into the camera as the system buzzed. "My name is Colonel Jonathon Lander, and I'm here to see Agent Carter," he said with a flawless British accent.

The door buzzed and a man wearing fatigues opened it. "Right this way, gentlemen," he said motioning for them to come in.

The door closed behind them as they walked in. The solider verified their credentials once more and then escorted them through the vault door. He brought them to a conference room and said he would let Agent Carter know that they had arrived.

The men took their seats. Moments later, Sierra Carter entered. Her brown hair was up in a ponytail and she also was wearing fatigues. Jäger and Simmons both stood to greet her. "Thank you for seeing us on such short notice, Agent Carter."

"May I see your credentials, sir?" Carter asked.

"Of course," Jäger said as he nodded for Simmons to follow suit in handing them to Carter.

Carter inspected the IDs and paperwork, glancing up suspiciously at Jäger as she handed them back. "What interest does G9 have here, Col. Lander?"

"May we sit?" Jäger asked as he put his credentials back into his pocket.

"Of course," Carter said as she took a seat at the conference table across from them.

"Thank you," Jäger said as he placed his cover on the table and sat. "As our visit request pointed out, you are holding two men of a national security interest to us at this time."

"And what interest is that exactly?"

"Alex Shepherd was known to work with the Kurds in Northern Syria and Iraq. We have reason to believe that he was radicalized in Libya and is working with a group of Americans to overthrow the American government," Jäger replied.

"And Mr. Reginald Jones?" Carter asked.

"If you mean your brother, Reginald *Carter*, then he is also suspected of working with this group," Jäger said. His face remained expressionless as he watched her shift uneasily in her chair.

"My brother?"

"Please don't try to play games, Agent Carter. We have been tracking them for quite some time."

"What sort of plot is he accused of?"

"The destabilization of Western governments," Simmons interjected.

"He's working with a group called Odin. Are you familiar with them?"

"No," Carter lied.

Jäger smiled. "Of course you are. You were the reason your brother joined Odin, Agent Carter."

"Why should I believe any of this?"

Jäger shrugged. "It doesn't matter if you do or not. I must speak with these men, and take them into custody if necessary. I have received proper authorization from your superiors and am merely having this chat with you as a courtesy, given your relationship with Mr. Carter."

"Odin is not a terrorist organization," Carter replied.

"It wasn't," Jäger said. "But recently the organization has splintered. The group went rogue. We are monitoring a threat to the United States as we speak."

"What type of threat?"

"Of that, we are not sure," Simmons answered. "But we believe it is a threat to the nation's infrastructure."

"It's why we must speak to your brother and Mr. Shepherd immediately, Agent Carter," Jäger said. "We don't have the luxury of time."

"Of course," Carter said as she stood. "Right this way."

Jäger and Simmons stood and followed Carter out of the room. She escorted them down the hallway to the room where her brother and Shepherd had been staying. Knocking on the door, she slowly opened it. "Gentlemen, you have a guest."

Carter froze as she entered the room and saw that it was empty. "Reginald? Alex?" she called.

"Where are they?" Jäger asked angrily.

"I don't know. They were here shortly before I met with you in the conference room," Carter said, pretending to look around the room. "Perhaps they've gone for some fresh air."

Jäger turned to Simmons. "They're trying to escape. Get this base on lockdown," he ordered.

"Straight away, sir," Simmons said as he hastily exited the room.

"I just can't imagine where they might have gone," Carter said, pretending to search the room.

Jäger turned to face Carter. He was easily a half foot taller than the young MI-6 agent. Before she could react, Jäger launched a knifehand attack into her throat. He was careful not to crush her windpipe, but the blow incapacitated Carter as she fell to her knees gasping for air.

"Of course I am no fool," Jäger said, losing the British accent. "They are likely miles away by now."

Jäger pulled out a pair of handcuffs and restrained Carter's hands behind her back. "But don't worry, Agent Carter. You will lead your brother and his friend to me."

* * *

"That's him!" Shepherd yelled as they watched the front gate security camera zoom in on the backseat occupant. "That's the guy who shot Tuna!"

"You're sure?" Carter asked. "His credentials check out fully. MI-5 does have a record of a Colonel Lander and the request for an interview is authentic."

"I'm telling you, that's him," Shepherd replied.

"Can you take him into custody?" Cowboy asked, watching the man look directly at the camera as the car proceeded through the gate.

"Not without cause," Carter replied, shaking her head. "His requests have been fully authenticated and my boss directed me to accommodate him. I would need proof."

"Let me fucking talk to him," Shepherd growled. "I'll get some answers."

"No," Carter said. "You both need to leave."

"We're staying here with you," Cowboy said. "If this guy is as dangerous as we think he is, I'm not leaving you alone to deal with him."

"I can take care of myself," Carter said. "Besides, he may be able to lead us to your colleagues."

"You're going to use yourself as bait?" Cowboy asked.

"I'm going to give you both time to get out of his path, and then we're going to track him," Carter replied. "Now, go. I've ordered a helicopter to take you to London. You'll be safe there."

Cowboy and Carter hugged. One of Carter's subordinates walked in to report that Colonel Lander and company had arrived.

"Take care of yourself," Cowboy said as they ended their embrace. Carter handed him something as Shepherd zipped his canvas bag. He couldn't see what it was and didn't have time to ask.

"It was nice meeting you, ma'am," Shepherd said with a hint of his southern accent. "I'm sure you can take care of this asshole, but if he hurts you, I'm going to fucking kill him. You can let him know that if you'd like. With all due respect, of course."

"I'll be fine, boys, now go!" Carter ordered.

The two men did as they were told, grabbing their gear and heading out the rear access. They jogged to the helicopter pad where a British Royal Air Force Puma HC2 cargo helicopter was waiting.

They greeted the crew chief and tossed their gear into the open side cargo door. The crew chief checked their paperwork and completed the preflight as they hopped on board.

"Mind if we hitch a ride?" Cowboy asked.

The pilots laughed and gave him a thumbs-up. "I'll start the meter," one of the pilots said.

As they strapped in, the helicopter's turbine engines spooled. Moments later, the giant rotor blades started to turn. After completing their pre-takeoff checks, the pilots received their takeoff clearance and the helicopter lifted off.

The helicopter made a turn over the MI-6 building as it climbed out. Shepherd saw two men exit escorting a prisoner with a hood over the head. He tapped Cowboy and pointed. "They're fucking taking her!"

"It's ok, mate," Cowboy said over the intercom while making a pained expression.

"What do you mean, it's ok?" Shepherd shot back. "That asshole has her!"

Cowboy pulled out his smartphone and unlocked it. He opened a map and showed Shepherd the blue dot. "Sierra gave this to me on the way out. She's wearing a tracker, mate."

"And what if this asshole finds it?"

"Then we're right fucked," Cowboy replied.

CHAPTER NINETEEN

The basement was more massive than Decker had expected. The first section housed Odin's massive servers. She imagined that was where Coolio had spent most of his time, coordinating Odin missions as the team's computer guy.

In the second section, the basement housed an armory with state of the art weapons and body armor, specialized equipment like micro-drones and night vision goggles, and skydiving gear with wingsuits. The equipment all looked brand new. Everything was in pristine condition.

The final section of the basement was a living area. There were bunks and food stores. It looked like Odin had set up provisions to last the entire team months. For one man, it could seemingly last years.

Decker sat next to Tanner at a table across from the man who'd made a habit out of being presumed dead. "So explain to me how you managed to survive down here without anyone knowing," she said as she studied the man.

"There's an escape chute under my desk with a mechanical trap door. Or, I guess I should say, *was*. The chute paralleled the building's support beams and then made a turn at the basement to slow down before landing back by that door on an inflated cushion system," Lyons said, pointing to a door behind him. "I heard an explosion and looked up to see a giant fireball headed for me. Barely made it down here, but not before getting a few burns."

Decker saw that Jeff Lyons had minor burns on his arms and bald head. She still couldn't believe that the billionaire leader of Odin had somehow managed to survive. "So why have you been hiding down here all this time?" Decker asked.

"A couple of reasons, actually. First, and most importantly, people are trying to kill me. Not just trying, but some of them are convinced that they succeeded. And second, well, the building collapse has limited my options a bit since the satellite communications and all of our servers eventually went down with the building," Lyons explained. "Can I get you ladies some water?"

"Who's trying to kill you?" Tanner asked as she and Decker both politely declined the water.

"It's complicated," Lyons said. "And, well, no offense, but I don't know you well enough to get into the gritty details."

"But you know me," Decker interjected. "And because of you, Cal is missing. So you'd better start talking."

"Then we can speak in private, but I—"

"I'll vouch for Special Agent Tanner," Decker snapped. "Start talking."

"Alright then," Lyons said, leaning back in his chair. "Where to begin? Well, for starters, we're all fucked."

"Get to it, Lyons," Decker said angrily.

"Michelle, I know you know about Odin. Agent Tanner, let's just call it a secret group run by four billionaires that has been influencing the world landscape for the last hundred years," Lyons said looking at Tanner. "Until recently, that is."

"I'd like to think we've been good guys the whole time, but to be honest, I think we're more gray area than anything. And while I have tried to keep us on the light side of the gray, in recent years things have gotten a bit darker. And I've tried to fight it," Lyons continued.

"What does that even mean?" Tanner asked. "Paramilitary?"

Lyons held up a finger and then stood. He stepped away from the table momentarily before returning with a piece of paper. He drew four circles and labeled them MONEY, INFLUENCE, INFORMATION, and DIRECT ACTION.

"Odin was formed by two really rich guys in 1915 as a direct action group. That means guys with guns doing bad things to even worse people. It stayed that way until after World War II, when the Stevens and Cruz families married in. They were also extremely wealthy, and had similar world visions to my great grandfather Charles Witherbee and the Stone family. So the two became four.

"Together, their view of what Odin was changed. It went from assisting in conflicts and doing things the governments refused to do, to actively influencing the world. The 1950s were a much different time. The Cold War had just kicked off, and isolationism wasn't really an option anymore," Lyons said as he pointed to the information circle. "So we bought media."

"The reason we bought media groups was to fight the communists. You may remember Senator McCarthy trying to root out communists in Hollywood, and history has painted him as a villain. Well, to be honest, he was mostly right. The Soviets were actively using our media against us, to break us down from within and cause the divide you see today. They were trying to play the long game because they knew our countries would never go toe to toe on the battlefield," Lyons explained. "So the Stevens family focused on building a media empire that could fight back in the information fight."

Lyons pointed to the circle labeled MONEY. "Money is a much more difficult thing. You can control entire countries by manipulating their currency. My great grandfather was one of the nation's best investment bankers. And I hate to say it, but he put us on the path of abandoning the gold standard. It was Charles Witherbee that put forth the initiative in the thirties, and my grandfather who helped drive the final nail in the gold standard coffin in 1971. It was meant to stabilize the world, but I believe it failed miserably."

Lyons moved to the circle labeled INFLUENCE. "Influence. That was the Cruz family legacy. I can't think of a single politician elected in this country in the last fifty years that doesn't have some tie to Walter Cruz or his father. He even has a hand in other countries. It's crazy. He's the man behind the proverbial curtain."

"That seems like something out of a movie," Tanner commented.

"Art tends to imitate life," Lyons said. "Or in this case, art imitates the Stevens family."

"I knew it," Decker said. "I knew Odin was bad news. No one group should work outside the law. No one group should be unchecked. My gut told me something was up."

"I'm sorry," Lyons replied. "I really am. For a while, Odin was a good thing. We helped bring down the Soviet Union. We helped find and kill Osama Bin Laden. We got our hands dirty when no one else would, and averted a third world war more times than I can count. We stopped a nuclear holocaust."

"But?" Decker asked.

"Sadly, we lost control," Lyons said. "We lost control as individuals. We lost control as a group. We lost control of everything. I've had a lot of time to reflect since I've been down here, and I'm just as much to blame as everyone else. "

"What happened?" Decker asked.

Lyons pointed to the piece of paper. "In every aspect of Odin, we started losing our grip on reality. On the money side, the fiat currency system we had created began to become a problem. The Chinese became one of our biggest creditors. We risked a global meltdown and hostile takeover financially, and it nearly happened in 2008."

"Social media pretty much killed our influence and information. Grass roots movements fueled by social media took power away. And instead of giving it to the middle of society, it gave power to the fringe. Whereas we had managed to keep the influence mostly centered for the last sixty years, the social media movement gave an overwhelming voice to the extremes."

"And then it took away our information. People stopped relying on media outlets. Blogs and social media posts trumped news articles. We could no longer control the information, and we couldn't protect it from outside influence either. It was a downward spiral."

"Even direct action – the thing that I focused on. As control started slipping from the other four, Stone, Stevens, and Cruz stopped using direct action teams. They thought it was a waste of time and money in the information age. I was the only one left, and I thrived on it. I thought I was a superhero. I guess my hubris finally caught up with me."

CHAPTER TWENTY

Y ou're still not telling us what happened," Decker pushed as she glared at the suddenly-alive billionaire sitting across from her.

Lyons let out a pained sigh. "Ok, well, about ten years ago Walter had an idea. We saw the storm building with the national debt and the Chinese. We thought maybe we could kill two birds with one stone – take the Chinese down a notch or two on the world stage and get Americans to focus and stop spending themselves into oblivion. So we started grooming a candidate."

"Don't tell me…"

Lyons nodded. "He was already working with them in the oil industry. It made perfect sense. We made a few indirect introductions and made sure he was selected as Secretary of

Defense. From there, we set him along the path to the White House. Kerry Johnson was going to be the man that exposed the Chinese influence for what it was and reset American apathy toward that country."

"Kerry Johnson?" Decker yelled, lunging across the table and grabbing Lyons by his collar. "You son of a bitch!"

Tanner helped restrain Decker as Lyons freed himself. "We fucked up. I freely admit it. We completely underestimated the Chinese espionage ability and the ambitions of Kerry Johnson. We lost control."

"They tried to kill the President, you stupid asshole!" Decker yelled.

"We had no idea they were planning that. We thought they were going to let Clifton's term run its course and then push Johnson into office. That's when we were going to let it come out and show the world what the Chinese were capable of. I didn't like the plan, but I was too busy chasing Al Qaeda around the desert to really care. The Chinese didn't seem like a threat to me," Lyons explained. "But when I found out, I assembled a team to try to fix it. We were too late. Luckily, in this case, you and Cal saved the day."

"You dumb shit," Decker growled. "I can't believe how stupid you could be!"

"It gets worse," Lyons said sheepishly. "With the rise of ISIS, we started fighting a two-front war. On one side of the world, you have radical Islamic terrorists trying to impose their twisted caliphate on the rest of the world, and on the other, a nation that is growing increasingly divided. I don't know if you've been watching the news, but we're one major incident away from a full blown civil war."

"What did you do now?" Decker asked angrily.

Lyons withdrew slightly, afraid of Decker's wrath. "This time, I tried to stop it. That's how we got here."

"Stop what?" Tanner asked.

"Helios," Lyons said. "It's an advanced technology we've spent years and probably upwards of a billion dollars developing. You've heard of IBM's Watson?"

"Is that the cloud-based super computer thing IBM is always advertising?" Tanner asked.

"Pretty close. Well, that system has sixteen terabytes of ram. Helios has a hundred and twenty eight. It occupies an entire basement much like this, but it's tied into everything."

"Everything?" Decker asked.

"NSA, CIA, FBI, MI-6, Soviet FSB, Google, Apple, Microsoft – if you name it and it's electronic, Helios has it or is connected to it, up to the highest levels of classification of every system out there. It can generate hacks into any system within hours," Lyons said. "Like I said, we're fucked."

"Why are we fucked?" Tanner asked.

"The original intent of the system was to recapture some of the influences we were losing. To learn the trends and figure out how we could adapt and make the world a better place. But what we soon learned was that the world is getting too far gone. With highly contested local elections, the BREXIT in the EU, tensions with the Russians in the Middle East, and the Chinese problem, it had become unfixable. There was too much of a disparity," Lyons said, shaking his head. "Cruz and Stone believed we were too far gone."

"So what?" Decker asked.

"Sometimes the only way to fix something is to start over. Like a computer with a virus, the hard drive needs to be wiped clean. That's what Helios could do. Start over," Lyons explained.

"How?"

"Helios knows everything. Anything you've ever said within hearing distance of an electronic device. Anything you've searched for on the internet. Basically, if you've touched an electronic device in your life, Helios knows everything about you.

And it knows most of it even if you haven't…which includes your deepest secrets."

"And politicians," Decker added.

"Everyone," Lyons said. "And what it doesn't know, it can perfectly recreate. It has built huge databases of words said by virtually anyone. It can precisely recreate entire conversations without either party even knowing what was said."

"That explains the phone call from Cal to the ISIS terrorist," Decker said to Tanner.

"It doesn't surprise me," Lyons said. "They can use it for whatever they want."

"So how does this wipe the slate clean and force people to start over?" Decker asked.

"Society is based on trust," Tanner answered. "That's how governments run. If all of our secrets are out in the open, then no one feels protected. Too much information is just as bad as not enough."

"Exactly," Lyons replied. "Helios built an algorithm to release the data. It's projected to cause a complete collapse of the U.S. government in months."

"But why? What good does that do?" Decker asked.

"Because they want to rebuild it. People want to be governed. Anarchy doesn't work forever. Helios had even calculated the rebuilding method to ensure control."

"That is idiotic," Decker snapped. "Holy shit."

"It's frightening," Tanner said. "We learned about this on a smaller scale during the cyber warfare lessons at the academy. My God."

Lyons nodded. "Which is why I wanted to stop it. Cruz and Stone were leading the charge. They are convinced that the U.S. needs to be wiped clean to avoid a world war. They've started to believe that globalism is the next answer. Stevens and I were very much against it."

"What happened to Stevens?" Tanner asked.

"Died of natural causes not too long ago."

"Leaving only you to stand in their way," Tanner said.

"I had a different plan," Lyons said. "I was going to run for President. Go in as an outsider and try to fix some of the corruption. Unite people and stop the divisive rhetoric."

"Why wouldn't they like that?" Decker asked. "You're one of them!"

Lyons shook his head. "Not anymore. Ever since Midway, I've been on the outs. Even though we never made it there, Odin died on that island. It was only a matter of time."

"When are they going to unleash this Helios, or whatever it is?" Tanner asked. "I need to warn Washington."

"In the coming weeks," Lyons said. "But it's no use. Helios can literally generate anything. They can declare you a terrorist and issue a FISA warrant for you without ever even seeing a FISA court. Your whole identity could be wiped clean. There is no way to stop it."

"We have to destroy it," Decker said. "But first we need to find my husband."

"Do you know where Helios is?" Tanner asked.

Lyons shook his head. "That's not something I was read in on."

"What about Mr. Martin? Do you think they have him?" Tanner asked.

"I have no way of knowing from down here. We need to get to my compound," Lyons said. "Without anyone knowing I'm alive."

"Wait a minute," Tanner said. "How did they identify your body at the morgue? Won't they figure that out soon anyway?"

"I have someone I trust on the outside," Lyons said. "Before the servers went down, I was able to get out a message to take care of it. Charred cadavers with forged dental records are often hard to tell. He should be waiting at my estate with someone who can help."

"So is Kruger still alive too then?" Decker asked.

Lyons gave her a confused look. "Kruger isn't the one who contacted you?"

"His body was at the morgue too," Tanner said.

"Goddammit," Lyons replied, hanging his head. "Then, no, Kruger is dead."

"Or they have him too," Lyons added.

CHAPTER TWENTY-ONE

Decker led the way as the vault door opened. She raised the Sig 516 rifle she had acquired from the armory and ascended the stairs. She maneuvered around the debris, using the rail-mounted flashlight to briefly illuminate her path as she cleared for threats.

Lyons and Tanner followed in a single file, each carrying their own rifle as they climbed out of the basement scanning their sectors. They had taken what they could from the armory for their trip, each donning Odin's experimental carbon-nanotube lightweight body armor, a holstered Sig P320 handgun, and a lightweight backpack carrying extra magazines, food, and water.

Because the armor was custom-fit, Decker had to make do with wearing the armor that had been custom made for the Odin pilot "Jenny." It was slightly small and constricting, but it was good enough and much better than the heavy ceramic plates as an alternative. Tanner was just the right size to wear former Filipino commando Cuda's armor.

They moved quickly across the debris field toward the parking lot where Decker had found Kruger's truck. Lyons had stashed an up-armored Yukon Denali at the rear of the parking lot with a fake registration. Decker was impressed at how much planning Lyons had done for a situation like this, but she figured a billionaire, caught up in the mess he was in, would need multiple contingency plans.

Reaching the SUV, Lyons unlocked the door and tossed his bag into the backseat. "Ok, last check, no cell phones, smart watches, pagers, or anything that can emit a signal, right?"

Decker checked her pockets a final time. She had left her phone in the rental car, but just wanted to be sure. Tanner had left her phone in the vault. Lyons warned that their phones could be used to track them, even if turned off. Helios could activate any phone. Even though Decker hoped Spectre might somehow call, having her phone on her was just too big of a risk. "Nope," she said.

Tanner gave a thumbs-up, also indicating that her phone was gone. As she started to put her bag in the SUV, she suddenly stopped and took off her watch. "Good point, I almost forgot. This is a smartwatch."

"I'll buy you a new one," Lyons said before taking it from her and throwing it across the parking lot. "I'm good for it."

Tanner watched her smartwatch land between two cars. "But I just got it."

Decker threw her bag in the back and turned to Lyons. "Are you driving?"

"No," Lyons said, shaking his head. "They'll use the traffic cameras and facial recognition. It's best if you and Agent Tanner sit up front. I'll give you directions."

Decker gestured for Tanner to drive. She thought it would be better for the young agent to drive given her familiarity with the area and current FBI credentials in case they ran into law enforcement. Decker unslung her rifle and walked around to the passenger side. She placed the short barrel rifle on the floorboard as she took her place in the front passenger seat.

"Where to?" Tanner asked as she adjusted the mirrors.

"I'll give you turn-by-turn," Lyons said. "Take a left out of the parking lot."

Tanner did as instructed. They drove in relative silence for a little over an hour as Lyons gave directions from the back seat. The route took slightly longer, Lyons explained, because he wanted to make sure they weren't being followed.

Decker saw several traffic cameras as they made their way out of Falls Church. She couldn't help but wonder if Lyons had been exaggerating about the capabilities of the computer Lyons's colleagues had developed. Was it really possible to tap into existing traffic cameras with terrible resolution and somehow manage facial recognition through a moving vehicle? If so, it was beyond frightening.

But Decker could also see the applications in law enforcement. License plate reader technology had already been a game changer in finding suspects, but having the ability to see their faces? Suspects on the run could be located within minutes. There would be no way to avoid capture short of hiding in the woods.

They arrived at Lyons's secluded compound just after midnight. Lyons gave Tanner a six digit combination to enter and the large iron gates with the initials J.L. automatically opened, revealing the mile-long driveway to the Lyons estate.

At the end of the paved road, another gate came into view. This time, Decker could see the multi-story compound. There was an empty guard shack and call box. "Now what?" Tanner asked as she stopped at the gate.

Lyons stepped out of the vehicle. He opened the callbox, revealing a phone and handprint scanner. He placed his hand on it. Moments later, the gates opened and a female voice said, "Welcome, Mr. Lyons."

"Fancy," Decker said.

"So do I just park anywhere?" Tanner asked as she approached the circle drive in front of the house.

"Behind the Ferrari would be fine," Lyons said as he leaned over the front seat center console.

"Uhh… Which one?"

"That one," Lyons said, pointing at a black Ferrari 458 Spider.

"I'm in the wrong business," Tanner said as she parked behind the Ferraris. "Is that a 550 Maranello and…Holy shit! A Ferrari LaFerrari?"

"Yeah, I have had it a few years," Lyons said as he grabbed his gear and opened the door.

Tanner grabbed her bag and rifle and walked toward the 458 Spider. "You just leave them out like this all day?"

"I usually have someone that tends to the stable, but they were all sent home under the protocol I enacted before comms went down," Lyons said as he headed toward the front door.

"He *has people for that*," Tanner said mockingly to Decker. "Wow."

"So who's the mystery guy that can help us?" Decker asked as she followed Lyons to the front door.

"One second." Lyons opened a hidden access panel, revealing a thumbprint and retinal scanner. He went through the authentication steps and once again access was granted. He pushed open the door and said, "Welcome to my humble abode, ladies."

As they entered, a small-statured man limped from around the corner carrying three bottles of water. He slowly moved across the marble floors, favoring his left leg as he hobbled toward them.

"I thought you might be thirsty, boss," he said as he came into view.

"Thank you for doing what I asked," Lyons replied as he accepted a bottle of water and patted the man on the shoulder.

The man handed Decker a bottle of water and then stopped as he turned to Tanner. "Hey! That's my armor!" he said, pointing to the name plate that said *CUDA* on the chest.

"Thanks for letting me borrow it," Tanner replied.

"Michelle, you remember Cuda, don't you?" Lyons asked.

"I'm not sure. We may have met once," Decker said, shaking the Filipino commando's hand. She could see scars on his arms and face. He looked like he was recovering from a bad accident of some sort. "I'm Michelle."

"And this is Special Agent Maddie Tanner," Decker said, turning to the young agent.

"Nice to meet you," Cuda said before turning back to Lyons. "Big trouble, boss."

"How's he doing?" Lyons asked as Cuda turned and started walking.

"Better," Cuda said. "He was up and working this afternoon, but Doc gave him morphine to help him sleep. He's worried about internal injuries."

"We can't risk a hospital again," Lyons said.

Decker and Tanner peeled off their armor as they followed Lyons and Cuda through the massive house. Decker recognized most of it from her time there with Spectre after he had been stabbed in a Florida prison and rescued by Kruger. Lyons led them to the same infirmary that they had used to nurse Spectre back to health after losing his kidney.

Lyons put a finger to his mouth as he opened the makeshift hospital room door, revealing Coolio lying in a hospital bed. He was attached to a heart monitor and multiple IVs. A closed laptop sat on a stand next to his bed.

"He's alive," Decker whispered incredulously under her breath. "Thank God."

Cuda looked back at Decker and frowned. "He's doing better. But Doc says he's still in bad shape."

"Thank you for doing that, Cuda," Lyons said in a low register. "You saved both of us."

Cuda shook his head. "Part of the job, boss."

They all followed Lyons out of the room and he closed the door behind them. "How are you feeling?" Lyons asked as he turned to Cuda. "You should be resting too."

"Better," Cuda said. "This sure beats physical therapy."

"If you don't mind me asking, what happened to you?" Tanner asked.

"He had a bit of a mishap about three months ago," Lyons said. "We've had him here recovering ever since. This team has taken a lot of lumps lately."

"Car accident?" Tanner pressed.

"Actually, a building fell on me," Cuda said as he exchanged a knowing look with Lyons.

CHAPTER TWENTY-TWO

O kay, gents, your story checks out," Agent Alfred Pierson said as he returned to his office holding a folder. "I spoke to the real Colonel Lander. He's on holiday in Brussels this week and has no idea about either of you."

The redheaded MI-5 agent sat down across from Shepherd and Cowboy and opened the folder. He pulled out two service photos, one of the actual Colonel Lander and one of the imposter that had taken Sierra Carter.

"The forgery is impeccable," Pierson said. "Every electronic database we have indicated that this was the real Colonel Lander, complete with fingerprints and retinal information. Someone at the MI-5 office had to go down to the paper archives to find this picture. Even facial recognition software matched him as Colonel Lander."

Cowboy pulled the phone out of his pocket and put it on the table, spinning it around so Pierson could see the blue dot hovering over Enderby Wharf next to the South Thames River. He had been keeping an eye on Sierra's tracker since leaving the RAF base and making the short flight to London.

"This is where he's taken her. We need to get to my sister before they move again," Cowboy said, pointing at the screen.

"The request will have to be routed through the appropriate channels," Pierson replied.

"Give us weapons, armor and a car, and we'll do it ourselves," Shepherd said.

"I'm sorry but I can't do that," Pierson said, shaking his head. "Let me see what I can do."

"We need to move *now*, mate," Cowboy reiterated.

Pierson picked up his folder and headed for the door. "Let me see what I can come up with."

Cowboy picked up the phone from the table, staring at the dot as Pierson left the room. Shepherd leaned over and whispered, "We need a plan to get the fuck out of here."

Cowboy nodded as he stuffed the phone into his pocket.

"No offense, but I don't trust these people," Shepherd said. "For all we know, they could be in on it too."

"I don't like it any more than you do. It's my sister out there and we don't even know what we're up against," Cowboy said.

"I'm just saying. The asshole who has her could be manipulating any number of systems. Obviously that airbase back there was pretty secure. If he could forge his identity like that, who knows what they are capable of. I don't like it."

"Let's just see what he comes back with," Cowboy said reassuringly. "Sierra works for a good group."

Shepherd folded his arms and sat back in his chair. "Fine, but the clock is ticking."

Moments later the door opened and Pierson entered, followed by a man in military fatigues. "Gents, we have a green light. This is Captain Smith. He will be leading the operation to retrieve Agent Carter."

"Gentlemen," Smith said as he and Pierson sat down across from them.

"May I see your tracker?" Smith asked.

Cowboy pulled it out of his pocket and unlocked it. The blue dot still hovered over a warehouse in Enderby Wharf.

"What do you know about the man that has her?" Smith asked.

"As much as you do," Cowboy said.

"We don't know shit except he put a bullet in the head of at least one of our friends," Shepherd added. "And we don't have time to sit around and wait."

"I have a tactical team on standby and drone reconnaissance missions ordered. Once we can confirm that your sister is there, we will move in at nightfall," Smith said.

"She'll be gone or dead by then," Shepherd said. "I watched this asshole put a bullet in a man's head without so much as flinching."

"He's right," Cowboy said. "If this man is as cunning an adversary as we have seen so far, he will have moved well before we get optimal conditions for an assault."

"The director has given authorization for the use of any and all assets to retrieve Agent Carter," Agent Pierson said. "Captain, it is up to you."

"Right," Smith said as he stood. "Then I'll get to it."

"May I?" Smith asked as he held up the smartphone.

"Of course," Cowboy said.

"My analysts will confirm that the signal is valid and then we will begin planning the mission," Smith said as he held the smartphone.

"We want in on it," Shepherd said.

"Of course," Smith said with a grin as he turned to walk out.

* * *

"Alpha One is in position," came the call over the tactical frequency.

"We should be out there," Shepherd said as he sat next to Cowboy and Agent Pierson in the control van. They were watching the various feeds from body cameras, an overhead drone, and the surveillance cameras they had tapped into as Captain Smith led his six-man team into position.

"You're lucky I could even get you here," Pierson said before keying up his radio. "Alpha One this is Zero, you are a go. I repeat, you are a go."

"Roger, Alpha One is a go," Smith replied.

Shepherd watched as the team moved to the entry point and prepared to breach the two-story warehouse. It was still daylight. They had opted for the fastest possible mission to ensure Sierra's safety. They had security camera footage of the car arriving at the warehouse and confirmation that she had arrived.

They were moving in six hours after Sierra had arrived, but the local cameras showed no movement out of the facility. Thermal drone imagery showed six contacts, one of whom appeared to be a hostage. The mission was greenlighted as soon as they had confirmation. Captain Smith had agreed to personally oversee Sierra's safe return.

The team breached the door and moved in with speed and efficiency. They had briefed the possibility of booby-traps and were careful to watch for them as they moved from room to room on the first floor.

"Alpha One, this is Zero, you're clear on the first floor. All targets and the package appear to be on the second floor," Pierson advised over the tactical frequency.

Two mic clicks from Smith acknowledged the message as they moved toward the stairs. The drone's real time infrared footage showed two men inside the room at the top of the stairs guarding the door, while two others were on the other side of the room and a fifth was talking to the hostage in the center of the room.

The team stacked up at the doorway at the top of the stairs. The breacher prepared a charge to blow the lock on the door while Smith readied a flashbang grenade. Smith's bodycam video showed him hold up his fingers and silently countdown from three. As he made a clenched fist, the charge detonated and the door was kicked open.

"Don't fuck it up, mates," Cowboy said under his breath as he watched anxiously.

Smith tossed in the flashbang and then they entered the room. Smith button-hooked right while the others alternated left, right and center as they followed.

"Motherfucker!" Shepherd yelled as the smoke cleared. The room was completely empty, despite the drone footage still showing the same contacts.

"Alpha One clear," Smith reported. "We'll keep looking but there's no one up here. We'll keep moving."

"How is that even possible?" Pierson asked, looking at Shepherd and Cowboy.

As Pierson keyed the mic to respond, there was a loud crash at the rear door of the van. Two smoke grenades rolled into the crowded van. Shepherd tried to cover his mouth as he searched for a weapon.

"Tear gas!" Cowboy yelled.

Pierson drew his weapon toward the entrance. Shepherd heard the suppressed register of a handgun as Pierson fell into the video monitors and dropped his weapon. Shepherd's eyes and skin burned as he struggled to breathe.

Three men entered wearing gas masks. Shepherd and Cowboy tried to fight but were both taken down with Tasers. They were restrained and given tranquilizers, then the men dragged them out of the van.

CHAPTER TWENTY-THREE

Spectre woke up with a terrible hangover. His head was throbbing. His mouth was dry. He rolled over in the bed, trying once again to make sense of where he was and what had happened. He was naked except for a pair of boxers.

He sat up, wincing as his head pounded. The room was almost completely dark except for a sliver of light creeping through the nearby curtains. As his eyes adjusted, he realized he was in another hotel room, but this time he was alone.

Spectre tried to stand, but immediately sat back down as his blood pressure dropped and he started to feel light-headed. He gave it a moment and then tried again, walking over to the window and opening the curtains.

He was greeted with a view of Times Square. It was early morning, but the sidewalks and streets were already busy with people making their morning commute. Spectre turned back to the room. It was a typical hotel room like any other he had stayed in on the road with the airline.

As his eyes adjusted, he saw his suitcase sitting on a stand near the TV. His airline crew tags were visible and it had been unzipped. He flipped it open, and saw that all of his clothes were still there. Spectre turned to the closet and saw his uniform, neatly pressed hanging in the closet. *What the fuck happened?*

Spectre walked into the bathroom. His shaving kit was on the sink and his toothbrush, toothpaste, and razor were lying next to it. It was all laid out as if he had been on a layover with his airline.

He reached into the shaving kit and found the ibuprofen bottle he always brought with him. He shook out four tablets and downed them with water from the faucet. He paused, standing over the sink as the water kept running.

Spectre tried to remember what had happened. Everything was hazy. He remembered his last trip and then getting a call from Michelle. He remembered jumpseating to Washington D.C., but everything after that was a blur. It all felt like a dream.

Turning off the water, Spectre walked back to the bed. He saw his cell phone plugged in to its charger on the nightstand. He picked it up and saw a missed call. *Crew Scheduling? Why was the airline calling him?*

As he stared at the voicemail notification, his phone rang. The caller ID said it was Crew Scheduling again. Spectre reluctantly answered.

"Hello?"

"Hello, First Officer Martin, this is Becky with Crew Scheduling, how are you this morning?"

Spectre grunted, still trying to shake the cobwebs.

"Yes, good morning, First Officer, I'm glad I reached you, otherwise I would have had to give you a missed assignment.

You've been junior manned for a sequence that deadheads from New Orleans to LaGuardia and then continues from LaGuardia to D.C. and back to New Orleans," the crew scheduler said.

"Junior manned?" Spectre mumbled. It meant he was the most junior pilot on reserve with the airline, typically within a two-hour callout. Before heading to D.C., he had called his Chief Pilot and told him about the "family emergency" in D.C. He wasn't supposed to be on call-out.

"Yes, sir. I show you as the most junior person available this morning. I'm sorry. Will you please verify the assignment?" she asked.

"I…I guess…"

"Perfect. Your flight is scheduled to leave New Orleans at eight a.m., and I will update your schedule."

"I'm already in New York," Spectre said slowly.

"Even better! I'll no show you for the deadhead and you can pick up the trip from LaGuardia. It's a one p.m. sign-in. That's pretty lucky that you were already there and the FO on that trip got sick," she said with a chuckle. "Well, thanks again. Is there anything else I can help you with?"

"No," Spectre said as he hung up the phone.

As the call ended, Spectre scrolled through his frequently used contacts and dialed Decker's cell phone. It went straight to voicemail.

Spectre cursed under his breath and then called Bear.

"Well I guess you're not dead, so that means you're just an asshole!" Bear answered, using his standard *Are you dead or just an asshole* opener when Spectre hadn't called him in a while.

"Bear, have you heard from Michelle?" Spectre asked.

"Not since last night, what's up?"

"How's Part Two?" Spectre asked, referring to his infant son.

"Slept better than I did last night. Getting old sucks."

"What did Michelle tell you last night?"

"Oh, you know, the usual. D.C. is still a cesspool. You're missing. Same story, different day."

"Missing?"

"Well, she said she didn't know where you were. Which, knowing you, I assumed to mean that you had gone off on another half-cocked plan of yours to save freedom or something," Bear said casually. "I thought you gave that shit up. So where the hell are you?"

"New York. I think."

"You *think*?"

Spectre rubbed his eye. His head was still throbbing, but the ibuprofen had started to ease the pain. "It's been a long few days. Actually, what day is it?"

"It's Wednesday, Cal. Holy shit. Did you go out on a bender last night or something? And how did you end up in New York?"

"I honestly have no idea," Spectre replied truthfully.

"Well, shit, son, be careful. You spend too much time up there and you'll turn into a bleeding heart liberal screaming for more government. Don't get too indoctrinated, whatever you do," Bear said with a chuckle.

"I won't. Listen, I should probably go. I need to get back to D.C. and find Michelle. She's not answering," Spectre said.

"You want me to text you if I hear from her?"

"Please do."

"OK, I will," Bear said.

"Thanks, I'll talk to you later," Spectre said and hung up the phone.

Spectre plugged the phone back into the charger. He picked up the remote and turned on the TV, changing the channel to the local news in hopes of recaging his brain and figuring out what the hell was going on.

As Spectre turned up the volume, the weatherman finished the week's forecast and turned it back over to the anchors. A picture of President Madeline Clifton appeared on screen and the anchor spoke of the president's plan to visit with business leaders to discuss corporate tax reform in Washington the next day.

The station cut to a video of President Clifton giving a speech highlighting her plan. Spectre's face suddenly turned red and his fists clenched. He was filled with rage. He had no idea why, but the sight of President Clifton made his blood boil as images of her and former Vice President Johnson flashed in his mind.

"She needs to die," Spectre said angrily as he turned off the TV.

CHAPTER TWENTY-FOUR

T he first stop Decker made, after waking up and taking a shower, was the mansion's gourmet kitchen. She had tossed and turned most of the night, worrying about Spectre and where they might have taken him. Her gut was telling her something bad had happened, causing her mind to run through a million different scenarios as she struggled to sleep.

Decker was still familiar with the house from her time there with Spectre a year earlier. She made a pot of coffee and then poured herself a cup in a Lyons Tactical Group mug she found in a cabinet. As she savored her first sip, she made her way down to the infirmary where Coolio was recovering from his injuries.

She slowly pushed the door open and sat down in the chair next to Coolio's bed, careful not to wake him. It brought back a flood of memories. She thought back to sitting in that same chair waiting and praying that Spectre would be ok after nearly dying from an assassination attempt in a federal prison.

They had been through so much together. They had survived assassination attempts, Presidential aircraft hijackings, and kidnappings. But now, Decker couldn't help but wonder if their luck had finally run out. Her gut still told her something was horribly wrong. *This time it's different.*

Coolio stirred as the morning light peaked through the curtain. Decker tiptoed around the bed to close it, but not before Coolio groaned and said, "Good morning. What time is it?"

"After seven," Decker said as she pulled the curtains shut. "Sorry, I didn't mean to wake you."

"It's OK, I need to get to work anyway," Coolio said as he tried to sit up in the bed. "Can you hand me my laptop?"

"You need to rest. Whatever work you have can wait."

Coolio shook his head as he tried to reach for his laptop. Seeing his struggle, Decker hurried to the bedside table and handed it to him. "It really can't," he said as he took it from her. "I've been finding a lot of anomalies in the system. Someone is setting the boss up."

"You need to talk to Jeff," Decker said. "The other billionaires of Odin have some kind of computer system that can tap into everything and manipulate data. He can explain it to you when you feel better."

"That explains a lot," Coolio said. "I've been seeing data artifacts at multiple levels, even at the highest levels of classification. It's almost untraceable."

"Almost? Could you trace the origin?"

"Maybe. But I'd need more horsepower than this Prius here," Coolio said, holding up his laptop.

"What have you found so far?"

"Autopsy report for Kruger, but it doesn't make sense," Coolio said, shaking his head as he turned his laptop screen so

Decker could see it. "It says he was burned and found in the building. Died of internal injuries from the trauma."

"It's horrible."

"It would be, but unless he went back into the building after he rescued me, it's not possible," Coolio said. "He's the one that carried me out."

"So Kruger's not dead?" Decker asked with a look of shock.

"I don't think so," Coolio said.

"So where is he?" Decker asked.

"That part, I don't know," Coolio replied.

"Can you find my husband?" Decker asked.

"Spectre is missing too?" Coolio asked with a look of concern as he started typing. "Jesus, what the hell is happening?"

"It's complicated," Lyons said as he entered the room with Cuda. "How are you doing, buddy?"

"I feel like I got hit by a bus," Coolio said. "But I'm ok."

"Did you know Kruger saved Coolio?" Decker asked Lyons as he passed her to check on Coolio.

"What?" Lyons asked.

"Autopsy says he was burned in the building," Decker said.

"But I'm pretty sure he's the one that saved me," Coolio added.

Lyons turned to Cuda. "Did you do anything for Kruger?"

"No, boss," Cuda said. "Just you and Coolio. The others were killed in the building."

"So you didn't fake Kruger's death too?" Decker asked.

"Nope," Cuda replied.

"So they probably have him too," Lyons said. "Fuck!"

"Who is *they*?" Decker asked.

"It had to be Stone or Cruz. I'm not sure why they would want him, but they are the only ones that make sense," Lyons explained.

"Ok, I think I have something on Spectre," Coolio said as he continued working on his computer. "Does he work for GulfJet airlines?"

"Yeah, but he took leave to go deal with this," Decker said.

"Well, he's listed as the First Officer for Gulfjet Flight Ten Seventeen from LaGuardia to Ronald Reagan National this afternoon. Looks like he continues on to New Orleans after that," Coolio said.

"That's not possible," Decker said.

"One second," Coolio replied as he continued working. "Well, his cell phone pings in downtown New York. Let me pull up his call records."

"He's in New York?" Decker asked incredulously. "How?"

"Looks like he received a phone call from a number registered to GulfJet, and then called you and a Mr. Charles Jennings. Do you know him?"

"Bear," Decker said, silently cursing herself for turning her phone off and leaving it behind. "Is Spectre still wanted by the FBI?"

"I'll check," Coolio said.

"Wanted?" Lyons asked.

"Yeah, the FBI stopped me getting off the plane because they think he beat up Agent Tanner and took off to work with a terrorist," Decker said, rolling her eyes.

"Nope," Coolio said. "No BOLOs, no advisories, not on the no-fly list. His history is clean."

"See what else you can find," Lyons directed.

As Coolio continued looking for clues, Tanner suddenly burst into the room with her government-issued Glock 17M in hand. "Guys, we have a problem. Your security system went off in the house. We've got company. Looks like six men armed with rifles."

Coolio quickly pulled up the compound's security system on his laptop. "Main gate has been disabled. Looks like they're on the north end of the mansion. How did they bypass the perimeter sensors?"

"I'll explain later," Lyons said. "Cuda, grab a rifle and stay here. We can't move Coolio."

"Copy that, boss," Cuda said as he bolted out of the room. Moments later he returned wearing a traditional plate carrier and carrying an H&K 416 rifle.

Lyons turned to Decker and Tanner. "You ladies up for it?"

Before either could respond, the power was suddenly cut. The room was still dark from the closed blinds, but the ambient lighting was enough to see each other.

"Looks like we don't have a choice," Decker said.

"I'm down," Tanner added as she started for the door with her handgun at the low ready.

Decker drew her Sig P320 from its holster and followed. Lyons followed and the three moved to the small armory next door. The compound had several armories strategically placed throughout each area. Lyons unlocked the door by entering his six-digit code and then went to work handing out plate carriers and rifles with spare magazines.

"I know these might be a little big for you, but try to get them as tight as you can. It's better than nothing," Lyons said, indicating the plate carriers. "We can't get to the armor skin shirts you had yesterday."

"We'll move in a wedge. I'll take point. You two take left and right. Maddie, remember your active shooter drills?" Decker asked, taking charge. "It'll be just like that."

"Got it," Tanner said.

"Yes, ma'am," Lyons said with a grin. "Lead the way."

Lyons and Tanner each took a side as Decker led them down the hallway. Reaching the doorway to the kitchen, Decker stopped short and nodded for Lyons on her left to slice the pie with her. They moved in an arc around the door way, looking for threats inside until they reached the other side.

After a silent countdown, Decker went in first and turned left while Tanner and Lyons followed. As she continued moving forward, Decker saw a man searching the room and fired two shots, hitting him in the neck and temple. He collapsed and dropped his rifle.

The trio split up and took cover behind the two large islands in the center of the kitchen. Two men who had been searching the house heard the shots, entered the kitchen and started firing at them. Lyons leaned around the corner of his cover and fired three shots, dropping one of them as the other took cover.

Decker motioned to Lyons and Tanner. They needed to keep moving and couldn't afford to get pinned down. Lyons laid down cover fire as Decker stood and moved toward the remaining threat. The attacker stood, firing off a round just as Decker dropped him.

The round hit her in the center of her chest plate, knocking the wind out of her and causing her to stumble as she took cover at the edge of the kitchen. Tanner took cover next to her while Lyons stood against the wall at the other side of the kitchen's entryway.

"You ok?" Tanner asked.

Decker nodded as she grimaced and tried to catch her breath. "I'll take point," Tanner said.

Lyons and Decker exchanged a shrug as Tanner moved forward and entered the doorway to the dining room. Lyons followed and moved left as Tanner went right. Decker pushed through the pain, raised her rifle, and entered into the dining area behind them. She went straight ahead as the other two cleared their respective sides.

The dining area was clear. Decker followed Tanner and Lyons to the next doorway leading to the living area. Tanner entered first. As she did, she was blindsided by a rifle butt that missed her head and hit her in the neck. She stumbled to the side, trying to get her rifle up, but the attacker was too quick and parried her muzzle.

Lyons moved in behind her, immediately sidestepping the fight as he zeroed in on another attacker training his rifle on Tanner. He fired three rounds, hitting the man in the chest plate and two rounds in the throat before turning to clear the rest of the room.

Decker moved in behind them. As she aimed for Tanner's assailant, Tanner swept his leg from beneath him and drew her handgun, firing four shots and killing the man. When she saw that Tanner had everything under control, Decker pushed past her in line with Lyons to finish clearing the room.

Shaking off the blow to the neck and wiping the blood splatter off her face, Tanner moved forward with her handgun up. She was the first to see the final attacker moving toward them. She fired six shots, hitting the man center of mass as he stumbled back. Decker and Lyons both followed up with shots and a well-placed headshot finally brought the man down.

The team continued clearing the house, going room to room as a team to ensure that Tanner's initial assessment of six attackers had been correct. When they reached and cleared the last bedroom, Decker turned to Tanner and said, "Nice job, rookie."

"Yeah, really nice work. There's hope for you yet," Lyons said with a grin.

"Thanks, but—"

Before Tanner could finish, the sound of shattering glass and the register of a high power rifle stopped her. Decker watched in horror as Tanner's eyes widened and she fell to her knees.

"Sniper!" Lyons yelled as they dove for cover.

CHAPTER TWENTY-FIVE

Kruger was weak. He had been given only small amounts of water since he had been in captivity, and no food. He had no idea how long he had been there, but he guessed it had to be pushing two or three days.

At some point earlier in the day, his captors had removed him from the chains suspended from the ceiling. They had put him in a cell just big enough to stand up in. He was starting to get delirious from the exhaustion and dehydration.

He had to dig deep into his training. He had been here before. He knew the game and had been on both sides of the resistance coin. Kruger knew how to break someone down – to bend them to his will. It was exactly what they were trying to do to him. They would weaken his resolve until he was pliable.

Kruger tried to stay strong, but he knew it was just a matter of time. It was what he had told every prisoner. You might last a day, a week, or a month, but everyone gives up eventually. Kruger wondered how long he would last. And for what?

He still had no idea who these people were. He didn't know what they wanted. They didn't appear to be radical Islamic terrorists trying to exact revenge for everything he had done over the years. They had no distinguishing characteristics at all. They were just cold, emotionless professionals.

Kruger's focus was waning. He needed to get to his people and formulate an escape plan, but the tactics being used against him were starting to work. He was starting to only care about himself and escaping the misery. He had been planning to walk away from it all when the building attack happened anyway.

As Kruger struggled to fight off the doubts in his mind, he heard the basement door open. Boots clanged against the metal stairs. Kruger wobbled as he tried to maintain balance in his standing room-only cell.

"I see your accommodations have improved, Mr. Mack," the voice in the darkness said. "How have you fared in my absence?"

The man came into view in the dimly lit basement. It was the same man that had threatened to deal with him before. A man who appeared to be a soulless devil with eyes as black as night.

Kruger said nothing as the man stopped in front of the cell. "I'm sure you understand what's going on by now, Mr. Mack. You were an interrogator once, weren't you?"

"Cut the bullshit. What do you want?" Kruger asked.

The man smiled as he stood in front of the caged operator. "You will learn my intent in due time, Mr. Mack. But first, I must ensure your cooperation."

"Good luck," Kruger growled defiantly.

"Perhaps an exercise in trust is in order," the man said. "My name is Jäger, and I am your salvation."

"Go fuck yourself, Jäger," Kruger shot back.

Jäger ignored Kruger as he pulled a key from his pocket and unlocked the cell. "Perhaps talking face to face will help," he said.

Jäger opened the cell and stepped back. Kruger stood, still wobbling as he tried to maintain his balance. Jäger motioned for him to step forward. "Please, come out. Let us talk as men."

Kruger stumbled out of his cage. His legs were weak. His body was numb, but the man in front of him invoked an undeniable rage. "What do you want, bub?" he asked as he stopped a few feet from Jäger.

Jäger stepped forward, closing the gap to within a foot. He was much smaller in stature than the bearded operator – at least three inches shorter and forty pounds of muscle lighter. He stood up straight, facing off with the weakened man before him.

"Your compliance," Jäger said. "And your absolute devotion to our cause, of course."

"What cause is that?"

"You will see soon enough," Jäger said. "But first, I must ensure your cooperation. And to do that, I'm afraid I may have to use your team to convince you. Perhaps I'll start with the woman you call Jenny."

The rage Kruger felt reached a tipping point. He lunged forward, trying to grab Jäger's throat. Jäger was much quicker, sidestepping Kruger's advance and ducking under Kruger's arm, countering with an uppercut to the gut.

Kruger stumbled under his own momentum, falling onto the hard concrete as the blow knocked the wind out of him. He tried to get to his feet, but not before Jäger outmaneuvered him once again.

Jäger kicked Kruger in the chest with the instep of his foot, sending him flying onto his back. Jäger laughed as he walked up to Kruger and stood over him. "You are not the man everyone thinks you are."

The rage was overwhelming. Kruger channeled it into every last ounce of strength he had left, spinning around on his back and sweeping Jäger's leg from beneath him.

The move caught Jäger off guard. He tried to break his own fall, but failed. Kruger was instantly on top of him, pummeling Jäger's face with blow after blow.

Jäger laughed as his face bloodied. Kruger was too weak to have any lasting effect, and with each strike, he lost power in his punch. Jäger knocked him off balance, causing him to fall face first into the concrete, this time unable to get back up before Jäger had gained the advantage.

Calmly picking himself up, Jäger moved toward Kruger. Kruger tried to get up once again, but Jäger kicked him in the face. The hit dazed him and he fell onto his back. Jäger stood over him, still laughing as he put his boot on Kruger's throat.

"I want you to remember this moment, Mr. Mack," Jäger said as he applied pressure to Kruger's windpipe. "It is the moment that you fell. You are weak, and while I don't believe you are worthy of joining our cause, I must still extend the offer. My superiors demand it."

Kruger gasped for air and swung his arms wildly in the air as Jäger applied even more pressure. "As I told you, I am your salvation. Heed my words, and you will have life. Resist, and you and your teammates will die."

Jäger removed the boot from Kruger's neck. He squatted down as Kruger tried to catch his breath. "But know this. If you resist, I won't kill you quickly. I will make you watch me kill your friends one by one. They will know that you failed them. They will know that their deaths are on your hands."

Standing, Jäger turned toward the door and said, "Choose wisely, my friend."

CHAPTER TWENTY-SIX

T he entire security system is down and I can't get into the closed-circuit video feeds," Coolio said as he worked feverishly from his hospital bed. "It's been too long. They should have been back by now."

Cuda stood with his rifle trained out the doorway and down the hall. "The gunfire has stopped," he said as he c-clamped the muzzle of his rifle against the doorframe and looked back at Coolio.

"That's what worries me," Coolio said. "It's been a few minutes, and there's only been a few sporadic shots. We should have sent them out with radios."

"No time," Cuda said, returning his attention to his sector. "Now we wait."

"I'm blind in here," Coolio said. "I need to get eyes on to help them."

"We stay," Cuda said.

"They have shut down everything," Coolio said. "Wait! I think I found something."

Cuda looked back at Coolio as the computer analyst worked hastily on his laptop. "Got it! Holy shit it worked."

"What worked?" Cuda asked, splitting his attention between Coolio and the hallway he was monitoring.

"I found the WiFi signal of the drone these guys are using and hacked it. Looks like a quadcopter. I think I can take over and use it to find out what's going on."

Coolio continued working, finally pulling up the control interface to the drone. With a few keystrokes, he was able to commandeer the drone. "Got it!"

He made it climb, zooming out as he attempted to get a big-picture layout of the battlespace. He started with the front of the house. Zooming in, he saw several windows shattered and the front door open.

Coolio descended the drone slightly to get a better look and zoomed in on the shattered windows as he moved the drone east along the front of the house. He stopped on a second floor bedroom where he saw Jeff Lyons behind cover with his rifle pointing toward the window.

"Someone is down!" Coolio yelled. He zoomed in as much as the drone's camera would allow. The grainy picture showed someone in the back of the room with long hair lying on the floor and another woman on her knees administering first aid, but Coolio couldn't tell who was who.

The woman administering first aid suddenly hit the ground in what looked like a delayed reaction as Coolio heard the faint register of another rifle outside. It was followed by Lyons peeking out from behind cover and firing his own shots back.

"They're pinned down," Coolio reported. "Looks like a sniper!"

"Can you find the sniper?" Cuda asked over his shoulder.

"Standby," Coolio said. He flew the drone higher and zoomed out, starting a tedious scan for a sniper he assumed would be well-hidden. The drone had no FLIR or thermal capabilities, so he was forced to use the grainy color image in a high stakes game of 'Where's Waldo?'

"Got him!" Coolio said as the drone hovered over a vehicle outside the front gate. It was a half-ton pickup truck. The sniper stood in the bed of the truck with his rifle perched on the roof.

"He's in a truck just outside the front gate. Maybe three hundred meters."

"Let me see," Cuda said, leaving his post and walking to Coolio's bed.

As Coolio showed Cuda the video, the sniper suddenly looked down at his phone and realized he had lost control. Coolio tried to maneuver out of the way, but the man raised his rifle toward the drone. Coolio heard the shot and then the video went black.

Cuda picked the handgun he had given Coolio earlier up off the bedside table and handed it to him. "You will be ok," he said.

Coolio nervously accepted the handgun. "Let's hope I don't have to use it. I haven't shot one of these since last year's qualifying."

"I have to stop him," Cuda said.

"Good luck," Coolio replied.

Cuda nodded stoically and raised his rifle as he headed to the door. He paused for a moment at the doorway he had previously been monitoring, verifying once more that the hallway was clear before leaving Coolio's room.

He moved methodically, but more slowly than he was used to. He had nearly died in Iraq a few months prior and was still recovering from broken ribs, internal bleeding, and a concussion.

If you asked his doctors, it was still far too early to be moving so much, much less trying to take down a sniper.

But Cuda pushed through the pain and stiffness. He had a job to do, and his teammates were depending on him. It was a level of toughness that had been instilled in him during his time as a Filipino Commando, and reinforced by Odin. He would have plenty of time to lick his wounds later.

Cuda reached the doorway at the end of the hall that led to the outside. He paused for a moment to catch his breath and then pushed it open. He turned left and headed for the supply building next to the outdoor dynamic shooting range.

He did his best to sprint across the open area, stopping just as he hit the wall of the supply building. He felt like his years of conditioning and training were gone. Cuda stopped to catch his breath as he looked around the corner at his next intended point of cover.

The truck that the sniper had been using was barely visible in the distance, just past the front gate and guard shack. Cuda planned to arc around the shooting grounds and hop the fence in an attempt to sneak up on the sniper, hoping he got to him before any more of his teammates were taken out.

Cuda moved from the supply building and ran to the outer perimeter of the reconfigurable shoothouse on the south side of the shooting grounds. As he stopped, he heard another volley of gunfire. It sounded like one shot from the sniper followed by a three-round burst of return fire in the sniper's general direction. Cuda knew he had to hurry.

Leaving cover, Cuda ran straight to the perimeter fence and slung his rifle across his back. His adrenaline was pumping as he pushed through the pain and made it over the fence. Cuda dropped to a knee, unslung his rifle, and looked out toward the sniper's position through his rifle's holographic sight. He could now clearly make out the man standing up with the rifle perched atop the truck's cab.

Cuda had a fair shot from his vantage point, but didn't want to risk it. There was nothing but open field between the sniper and him. If he missed or failed to kill the sniper, he wouldn't get a second chance. And at that range, he wasn't confident in his ability to score a killshot using a holographic sight against a sniper wearing body armor.

Crouching in the tall grass, Cuda moved as stealthily as he could to flank the shooter. He kept his rifle trained on the sniper and watched as the sniper and Lyons traded more shots. Cuda had to give it to the sniper, he was at least patient.

Cuda closed to within a hundred meters of the sniper. He was directly behind the pickup truck. His lungs burned and he could barely breathe, but he pushed through as he approached his prey.

Reaching the lowered tailgate, Cuda swung his rifle around behind his back on its single point sling and drew his fixed blade knife. He spun it around in his hand blade down as he climbed up into the bed of the truck. Cuda had opted for stealth, unsure if there were other mercenaries the drone footage had missed in the area.

Cuda stumbled as he stood on the tail gate. Despite the adrenaline, his condition was still poor. The movement of the truck startled the sniper and caused him to turn around.

Drawing his handgun from his chest rig, the sniper turned to face Cuda. Cuda lunged forward, raising his blade to strike from above, but not before the sniper fired two rounds from the hip.

One round struck Cuda in the armor and the other just below it in his abdomen. Cuda pushed forward, driving the knife into sniper between his collarbone and neck. The sniper managed to fire another shot into Cuda's abdomen as Cuda withdrew the bloody blade and fell forward.

Using every ounce of strength he had remaining Cuda drove the knife down again into the sniper's throat. Cuda's bodyweight pinned the dying sniper onto the cab of the truck as they both struggled through their injuries.

Cuda pushed the blade forward, severing the sniper's jugular and slicing through his throat. The sniper dropped his gun as they both fell over the side of the truck and onto the grass. Cuda looked to his left and saw the sniper's lifeless eyes staring back at him. He had managed to stop the threat.

He breathed a sigh of relief, but the pain from the gunshot wounds grew. His breathing became labored as he rolled onto his stomach to try to pick himself up and move back to the house. Grunting through the pain, Cuda made it to his knees. He grabbed his gut, feeling the blood pouring from the bullet wounds.

Cuda tried to stand, but he felt himself letting go. The blue skies started to dim as his vision started to blur. He fell over to his side and rolled onto his back. He was too weak to move.

Closing his eyes, Cuda said a prayer as he slipped away.

CHAPTER TWENTY-SEVEN

He should have stayed with Coolio," Lyons said as he stood over Cuda's lifeless body. "Goddammit!"

Decker put her hand on his shoulder. After confirming the sniper threat had ended, they had moved Tanner to the infirmary with Coolio and called Odin's private doctor. The sniper's bullet had passed through and through Tanner's shoulder. They had bandaged and packed it as best they could, but Lyons felt a professional consult would be best.

They had gone back expecting to find Cuda right where they had left him with Coolio, but instead it had been Coolio that had told them about Cuda's heroics. How he had been determined to save the team and went out to take on the sniper alone.

"This is all my fault," Lyons said as he squatted down next to Cuda. "All of this is my fault."

Decker walked to the front seat of the truck, looking for clues. It was completely empty, except for shards of glass from some of the shots Lyons had taken to return fire. "The keys are still in the ignition," Decker said as she walked back to Lyons. "We can use the truck to get Cuda back to the infirmary."

Lyons nodded slowly and then moved to lift Cuda's shoulders as Decker grabbed his legs. They gently lifted him into the bed of the truck. Fresh blood from Cuda's fight with the sniper still smeared the bed of the white pickup.

After raising the tailgate, Lyons walked over to the body of the sniper and squatted down. The sniper was a white male. He was clean shaven with dark brown hair. There were no patches or identifying marks on his body armor or clothing.

Lyons pulled out his smartphone and snapped several pictures before taking shotgun in the truck next to Decker.

"I thought we weren't supposed to have phones here?" Decker asked as Lyons studied the picture.

"Sim card is removed and it's in airplane mode," Lyons said. "I'm hoping Coolio can use this picture to find out who these guys are."

"If you say so," Decker said with a shrug as she started the truck's diesel engine and backed it away from the fence line.

"Do you trust Agent Tanner?" Lyons asked as they slowly made their way down the driveway.

"Why do you ask?"

"She's the only person here I haven't had a chance to properly vet."

"You vetted me?"

"I like to know everyone I deal with, Michelle. It's nothing personal," Lyons replied. "But I didn't have that luxury with Agent Tanner, given the circumstances."

"She's young, but she's a good agent. Hell, she just took a bullet for us, if you're thinking she led them here," Decker said.

"You're right," Lyons replied. "I'm just trying to figure out how this all happened."

Lyons directed Decker to pull up next to the range storage building. "He will get a proper burial, but until then I have a cold storage locker in this building. Let's unload him."

Decker helped Lyons unload Cuda's body. They gently placed it in the meat locker and closed the door. Lyons locked the door and then they walked back to the infirmary.

They found Tanner sitting next to Coolio, holding pressure on her bandaged left shoulder as the two seemed to be getting along, joking and talking about video games. When Coolio saw Lyons's face, he immediately turned serious.

"Did you find Cuda? Is he ok, boss?" Coolio asked.

Lyons shook his head. "He managed to take out the sniper, but he was shot several times. He's gone."

"Damn," Coolio said softly. "That sucks."

Lyons pulled out his phone and handed it to Coolio. "I took a picture of the sniper. Can you run him and see what you can find about these guys?"

Coolio nodded solemnly. "Can you hand me that USB cable?" he asked, pointing to the cable sitting on the chair.

Decker picked it up off the chair and handed it to the young hacker. Coolio plugged his computer into the phone and went to work downloading and analyzing the picture.

"Are you ok?" Decker asked as she turned to Agent Tanner.

"It's just a flesh wound," Tanner said with a nervous laugh. "Hurts like a bitch though."

"I bet."

"Have you ever been shot?"

"Nope," Decker said.

Tanner grinned at the realization that she had been through something her idol hadn't. "I don't recommend it."

"Got something!" Coolio said as he continued working on his laptop. "Holy shit!"

"What is it?" Lyons asked. They all crowded around Coolio as he pulled up personnel files on the sniper.

"The sniper's name is Caleb Goodwin, former Marine Recon. Honorable Discharge in 2012. Looks like he's been working for a group called The Ziffler Group out of Kentucky," Coolio said.

"Shit!" Lyons said.

"Do you know them?" Decker asked.

Lyons nodded. "Coolio, can you get into the CIA database and see if they've been hired recently? It will probably be Special Access Required level stuff."

"That may take a while, boss, especially with this laptop," Coolio said.

"What's the Ziffler Group?" Decker asked.

"Private military contractors that the CIA uses to do their dirty work. A wet-work team," Lyons said with a frown.

"Doesn't everyone think you're dead? Why would a wet-work team come here?" Tanner chimed in.

"They obviously figured out I'm alive somehow," Lyons said.

"The CIA wants you dead?" Decker asked. "After all you did for the Director?"

Lyons shook his head. "He probably doesn't even know about it. In fact, I bet no one does."

"How is that possible?" Tanner asked.

"Helios," Lyons said.

"What's Helios?" Coolio asked without looking up from his computer.

"A supercomputer that can manipulate, access, or infiltrate any computer system in the world," Decker answered.

Coolio suddenly stopped working and looked up at Lyons. "Seriously?"

Lyons nodded shamefully. "I'm sorry."

"Wow," Coolio said. "That explains so much."

"What does it explain?" Tanner asked.

"Everything," Coolio said. "All the artifacts I've been seeing. The broken files in our system. That transmission from our server about our missions in Iraq. It was like someone was sending our files out from within but I could never traceroute it."

Coolio stared accusingly at Lyons. "You knew about this?"

"I'm sorry," Lyons repeated.

"And you didn't tell me?"

"I was hoping to stop it," Lyons said.

"I'm not mad about that, but you've created the single greatest hacking tool in human history and I'm the last to know? What the shit! What are the specs? What kind of processor? Liquid cooled?"

"We can talk about it later," Lyons said. "For now, we need to get a handle on who's trying to kill us."

"Right," Coolio said as he returned to his laptop.

Decker turned to Lyons. "If Cal is on his way to D.C., we need to get to him."

Coolio looked up once more. "Oh, right. While y'all were out, I confirmed the crew listings for his flights. He's definitely going to DCA this afternoon and then New Orleans. Assuming it's all real."

"Why would he be flying?" Tanner asked.

"Great question," Decker said. "And he took off work to deal with this. Why would they have him on duty? And from New York? He hates that job. No way would he pick up a trip at a time like this."

"Maybe he was just using it as a way to get home?" Tanner asked.

Decker shook her head. "He could have gotten a ride on the jumpseat. And, Coolio, you said the flight goes to New Orleans? How long is he on the ground?"

"Forty-five minutes," Coolio answered.

"Not a chance," Decker said. "That's not something my husband would do."

"This smells like something Cruz would do," Lyons said. "If Spectre was in New York, that's who had him. I bet he wants Spectre in D.C. for something."

"Yeah, but why? It's not like Cal would do anything for him," Decker said. "He doesn't even know the guy."

"It may not matter," Lyons said with a pained expression.

"Oh come on! What other kind of stuff are you guys doing?"

Lyons sighed. "Have you ever heard of a drug called 'The Devil's Breath'?"

"Scopolamine," Tanner answered. "It's made in South America, but rarely used because even a slight overdose is lethal. It can make people susceptible to suggestion without a memory of the event."

Lyons nodded. "Well, part of our project involved a synthetic version of scopolamine. Cruz had a chemist develop a slightly less dangerous version that makes the subject more easily convinced. It's delivered in the water supply. It was Phase Two of the Helios plan. Basically, if you could suggest something and make people believe it was their own idea without actually remembering what led them to that thought, you could control the masses."

"You guys are morons," Decker said angrily. "Absolute morons. What did you do to my husband?"

"I don't know," Lyons said, holding his hands up defensively. "But if they had Spectre, it's possible they are trying to get him to do something. It's what Cruz does. And, given Spectre's history and skills, just about anything is on the table."

"What skills?" Tanner asked.

Lyons laughed. "What skills doesn't he have? Expert marksman, black belt in Krav Maga, trained by elite special forces in close quarters combat, survival, evasion, and resistance. And he was a fighter pilot. Literally anything is on the table."

"I knew he was badass, but damn," Tanner said, turning to Decker. "I can see why you two married each other."

"Cal can also be slightly…impulsive. If he believes in something, he will stop at nothing to get it done. We have to get to him," Decker said.

Ha! Got it!" Coolio yelled abruptly. "I'm in!"

"That was fast," Tanner said.

"We don't need no stinkin' supercomputer," Coolio said with a sly grin. "Here we go."

Coolio pulled up the CIA order that sent the kill team to the Lyons Estate. "Looks like it was a kill order on you, Michelle."

"What?" Decker asked with a shocked look. "Why?"

"Doesn't say why. Just identifies you as a primary and Maddie here as a secondary target," Coolio said as he clicked through the file. "Looks like they got a traffic camera facial recognition ID on both of you and compared it with the plate readers to track you here."

"Son of a bitch," Lyons said. "So they don't know I'm alive."

Decker glared at Lyons. "*That's* what you took out of that?"

"We can use that to our advantage," Lyons said. "Sorry, I didn't mean to be crass."

"I need to go stop my husband from doing something stupid," Decker said. "Kill order or not."

"I'll go with you," Tanner said.

"You're injured," Decker replied. "You stay here with Coolio."

"I'll go with you instead," Lyons said.

Decker shook her head. "You're *dead*, remember?"

"But how are you planning to get there? They found you with traffic cameras, remember?" Tanner asked. "And when they find out that their first team failed, there will be more."

"I'll deal with them."

"Let me fly you there," Lyons said. "I have a helicopter on the property. I'll fly you in."

"You have a helicopter here?" Tanner asked incredulously.

"Of course I do, honey," Lyons said with a grin and a wink. "I'm rich."

CHAPTER TWENTY EIGHT

Lajes Air Base, Portugal

It was early evening in Lajes when the Bombardier Challenger 650 luxury business jet lowered its landing gear on final approach. The Portuguese island was often used as a primary divert for military and commercial aircraft crossing the Atlantic, but this evening it was being used as a neutral meeting site for some of the world's most powerful people.

The Challenger touched down fifteen hundred feet down the ten thousand foot runway and slowed. It turned onto the parallel taxiway and taxied to a secluded hangar on the northwest side of the airfield near a United States Air Force hangar. As the jet pulled to a stop next to a Gulfstream G650ER business jet, the pilots shut down both engines and the stairs lowered.

Jäger adjusted his suit as he descended the stairs alone. He walked to the nearby Gulfstream. The man guarding it was wearing a suit as well, but also had an earpiece and was carrying an H&K MP-5. Jäger nodded and the man stepped aside, allowing Jäger to ascend the stairs and enter the aircraft.

As he entered, Jäger found Nicholas Stone sitting next to a very attractive Italian woman on a sofa. They were sharing a bottle of wine and eating caviar as the Israeli assassin approached.

"Glad you made it," Stone said before dismissing the woman to the rear of the aircraft. He gave her a pat on the butt as she adjusted her skin tight dress and blew him a kiss.

When she was out of earshot, Stone invited Jäger to sit on the couch across from him. "How are our guests?" he asked.

"You should let me kill them," Jäger said matter-of-factly.

Stone's expression soured. "That's no way to speak of our guests. Have you made no progress?"

Jäger's face remained expressionless. "These are not your average citizens. They are highly trained and extremely lethal. Although I believe Mack is weak, his willpower is impressive."

"Then you should have no problem convincing them to join our cause," Stone said dismissively as he poured more wine into his glass.

"I do not understand why they are necessary. They will only cause complications."

"Let me worry about the big picture, my boy," Stone replied. "You just get me results. Now, what about our little problem in America?"

"I just received word that the CIA's team was unsuccessful. After the meeting, I intend to go there myself to dispatch them," Jäger replied.

Stone smiled. "Don't," he said as he held up a finger. "I spoke to Cruz before leaving. I will ask him when he gets here, but he mentioned that he had Martin under control. The wife should be of no consequence in that case."

"There are too many loose ends," Jäger replied. "Every time you use that system to attempt to resolve a problem, it creates even more. Let me handle it personally."

Stone shook his head. "Your priority is in Poland. I want them turned as quickly as possible."

Jäger started to argue, but then thought better of it. "Yes, sir."

"Very good," Stone said, as he leaned back on the couch to look out the window. "And speaking of the devil, Walter is here."

Jäger turned to see a black and white Bombardier Global 6000 business jet taxi next to his Challenger. As the aircraft came to a stop, the stairs were lowered and Cruz hobbled down them followed by a security entourage.

Moments later, Cruz walked into the cabin and sat down on the couch next to Stone, winded from the short jaunt. "No need to get up or anything. Good to see you too, Nick," he said as he tried to catch his breath.

"Would you like some wine?" Stone asked, holding up the glass.

"I'm fine," Cruz said. "You shouldn't be drinking during a meeting like this."

Stone took a drink in response. "Sharpens the mind."

"When will our friends be here?" Cruz said. "I'd like to get back to D.C. for an event."

"Ah, yes," Stone said. "I was just telling our associate about your successes there."

"Martin?" Cruz asked. "I think he will do as we ask."

"Forgive me for asking, but what will you have him do?" Jäger asked.

Cruz looked at Stone as if to ask permission to answer. Stone nodded and Cruz turned to Jäger. "He's going to kill the President."

"Is this true?" Jäger asked Stone.

Stone laughed. "Of course not," he said. "Martin won't even come close."

Cruz nodded with a nervous chuckle.

"So why do you need him?" Jäger asked.

"We don't," Cruz answered. "Or at least, we *didn't*. But when I learned that he was snooping around Jeff's building, I realized it was too good an opportunity to pass up. He could be the catalyst to kick this whole thing off."

"How?" Jäger asked. "I have read his file, but I do not see how he is of any value here."

"Martin was awarded the Presidential Medal of Freedom," Stone answered with a knowing grin.

"Yes, I know," Jäger said.

"Think, my boy," Stone said. "Martin also killed Vice President Johnson. The two had quite the history."

"But aren't you worried that would lead to you?" Jäger asked.

"Quite the opposite," Cruz said. "We're going to leave the breadcrumbs and let the American people make the connection."

"Perhaps you are right. I am just a soldier and this is beyond my comprehension," Jäger said.

"It's quite simple," said Stone. "The hero's fall from grace. He was already framed once for the murder of Senator Wilson, except that was covered up. His attempt will become a public spectacle, leading the media to everything Johnson did with the Chinese. We'll use our systems to create the link tying Clifton to it all, vindicating Martin. And Martin will once again become a hero for exposing the corruption."

"To what end?" Jäger asked. "And why not just connect the dots without him?"

"Because the American public is stupid," Cruz said. "They thrive off drama. If you tell them that someone is bad, they'll forget about it in two days. But an assassination attempt? That's weeks' worth of headlines. He'll be the underdog, and America loves an underdog."

"And as a result, the office of the President of the United States will be shaken. It will be a scandal worse than Nixon. Combine that with Helios, and we may be talking about complete success with Helios in six months instead of two years," Stone added.

As Jäger started to question their plan further, he heard another jet pull up next to their trio of luxury business jets. It was a white Dassault Falcon 900LX bearing no registration or N-number on the tail.

Moments later, another man dressed in a dark suit entered Stone's Gulfstream. Jäger recognized him as Borya Medvev, a high level Russian FSB agent he had worked both with, and against, in years past.

Jäger, Stone, and Cruz stood, shaking the Russian spy's hand as they exchanged greetings. Stone excused himself, returning with four shot glasses and a bottle of vodka from the bar.

Jäger politely declined, and the other three toasted before sitting down at the couches.

"I trust your flight was OK?" Stone asked.

"Was good," Medvev said in his thick Russian accent. "But I must return soon."

"Of course," Stone said. "We all have places to be, so let's get started."

"What about our Chinese friend?" Cruz asked Stone.

Stone shrugged. "Couldn't make it. Made up some bullshit excuse about North Korea, but I think the Politiburo is still butthurt about their failed Midway operation and Clifton dropping a concrete bomb in their backyard."

"Won't we need them eventually?" Cruz asked.

"Let's sidebar that," Stone said before turning back to Medvev. "Our friend's time is very valuable."

"How may I help you?" Medvev asked.

"As you know, Helios will be going live in six days," Stone said.

"Yes, of course, the supercomputer," Medvev.

"Right," Stone said. "And of course, this is very beneficial to Russia. A more level playing field is beneficial to everyone, really."

Medvev nodded.

"And of course, the current strategic interests Russia has in the Ukraine and the naval port Tartus in Syria will be up for grabs with America out of the way," Stone continued.

"Da," Medvev replied.

"And I know you will want to take advantage of this power shift as quickly as possible," Stone said.

"Da."

"I'm going to ask you not to," Stone said. "It's very important, in fact, that Russia not change anything."

"And why is that?" Medvev asked. "We have given you all of the assistance you have asked for. Why would we not take advantage of the fruits of our labor?"

"Because if the rest of the world somehow finds out that you were involved, it will start a world war," Cruz interjected. "We can't afford that."

"And we will crush them," Medvev said.

"And the entire project will fail," Stone replied. "Americans *love* war. Look at World War II. The military was weak. The naval fleet was nearly destroyed, but they made it work and won on two fronts. War seems to solidify American resolve and patriotism, which is the exact opposite of what we are going for here."

"We need people to lose faith in the system so that we can build a new one. It must collapse from within in order to assure success," Cruz added.

"And if this new government takes same stance against Russia?" Medvev asked.

"It won't," Stone replied. "We will have direct control, even more so than we have had in the past."

"Is big risk," Medvev said.

"And your people have to keep their mouths shut," Stone said.

"In Russia we are not worried about media like U.S. No one will talk. And, of course, only I and the Prime Minister know," Medvev said. "No problems."

"Good," Stone said as he poured three more shots. "Then let us toast to new beginnings. To Helios!"

"To Helios!" Cruz and Medvev replied.

CHAPTER TWENTY-NINE

The cell was barely bigger than 3 x 5 with a honey bucket in the corner for bodily functions. There was no bed or cot to sleep on and the floors were hardwood. They had taken his shoes and changed him into an orange jumpsuit.

Shepherd sat up as he slowly shook off the effects of whatever drug they had given him. He felt like he was in a haze as he tried to process his surroundings. The last thing he remembered was watching the MI-5 team raid the empty building. He had no idea where he was or how he had gotten there.

He slowly stood. His body ached and his legs felt weak beneath him as he gained his footing on the damp wood floors. Shepherd walked to the cell's door and looked out the small opening with two bars.

Shepherd looked through the opening and saw a guard wearing a duty belt with a Taser, collapsible baton, and pepper spray. "Hey, you," Shepherd said with a whistle.

The guard turned and walked up to the peephole. "What do you want?"

"Where am I?"

The guard smiled. "Purgatory."

"What do you want?" Shepherd asked.

"Compliance," the guard said. He had a hint of an accent that Shepherd couldn't quite place.

"Where are the others?"

"You will soon find out," the guard said before sliding the opening in the door closed.

Shepherd stepped back from the door. He searched the room for possible escape routes but came up with nothing. There was no window or vents that might lead to other rooms or the outside.

As Shepherd continued looking around the room, he heard a faint tapping on the wall to his left. There was a distinct pattern to it as he leaned in closer. *Morse code.*

"Hello!" Shepherd yelled. "Cowboy?"

The tapping continued, growing more intense as the message was repeated.

"Yeah, sorry, dude. I don't know Morse code," Shepherd said.

"Bloody hell, mate, c'mon!" Shepherd heard a muffled voice say on the other side of the wall.

"Jesus, Cowboy, what the hell is going on here?" Shepherd asked through the wall.

"Keep your voice down," Cowboy replied. "I'm not sure."

"We need to get out of here," Shepherd said.

Before Cowboy could respond, Shepherd's door suddenly opened. Two men entered. Shepherd turned to square off with them, but the same man that Shepherd had spoken to earlier already had his Taser drawn.

With a sickening pop, the cartridge deployed and Shepherd rode the lightning for five seconds. His body tensed as the guards secured his hands with zipties and put a hood on his head. They ripped the Taser prongs from his skin and dragged him to his feet, forcing him out of the room as he recovered from the tasing.

He heard the groans of others as he was half-dragged down a flight of stairs and forced to his knees. His hood was ripped from his head and a bright light shined in his face.

As his eyes started to adjust, he made out a man standing in a cage a few feet away. To his left and right were more people on their knees. The guards ripped off their hoods. He saw Cowboy and Jenny to his right. As he looked to his left, he realized it was Tuna and Waldo kneeling next to him. *They're alive!*

A man wearing a well-tailored suit walked in behind them and walked up to the cage. He removed his coat and draped it over a nearby folding chair before unlocking the cage's door. The man inside stumbled out. Blood stained his nearly naked body. *Kruger!*

"Mr. Mack, these are your teammates, are they not?" the man said with a thick accent. As he walked into the light, Shepherd immediately recognized him as the man he thought had shot Tuna.

Kruger said nothing. Instead, he just stood there with a blank expression. He looked beaten and broken. Shepherd had never imagined the one they called the angry bearded ginger could look so broken. He was like a zombie as he stared at the man taunting him.

"For those of you that don't know me, my name is Jäger. I am your salvation," Jäger said. "Comply, and you will be saved. Resist, and you will die. It is very simple."

"I'm going to kill you, bub," Kruger mumbled weakly.

Jäger smiled. "Of course you are," he said as he drew a handgun from his shoulder holster. "Would you like to do it now?"

He flipped the gun around in his hand, as if to offer the weapon to Kruger. Kruger weakly grabbed for it, but Jäger was too quick. He sidestepped the weakened operator and struck him in the forehead with the butt of the gun.

Kruger stumbled forward and dropped to a knee as Jäger laughed at him. It was a sinister laugh, unlike anything Shepherd had ever heard.

"How many times must you learn the same lesson?" Jäger asked. He spun the weapon back around in his hand and pointed it at the hostages on their knees. "Perhaps it is not your life that you care most about."

"Stop," Kruger muttered.

"Ah ha!" Jäger said. "Now we're making progress."

He stepped forward, pointing the weapon at Waldo's head. "Who's your favorite? Who will force you to submit?"

"No," Kruger groaned.

"No?" Jäger said as he pulled the trigger. The register was deafening in the confined basement space.

"You motherfucker!" Kruger yelled.

Jäger laughed as he moved to Tuna. "How about this gentleman?"

"Please," Kruger mumbled.

"I see," Jäger said.

Jäger sidestepped to Shepherd and pointed the gun at his forehead. "I'm new, so you might as well move on, jack," Shepherd said. "It ain't me."

Jäger pressed the hot barrel into Shepherd's forehead and leaned in. "Will you be a problem as well?"

"Always have been," Shepherd said defiantly. "I've got nothing to lose."

"We'll see about that," Jäger said with a wicked grin.

He removed the gun from Shepherd's forehead and sidestepped to Cowboy. "What about this one?" he asked as he looked back to gauge Kruger's reaction.

"Where is my sister?" Cowboy asked.

"Relax," Jäger said. "I already know your weakness. You will do what I say for that very reason."

Jäger moved on to Jenny, moving a lock of her brown hair out of her face with the barrel of his gun. She knelt stoically, saying nothing as she stared up at the monster threatening her.

"No!" Kruger managed.

Jäger looked back at Kruger as the bearded ginger struggled to stand. "I believe we have found a soft spot," Jäger said.

Kruger finally stood and stumbled toward Jäger. "Don't!" he said.

Jenny closed her eyes as Jäger pressed the barrel into her head. "What recourse do you have, Mr. Mack?"

Kruger froze. "Please," he said weakly.

"Please what?" Jäger asked.

"Please...don't hurt them," Kruger said.

Jäger smiled once again. "It's quite simple. Join me. Join our cause and all will be forgiven."

Kruger stood, staring at Jäger. His body slouched and he was listing slightly. Jäger holstered his weapon and turned toward him.

"Will you join me?" he asked as he held out his hand.

"OK," Kruger said as he took Jäger's hand.

As the two men shook hands, Kruger stepped forward. Using every ounce of strength he had remaining, he gouged Jäger in the eyes with his left hand, catching the assassin off guard. Before he could react, Kruger removed the handgun from its holster and shot Jäger twice in the chest at point blank range.

Jäger fell backward, dragging Kruger down with him. As he fell, Kruger turned and fired at the guard standing behind Shepherd, hitting him in the throat.

Seizing the opportunity, Tuna stood and then fell back on his hands, breaking the Flexcuffs and freeing his hands. He turned and attacked the guard behind him, driving his palm into the man's nose and following up with a groin kick.

Cowboy freed himself as well and then helped Jenny. Tuna ran to help Kruger who had collapsed of exhaustion.

"A little help here, fellas," Shepherd said as he stood with his hands still bound behind his back.

"Didn't we teach you how to get out of that?" Cowboy asked.

"Shit, I don't remember," Shepherd said as he fought against his restraints.

After freeing Jenny, Cowboy helped Shepherd. "We have to find Sierra."

"I think she was in the cell across from mine," Jenny said.

Tuna helped Kruger up and put Kruger's arm over his shoulder. Kruger handed the gun to Tuna. "Take this."

Tuna pulled the spare magazine from Jäger's holster and handed both to Cowboy. "Lead the way. I've got him."

Cowboy nodded as he raised the weapon and headed up the stairs. As he reached the top, a guard burst in. Cowboy fired two rounds, dropping him as they continued out of the basement.

Their movements were slowed by Kruger. He was weak and had used every remaining ounce of energy against Jäger. Shepherd joined Tuna in helping Kruger out of the basement and into the holding cell area.

Jenny pulled the keys off the dead guard. When they reached the top of the stairs, Cowboy gave a silent countdown and then entered the hallway. He fired three more rounds, dropping the nearest guard before yelling, "Reloading!"

He quickly swapped magazines and then moved down the hallway. When it was clear, he motioned for Jenny to open Sierra's cell.

They found Sierra still sedated. Shepherd swapped positions with Jenny and walked in, throwing the British spy over his shoulder in a fireman's carry. "I've got her. Let's roll."

They made it out of the compound without further resistance. The sun had just set. Its orange afterglow illuminated the Challenger jet sitting a few hundred yards from the interrogation facility. "Can you fly it?" Cowboy asked Jenny.

"If I can start it, sure," Jenny replied.

As the team ran toward the aircraft, two men wearing white uniforms exited the building. They had come out to investigate the gunshots, but immediately retreated back inside when Cowboy pointed his gun at them.

They helped Kruger onto one of the couches in the rear of the aircraft as Jenny took the left seat in the cockpit. Moments later, the auxiliary power unit spun to life.

"I got it!" she yelled. "We're out of here."

CHAPTER THIRTY

He had at least one broken rib, maybe two. As Jäger rolled to his stomach and picked himself up, he gingerly unbuttoned his shirt, revealing the Level IIIA Kevlar vest he had been wearing. He pulled out the two 9MM rounds as he coughed and wheezed.

Discarding the rounds, Jäger slowly took off his tie and the white button-down shirt and gently placed them on a nearby chair. He removed the vest and tossed it aside. His chest was black and blue. He was sure he had broken a rib as he inspected his injuries.

He put the shirt back on and tucked it back into his charcoal trousers. He stepped over the body of one of the German contractors he had hired and walked to where he had left his coat hanging. He gingerly put it on, stuffing his tie into one of the pockets as he shook off the pain.

Jäger climbed the stairs and stepped over another body as he entered the detainee holding area. All of the cells were empty and his men were dead. He had only brought a small contingent of guards to man the Cold War facility. They had proven insufficient.

He opened the door and walked out into the cool evening air. His Challenger jet was gone, as expected. He had grown fond of traveling in its luxury and knew he would miss it. Jäger checked his watch and then pulled the tie from his pocket. He flipped up his collar and wrapped the tie around his neck as he began tying it.

In the distance, he could hear the thump of rotor blades approaching. As he finished tying the Windsor knot, a Eurocopter EC-135 helicopter turned on its spotlight and landed on the asphalt in front of him.

The helicopter turned off its light as it touched down. Jäger shielded his eyes from the dust and debris as he walked toward it. He opened the side door, climbed aboard and sat down in the luxury seating.

A middle aged man in a dark suit sitting across from him handed Jäger a headset. "You seem to be moving slowly, are you ok?" the man asked in a thick Russian accent.

"I am fine," Jäger replied.

The helicopter lifted off and did a pedal turn before climbing away from the forgotten interrogation facility.

"Is everything on schedule?"

"Of course," Jäger replied. "It is all going as planned."

* * *

A pair of Eurofighter Typhoon fighter jets intercepted the stolen Challenger as it crossed into German airspace. After a brief exchange of flashlight signals between Jenny and the lead pilot, and a short chat on the emergency frequency of 121.5, they were instructed to land at Celle Air Base.

The fighters escorted them until short final and then peeled off as Jenny made a smooth landing. She stopped straight ahead on the runway as a convoy of military and police vehicles surrounded the aircraft with lights flashing.

"We're here," Jenny said as she turned back to her passengers.

Sierra Carter was standing right behind her, looking out at the sea of armed men pointing rifles with mounted flashlights at them. "Don't worry. I was able to contact MI-6 using the plane's satellite phone. They should be here soon."

"It doesn't look like they got the memo," Jenny replied, nodding to soldiers who could now be heard yelling in German.

"Hey guys, I don't speak German, but it sounds like they're saying 'Get the fuck out now or we're going to shoot you,'" Shepherd reported.

Kruger stood and hobbled to the front of the aircraft. "Let's get this over with," he grumbled as he opened the door. The air stairs lowered. Kruger raised his hands as the soldiers shouted instructions at him. He descended the stairs, then limped a few yards away from the aircraft and dropped to his knees with his hands over his head.

Cowboy, Tuna, and Shepherd followed. They formed a line next to Kruger, each with their hands over their head and sitting on their knees. Kruger wobbled as he struggled to stay upright. His eyes were closed as he waited for the inevitable.

Jenny and Sierra filed out last. Sierra attempted to yell out that she was MI-6 in German, but her statements were drowned out by the commands being shouted at them. They took their place next to Kruger and assumed the position.

When they were all out, the soldiers shouted commands for a few more minutes. When no one answered, they sent three men in to search the aircraft while the rest secured the prisoners. Upon reaching Kruger, a soldier shoved a boot into his back, driving him face first into the runway. Too weak to catch his fall, the blow knocked him unconscious.

"Hey asshole, we won the war, so show a little respect," Cowboy said as he watched Kruger fall.

The soldiers responded by forcefully grabbing Cowboy's arms and laying him out on the pavement. One soldier put his knee on the back of Cowboy's neck while the other restrained his hands behind his back with Flexcuffs.

After the entire team was secure, they were helped to their feet and placed in a prisoner transport vehicle. Kruger was put on a stretcher and taken to a nearby ambulance.

"I thought you said you called your boys at MI-6?" Cowboy asked Sierra as the door was closed and the transport started to move.

"They'll be here," Sierra said confidently.

"They couldn't put in a good word or something to stop Kruger from getting knocked out?" Shepherd asked.

"Standard procedure," she replied. "And besides, Kruger needs to go to the hospital."

"Well, it would've been nice to have him go conscious and under his own power," Tuna interjected. "That was just bullshit."

"I don't trust any of these fuckers," Shepherd said. "How do we know they're not all part of this?"

"We don't," Cowboy said. "It's a bloody mess."

"They'll be here," Sierra reiterated. "We will get this all sorted out."

"So what do we do until then, boss?" Shepherd asked Tuna.

"The only thing we can do," Tuna replied. "We wait."

CHAPTER THIRTY-ONE

S pectre took a cab to the airport two hours before his scheduled departure time. He arrived at LaGuardia a half hour before his scheduled sign-in time and made it through security with no issues.

He tried calling Decker's cell phone but was immediately greeted by her voicemail message once again. As before, he called Bear and confirmed that everything was OK back home, but he also had not heard from her.

Spectre used the airline-provided application on his phone to sign in for his trip and found the departure gate. He was still twenty minutes early and the gate agent had not yet arrived to let him on the aircraft.

He heard President Clifton's voice on a nearby TV and turned to face the wall-mounted LCD. She was answering questions in a press conference about an upcoming trade agreement, but Spectre didn't pay attention to what she was saying. The sight of her once again made his blood boil.

Spectre could feel his blood pressure rising as he clenched his fists and jaw. He couldn't shake the feeling. He had no idea why he hated her, but for some reason he associated her with Kerry Johnson which ignited a visceral hatred that coursed through his veins.

He felt someone grab his shoulder and immediately turned around, raising his fist as the rage reached a boiling point. "Easy, guy," a man said as he immediately withdrew and threw up his hands to defend himself.

As Spectre calmed, he realized it was another pilot with his airline. He was wearing the uniform green shirt, blue tie, and charcoal pants. He wore four stripe epaulets on his shoulder, signifying he was a captain for the airline.

"Sorry I startled you," he said as Spectre started to calm. "I just wanted to introduce myself. I'm Tom Haskins. I think we're flying together to DCA and then back to New Orleans. Unless you're deadheading?"

Spectre collected himself and extended his hand. "It's OK, just caught me off guard. I'm Cal Martin. I am flying with you today."

Haskins shook Spectre's hand. "You must've been a military guy. Air Force? Navy?"

"Air Force," Spectre said as he grabbed the handle of his rollaboard and started walking toward the gate with the captain. "How can you tell?"

"All you military guys are jumpy," Haskins replied. "I'd love to hear your war stories. I'm just a straight civilian. I flew corporate before this."

"Cool," Spectre said as they reached the gate agent's podium. She had just arrived and logged into her station. Spectre and the captain both scanned their badges and headed down the jetbridge.

Spectre stowed his bags in the first class closet and grabbed his reflective vest that he would wear for the preflight inspection. "Give me your vest. I'll grab the walk around," the captain said after stowing his own bag in the cockpit.

Spectre thanked him and then headed for the cockpit. The jet had just landed thirty minutes prior, so the battery was already on and the auxiliary power unit running. Spectre began his preflight checks and started setting up the navigation systems for the flight to Reagan Washington National Airport.

The captain returned just as Spectre finished loading and checking the route. Passengers began to board as Spectre and the captain went through the Before Starting Engines checklist and verified the clearance that printed out on the ACARS printer.

They completed the checklist and then Spectre called for pushback clearance as the captain established communications with the crew chief. The controller cleared them to push and they were on their way.

"Alright, cleared to start number two when you're ready," Haskins said.

Spectre was staring at the New York skyline in the distance when Haskins looked over at him. "You ok, guy?" Haskins asked.

"Huh?" Spectre said, snapping out of his daydream. He still felt like he was in a haze. The skyline triggered vague memories of a meeting in a private office overlooking Manhattan, but he couldn't remember what the meeting was about or with whom. He felt like he was in some kind of dreamlike trance and nothing seemed to register.

"I said you can start number two," Haskins repeated and then pointed up at the engine ignitor switches on the overhead panel. "Whenever you're ready."

"Oh, yeah," Spectre said. He reached up and turned the ignitor switch on the number two engine. "Sorry."

The rest of the start sequence went uneventfully. They taxied out behind the long line of aircraft and waited for takeoff. The captain decided to fly the first leg, leaving Spectre the Pilot Monitoring (PM) responsibilities. When the line of aircraft finally cleared, tower cleared them to lineup and wait on the runway.

Tower cleared them for takeoff. The captain ran up the engines to forty percent N1, then pressed the TOGA button and the throttles moved forward. Despite his duties as pilot monitoring, Spectre caught himself looking over at the skyline once more. He couldn't seem to focus as their 737 started to accelerate down the runway.

"Thrust is set at ninety-two point eight," the captain said, trying to get Spectre engaged. As the Pilot Monitoring, it was Spectre's job to call out that the engines had stabilized at the desired thrust setting.

"Sorry," Spectre said as he looked up at the digital displays and tried to get back into it. "There's eighty knots."

"Checked," came the reply.

Spectre managed to focus for the rest of the takeoff and departure, making the required calls and completing the appropriate checklist items as they left New York's airspace. As they leveled off at cruising altitude, the captain once again noticed Spectre daydreaming out the window.

"Did you leave a girlfriend back there or something?" Haskins asked with a sly grin.

"No, sorry. Just have a lot on my mind," Spectre replied. "Trying to sort a few things out."

"Divorce?" Haskins asked. "Because believe me, after about the third one, you stop caring as much. Hell, my last one cost me two hundred grand."

"No," Spectre replied.

Taking the hint, Haskins pulled out a newspaper from his kit bag and began reading. They flew the rest of the relatively short flight in silence, aside from the mandatory checklist items. They landed at Reagan National and taxied to their gate.

After completing the engine shut down checklist, the captain said goodbye to the passengers. Spectre checked his phone once again, but there were still no voicemails or messages from Decker.

After the last passenger was off, Spectre started for the jetbridge. "Where are you heading?" the captain asked. "Food run?"

"I just need a minute," Spectre said.

"OK, but just be back in fifteen minutes. We only have a forty minute turn."

Spectre nodded and continued up the jetbridge. He entered the busy terminal and came face to face with another row of screens. The cable news network was rebroadcasting President Clifton's speech from earlier.

Trying to shake off the rage, Spectre headed down the concourse and out the terminal exit. He took the escalator down to baggage claim and walked out to the taxi stand where the first taxi driver eagerly opened the door for him.

"No luggage?" the man with a Middle Eastern accent asked.

"No," Spectre said as he sat in the back.

"Where to?"

"The White House."

CHAPTER THIRTY-TWO

Tanner and Decker drove to the Washington National Airport after Lyons's personal doctor had a chance to examine Tanner's gunshot wound. The bullet had gone through and through, missing any vital organs or bone. She would be OK, except for some limited mobility and soreness in her left shoulder until the wound healed.

They had considered having Lyons fly them in his Eurocopter AS350 helicopter, but after discussing the clearance requirements to get into Reagan and the potential for Lyons to be discovered alive, they decided it would just be faster to drive.

That didn't, however, alleviate the security concerns associated with driving. They had already been found once using facial recognition and traffic cameras. Lyons loaned them his Ferrari 550 Maranello which had a fake registration and a license plate cover that distorted it from plate readers. They both wore hats and sunglasses, and Coolio did his best to hack into cameras ahead of them and disable the cameras temporarily as they passed.

They arrived at the short term airport parking garage a few minutes after Spectre's scheduled land time. Decker parked the car and the two moved as quickly as they could into the terminal and to the security checkpoint.

Tanner flashed her badge and notified the officer sitting at the podium near the passenger exit that she was carrying her weapon. The officer nodded and asked her to sign the logbook.

"What about her?" he asked, nodding to Decker as Tanner filled out the paperwork.

"She's with me," Tanner said.

Decker pulled out her credentials from the Jefferson Parish Sheriff's Office and showed them to the officer.

"Is this official business?" the officer asked.

"It is," Tanner said.

"Anything I should know about?"

"Just need to interview someone on a flight that's arriving. It's regarding a missing person case," Tanner explained.

The officer picked up his radio. "I'll let the station chief know."

"That's quite alright," Tanner said. "Just routine."

The officer hesitated and then put the radio back down. Decker confirmed that she was unarmed and they were cleared into the secure area.

Decker took off at a jog as she looked at her watch and realized the flight had been at the gate for at least twenty minutes. She pushed through the crowd of people as a feeling of dread came over her that she might be too late.

Reaching the gate, her fears were temporary alleviated. There was a long line of passengers standing at the gate and the sign indicating departure time and destination showed that the flight was delayed.

Decker ignored the complaints of the angry passengers and pushed to the front of the line. She flashed her badge at the gate agent as Tanner met her at the podium. "I need to speak to the first officer of this flight. Cal Martin."

"You and me both, sister," the woman said as she picked up a phone. "I've been paging him for the last ten minutes. These people should've already started boarding by now and I'm not taking this delay. Excuse me."

"We're too late," Decker said as she turned to Tanner.

"What about him?" Tanner asked, pointing to a man wearing a pilot's uniform and talking on his cell phone next to the jetbridge door. "Think he might know something?"

"I'll ask," Decker said. "Stay here with the agent."

Decker walked up to the pilot who raised a finger and turned away. "Excuse me," Decker persisted.

"Ma'am, you'll have to talk to the gate agent," he said with a tone of frustration. "We're doing all we can."

"Are you the captain?" Decker asked.

"Hold on one second please," the pilot said on his phone call before turning back to Decker. "Yes, I am. Now, please, go wait in line like everyone else."

"Cal Martin is my husband," Decker said. "He's your first officer on this flight, right?"

"Jesus. Ok, hold on," the captain said before returning to his phone call. "Hey, let me call you back."

"Do you know where he is?" he asked in a hushed tone as he shoved his phone into his pocket. "We're already looking at a delay because of him."

Decker looked over at Tanner and waved for her to come over. She turned back to the captain and said, "We were hoping you could tell us what happened."

"Who's she?" the captain asked.

"Special Agent Tanner with the FBI," Tanner said, pulling out her credentials. "What can you tell us about Mr. Martin?"

"Captain Tom Haskins," the captain said, pointing to the ID badge clipped to his shirt. "I was paired with Cal for a two leg flight back to New Orleans today."

"From New York?" Decker asked.

"Yes, ma'am."

"Don't most flights originate from New Orleans?" Decker asked.

"They do, but I guess my FO was reassigned or sick, because they pulled him off the trip last night when we were at dinner. This is the last day of my three-day."

"And you had the same co-pilot the first two days?" Tanner asked.

"Yeah, that's typically how it works around here, unless something happens or the company changes their mind," Haskins replied.

"When did you last see Cal?" Decker asked.

"After we said goodbye to the folks. He just walked off. He's a real quiet guy, so I figured he was just going to get coffee or a snack or something. I told him to come back soon because we had a tight turnaround here. He didn't take his bags with him, so I didn't think anything of it. Hell, his cell phone is still sitting next to his company iPad."

"He had bags with him?" Tanner asked.

Haskins nodded. "All still on the airplane. That's why it doesn't make sense."

"Can you go get his phone please?" Decker asked.

"Sure," Haskins said. He turned and punched in his code on the jetbridge door before heading down to the aircraft.

Tanner turned to whisper to Decker. "I'm ninety-nine percent sure Spectre's bags were still in my Tahoe when he went missing. When I came to and they put me on the stretcher, I saw the crime lab guys removing them from the back."

"So he either bought new bags or somehow managed to get them out," Decker said.

Haskins returned wheeling Spectre's bag up the jetbridge. He handed the phone to Decker. She unlocked it and saw that he had tried calling her cell phone multiple times and had connected with Bear earlier in the day.

"Did he say anything in the air? Do anything weird?" Tanner asked as Decker went through the phone.

"He seemed distracted. Missed a few checklist items here and there. I had to prompt him a few times," Haskins said. "But that's not unusual for a new first officer. It takes some getting used to."

"We need to get moving," Decker said to Tanner. "Maybe Coolio can use the cameras to find him."

"Special Agent Tanner!" they heard behind them.

Decker and Tanner turned around to see Special Agent Nickerson with four uniformed airport police officers and another man in tactical pants and a polo shirt.

"Shit," Decker hissed.

"And Michelle Martin," Nickerson said as he closed to within a few feet. "Long time, no see."

"We don't have time for this," Decker said.

"Sure you do," Nickerson said with a sly smile. "Let's chat."

"I insist," he added as he grabbed Decker's wrist.

CHAPTER THIRTY-THREE

They had been in holding cells for several hours before Sierra Carter's friends showed up to bail them out. Shepherd was getting tired of being a prisoner. It seemed to be a common occurrence ever since he had volunteered to go to Iraq to fight with the Kurdish People's Protection Groups.

Upon arrival at their temporary jail cells, they were searched, fed, and allowed to shower. The conditions were much more humane than what they had endured at the previous location, but in Shepherd's mind jail was still jail. It wasn't something he had signed up for.

He had managed a short nap before his cell door was opened and he was escorted with the others to an empty hangar where Captain Smith and a man in a business suit were chatting with

German officers. Once in the hangar, their restraints were removed and they were each given a bottle of water.

Sierra Carter and Cowboy walked up to the two Brits as the rest of the team congregated near the open hangar door.

"Where's Kruger?" Shepherd asked as he rejoined his team.

Tuna pointed behind Shepherd where Kruger walked in as if on cue. He fought off an orderly that was clearly upset that he chose to walk from the ambulance instead of riding in the wheelchair. He was walking with a limp, but appeared noticeably stronger than when they had last seen him.

"You folks OK?" he asked as he approached the group.

"We're fine. But what about *you?*" Tuna asked, tapping Kruger's shoulder.

"Just need some Motrin and a bottle of water and I'll be fine," he replied.

Shepherd offered him the bottle of water the Germans had just handed out. "Here."

"Army joke," Kruger said, turning it down. "So who's in charge here?"

"Cowboy's hot sister," Shepherd said, nodding to Sierra and Cowboy talking with the Brits and Germans.

Kruger turned and headed toward them. His gait was still labored, but purposeful. He looked like a new man compared to what Shepherd had seen in the basement of that Polish prison site. The rest of the team followed him as he approached the group.

"Kruger!" Cowboy said as he interrupted their conversation with the Germans and turned to greet him. "You look a lot better, mate."

"Cowboy," he said, shaking the British operator's hand.

"It's nice to see you up and about, Frederick," Sierra said with a shy smile. "How are you feeling?"

"I'll be fine. Who are they?" Kruger asked, indicating the two Brits still talking to the German officer.

"MI-6," Sierra replied. "Captain Smith is with the tactical response team and the man in the suit is Kenneth Worthington. He's my superior."

The German officer excused himself. Sierra turned and introduced Smith and Worthington to Kruger. "He's with the group I told you about," she said.

"I thought you were a myth," Worthington said as he shook Kruger's hand. "I've heard a great deal about you."

"Just your average guy," Kruger said.

"Good to see you. By all accounts, you're a dead man," Smith said.

"I was," Kruger replied. "Now I'm back."

"Don't worry, we will get you medical care in London," Worthington said.

"No. We need to get back to Virginia," Kruger said before turning to Cowboy. "Have you heard anything from Coolio?"

"I'm sorry mate, but we thought he died with you," Cowboy said. "At least that's what the reports said."

"We need to find him," Kruger said. "He was alive when I put him on that stretcher. If the assholes who captured us have him, we need to get to him."

"You can square all of that away after a thorough debrief," Worthington said. "We'd like you to come back to London so we can get a handle on what's being planned."

"Well, at least one of those cunts is dead already," Cowboy said.

"He's not dead," Kruger said.

"What?" Sierra asked as she stepped up to Kruger. "What do you mean he's not dead? They said you shot him."

"I did," Kruger said. "But he was wearing a vest."

"Wait, so why didn't you kill that fucker?" Shepherd asked. He and the rest of the team had been standing within earshot listening to their conversation.

"The whole thing was a setup," Kruger said. "It's an advanced interrogation technique. He's been trying to break me down for days – trying to weaken my resolve and to show me that he was in control."

"He wanted you to shoot him?" Shepherd asked.

"No, he wanted me to escape," Kruger said. "He wanted all of us to escape."

"But what about Waldo?" Shepherd asked. "He shot him in cold blood!"

"Waldo proved too weak and submitted. Whatever he's planning, he needs us to think we're resisting him."

"Hold on a second," Tuna interjected. "Now, granted, I didn't get as much face to face time as you did, but what you're suggesting is insane. This guy spends days beating you down just to let you escape? Just to let *us* escape? Why?"

Kruger shrugged. "I don't know. I didn't get a chance to look at his master plan, but I'm telling you, what he did was straight out of a fairly advanced playbook. And he's not an inexperienced operator. No way would it have been that easy to get the drop on him like that."

"Back to my original question, then. Why didn't you put a bullet in his head so we don't have to deal with him again?" Shepherd asked.

"You were a cop, right?" Kruger asked. "You shoot to stop the threat, and at the time he was neutralized."

"I don't think that applies to psychopaths that kill people in cold blood like that," Shepherd shot back. "At least not in my book."

"If I had killed him, it would be that much harder to figure out what he's planning and to stop him," Kruger said.

"How?" Shepherd asked.

Kruger looked at Worthington. "Send a team to the site. I guarantee you'll find a half dozen bodies but no Jäger. When you confirm it, start working from when we left in his jet with the satellite feed. Find out where he went. But in the meantime, we need to go back to Virginia."

"We need to go back to London," Sierra interjected.

"*You* can go back to London," Kruger replied. "I am going to find a way to get back to Virginia. There's no way they transported Coolio in the condition he was in, so if he's being held somewhere, that's a good starting point."

"I don't know about you guys, but I miss America," Shepherd said. "I'll stick with the boss."

Kruger turned to Sierra. "You can debrief us on the way there if you like. Just get us a jet and let's go."

"And what if you're right?" Sierra asked. "What if he did manage to escape and he's in Europe?"

Kruger pointed to Captain Smith. "Send this guy after him. He can handle it."

CHAPTER THIRTY-FOUR

The taxi dropped Spectre off at 15th Street and Pennsylvania Avenue. After crossing the street, he filed in behind a group of tourists entering through the Visitors Entrance for a scheduled tour of the White House.

He stood in line for twenty minutes before it was his turn in front of the uniformed Secret Service officer checking identification behind bulletproof glass. Spectre handed her his driver's license and she entered his information into her computer.

"You're not on the cleared list with this tour," she said, looking up from her computer.

"I need to speak to the President," Spectre replied.

The officer raised an eyebrow as she studied Spectre. Spectre could feel another officer approach behind him, having overheard the conversation. He suddenly felt claustrophobic.

"We get that a lot, sir, but that's not how that works," she said. "This is the entrance for tours. In order to get a tour, you'll need to get with your local Congressman and set it up. Where are you from?"

"Louisiana," Spectre replied. Spectre didn't look back, but he could see the reflection of the other officer just a few feet behind him.

"I'll look up his information for you," she said, nodding to the officer behind Spectre as she went back to work on her computer.

"So what do you need to talk to President Clifton about?" the male officer behind Spectre asked.

Spectre turned to face the officer. He was a few inches taller than Spectre and in reasonably good shape. He was wearing a plate carrier with a SECRET SERVICE patch on the chest. Spectre's Krav Maga and Project Archangel training made him instinctively size up the officer as he calculated his options of escape.

"That's classified," Spectre replied casually.

"Let me guess, you could tell me but then you'd have to kill me?" the officer asked with a grin as he stuck his thumbs under the plate carrier he was wearing over his uniform.

"Hold on a second," the woman behind the counter said before Spectre could reply.

"Sir, you do have a meeting with President Clifton at 4 p.m.," she said. "You need to go to the appointment gate, Mr. Martin. I'm sorry for the confusion."

Spectre was confused. He didn't know of an appointment, and didn't really have a plan of how to get into the White House beyond his current attempts. His mind still seemed foggy, like he was walking in a dream.

"I'll take you to the East Appointment Gate. It's not that far from here," the male officer said.

The female officer handed Spectre's ID back to him and apologized once again. Spectre turned and followed the male officer out the door and they turned toward the appointment entrance.

"Cal Martin," the officer said as if trying to remember where he'd heard the name. "Where have I seen you before?"

"I've been here once. Long time ago."

"That's it!" the officer replied. "Presidential Medal of Freedom for saving the President on Midway. I knew it!"

"I guess so," Spectre replied as they kept walking.

"A lot of good agents died on that island. What was it like?"

"It sucked."

The officer shook his head. "It's incredible. Worst day in the history of the Secret Service, but somehow she made it to safety. And to think ISIS was behind something like that."

"They weren't," Spectre said.

"Really?"

"Really."

"Is that classified too?"

"Yup."

"Fair enough," the officer said as they reached the East Appointment Gate. It was a smaller building with both uniformed officers and Secret Service agents wearing their trademark dark suits. "Well, it was an honor to meet you, sir."

"Thanks," Spectre said as the officer held the door open for him.

Spectre walked into the building and greeted the attendant as before. The uniformed officer once again took his identification, but this time asked him to have a seat in the waiting area.

As he took his seat, Spectre looked up to see a TV that appeared to be running programs from the White House's press team. It showed the President's public agenda for the next several days and then cut to the new Vice President giving a speech at Kennedy Space Center about funding a manned mission to Mars.

"Mr. Martin," the officer said, motioning for him to approach the two-way glass.

"Here's your visitor badge and ID," he said, passing them through the slot. "You'll need to wear the badge at all times, and you'll be escorted the entire time you're here."

He passed another piece of paper through the slot. "This is the code of conduct. Please read through this, initial each line, sign, and date."

As Spectre went through the form, he suddenly heard President Clifton's voice on the TV overhead. He looked up to see her delivering remarks about their ongoing meetings with China about artificial islands in the South Pacific.

Spectre dropped the pen. It rolled off the ledge and onto the floor. The thud caused the officer to look up at Spectre. His face felt flush and the hand that had just been holding the pen was now trembling.

"Sir, are you OK?" the officer asked.

Spectre stepped back. He closed his eyes, trying to block out the stimulus that was causing his sudden rage. His conscious seemed to be fighting his subconscious as he thought about President Clifton. He felt a visceral rage and hatred toward the woman, wanting to kill her for everything she had done, just like Vice President Johnson.

But on the other hand, Spectre had a nagging thought that it was all just a dream. That he had no real reason to hate her. That something —*someone* was driving these thoughts. He felt like he was losing control.

"Sir?" the officer repeated.

Two Secret Service agents approached Spectre in a non-threatening manner. They seemed to be more concerned about his own health and safety, unaware of what he was capable of.

"You need to arrest me," Spectre said, gritting his teeth as he turned to the agents.

"Say that again?" the agent to his right asked. "You want us to arrest you, sir?"

"I'm here to kill the President," Spectre growled.

Within seconds, Spectre was face down on the polished concrete floor. He didn't resist as they restrained him and searched him for weapons. He started to calm as he no longer heard the President's voice on the TV overhead.

"Let's go have a chat," the agent said as they picked him up.

A wave of relief rushed over Spectre. "Thank God," he mumbled as they removed him from the check-in room.

CHAPTER THIRTY-FIVE

A m I under arrest?" Decker asked as she sat across from Nickerson. She and Tanner had been cuffed and taken to a different location from her first visit with Nickerson. The sign on the door indicated that it was the office of the airport chief of security. His name was Ron Maxwell and he was standing behind Nickerson.

Nickerson nodded to Maxwell. He removed the cuffs from both Tanner and Decker. "Your weapon is in secure storage," he added, as he put both sets of cuffs down on the desk between Nickerson and the ladies.

"You didn't answer my question," Decker said. "Are we free to go?"

"What are you doing here, Tanner?" Nickerson asked, ignoring Decker's questions. "You're supposed to be in the hospital, or at the very least on sick leave."

Decker slammed her hand down on the desk. "Hey!" she yelled. "Look at me!"

"We don't have time for this bullshit," Decker said as Nickerson withdrew slightly. "Now, you either tell us what we're being charged with, or we're out of here."

"You are being detained," Nickerson said. "I had the cuffs removed as a courtesy."

"On what grounds?"

"Well, for starters, you were in the secure area of the airport without having properly gone through security," Maxwell said, speaking up for the first time since they had been removed from the gate. "That's a felony."

"I'm a federal agent," Tanner said.

"You are," Maxwell said before pointing to Decker. "But she's not."

"Is she not allowed to escort me?" Decker asked and then turned to Nickerson. "Do we really have to play these games? How did you find us?"

"Officer Davis reported you to me," Maxwell said. "He said you two seemed suspicious and wanted a second opinion."

"And you?" Decker asked, still looking at Nickerson. "Do you just live at the airport now?"

"I happened to be in the area when Chief Maxwell gave me a call," Nickerson said.

It was subtle, but Decker noticed a slight twitch in his face – a tell. Nickerson was lying. He knew they were going to be there. He had been waiting for them. Every warning bell in her head was suddenly going off all at once. They needed to get out of there. They needed to escape.

"Is that so?" Decker asked. She turned and looked at Tanner. The expression on Tanner's face said it all. She had caught it too. Decker hoped they were on the same page.

"So why were you here?" Nickerson asked.

"I wanted to meet someone on the flight."

"Your husband?"

"Are you still investigating him?"

"You were in the FBI, Mrs. Martin. Do you think something as serious as assaulting a federal agent would be dropped so quickly?" Nickerson replied.

That's it. The hair on the back of her neck was standing up. Coolio had told them that the charges had mysteriously been removed and the files purged. Nickerson was lying. The same tell as before reared its ugly head.

"Then I guess we have nothing left to discuss," Decker said.

"Oh, but we do. Where have you ladies been the last couple of days?" Nickerson asked as he turned to Tanner. "You've had us worried sick, you know."

"Did you meet with him?" Nickerson added. "What about his friends? We know he's not working alone."

"Charge me or release me, but I think we're done here," Decker said as she started to stand.

"Sit down," Nickerson ordered. He also stood and sidestepped to the side of the desk where he could get to her.

Decker remained standing, staring down Nickerson as she squared up against him.

"Can you give us a moment, Chief?" Nickerson said without turning away from Decker.

"Are you sure?" he asked.

"I'll be fine," Nickerson replied.

Maxwell tiptoed between Nickerson and Decker and left the office, closing the door behind him.

Nickerson waited until the door was closed and then said, "You know where he is, don't you?"

"I already told you, I—"

Nickerson drew his Glock and pointed it at Decker's forehead. "No you dumb bitch, not Martin. I know where he is. You were with Lyons. He's alive, isn't he? That's why you went to Falls Church?"

Decker eyed Tanner as she started to move. She gently shook her head, telling the young agent to stay put.

"Listen to your friend, sweetheart," Nickerson said without taking his eyes off Decker. "This is not your fight."

"Where is my husband?" Decker asked, seemingly unfazed by the fact that she was staring down the barrel of a loaded gun.

Nickerson smiled. "He'll either be in jail or dead very soon. Now answer the question or little Calvin Junior becomes an orphan today."

Decker watched as Nickerson's trigger finger slid into the guard and rested on the trigger. The mention of her son made her furious. She was done negotiating.

Raising her hands as if to surrender, Decker grabbed Nickerson's wrist with her left hand and the slide of the gun with her right in one smooth motion. She pushed the weapon away with her left hand while twisting it with her right, careful not to put Tanner in the line of fire.

Nickerson's finger snapped with a satisfying crack as it got stuck in the trigger guard and Decker ripped the weapon from his grip. As she pulled the gun away, she struck him in the temple with the barrel before stepping back, rotating the gun in her hand, and pointing it at him.

Nickerson screamed out in agony as he stumbled from the blow to the head while holding his newly deformed finger. Seizing the opportunity, Tanner stood and swept his leg from underneath him as she grabbed his head and slammed it into the desk. The blow knocked him out cold.

"Nice," Decker said with a look of approval. "Let's get out of here."

Decker dropped the magazine and racked the slide, ejecting the round. She pointed the weapon in a safe direction and pulled the trigger. Pulling the slide back far enough to activate the take down, she removed the slide and took out the barrel, tossing it to one corner of the room as she dropped the frame and tossed the slide to the other corner.

Tanner slowly opened the door and exited first. Decker followed and closed the door behind them. Maxwell was standing in the hall talking to someone with his back turned to them. They moved quickly out of the office and into the baggage claim office. As they made it to the automatic door, they heard Maxwell yelling out at them. He had obviously discovered Nickerson's unconscious body.

Decker and Tanner ran through the automatic doors. They dodged taxis, airport shuttles, and buses as they ran across the divided street to the parking garage. As they reached the Ferrari, Tanner pulled out the keys and offered them to Decker.

"You're doing a great job," Decker said. "Just get us to the White House."

Tanner smiled and jumped in the driver's seat, firing up the Ferrari's V-12 engine. She backed out of the spot and sped through the parking garage, clearing the pay kiosks at the bottom before Nickerson or Maxwell could lock it down.

They sped down the George Washington Memorial Parkway and onto I-395 uneventfully. Decker and Tanner both watched out for police cars or unmarked government vehicles the entire time as they weaved through traffic, but none ever appeared. The pursuit was over, at least for the time being.

But Decker couldn't relax. Nickerson's threats had stuck with her. The people behind this were planning to kill her husband. She had to save him.

CHAPTER THIRTY-SIX

President Madeline Clifton was sitting at her desk in the Oval Office when she heard her Chief of Staff Todd Plonski enter the room. She had been reviewing a National Security Brief on the ongoing Chinese threat in the South Pacific.

"Madame President," he said softly as he interrupted her.

"What is it, Todd?" she asked as she looked up from the folder marked TOP SECRET.

"Your 4 p.m. appointment has cancelled," he said as he walked up to her desk.

Clifton looked up at the clock. It was ten minutes after 4 p.m. "I wasn't aware I had a four o'clock."

"Me neither, ma'am. I must have overlooked it, but it's apparently been on the books for a few months."

"Have a seat," Clifton offered. "You make me nervous when you stand there like that. Who was the appointment with?"

Plonski took a seat in the plush leather chair across from Clifton's desk. "Apparently you were supposed to meet Cal Martin today, ma'am."

Clifton closed the folder on her desk and folded her hands over it as she gave Plonski a look of astonishment. "*The* Cal Martin? Michelle Decker's husband Cal Martin?"

"Yes, ma'am," Plonski said as he sat back and crossed his right leg over his left.

"Well, what did he want?"

Plonski pulled out his phone and opened his digital calendar. "The meeting itinerary was a simple meet and greet. No further details."

"So where is he?"

"That's just it. The Secret Service detained him about a half hour ago because he threatened to kill you while he was signing in," Plonski said with a look of disbelief. "Now, how does that make sense?"

"It doesn't. Where is he now?"

"The Secret Service is interviewing him on the east side."

Clifton turned slightly to her left and yelled, "Ned!" Within seconds, Special Agent Ned Landry, the agent in charge of her protective detail appeared.

"Yes, ma'am?" the balding senior agent asked in a thick southern accent.

"What do you know about the arrest of Cal Martin?"

"From what I've been told, ma'am, he attempted to sign in at the Visitors Center and was escorted to the Appointment Entrance. While being checked in there, he suddenly demanded that agents arrest him and said that he was going to kill you," Landry said. "Very strange."

"What did he say when your people interviewed him?" Clifton asked.

"I haven't heard anything yet, ma'am, but I can find out."

Clifton thought about it for a moment and then said, "No, I want you to bring him here."

Landry's eyes widened. "Excuse me, ma'am? I don't think I heard you correctly. It sounded like you wanted me to bring him here."

"That's exactly what I said, Agent Landry. Please make it happen."

Landry shook his head in protest. "Absolutely not, ma'am. Respectfully, I cannot allow someone that just threatened you to come in here. I simply cannot honor that request, ma'am."

"Perhaps I was unclear," Clifton said, her tone growing more irritated. "I wasn't making a request. I am directing you to bring him to this office because I would like to speak with him."

"But ma'am…"

"You have handcuffs on him, do you not?"

"Yes, ma'am."

"And body scanners you can use to determine if he's carrying a bomb?"

"Yes, ma'am."

"Then bring him to me," Clifton ordered. "And don't make me wait."

Landry let out a defeated sigh and nodded. He walked out the door as he pulled out his cell phone.

"You really want to see him?" Plonski asked.

"That man has a knack of getting into trouble. He sniffed out Kerry's dealings with the Chinese and nearly took down our entire administration. I thought he was tucked away in some Air Force squadron. Which means, if he's back, something's going on and I want to know about it," Clifton explained.

"Apparently he's been on the schedule for months though," Plonski said.

"Which also makes no sense. That's why I want to talk with him. If he wants to kill me, I want to know why," Clifton said.

"The Secret Service is going to hate this."

"They'll be fine. Now," Clifton said as she turned back to her folder, "let's talk about this briefing while I have you here."

Clifton and Plonski discussed the brief in detail, going over the policy matters and the road going forward. Although Clifton had decided to stay for only one term after the Midway Island incident, she intended to leave the next President with a workable policy in dealing with the growing aspirations of the Chinese.

As they wrapped up their talk, Agent Landry arrived with Martin. He was in a wheelchair with his hands and legs securely strapped to the framework with leather straps. Six agents accompanied Landry in escorting Martin into the Oval Office.

"Against my better judgement, Cal Martin is here to see you, ma'am," Landry announced.

Spectre's eyes were closed as they wheeled him next to Clifton's desk.

"Is he sedated?" Clifton asked.

"No, ma'am," Landry replied. "He's been like this since we strapped him down."

Clifton stood and walked over to Spectre. "Cal," she said softly as she stood next to him.

Spectre opened his eyes. He appeared confused and disoriented. As he saw Clifton, his muscles flexed and he pulled against his restraints. His breathing became shallow and rapid and his face turned red.

"Cal," Clifton repeated. As the episode grew more intense, one of the agents gently pulled President Clifton away from Spectre.

"Has he been seen by medical?" she asked.

"Only a basic work-up. They didn't find anything unusual," Landry answered.

"Who interviewed him?" Clifton asked.

"I did, ma'am," an agent answered. "I'm Special Agent Case."

"What did he tell you?"

"He didn't remember anything. He said he only remembered getting out of the taxi, but he couldn't tell me why he was here to see you," Case said.

Spectre suddenly calmed. His eyes darted around the room, shifting from agent to agent as he tried to make sense of his surroundings. "Where am I?"

"Cal," Clifton said as she moved the agent out of the way. "Do you remember me?"

Spectre felt nothing as he looked at the President. "President Clifton?" he asked with a look of confusion. "Where am I?"

"The Oval Office. You had an appointment to see me today."

"I did?" Spectre asked.

Clifton looked at Landry and stepped back to whisper in his ear. "You're good at telling if people are lying, right? What do you think?"

"How did I get here?" Spectre asked. "What happened?"

Landry shrugged as they turned back to Spectre. "What's the last thing you remember?" Landry asked.

Spectre stared at Agent Landry for a moment and then said, "Getting tased."

Landry looked back at the President. "He wasn't tased, ma'am. But he doesn't appear to be lying."

"Jesus my head is killing me," Spectre said. "Why am I strapped to this chair?"

"Who tased you?" Landry asked.

"I don't know," Spectre said, still wincing from the headache. "I was at the morgue with that FBI agent...I forget her name...Tanning? Tanner? That's it, Agent Tanner."

"What morgue?" Clifton asked.

"In Virginia," Spectre said before stopping as he looked down. "Wait, why am I in uniform? What the hell is going on here?"

"Get Dr. Rabito here," Clifton said. "Get him to our infirmary."

"Ma'am, I don't think that—"

Clifton interrupted Landry again. "Not a request, Agent Landry. This man needs medical attention and bloodwork done. He's obviously on something."

"Yes, ma'am," Landry replied.

"And find out who Agent Tanner is," Clifton added.

CHAPTER THIRTY-SEVEN

The team huddled around Kruger as they waited for the secure video teleconference to connect. They were flying at thirty-seven thousand feet above the Atlantic in an MI-6-provided Hawker 900XP business jet. Sierra Carter and her team had stayed behind, promising to update Kruger as soon as they had information on the mysterious man named Jäger from the interrogation facility.

Kruger found himself wishing Coolio were around to help him get the software set up. He missed the quirky little MIT-graduate. He hoped Jäger and whoever else was involved hadn't hurt or killed him. Kruger's first priority was to find Coolio and then make sure whoever was responsible for all of this died a slow, painful death. He already had a few ideas in mind of how to make that happen.

The video teleconference finally connected after a bit of clicking around on the laptop and help from the peanut gallery sitting and standing behind him at the Hawker's luxury table. Sierra Carter appeared on screen and said hello. There was a slight lag between her mouth moving and the audio due to the speed of the Hawker's satellite internet connection.

"What did you find at the site?" Kruger asked.

"Lots," Sierra began. "It's a former CIA black site that was decommissioned in 1998. We went through the records and it was purchased shortly after by a holding company based in Sweden. We did a little digging, but it was a total dead end. Other than a name on the deed, the company doesn't exist."

"I'm not surprised," Kruger said. "What about on the ground?"

"I didn't personally go there, but from the video I saw, it looked like it was still being used. Maybe even by the CIA. I've reached out to Langley, but no response yet. We still have people looking the place over. We found lots of bodies, but no one matching the description of the man called Jäger. Having seen him myself, I had them live stream the faces of each body they found."

"What do you know about this guy?" Kruger asked.

"He's a ghost," Sierra replied with a frown. "We pulled the security camera footage from when he abducted me and found nothing. Not a single match from any angle, and we had a few pretty clear shots of him."

"So we know nothing," Kruger said.

"We found a secure server room of some sort. Lots of computer equipment with video chat capabilities. Unfortunately, breaking in triggered a series of small charges that destroyed most of it. We may be able to do a bit of forensics on the hard drives back in London, but that will take months."

"We don't have months."

"Right," Sierra said.

"What about Jäger? If he's not dead, do you know where he is?"

"About that," Sierra said. "We actually did have a satellite over the area at the time, and we found where you took off. There is nothing after that."

"What do you mean nothing?"

"We're dealing with people with high level access, Mr. Mack. It's barely perceptible, but shortly after you took off, the satellite feed enters a loop for about fifteen minutes. Long enough for someone to escape, but it gives us nothing to go on. Or it didn't at first," Sierra explained.

"Given the time of the loop, I had a hunch that he may have exfiltrated via helicopter. Local air traffic control feeds showed the same artifacts as the satellite, so I reached out to a friend with the missile defense project at the European Interceptor Site in Redzikowo. The Aegis Ballistic Missile Defense System isn't quite online, but the radar is up and running doing test trials. So I had him look for targets at the time of the satellite feed anomaly," Sierra continued.

"And you found him?"

"Slow moving helicopter target arrives five minutes into the loop and departs to the northeast. I then matched it with the ATC feed outside the area and matched it to a helicopter on a diplomatic flight plan headed to Minsk," Sierra said with a smile.

"Are you sending a team?"

Sierra shook her head. "Minsk was just a refueling point. The final destination is Moscow, and there's no way I can get that approved. At least not without more evidence of what they're planning."

"The fucking Russians?" Shepherd asked, breaking the silence from the team watching over Kruger's shoulder. "They're doing all of this?"

"We currently have no intel to connect them at this time. It may simply be a diversion. So far, we have nothing concrete to connect Jäger to the current threat," Sierra answered.

"Can the Russians hack our satellite feeds and do what this guy did?" Kruger asked.

"If they can, we're not aware of that capability," Sierra replied.

"So it's an inside job."

"It's an American satellite," Sierra said.

"And a CIA black site," Kruger added.

"We're going to keep digging, but for right now, we're at a dead end."

"Thank you, Sierra. I appreciate all your help. Please let us know if you find anything else," Kruger said.

"Will do. Safe travels," Sierra said before signing off.

Kruger closed the laptop and turned to face the group.

"What now, boss?" Tuna asked, seated on the leather couch across from the desk.

"We find Coolio and get in comms with Cuda."

"Do you think they're still alive?" Shepherd asked. "Given all of this, I mean."

"Coolio was alive when I put him in the ambulance. He wasn't trapped or burned in the building. I think they did the same thing to him that they did with me. And Cuda was at home when the explosion happened. Unless they tapped him at his house, he should still be alive," Kruger explained.

"Do you think this Jäger bloke is GRU or FSB?" Cowboy asked. The GRU was the Russian Main Intelligence Agency, Russia's largest foreign intelligence service while the FSB was responsible for state security and counterespionage.

Kruger shrugged. "It doesn't matter to me. He's going to die one way or another, regardless of what flag they drape over his coffin when this is all said and done."

CHAPTER THIRTY-EIGHT

Decker knew she was taking a major risk when she and Tanner walked into the Robert F. Kennedy Department of Justice building. She was betting her freedom and potentially her life on Coolio's intel that the charges against Spectre had been dropped. And she was relying on a little luck that Nickerson hadn't managed to put out a Be On Lookout (BOLO) notice for her yet.

It was a gamble, but Decker believed that U.S. Attorney General Jennifer Chase was her best chance at putting a stop to this madness. Decker and Chase had been friends ever since their showdown with former Vice President Kerry Johnson in the Oval Office, and his subsequent outing as a traitor to the United States.

Her gut told her Chase was a person that could be trusted and could help them find Spectre. She hoped she wasn't wrong.

Decker and Tanner walked in and showed their IDs to the security officer. They passed through the metal detectors and proceeded to the reception desk where Decker introduced herself and told the officer she was there to see the Attorney General. The officer took her ID and picked up the phone, dialing Attorney General Chase's secretary.

As the officer waited on hold, Decker looked up at the wall clock. It was just after 4:30 p.m. Time was a luxury they did not have. She hoped whatever was going on inside Spectre's head hadn't caused him to do something that would get him killed.

"Do you have an appointment?" the officer asked after a brief conversation with the secretary.

"No, but please tell her it's Michelle Decker and this is an emergency," Decker said urgently.

The officer relayed the information and then hung up the phone after a brief exchange. "She said she'd call me back. Please wait a moment."

Tanner pulled Decker away from the desk and whispered, "Are you sure this is the right play? Maybe we could find a phone and call Coolio to track him down?"

Decker shook her head. "Phones aren't safe and we don't have anyone left to trust. Jen has resources to help us find him."

"It's obviously your call," Tanner said. "But I'd hate to run into another goon like Nickerson."

"Ma'am," the officer interrupted.

"Yes?" Decker asked, turning back to the desk.

The officer handed them each a visitor badge. "The Attorney General will see you now. Do you know how to get there?"

"We'll find it," Decker said as she clipped the badge to her shirt.

Tanner followed Decker through the lobby to the elevator. They took it to the U.S. Attorney's Office and were greeted by the receptionist. "Mrs. Martin?" the young man asked.

"We're here to see Attorney General Chase," Decker announced.

"Right this way. Can I get you some water?" he asked as he stood to usher them in.

"Sure," Decker said.

They walked in and Jennifer Chase stood from behind her desk. She walked up and hugged Decker before Decker introduced her to Tanner. Chase invited them to sit as she sat behind her desk. The receptionist returned with two bottles of cold water and excused himself before closing the door behind him.

"Are you OK?" Chase asked with a look of concern. "They said it was an emergency."

"Cal is missing and something is going on," Decker said with a pained expression.

"Is that why the FBI is involved?" Chase asked.

"Oh, no ma'am," Tanner said. "I'm not here on official business."

"Ok, honey, start from the beginning," Chase said. "Let's see if we can figure this out."

Decker started from the beginning when she learned that the office building in Falls Church had exploded. She explained Spectre's involvement and how she had been detained upon exiting the aircraft in D.C. with Nickerson claiming that Spectre was under investigation by order of the Director of the FBI himself. She was careful to leave out the details of Odin and Lyons's status, but told the story of Nickerson and the gun to her head in the office at the airport.

"I'll have his badge," Chase said angrily before turning to Tanner. "And what happened to your shoulder? Did he do that too?"

Tanner looked down to see that the bandage was starting to bleed through her shirt slightly. "That's another story, ma'am," Tanner said.

"So Cal somehow ended up in New York and flew a flight to Reagan? And now you don't know where he is?" Chase asked.

"I think he's been drugged," Decker said.

"By whom?"

Decker shifted uneasily in her chair. "Well, in a roundabout way, the same people who were behind Kerry Johnson."

"What?" Chase yelped. "You're kidding, right?"

"It's very complicated, Jen. You'll just have to trust me until we can sort this out. But first I want to make sure we find Cal. And then I will turn myself in to you if it comes down to that," Decker said.

"You don't have to turn yourself in to anyone. Let's start with the FBI Director and make sure your husband really isn't a wanted man," Chase said as she picked up the phone. "One sec."

As Chase dialed the number, Tanner turned to Decker. "I still can't believe you are friends with the Attorney General. That's amazing."

"If we get out of this, remind me and I'll tell you the story," Decker said. Although she was young and a bit naïve, Tanner had started to grow on Decker. She reminded Decker of herself when she was a young prosecutor before getting bored and joining the FBI.

Tanner's face lit up. "That would be awesome."

"We need to get someone to look at that bandage," Decker said, pointing to the small bloodstain on Tanner's shirt. "Shouldn't be bleeding through like that."

After a short conversation, Chase hung up the phone. "Well, I found your husband," she said.

"You did?" Decker asked excitedly. "Is he OK? Where is he?"

"He's receiving medical care in Secret Service custody. In fact, the Director thought that's what I was calling about. Apparently Cal threatened to kill President Clifton."

"Goddammit," Decker said softly.

"That's not all," Chase said. "Clifton insisted that they meet. He has no memory of anything. She ordered lab work and medical treatment for him. She thinks he was drugged."

"When did this happen? Where is he now?"

"Just a few minutes ago. Schultz said he had just gotten off the phone with President Clifton when I called," Chase explained and then turned to Tanner. "You said your name is Tanner, right?"

"Yes, ma'am."

"Madison Tanner? Special Agent with the D.C. field office? Assigned to escort Cal to the collapsed building in Falls Church?" Chase asked.

"Yes, ma'am," Tanner replied, confused at the line of questioning since all of that had already been established.

"The President would like to speak with you," Chase said.

"She would?" Tanner asked.

"Yes," Chase said as she stood from behind her desk. "Let's go. And I'll make sure you get to see your husband, Michelle."

"Thank you, Jen," Decker said as she stood to follow the Attorney General.

"I don't know what you guys have gotten yourselves into this time, but you definitely have the leader of the free world's attention," Chase said.

CHAPTER THIRTY-NINE

Jäger's satellite phone rang as he stood in the hangar waiting for the helicopter to be refueled. He answered, immediately recognizing the voice of Stone as his boss opened with a profanity-infused tirade.

"Where the fuck are you?" Stone asked as he finally became understandable.

"I am on my way to meet with our associates as you directed, sir," Jäger replied calmly.

"MI-6 has Mack and his team. And I'm just now hearing that MI-6 is crawling around the Poland site. Did you know about this? What the fuck is going on over there?"

"I had not heard about MI-6, but I will—"

"You will get your ass back to America and personally take care of this. This is a fucking disaster."

"Yes, sir," Jäger replied. He considered pointing out that he had requested to do just that in the first place, but thought better of it. The old man likely didn't even remember that conversation.

"Please tell me what the hell happened in Poland? How did they escape? How did the site get compromised?"

"As I said, I have been traveling, sir. I will find out."

"How successful were you before you left?"

"They were coming around, sir. As I told you, turning someone takes time. It would have been much easier just to kill them."

There was a pause as Stone seemed to consider the options. "Fine. Kill them," he said finally.

"Are you sure?"

Stone hesitated again and then said, "Yes. Fuck'em. They had their chance. They could have been valuable assets, especially Mack. We needed a good tactical team to work outside of Helios. But we don't have time for this shit. Tie up the loose ends."

"I will need to use the system to find them, and—"

"Don't bother. I already did. MI-6 gave them a plane and they're flying to the United States as we speak. I'll send you a copy of their flight plan. You need to get there now. Don't worry about the Russians."

"Yes, sir," Jäger replied. "Will that be all, sir?"

"Just get it done," Stone said before hanging up.

As Jäger stuffed his phone back into the inside pocket of his coat, Borya Medvev approached. The GRU operative was wearing a three-piece suit. He walked up to Jäger and stopped as if waiting for an explanation for the phone call.

"What have you learned?" Medvev asked. "Was that your boss?"

"I must return to America," Jäger said.

"We can continue to Moscow or I can arrange for transportation from here if you'd like."

"I should go from here," Jäger replied. He knew Stone would be keeping tabs on him and would expect him to use the quickest method available to get back to the United States.

"Is everything as planned?"

"Yes," Jäger answered. "He only knows that MI-6 discovered the interrogation facility."

"Good," Medvev said. "What will he have you do in the United States?"

"He wants me to tie up loose ends. I think he is afraid that they will discover him and turn against him."

"Do you think they can?"

"The one they call Kruger – Fred Mack – I believe he can. I could see it very clearly in his eyes," Jäger replied, thinking back to his sessions with the bearded operator.

Medvev smiled. "You must first discover the location of the computer system."

Jäger nodded. Although he had been allowed frequent access to the capabilities of Helios, Cruz and Stone had been tight-lipped about the physical location of the hardware powering it. "I will find it," Jäger said confidently.

"Good," Medvev said. "Then let us find suitable transportation for you to go back to America. You have much work to do."

* * *

After ending the call with Jäger, Stone dialed Cruz's personal line. On the second ring, Cruz answered. "What is it?"

"Your boy somehow managed to let Mack and his team escape," Stone said angrily.

"He told you this?" Cruz asked.

"No, even worse. I had to tell *him*. He had no idea."

"How could he not know?" Cruz asked.

"Because he said he was on his way to Moscow."

"For what?"

"I sent him to stress the importance of Russian cooperation to Medvev. I didn't get a warm fuzzy that he fully understood after our meeting," Stone explained.

"Sounds like this is your fault, then," Cruz replied tersely. "So what are you going to do to fix it?"

"Mack's team is on an MI-6 flight on the way to America. I'm sending Jäger to handle them personally."

"So you're giving up on using them?"

"We're out of time," Stone replied.

"Well, while he's there, he can take care of another loose end for us," Cruz said.

"Who?"

"Michelle Decker-Martin. I just found out she had a meeting with the Attorney General," Cruz replied.

"Let me guess, your wild idea of having her husband try to assassinate the President didn't work?"

"No, it worked," Cruz snapped. "Martin did exactly what I wanted him to. Except I'm hearing he tried to turn himself in instead of actually going through with it. That doesn't really matter though. He's where I need him to be. I'll manipulate a few things and get the press rolling on it. It will have the same effect in the end. They will follow the bread crumbs."

"Then why are you worried about his wife?"

"She's a wild card. After what she did with Kerry Johnson, I just don't feel like leaving it up to chance. We can have Jäger take her out and make it look like a suicide. Make her ashamed of what her husband did. It'll just sweeten the story and keep her from getting in our way. We are less than a week away. It's time to start tying up the loose ends," Cruz explained.

Stone let out a soft sigh. "Are you sure this is a good idea? Is this really what we're doing these days? Killing national heroes?"

"You have to break a few eggs to make an omelet. The country is too far gone. We both know it. The only way to save it is to give it a good flush and start over. I don't like it any more than you do, but this is not our fault. We don't have a choice. The people decided a long time ago. Our hands are tied," Cruz replied.

"You're right," Stone said. "We did everything we could. We'll be saving more lives in the long run. I wish Jeff had seen it like that."

"Lyons was a stubborn boy," Cruz replied. "We gave him every chance as well, but you can only lead a horse to water. Now, let's push the doubts aside and get moving. We have a lot of work to do today."

"I'll call Jäger back. Ciao."

<u>CHAPTER FORTY</u>

Lyons had just finished burying Cuda when he heard a helicopter approaching from the north. Like most of the members of Odin, Cuda had no family or friends outside of the team. Although he would have preferred to give Cuda a proper burial, Lyons wanted to respect Cuda's Muslim faith and bury him as soon as possible. Lyons also didn't know if the circumstances would allow the team to be together again in the near future, and he was starting to go stir crazy in the room with Coolio as they waited for word.

As the sound of the helicopter grew louder, Lyons tossed aside the shovel and said a quick prayer for Cuda. He ran to the John Deere Gator utility vehicle and headed back to the compound. Looking back over his shoulder, he saw the helicopter clearly headed toward them. He knew he needed to get to Coolio and get them both to safety.

Arriving at the compound, Lyons parked the Gator, grabbed his rifle, and headed straight for Coolio's room. Coolio was sleeping with his laptop on his lap when Lyons walked into the room.

"Coolio, wakeup, bud, we have to move," Lyons said, gently shaking his shoulder.

"What time is it?" Coolio asked lazily.

"We've got visitors," Lyons said, slinging his rifle over his shoulder. "We need to move."

Coolio started to get up, but Lyons moved the laptop out of the way and picked him up instead. Hoisting him up like a child, Lyons turned and put him in a nearby wheelchair.

"Wait!" Coolio said. "I should bring my laptop."

Lyons grabbed the laptop and handed it to Coolio who opened it and logged in. "I've got the camera feeds on the house up. Looks like a helicopter landed on the north side."

"That's why we need to move," Lyons said as he wheeled Coolio out of the room.

"Are we going to fight them?"

Lyons broke into a light jog as he pushed Coolio down the hallway and into the kitchen. "No, we don't have the firepower."

"Where are we going?"

"You'll see. Just keep an eye on them and let me know if they get close."

"Uhh...They're getting close," Coolio said as he watched the armed men approach the house.

Lyons pushed Coolio through the kitchen and dining areas and into the east wing of the house. Entering the large master bedroom, Lyons set the parking brake on Coolio's chair and disappeared into the large walk in closet. Moments later, he returned and picked Coolio up out of the chair as the young hacker clung to his laptop.

"This is humiliating," Coolio said as Lyons carried him like a baby. "I'm not a child."

Lyons carried Coolio into the narrow doorway for the walk-in closet since it was too narrow for the wheelchair to pass. He had removed the false panel and opened the steel vault door to this safe room. Lyons carried Coolio into the room and gently placed him on the leather sofa next to the wall. He turned back to the entrance, closed the door, and locked it.

The room was stocked with MREs, cases of bottled water, and snacks. There was a small safe with four rifles and two handguns along with a few thousand rounds of ammunition. On the wall was an LED TV with video feeds of the outside security cameras, and in the corner of the room, Lyons had a toilet with a small curtain installed.

"The walls are reinforced steel and Kevlar. There's a ventilation system for air and air scrubbers. We have enough bottled water and food to last two weeks, but we also have running water and sewage as long as it stays connected," Lyons explained.

"What about electricity?" Coolio asked.

Hooked up to the main system, but there's also a backup generator on the other side of the back wall right there. It has enough fuel for about a week, but it's the most vulnerable to being shut down," Lyons replied.

"Great. So we're in a prison for who knows how long," Coolio said as he opened his laptop. "I don't have a charger for this thing."

"Got it covered," Lyons said as he walked to a nearby storage locker. He pulled out a spare battery and charger and put them on the couch next to Coolio. "Will these work?"

"You really have everything in here," Coolio said. "But I have no WiFi signal. Do you have a LAN drop?"

Lyons grabbed an Ethernet cable from the locker and plugged one end into the wall. He handed the other end to Coolio. "See if you can find Spectre and the girls," Lyons said.

Coolio nodded as Lyons turned to the display of the various security cameras. He switched to the outside cameras with the remote. Armed men carrying H&K MP-7 subcompact machine guns descended on the house. They appeared to be trained operators. Lyons guessed they were another wet work team from the CIA there to finish the job.

Lyons followed them on the cameras from room to room as they cleared the compound. Lyons had no surveillance cameras in the master bedroom. He watched them enter on the hallway camera. Minutes later, he heard them attempt to open the door.

"They can't get in, right?" Coolio asked nervously.

"Not anytime soon," Lyons replied.

"Good," Coolio said, trying to stay preoccupied with his laptop as the noise outside the door grew louder. "I think I found Spectre."

Lyons walked over to Coolio and sat down next to him to look at the laptop. "Where is he?"

"Med Star Hospital on 19th Street in Washington, D.C.," Coolio said, reading from the laptop. "Looks like they've ordered lab work and a psychiatric evaluation."

"What about Michelle and Agent Tanner?"

"Nothing yet," Coolio said. "It's not that easy with just a laptop."

"Keep digging," Lyons said. "Good job."

Lyons returned his attention to the screen. He could tell the men had declared the area secure. They had set up a perimeter and were busy retrieving the bodies of the previous team. He breathed a sigh of relief as he saw men exit the master bedroom into the hallway.

That relief was short lived as he saw them return moments later carrying a backpack into the bedroom. Just before entering, he saw one of the men pull out a six inch brick from the backpack and realized what it was.

Lyons sprinted over to Coolio and picked him up. "What's going on?" Coolio asked frantically.

"C4! They're going to try to blow the door!" Lyons yelled as he ran to the opposite corner of the room with Coolio. He placed Coolio on the floor and shouldered his rifle, pointing it at the door.

"Get down!" Lyons yelled.

"Can they blow up the door?" Coolio asked frantically.

"We're about to find out."

CHAPTER FORTY-ONE

anner could not stop smiling as she and Decker entered the White House. She was like a little kid going to Disney World for the first time as they stepped into the West Wing. She had never been even as a visitor, always saying she would one day but never getting around to it.

Decker, however, did not share Tanner's enthusiasm. It brought back gut wrenching memories of facing off against the vile former Vice President named Kerry Johnson. And this visit was no different. She found herself once again appealing to the President to help her husband and the country. Decker wanted nothing more than to get Spectre, hop on the first flight back to New Orleans, and forget any of this ever happened.

The two followed Attorney General Chase as one of the President's aides escorted them through the hallways of the West Wing. The aide checked in with the President's secretary and they were immediately invited into the Oval Office.

As they walked in, the President was meeting with FBI Director Schultz and Chief of Staff Plonski. She stopped their conversation and walked up to Decker, giving her a gentle hug. "It's good to see you again."

"I wish it were under better circumstances," Decker said.

Tanner shyly said hello to the director of the FBI. He grunted an unintelligible response, obviously irritated by Tanner's involvement. Her face felt flush as she realized her career might be ending during the most incredible experience of her life.

Seeing the tension, Decker introduced Tanner to the President. "Special Agent Tanner has done quite well in this case," Decker added. "Very impressive."

The President nodded, then shook Tanner's hand, and acknowledged the Attorney General. With all the introductions out of the way, she invited everyone to sit on the two couches separated by a coffee table near the fireplace.

"Where is my husband?" Decker asked impatiently.

"He was taken to the hospital for evaluation and possible treatment. We think he may have been drugged," Plonski said.

"I'd like to see him as soon as possible," Decker said.

"Don't worry, dear," Clifton said in a motherly tone. "We will see to it that the two of you are reunited, but first I'd like to get a handle on what's going on here."

"And I'd like to know how you got involved in this, Agent Tanner," Director Schultz added.

"My husband was abducted by unknown parties while looking into the death of Jeff Lyons," Decker replied before Tanner could answer. "Agent Tanner was assigned as his escort as a personal favor to me."

"I am aware," the director replied, still focusing on Tanner. "But your Special Agent in Charge said you were on medical leave after that. You were supposed to be in the hospital."

"I asked her to help me, sir," Decker said. "I believed Agent Tanner would be best suited to assist me in finding my husband."

"Well, I don't think—"

"I don't care what you *think*, Director," Decker snapped. "Did you know that one of your agents falsely accused my husband of killing Lyons, assaulting Agent Tanner, and fleeing? Or that the same agent put a gun to my head and threatened me if I didn't tell him where we had been? Is that what they're teaching at Quantico these days?"

"Michelle," President Clifton said, trying to intervene. "Let's try to calm down. We all just want to find out what's going on."

"I'll tell you what's going on. Someone is falsifying government files to accuse my husband of a murder that the local authorities were investigating as an accident. Someone also sent a CIA hit team to try to kill us," Decker said. She knew she was dangerously close to crossing a line, and risking outing Lyons as being alive. But she wanted to lead President Clifton and Director Schultz down the right path.

"They did what?" Chase interjected. "You didn't mention a CIA team."

"We went to the estate of Jeff Lyons to try to find clues as to Cal's whereabouts. While we were there, a CIA hit squad showed up and tried to kill us," Decker said.

"Tried to kill you?" Schultz asked.

Tanner pulled down the collar of her shirt, revealing the blood-stained bandage. "Tried to kill us, sir," she said.

"Get Director Chapman on the phone," Clifton said, ordering her chief of staff to contact the Director of Central Intelligence.

"Yes, ma'am," Plonski said as he stood and walked to the President's desk.

"How do you know they were CIA?" Clifton asked.

"You'll just have to trust me, ma'am. I can't divulge that information right now," Decker said.

"OK, but why? What's the threat here?" Clifton asked. "Why would you be targeted? Why would Cal be abducted and then show up out of nowhere saying he wants to kill me?"

"I can assure you, ma'am, Cal has no intention of killing anyone," Decker said. "What I can tell you is that there's a looming national security threat out there that I believe Cal stumbled upon inadvertently while investigating the death of Lyons."

"Was Lyons involved in this plot?" Schultz asked. "There have been rumors of a threat involving his group, but no concrete intelligence."

"I believe he was targeted because he was aware of it," Decker said.

"He was planning to run for President. He and I had talked about it," Clifton said, shaking her head. "So what's this threat?"

"It's a cyber threat, ma'am," Tanner said nervously as she spoke up for the first time.

"From where?" Clifton asked.

Decker hesitated. She knew the answer, but trying to explain what Lyons had told them seemed almost too outlandish. She didn't want to risk being dismissed as a conspiracy theorist. It also risked outing Lyons and Odin, which she wanted to avoid for the safety of everyone involved.

"What aren't you telling me?" Clifton prodded.

"We're not sure what the origin of the threat is yet, ma'am," Tanner interjected as she and Decker exchanged a look. "But the nature of the threat involves an attack on infrastructure and the ability of our government to collect and interpret intelligence. We have seen multiple instances and artifacts of hacking or tampering with official government documents."

"Ma'am, Director Chapman is on the phone for you," Plonski said as Tanner finished.

"Ask him if he has any knowledge of the hit team," Decker said. "I'm willing to bet he can't find a single person in the agency who gave the order directly, but it definitely happened."

"And Director Schultz, did you personally give the arrest order issued for Cal Martin?" Tanner asked.

"I had no idea such an order even existed," Schultz confessed.

"Well, that was the reason given when I was detained. You personally tagged him as a suspect," Decker said.

Schultz made a sour face and shook his head. President Clifton walked to her desk and took the phone from Plonski.

"If the CIA is ordering operations on American soil against U.S. citizens, I'm going to go nuclear on them," Chase said to Decker as they waited for the President to finish her call.

"I don't think they did. I think there's someone out there hacking our computer systems and falsifying information, including voice and speech," Decker said.

"That seems unlikely," Schultz said. "That would take an amazing amount of processing power to break through our various levels of encryption and security. Besides, which system?"

"All of them, sir," Tanner said.

"All of them?" Schultz asked incredulously.

"That's how big this threat is," Decker answered.

President Clifton made a face as she hung up the phone and returned to the sitting area. "You're right. He didn't order it and no one with that kind of authority did. He's having his cyber analysts look into the order itself."

"The fact that such an order is even possible needs to be explored further," Chase said.

"Chapman also said there's another team assigned to that location for a cleanup operation," President Clifton said. "I told him to personally see to it that it's cancelled, but thankfully you're here with us."

Decker's stomach turned. Lyons and Coolio were still holed up there. They wouldn't be able to fend off another team by themselves. "He needs to call that team off now," she said.

"He will," Clifton said reassuringly. "He's working on it."

"*Now*," Decker insisted.

"What aren't you telling me?" Clifton asked again. "Who's in that compound?"

"We have a material witness that is staying there for the time being," Tanner said.

Decker snapped to Tanner, hoping the young agent knew what she was about to do.

"He's a cyber analyst that discovered the threat, ma'am. We were keeping him there until we could properly present the case to my superiors," Tanner added.

Decker nodded approvingly. She had to give it to the rookie, Tanner had a good head on her shoulders. She was liking her more and more every minute.

"I see," President Clifton said.

"And when were you planning on running this through your chain of command, Agent Tanner? You were not assigned this case," Director Schultz said.

"That's my fault," Decker said. "When we came across this information, I asked her to delay notifying her superiors until we could talk to Jen and get a handle on what's really going on, especially after what happened with Nickerson."

Schultz nodded, not willing to push the point any further with the realization that one of his agents had crossed the line against a national hero like Decker. Clifton motioned to Plonski and told him to get in touch with the CIA to make sure the stand down order was urgently passed.

"Director, get with Homeland and the applicable agencies and raise the Cyber Threat Level to Level Four Orange," Clifton directed. "At least until we get a better handle on this."

"Yes, ma'am," Schultz replied.

"And I'm sure I don't have to tell you this, but make sure this Agent Nickerson is properly dealt with," Clifton said.

"Already on it, ma'am."

Clifton turned to Decker. "As odd as these circumstances are, thank you for bringing them to my attention. Now, let's get you to your husband."

CHAPTER FORTY-TWO

The explosion shook the walls of Lyons's fortified panic room, but the door held. MRE packets fell from the racks and the concussion kicked up a cloud of dust. Lyons kept his rifle trained on the door as he waited for the operatives to gain entry.

"Jesus I can't hear anything!" Coolio yelled, trying to shake off the ringing in his ears.

"The door held," Lyons said, still keeping his rifle pointed at the door.

They heard what sounded like hammering on the door. The pounding continued for several minutes. Lyons held his position in front of Coolio, waiting for the team to gain entry and kick off a fight to the end.

There was a pause in the banging on the door. It seemed to last several minutes. "Are they gone?" Coolio asked nervously.

Seconds later, there was another explosion. This time, the racks holding the MREs and water fell over and the room went dark. Lyons did his best to shield Coolio as the blast rocked the small room.

Lyons flipped on the rail light of his rifle and pointed it at the door. It was still standing strong. He heard the pounding resume. He couldn't tell if they were using a battering ram or just trying to kick it in. Although it had somehow managed to survive two rounds of C4 explosions, Lyons knew they would eventually find their way in. It was just a matter of time.

The emergency lights finally kicked on. Lyons pushed away some of the debris, moving the broken shelves to in front of the door as a barrier. After a few minutes, the emergency generator finally came online and full power was restored.

The pounding on the door stopped again. Lyons and Coolio remained still. After fifteen minutes with no further reports, Lyons handed the rifle to Coolio. "Keep this on the door," he said.

Lyons turned the LED TV back on and checked the security cameras. The bodies from the previous shootout had all been removed. He cycled through every camera. There was no movement. He switched to the exterior cameras. The helicopter was gone. Whoever had just been trying to gain entry had apparently given up and gone home.

"So they're gone? Just like that?" Coolio asked.

"It appears that way," Lyons said as he continued cycling through cameras.

Coolio put the rifle down and Lyons helped him back to the couch. He plugged his laptop back into the Ethernet port and booted it up.

"I can't get into the CIA's databases," Coolio reported.

"I know, you need more horsepower," Lyons said dismissively. "Well, we don't have that here."

"No, I mean they locked it down. Looks like all government agencies have gone Cyber Threat Level Four."

"Shit," Lyons hissed. "Decker and Tanner. Tanner must have told her bosses about Helios."

"Yeah, you still haven't told me about that," Coolio said.

"I'll tell you on the flight out of here," Lyons said. "We're not staying."

"Where are we going?"

"I have an off-the-books cabin in the mountains in West Virginia. I've been doing some renovations on it, but it's should be a good place to hang out. We need to get going."

"What about Michelle and Maddie?"

Lyons shook his head. "If they warned them about Helios, then they probably told them I'm still alive. We can't hang around here and wait to find out. We need to get moving."

Lyons moved the debris out of the way and tried the door. He attempted the electronic release. The lock clicked open, but the door did not budge. Lyons tried putting his shoulder into it with no success.

"Are we stuck?" Coolio asked.

"Hold on," Lyons said.

He walked over to the emergency door lock release button and pressed it. There was another loud click. Lyons pushed on the door once more, but it didn't move.

"Yes," Lyons said. "We're fucking stuck."

"OK, then I'll call for help," Coolio said.

"Wait," Lyons replied as he considered their options. The truth was, they were out of options. They could last for weeks in the room, but with no promise of anyone ever coming for them, waiting seemed to be a dead end. If they called for help, they would give away their identity and Cruz and Stone would know he was still alive.

"Too late," Coolio said. "I already did it."

"What did you do?" Lyons asked angrily.

"I sent out a call for help," Coolio said. "I don't plan on dying in here."

"They'll know we're alive! You want to die out there instead?"

"Relax, boss," Coolio said with a sly grin. "I sent it to people who can help us without tipping anyone off."

Lyons stared at Coolio, not sure what to think about his sudden spurt of confidence.

"Now, tell me about Helios while we wait," Coolio added, as he closed his laptop and set it aside.

CHAPTER FORTY-THREE

Rebecca Mallory pushed a stray strand of her bright red hair out of the way as an email notification popped up on her desktop. As a cyber analyst for MI-6, she had been tasked by Sierra Carter to uncover the identity of the mysterious man they called Jäger.

The search had so far turned up nothing. Jäger was a ghost. He simply didn't exist. And even the files she had discovered, that had been altered, were done so well that it came down to a single line of code.

Mallory downed the last of her Rip-It energy drink as she minimized her window and opened her e-mail. A cyber analyst she had worked with from the States named Julio Meeks had gotten her hooked on the drink during a mission they had worked together several months earlier. He was part of a secret organization of paramilitary contractors. She wasn't quite sure what their charter was, but she knew they were based in America and would often work off-the-books operations.

The subject line read TPS REPORTS and the body of the e-mail was blank. Mallory's brow furrowed as she saw the sender: RipItGood0919@freemail.com. It was the covert e-mail address she and Julio had set up to communicate with each other in case of emergency. She knew the team had been in trouble, but no one had said anything to her about Julio.

She quickly opened the attachment. Her e-mail program couldn't decipher the format and prompted her to download it after warning her that it might contain viruses. She downloaded it to her desktop and then opened a program marked MALEEKS. It was a computer program the two had written together to encrypt and unencrypt messages they sent to each other.

The program used high level encryption that only they possessed the keys for. They had settled on MALEEKS as a program name, combining their last names after neither of them could come up with anything creative to call it. They were the only two people on the planet that could open the messages, which meant he was very worried about being intercepted.

When the program was ready, Mallory opened the attachment with it. Mallory smiled as the program's status bar zig-zagged around the screen in lieu of the traditional bar. She liked Julio's geeky sense of humor. She had enjoyed working with him because of it.

The e-mail opened. Mallory made sure no one was looking over her shoulder. She was alone in the work center. Confident that no one could see it, she maximized the email so she could read it.

"L-O-L, I'm not dead," Mallory said with a confused look as she read it softly to herself in her Irish accent. "Stuck in a safe room with the boss at his house. Door won't open. Please send help. Slow internet here. Don't know how much longer I can take it."

Mallory closed the e-mail. The program indicated that it was putting the e-mail through a cyber shredder and then closed. Mallory deleted the original file and then locked her computer. She darted out of the room and into the hallway, pushing past people as she headed for Sierra Carter's office in the heart of the vault.

Without knocking, Mallory opened the door and rushed into the office. She came face to face with the Minister of Defence Nigel Williams, who was standing across from Carter's desk. Mallory froze in her tracks as her eyes widened.

"I am so sorry, Minister, I had no idea," she said. "I just had news for Ms. Carter."

"It's quite alright," Williams said graciously. "I was on my way out anyway."

"Yes, sir," Mallory said. "So sorry."

Williams excused himself and exited Carter's office as he closed the door behind him. Carter gave Mallory a look of confusion as the excited cyber analyst waited to be called on.

"Well, what is it?" Carter asked finally.

"Right, sorry, ma'am," Mallory said. "I apologize for interrupting, but I just received a transmission that I think you'll be quite interested in."

"Out with it, Rebecca," Carter pushed. "I haven't got all day."

Mallory looked around nervously before whispering, "Julio Meeks just sent me an e-mail, ma'am."

Carter stepped around her desk and leaned in close. "The cyber analyst from Odin?"

"Yes, ma'am."

"Well, what did it say?"

"He said he's not dead. I'm not sure why he was telling me that, but he asked for help. It seems he's stuck in a safe room and the door won't open," Mallory said, still whispering.

"A safe room where?"

"His boss's house, and he's *with* his boss."

"With his boss?" Carter asked. "You mean Lyons is *alive?*"

"I don't know, ma'am, but that's what the e-mail said. He's stuck in a safe room with his boss."

"Are you sure it was him?"

"Ma'am, only two people in the world have the capability to send an e-mail in the manner he did, and I'm one of them," Mallory said proudly.

"Can I see it?"

"No, ma'am. It was wiped as soon as I closed it. For security."

"No, no. That's smart. Good idea. With the recent hacking, we don't know what may have been compromised."

"There is no way this was compromised, ma'am. I swear on it," Mallory said confidently.

"Come with me," Carter directed. She led the way out of her office and into the hallway. Carter walked with a purpose as she headed to the secure videoteleconference room.

She had Mallory close the door and lock it, then dialed Kruger and his team on the jet. After a few attempts, Cowboy answered.

"Hello, sis," he said.

"Where's Kruger?" Sierra asked.

"Sleeping," Cowboy replied. "We're about four hours out."

"Wake him, please."

"Are you crazy?" Cowboy asked. "I thought you loved me."

"I do, but this is very important. Now please, go get him."

"Bloody hell," Cowboy said as he disappeared from the screen.

Moments later, Kruger appeared on the screen. "What's up, Sierra?"

"We just received a transmission from your cyber analyst, Julio Meeks," Carter replied.

"Goddamn, that's good news! Did it seem like he was under duress? What did it say?"

Carter pulled Mallory into view, making her stand next to her as she made the introduction. "This is my cyber security analyst, Rebecca Mallory."

"Hello," Mallory said sheepishly.

"Mallory, please tell Mr. Mack what the message said," Carter said.

"He wanted me to know he wasn't dead, and then said he was stuck in a safe room in his boss's house with his boss," Mallory said.

"You're shitting me!" Kruger said with a look of shock. "Say that again."

"He wanted me to know—"

"No, the last part," Kruger interrupted.

"He's stuck in a safe room with his boss," Mallory repeated bashfully.

"Holy shit!" Kruger said. "He fucking survived. OK, who else knows about this?"

"Just us," Carter replied.

"Good, keep it that way. No one can know he's still alive. At least not yet."

"Copy that," Carter said.

"What did he mean about being stuck in a safe room?" Kruger asked.

"He said the door won't open," Mallory replied.

"Roger," Kruger replied. "Do me a favor and send him a reply that our ETA is about four hours. Ask him to send a threat assessment if he can, but don't compromise security if he can't. I don't want you two sending a hundred messages and getting discovered. And make sure no one uses real names in these e-mails."

"Right sir. Straight away," Mallory replied.

"Keep me updated," Kruger said. "Outstanding job, ladies."

"Talk soon, Kruger," Carter said before signing off.

CHAPTER FORTY-FOUR

They had been in the waiting area for over an hour by the time the Secret Service agent told Decker and Tanner that it was okay to meet Spectre. Despite Decker's protests and threats for legal action, the agents had refused her request to accompany Spectre during his psychological evaluation.

A senior agent escorted them to Spectre's room. They found him sitting in a chair next to his bed, wearing a white undershirt and the slacks from his airline uniform. The hospital gown he had been given was balled up on the bed. His room was under guard by two other agents.

"Cal!" Decker yelped as she entered the room and ran to him.

Spectre stood and hugged her. "Are you OK?" she asked after kissing him.

"I'm fine," Spectre replied before nodding to Tanner. "Hello Agent Tanner. Glad to see you're doing better."

"So you *do* remember?" Tanner asked.

"That's the last thing I remember," Spectre said.

Decker turned to the Secret Service agent that had escorted them in. "Can you please give us a moment?"

"Yes, ma'am," the agent replied.

Decker watched the agent as he exited the room and closed the door behind him. "Tell me everything. What happened?"

"I honestly don't know," Spectre said, shaking his head. "Everything is a blur after I found Agent Tanner unconscious."

"Do you remember flying here?" Tanner asked.

Spectre frowned. "Sort of. It all seems like a dream. I remember bits and pieces, but none of it seems connected to reality. It's really weird."

"We're going to get you out of here," Decker said. "It's not safe."

"What about you? Did you make it here OK?" Spectre asked. "How's Calvin?"

"He was fine when I left, but I haven't been able to call Bear."

"Why not?"

"Because our phones were being monitored. There's a CIA hit team out there trying to kill us, but it wasn't ordered by Director Chapman," Decker explained.

"Is that who killed Lyons?" Spectre asked. "And Coolio."

Decker exchanged a look with Tanner and then leaned in close. "They're not dead, sweetie," she whispered.

"What? No, I remember that part. I saw the burned bodies in the morgue."

"Cuda helped Coolio escape, and Jeff had a secret escape chute to the vault in the basement," Decker said. "They're alive, Cal. I saw them both."

"I don't understand," Spectre said. "I *saw* them."

Decker and Tanner made sure no one could overhear them and then explained everything they had learned from Lyons. She explained Odin's inner workings to him and the current plot by the other billionaires, as well as the attack by the CIA team and Cuda's unfortunate demise.

"Did you tell the President this stuff when you met with her?" Spectre asked.

"No. No one can know that they're alive. It's not safe."

"And you're officially assigned to this case now?" Spectre asked Tanner.

"As of the meeting with the director and President Clifton, yes," Tanner replied.

"Wow," Spectre said. "I feel like I've been in a coma and missed so much."

"Well, the important thing is that you're back now. We think the drug they're planning on using was what they gave you, so that's why you don't remember anything," Decker said.

"Jesus. I almost killed the President," Spectre said in disbelief. "Wow."

"You have to understand, though. Nothing is safe anymore. They can manipulate any government or civilian document to say whatever they want. They even created audio of you confirming killing Lyons with a terrorist group. You cannot trust anyone," Decker said.

"What happened to you?" Spectre asked, pointing to the blood stain on Tanner's shirt.

"Took a bullet," Tanner said proudly.

"Honey, we really need to get you a new shirt," Decker said.

"So how do I get out of this place?" Spectre asked. "Hospitals really aren't my thing."

"I'll go talk to the Secret Service, but the order from the President was to release you to my protective custody, and drop all charges," Tanner said.

"Thank you," Decker said. Tanner nodded and walked out of the room, closing the door behind her.

"You always manage to stumble upon these things," Decker said with a smile. "I'm going to have to keep you at home and make you my trophy husband."

"Believe me, I'm ready," Spectre replied. "I had no idea any of this would happen, but you know what? I say we just go home and forget about it."

"What about the threat?"

"You and I both know, there will *always* be a threat," Spectre replied. "Let the professionals handle it."

"And what if they can't?"

"Then we'll move in with Bear," Spectre said with a grin. "He's been preparing for a post-apocalyptic world like that his whole life. We'll just have to get used to the 'I told you so' reminders every day, but otherwise, it would be fine."

"Cal, I'm serious," Decker said sternly. "We can't just let this go."

"You always say that," Spectre said as he pushed a stray strand of hair from her face and caressed it gently.

"We have to ensure a future for our son," Decker said. "We can't just walk away knowing we could have done something to stop it."

Spectre let out a soft sigh. "Fine. We can start with finding the son of a bitch that drugged me."

"Thank you," Decker said.

She hugged Spectre and then gave him a kiss. As the two embraced, there was a gentle knock at the door.

"Come on in," Spectre said, thinking it might be Tanner trying to give them some privacy. "Can I leave yet?"

The door opened, revealing an older man. Spectre thought he recognized him, but wasn't sure. He had the strangest feeling of déjà vu. It all seemed very surreal.

"Who are you?" Decker asked.

"Hello, Michelle," he said as if he had known her for years. "It's good to see you again, Cal."

"I'm sorry, but who are you?" Spectre asked.

"You don't remember?" the man asked.

Spectre bladed his body, taking up a defensive posture in front of Decker as he grew tired of the game. "Who are you?" he demanded.

"My name is Walter Cruz," the man replied finally. "Let's chat, shall we?"

CHAPTER FORTY-FIVE

Kruger and his team landed at the Washington Dulles International Airport just after 7PM Eastern time. The vehicles and weapons Sierra had arranged to be waiting for them at the FBO were parked at the far end of the parking lot. Kruger retrieved the keys from the front desk attendant and they were on their way.

"You feeling ok, boss?" Tuna asked as they walked toward the two black, armored SUVs.

"I'm good," Kruger grumbled.

"You're limping and you have to be feeling like shit given what they did to you."

"I'll be fine," Kruger replied.

Tuna stopped and pulled him aside as the others continued to the vehicles. "Let me take point on this," Tuna said. "I know you're out for blood, but you're not a hundred percent."

"The threat assessment from Coolio is low," Kruger said.

"Based on what he can see with security cameras. We don't know what kind of shit we're walking into out there. You need to stay behind with Jenny and run command and control."

Kruger grumbled something unintelligible as he watched his team load up in the two SUVs. He knew Tuna was right. He was operating at half speed at best. Although half speed for Kruger was faster than ninety-nine percent of the population, he knew that he had to trust his team. They were among the best in the world.

"You know I'm right," Tuna said. "Let us handle it."

"Fine," Kruger said.

"Good call," Tuna said, smiling as he slapped Kruger on the shoulder. "Now let's roll."

"Ugh," Kruger groaned.

Kruger took shotgun in the lead vehicle as Tuna drove. Jenny rode with them while Cowboy and Shepherd took the second SUV. It was a twenty-minute drive to the Lyons Estate. The two vehicles parked at the gated entrance.

They exited and gathered around the hood of Kruger's vehicle. He placed the iPad Sierra had given them on the hood. While they had been in flight, Coolio had sent a schematic of the compound and grounds.

Kruger briefed the plan. Cowboy, Shepherd, and Tuna would take the second SUV down the main road and make a direct entry into the compound. Kruger and Jenny would be on comms, scouting ahead for improvised explosive devices and hostiles using the micro-UAV with Forward-Looking Infrared that Sierra's people had provided them.

Once inside, they would begin the slow process of clearing room to room. When they were satisfied that the building was clear, they would post a guard outside the master bedroom while the other two went to the outdoor storage building and retrieved the necessary tools to break into the panic room.

After gaining entry, they would exfil Coolio and Lyons, then move to an MI-6 safe house in Alexandria, Virginia. If all went well, Kruger hoped to have the team safely tucked away by midnight so they could rest, regroup, and plan their next mission.

"Questions?" Kruger asked as he finished briefing the plan.

Kruger made eye contact with each member of the team individually as he waited for a response. When none came, he said, "Alright then, be safe out there. Do good work."

* * *

"A vehicle just tripped the outermost perimeter sensor," Coolio reported. He was lying on the couch with his laptop on his lap.

"They're here," Lyons said. "Good."

"Thank God," Coolio said. "I don't think I could hold it any longer."

"You know that's a toilet in the corner, right?"

"No way, man, I'm not going in there," Coolio said with a look of disgust.

"Millennials," Lyons said with a snicker.

"I've got them on the outdoor cameras now," Coolio said. "Looks like they're moving toward us."

"You may have to hold it a little while longer," Lyons said. "They'll want to make sure the house is secure before they go to work on the door."

"Damn," Coolio said with a defeated look.

An alert popped up on Coolio's screen, notifying him of a change in Spectre's patient status. He opened it and said, "Looks like Spectre was just discharged from the hospital."

"Can you get into the hospital surveillance cameras and see if the girls were with him?" Lyons asked.

"I can try, but this connection is pretty bad. Plus it depends on how new the hospital camera system is. If it's one of the old closed circuit systems, there's no way."

"Try."

Lyons turned back to the surveillance cameras as Coolio went to work. He watched as the team went room to room, clearing the house as they made their way to the master bedroom. He saw Cowboy and Tuna enter the master bedroom as Shepherd covered the hallway. Moments later, Cowboy and Tuna emerged from the bedroom, leaving Shepherd to stand guard outside the door.

It took ten minutes for Cowboy and Tuna to return with the equipment. The sound of drilling was deafening as they worked to get the door open.

"Got it!" Coolio yelled over the noise. "That was easier than I thought."

"What do you have?" Lyons asked as he walked over to Coolio.

"I backtracked from the time of discharge. This is footage of him being wheeled out. Looks like two women are with him," Coolio said, turning the laptop toward him.

Coolio let the video play as the trio walked out of view. "Wait! Who's that?" Lyons said, pointing at a man exiting the elevator behind them.

"Who?" Coolio asked.

"Back up a few frames."

Coolio did as he was instructed, reversing the footage until Lyons told him to stop.

"Can you zoom in on his face and clean it up?"

"Geez, I don't know," Coolio said. "This is just a laptop and your home internet connection…"

"Try."

Coolio went to work, doing the best he could with the image. Lyons watched over his shoulder as the blurry image became slightly clearer.

"Fuck!" Lyons said as he recognized the face.

"Who is that?" Coolio asked.

"It's Walter Cruz," Lyons said angrily. "That son of a bitch!"

"What does that mean?"

"Remember Helios?"

"Yeah?"

"He's one of the men trying to use it."

"But Michelle, Spectre, and Agent Tanner were clearly OK. Wouldn't he have killed them?"

"Not if he was trying to get something from them," Lyons said.

"Like what?"

"Information or cooperation. That's what Cruz specializes in," Lyons said. "It's how he's doubled his fortune."

"Do you think they told him about us?"

"I don't know."

"Well, I don't think so," Coolio said confidently. "Spectre is tough and Michelle is even tougher."

"I don't doubt it, but Cruz likes to manipulate people. I don't trust him."

There was a loud banging accompanied by muffled yelling. The noise was followed by a brief silence before the panic room's large vault door fell down. As the dust settled, Cowboy and Tuna entered.

"Good to see ya, boss," Cowboy said.

"Jesus, Coolio, are you OK?" Tuna asked as he approached Coolio.

"Had a building fall on top of me. No big deal, really," Coolio replied.

"We need to get you out of here," Tuna said. "Kruger and Jenny are waiting at the estate entrance. We're going to use an MI-6 safe house."

"Kruger is alive?" Coolio asked excitedly.

"Well, he's seen better days, but he's alive," Tuna said.

"Good to hear," Lyons said. "We weren't sure."

"I'm assuming that wheelchair out there is yours?" Cowboy asked Coolio.

"Pimpin' ride, isn't it?" Coolio said.

"How did you guys get here?" Lyons asked.

"Two SUVs on loan from MI-6," Tuna replied.

"We can't go to their safe house. Tell Kruger to get down here. We'll take my helicopter to West Virginia."

"What's wrong with MI-6?" Cowboy asked.

"Nothing," Lyons said. "And I'm sure they mean well, but I doubt they ripped out the factory GPS systems in those vehicles. And I doubt their safe house is off the grid. Which means Helios can track us."

"What is Helios?" Tuna asked.

"A badass super computer!" Coolio answered.

"I'll explain later," Lyons said. "For now, we need to get to a safe location that's off the grid. I have a cabin in the mountains. Clear lines of sight, satellite communications only. Totally off the grid."

"What about Spectre and Decker?" Coolio asked.

"Wait, they're involved in this too?" Tuna asked.

"We can regroup and then figure out how to get to them," Lyons said.

"I'll radio Kruger," Tuna said as he walked out of the room.

CHAPTER FORTY-SIX

What exactly is your plan, again?" Kruger asked angrily as he and his team gathered around Lyons in the kitchen of his mansion. Lyons had just finished explaining the inner workings of Helios, the other Odin billionaires, and how they had gotten to this point.

"I have a cabin in the woods in West Virginia. It's off the grid and we can go there to regroup and work on finding the location of the Helios servers," Lyons said.

"And what about Spectre and Decker? You said you know where they are, right?"

"We know where they *were*," Coolio interjected. "I'd have to start looking for them again to know where they went."

"Do it," Kruger ordered.

"We can do that once we get to higher ground," Lyons said. "Right now, I'll get the helicopter ready and we can get moving."

"No," Kruger snapped. "We are not leaving them hanging in the wind."

"We won't, but right now, we are going to—"

Kruger slammed his fist down on the island between them. "You're not in charge here, bub. In fact, you're part of the reason all this is happening."

"Kruger—"

"Cuda and Waldo are dead because of you and your rich friends trying to be puppet masters. That shit stops now. You can have a seat at the table, but from here on out, your participation is advisory only. Is that clear?"

Everyone in the room had tensed up. Kruger was visibly angry, a sight that frightened even the most hardened operators among them. They all seemed to be waiting for Kruger to reach across the island and rip Lyons's throat out.

"Do you understand?" Kruger asked.

"Yes," Lyons said sheepishly.

"Good," Kruger said. "When we fix your mess, we can talk about the way ahead. So let's get back to business. You said they can track our vehicles?"

"Using the OnStar systems, yes," Lyons replied.

"Cowboy, you and Wolf get out there and start ripping them out. Find the circuit breakers and pull them. Rip off the antennas," Kruger ordered.

"Copy that," Cowboy said as he nodded to Shepherd and they headed out of the kitchen.

Kruger turned back to Lyons. "What kind of comm gear do you have at your cabin?"

"Satellite communications. Same stuff we use in theater," Lyons replied.

"Encrypted?"

"Yes."

"Do you have those encryption keys for the radios here?"

"I think so," Lyons replied.

Kruger nodded. "Good. I agree with you that this place is compromised. You and Coolio need to stay out of sight, so you, Jenny, and Coolio will fly out and work from your cabin."

"OK," Lyons said submissively.

"Coolio, what do you need to find the location of this server?" Kruger asked.

"If they're masking their IP addresses with a VPN of some sort, I'll need the actual device they're using to connect to it, and even then it will take some work," Coolio replied.

Kruger looked back at Lyons. "Do you have one of these devices?"

Lyons shook his head. "No. I knew about Helios but I was never involved in the testing. It wasn't supposed to be operational yet."

"OK, so who would have one?"

"Cruz or Stone, for starters. They may have given control to others, but it would be to people in their inner circles."

"Have you ever heard of someone named Jäger?"

Lyons sighed. "Yes."

"What do you know about him?"

"Former Israeli Mossad. He's been doing odd jobs for Cruz and Stone for years. I don't remember which one hired him, but he's their go-to guy when they want to go hands on without actually getting their own hands dirty," Lyons explained.

"Would he have access?"

Lyons shrugged. "If they're using him for their dirty work, probably."

"That explains why he was a ghost to MI-6," Jenny said. "He erased himself from the system."

"Kruger, you need to be *very* careful with this guy. He's dangerous," Lyons warned.

"I've met him," Kruger said.

"Then you know what I'm talking about. He's very cold and methodical. From what I understand, his parents were involved with the Russians after World War II and his father did work with the KGB before moving to Israel. There were rumors that he spied on Israel as a sleeper cell up until the day that he died, but no one could ever confirm it. I never heard anything about Jäger being involved with foreign agencies, but the apple doesn't fall far from the tree. I never trusted him," Lyons explained. "I didn't like how he left Mossad."

"How was that?" Tuna asked, speaking up for the first time.

"He was caught by our NCIS trying to steal intelligence on one of our newer carriers," Lyons said. "Israel claimed it was an unsanctioned operation and disavowed him."

"How long ago was this?" Kruger asked.

"Almost fifteen years," Lyons replied.

"Coolio, see if you can dig something up on that. I want to know everything we can on this guy," Kruger directed.

"Will do, boss," Coolio replied.

"In the meantime, if we can't find Jäger, we'll have to grab one of your buddies," Kruger said.

"You want to grab Cruz or Stone?" Lyons asked skeptically.

Kruger nodded. "Unless you have a better plan."

"Well, Stone lives in Italy, so it's going to be tough getting to him. Cruz has a penthouse in New York and properties that he frequents all over the eastern seaboard. We just saw him at the hospital with Spectre, so he's in the area right now. But they're both going to be heavily guarded, and with Helios, they'll see you coming from a mile away. I can't stress enough how dangerous this technology is."

"We'll figure that out in the battleplan. If Cruz is the only option here, then that's who we'll grab, but first we're going to find Spectre and Michelle," Kruger said.

"Please be careful," Lyons said. "Don't underestimate these people. They've been planning this for years."

"Noted," Kruger said. "Let's grab as much gear as we can and get moving."

Lyons and Jenny broke off to go preflight the helicopter, leaving Kruger with Coolio and Tuna.

"A little harsh on the guy. Ouch," Tuna said.

"People are dead because of what they're doing, and more people will die if we don't put a stop to it," Kruger said.

"Yeah, but they tried to kill him, too. I think he's on our side," Tuna said. "Just saying."

"Copy," Kruger said. "Do you think the team is up for this?"

"The team? Absolutely. I'm still worried about you, though."

"I'll be fine," Kruger said. "Coolio, what about you?"

"I hope he stocked up on Rip-Its," Coolio said. "But other than that, I'll be fine. Just a little sore."

"I'll help you to the helicopter," Kruger said as he walked behind Coolio's wheelchair. "Tuna, tell the troops we're rolling in fifteen."

CHAPTER FORTY-SEVEN

Jäger's plane landed at Washington Reagan National under a forged diplomatic clearance. A driver in a black luxury SUV was waiting to take him to the Ritz-Carlton Residences near downtown Washington, D.C.

Traffic was relatively light as they made their way to the city. The luxury apartments were located just off K-Street. At prices of up to three million, these apartments were home to some of the wealthiest people in Washington.

For most of the residents, it was a temporary home. Wealthy congressmen, lobbyists, and businessmen cycled in and out while Congress was in session. For Walter Cruz, it was one of his many luxury residences along the East coast.

It offered a spectacular view of the Potomac River while remaining within walking distance of the heart of the city. In addition to his own private security detail, the apartments boasted state of the art twenty-four hour manned security. It was one of Cruz's favorite places for that very reason.

The SUV dropped Jäger off at the entrance to the apartments. The doorman smiled as he opened the door for Jäger, who in turn handed him a five dollar bill. Jäger went to the security desk and showed the guard his pass that indicated he was a guest of Walter Cruz.

After a brief search in the computer system, the guard nodded approvingly and Jäger made his way to the elevator. He rode the elevator up to the fifth floor. Upon exiting, Jäger found one of the men from Cruz's security detail standing at the door to the apartment. The man recognized Jäger and stepped aside as he opened the door for him.

Jäger thanked him and then entered. Two more men were sitting in the living area watching TV. "Where is he?"

"Shower," one of the men said.

"Leave us," Jäger ordered.

The men didn't hesitate in complying with Jäger's order. They quickly exited as Jäger sat down in a chair facing the bedroom door. He waited patiently as he heard the shower turn off. A few minutes later, Cruz emerged wearing silk pajamas and a bathrobe.

He walked into the living area and was startled to see Jäger sitting there. "Jesus," he said as he clutched his chest.

"Hello Mr. Cruz," Jäger said.

"You scared the shit out of me," Cruz said, trying to catch his breath.

"Sit," Jäger said, motioning to the love seat across from him. "Let us chat."

"Stone sent you here, didn't he?" Cruz asked nervously as he stood motionless.

"*Sit,*" Jäger ordered once more.

Cruz nervously complied as he looked around the room.

"Your security detail has been relieved," Jäger said, noticing his search.

"You're too late. I already told them everything. Stone isn't going to get away with this," Cruz said. His voice was trembling and his hands were shaking.

Jäger smiled without saying a word, letting the old man continue to ramble.

"I told them everything about Helios. I told them about the plan. I even told them about you and how you killed Lyons. They've been talking to the President. They're going to stop it," Cruz continued.

"Now why would you do that?" Jäger asked calmly.

"Because your boss has lost his mind, that's why. I talked to him on the flight over here. He wants to give the Russians partial control. He wants to make them a partner. That was never part of the plan!"

"Where is the Helios server located, Mr. Cruz?" Jäger asked.

Cruz gave Jäger a look of confusion. "Why do you care? Ask your boss!"

"I am asking you," Jäger said.

"You know I don't know," Cruz said. "No one knows where it is. That's the point."

"Are you sure?" Jäger asked.

"Why are you asking? Stone wouldn't want to know that. He already knows that I don't know!"

"Very well," Jäger said. "I believe you."

"This is madness! Let me talk to Stone! We can work this out," Cruz pleaded.

"Would you prefer to die peacefully in your sleep, as Mr. Stevens? Or something more violent, like Mr. Lyons?" Jäger asked.

"You killed Oscar Stevens?" Cruz asked incredulously. He had thought that the eighty-five year old former Odin partner had died of natural causes, but he knew Jäger had set the charges that destroyed the building Lyons was in.

"I do as I am told," Jäger said calmly. "In this case, I am giving you the option."

Jäger watched Cruz's eyes dart between him and the door. "I have already told you, they will not come and help you. Please, make your choice quickly. I have a very busy schedule."

"You and Stone will burn in hell for this!" Cruz yelled defiantly.

"Of course," Jäger said. "Are you finished now?"

"I want to talk to my wife one more time," Cruz said.

"I'm afraid that won't be possible," Jäger said. "What is your choice?"

A tear rolled down Cruz's cheek as he started sobbing. "Please don't do this," he said between sobs.

Jäger pulled a syringe from his coat pocket and held it in his hand for Cruz to see. "Potassium Chloride," he said, holding it up. "You may feel some mild discomfort, but you will slip away peacefully."

"You won't get away with this," Cruz said softly.

Jäger stood and approached Cruz. "Would you like to lie down?"

Cruz nodded slowly. He reluctantly stood and shuffled to the bedroom, removing his robe as he crawled into bed. As he closed his eyes, Jäger jabbed the syringe into Cruz's neck and pushed the plunger.

Jäger watched as Cruz's breathing became labored. He clutched his chest as the potassium chloride started to take effect. In less than a minute, he was dead.

After verifying that the old man was dead, Jäger searched the room and found the tablet computer Cruz used to connect to

Helios. He put the syringe back in his coat and walked out, carrying the tablet.

Jäger casually walked out of the bedroom, closing the door behind him. He continued out of the apartment where the three guards were huddled around the door waiting to be let back in.

"Mr. Cruz has retired for the evening and does not wish to be disturbed," Jäger said.

The men nodded as two of them went back to their spots watching TV and the third resumed his post in the hallway. Jager called for the elevator as he plotted his next move. He would need to find and terminate the people Cruz had talked to before daybreak in order to prevent further complications.

CHAPTER FORTY-EIGHT

I don't trust that guy," Spectre said as he sat in the back seat of the unmarked Tahoe surveilling the safe house Cruz had told them about. "This feels like an ambush."

"After everything he told us, do you think he'd lie about this?" Tanner asked from the driver's seat. She looked over at Decker sitting shotgun, who was ignoring the debate and focusing on the townhouse with her night vision binoculars.

After their meeting with Cruz, Decker and Tanner had ditched Lyons's Ferrari and gone to the FBI field office to pick up Tanner's Tahoe. Spectre had gone on foot to a nearby hotel where he checked in and waited for the ladies to return. Once reunited, they cleaned up, ate, and headed for the townhouse in

Arlington that Cruz had told them MI-6 had allowed Kruger and his team to use as a safe house.

Spectre still had trouble believing any of it. The news that both Lyons and Kruger were still alive had come as a shock to him. Although he didn't remember much after, he was sure he had seen their bodies in the morgue. The fact that Tanner and Decker both claimed to have met with Lyons helped lend credibility to the narrative that they had faked their deaths, but Spectre was still skeptical. It all still seemed like a very lucid dream.

"We've been here for an hour and there hasn't been any movement," Spectre said. "Michelle, do you see anything?"

"Nothing yet," Decker said. They were parked on a one-way street in front of a townhouse for sale across from the safe house. Aside from a few other parked cars, the street was empty and all was quiet.

"I think we should start looking at other ways to find them," Spectre said, growing increasingly impatient. "Where did you say Lyons was?"

Before Decker could answer, four bright lights were suddenly shining into the dark-tinted windows of their vehicle. The windows were broken and the doors ripped open as Tanner, Decker, and Spectre were violently pulled from the vehicle and shoved face down onto the pavement. Although all three of them were armed, they had no chance to fight back due to the speed and surprise of the vehicle takedown.

"Michelle?" one of the men asked as he removed a knee from her back.

"Bloody hell, this is Spectre," a British voice said.

"Two girls and a guy? Are these the ones you were looking for?" a third voice asked.

"Shit. I'm so sorry, Michelle," Kruger said as he helped her to her feet. "We watched you guys surveilling us, but we couldn't see inside to make an ID."

"Dude, you're really alive!" Spectre said, staring at Kruger as Cowboy helped him up. "Holy shit."

"We need to get out of the street," Shepherd warned as he helped Tanner up.

"You assholes are going to have to explain the windows to my boss," Tanner said as she ripped away from Shepherd and brushed herself off.

"How did you find us?" Tuna asked.

"Let's talk inside," Decker replied.

Cowboy and Shepherd raised their rifles and covered as the team briskly moved across the street and into the townhouse. Although it looked like an average suburban residence on the outside, on the inside it looked more like a tactical operations center.

Hardened Pelican cases lined the walls of what should have been the entry and living area. There were computers set up in the dining area, and safes that Spectre could only assume contained classified information.

A table had been set up near the kitchen. Kruger escorted them to it with Tuna, as Shepherd and Cowboy went back to overwatch positions on the third floor.

"First off, where is Cruz?" Kruger asked, getting straight to the point as he sat at the head of the metal folding table.

"How did you know we talked to him?" Tanner asked with a look of shock.

"Coolio found Spectre's discharge video and Lyons pointed out that he was in the elevator behind you," Kruger said. "It's very important that we find him to stop what he has planned."

"Well, that's why he came to us," Decker said. "He wants immunity and help stopping Helios."

"Do you know what that is?" Spectre asked.

"Lyons told us," Kruger said. "Start from the beginning. What did he tell you, exactly?"

"Well, first of all, he's the asshole that kidnapped me and drugged me with some kind of date rape drug that used the power of suggestion and association to get me to do whatever he wanted," Spectre said. "He's lucky I didn't punch him in the throat."

"You're familiar with the real history of Odin, correct?" Decker asked as she grabbed Spectre's hand. "Did Lyons explain that to you?"

"He mentioned it," Kruger said gruffly.

"Well, Lyons gave us the rundown and it matched what Cruz told us. Long story short, what started out as a covert organization helping in tactical situations turned into an attempt to shape the future of America through various means – media, money, wars. The problem was that they started seeing their power wane with the invention of the internet and social media. Globalization presented a new problem altogether," Decker explained.

"Yeah, I heard this all before. It's bullshit," Kruger said.

"They started developing a supercomputer that could tap into any information source on the planet with the power to manipulate the data at their whim," Decker continued.

"Lyons explained all of this."

"Well, did he mention the Russians?"

"The Russians?" Tuna asked.

"I don't think so," Kruger said. "What about them?"

"Odin reached out to the Russians and Chinese. With their plan to destabilize America and essentially hit the reset button to drain the swamp and start over, they needed assurances that the Russians and Chinese wouldn't use it as an opportunity to start a war. They wanted balance, not to replace one superpower for another," Decker said. "So they brought the Russians on board."

"On board how?" Kruger asked.

"They wouldn't tell them where the physical location of the server is, but they promised access once they put their plan in motion. And threatened to topple their governments the same way if they refused to cooperate," Decker explained.

"We need to find that server," Kruger said. "Did he say where they have it?"

Decker shook her head. "None of the billionaires of Odin know where it's physically located. They were all given handheld devices and computer access to use it, but they intentionally compartmentalized it so one billionaire couldn't take over and cut the others out of the loop if things went south," Decker said.

"How the hell is that even possible?" Tuna asked.

"They used one of their tech companies in Silicon Valley to build it. And then, as one of its first acts, it created a government work document to randomly install itself into an empty government building," Decker said. "They set up the parameters and the installation as a server farm, but they masked the actual location so they wouldn't know. It could be anywhere."

"We need to get Cruz's device to Coolio," Kruger said. "Where is he?"

"He went to his apartment in downtown D.C. for the evening. We're going to meet with him tomorrow and take this to President Clifton," Decker said.

"How did he find you though? And what was the point of drugging Spectre?" Tuna asked.

Spectre sighed. "Because I killed Kerry Johnson. He thought that if he got me to kill, or at least attempt to kill the President, they could use it as an opportunity to bring to light Johnson's involvement with the Chinese and paint me as a martyr. He thought it would create a public spectacle that would make a big enough scandal to shake the foundations of government for when this thing goes live. People wouldn't trust anything that came from Washington while Congressional hearing after hearing took place. It was basically a diversion."

"But Spectre was strong-willed enough to turn himself in instead of trying, and Cruz found out that we met with the

Attorney General. He decided to come to us to help him get immunity," Decker said.

"Immunity from what? Why the change of heart?" Kruger asked.

"He and Stone met with the Russians in Lajes to discuss the transition of global power yesterday," Tanner said, speaking up for the first time. "After the meeting, he and Stone had a pretty heated discussion. He thinks Stone is going to give the Russians access to Helios, and that they'll weaponize it. He thinks once their hackers get access, they'll figure out where it is and take over."

"Jesus Christ," Tuna said. "This is a cluster."

"Cruz told you where we were?" Kruger asked, immediately thinking tactically.

"He knew you escaped and were working with MI-6. I guess Helios has access to their files too, because he gave us the address to this place," Decker said.

Kruger leaned forward. "Did he say anything about Jäger?"

Decker and Spectre looked at each other and then Decker shrugged. "That's not a name I've heard."

"What about the escape? What did he say specifically about that?" Kruger asked.

"He said they were going to try to get you to join them, but you escaped and found MI-6. He said we needed to link up with you because of how dangerous Stone and his people are," Decker replied.

"Did he mention letting us escape?" Kruger asked.

"He seemed to believe you did it on your own," Tanner answered.

"Yeah, he seemed quite impressed with it, actually," Decker added.

"So, he didn't know," Kruger said. "That explains why Jäger was headed to Moscow."

"Jäger was heading to Moscow?" Decker asked.

"He altered the satellite imagery, but MI-6 managed to find his helicopter flight from the secret facility in Poland to Minsk. It was scheduled to continue on to Moscow," Kruger said.

"Wait a second. Who is Jäger?" Spectre asked.

"Ex-Mossad operative working for Stone and Cruz," Kruger said. "Very dangerous man."

"Great," Spectre said. "Just what we needed."

"Did he mention where Stone might be?" Tuna asked.

Decker shrugged. "He said he has a villa in Rome, but didn't give us the address or anything. We can ask him tomorrow when we meet with POTUS."

"OK," Kruger said. "Do the meeting tomorrow. Make sure he gives you Stone's location and the device. If we can get those things to Coolio, we can grab Stone and find a physical location for this server."

"Are we going to be safe here?" Spectre asked.

Decker looked at Spectre. "Cruz said he deleted the MI-6 safe house, remember?"

"I still don't trust him," Spectre said as he looked back at Kruger. "What do you think?"

"We have guns, body armor, and extra gear here," Kruger said. "We'll manage until the morning, then we'll reposition to where Coolio and Lyons are staying. By the way, you didn't tell him Lyons is alive did you?"

"Of course not," Decker replied.

Kruger smiled through his thick red beard.

"Good girl."

CHAPTER FORTY-NINE

J äger stood at the end of the block watching the four-man team escort two women and a man across the street into the townhouse. He had only been standing there ten minutes when he heard the sound of breaking glass followed by yelling. He saw the takedown unfold, and recognized Kruger escorting them across the street. In a stroke of luck, he had been led right to his prisoners from Poland.

After leaving Cruz's apartment, Jäger had used Helios to create a search for Michelle Decker-Martin, Cal Martin, and Special Agent Madison Tanner. Within minutes, the system located Tanner in the parking lot of the Washington FBI field office. Using their parking lot security cameras, Jäger found the vehicle they were using and then Helios tracked the vehicle using its onboard GPS.

He arrived in the area not sure where they had gone. He saw the vehicle sitting on the street, but the windows were too dark to see inside and Jäger hadn't wanted to get closer for fear of alerting them to his presence. He wanted to see where they were going.

Jäger wasn't surprised to see Kruger and his team. It made sense that the trio would seek them out. But he was surprised that they were being so careless about meeting. He had expected more from the infamous operator named Kruger. The breaking glass and yelling meant Kruger and company obviously hadn't been expecting visitors. Jäger found himself wondering if Kruger suspected Jäger had survived and was afraid of being stalked.

The thought of Kruger cowering in fear made Jäger smile. After all he'd heard about the red-headed operator, Jäger still wasn't impressed. Granted, he had performed well during the escape, but Jäger's gamble had paid off. Kruger failed to go for the killshot, further demonstrating his weakness.

And now, here they were, out in the open and oblivious to the fact that they were being watched. They didn't even use a side or back door to get into the townhome. They walked right in through the front door as if coming home from work after a long day. Jäger just couldn't understand why Cruz and Stone had been so adamant about bringing them on board to their plan. He had at least a dozen men that were significantly more qualified.

Jäger felt his phone vibrating in his pocket. He noted the address and then turned away from the townhome, turning left onto the intersecting street as he answered the phone.

"Is it done?" the male voice asked.

"Yes. Cruz has been taken care of," Jäger replied as he walked back to the waiting SUV.

"Were there any complications?"

"Cruz sought the help of three individuals. They will be taken care of."

"And the others?"

"I just found them."

"You're sure your plan will work?"

"Although I don't believe he's as formidable as everyone else thinks, I still believe his team will lead us to the server."

"How can you be so sure?"

"Their hacker communicated with MI-6 using a very complicated code. Our system almost missed it."

"How will you take care of both? Do you need more men?"

"No," Jäger said. "I will have my men watch the house and deal with them all as necessary."

"What if they stay together?"

"Then they are more likely to lead us to the server."

"Very well," the man said. "I trust your judgment."

"As you should," Jäger replied. "I will be in touch."

Jäger hung up the phone without waiting for a reply. He entered the SUV and closed the door as he unbuttoned his coat.

"Where would you like me to take you, sir?" his driver asked.

"The hotel," Jäger replied.

The driver nodded and then pulled onto the street. Jäger pulled his phone from his pocket and dialed one of his men.

"Sir?" the man answered.

"Thomas, I am going to send you an address. I would like you and your men to perform surveillance of this building, but it is imperative that you remain hidden."

"Yes, sir. I will assemble a team immediately," Thomas replied.

"Send your best men," Jäger ordered. "If anyone leaves the location, I want them to be followed."

"Yes, sir. Not a problem."

"It is imperative that you impress upon your men that they must not be discovered. Do you understand, Thomas?"

"Yes, sir. Complete stealth."

"Very good. I will send you the information," Jäger said before ending the call.

Jäger leaned back in the leather seat and exhaled. Before he could relax, his phone rang yet again. He looked at the caller ID and groaned softly.

"Yes, Mr. Stone?" he asked as he answered.

"Cruz is dead! Where are you?" Stone asked frantically.

"I am on my way to the hotel, sir," Jäger replied.

"Did you know about this?" Stone asked.

"No, sir. This is the first I'm hearing of it," Jäger lied.

"The news is saying it was a heart attack, but I don't believe that shit. I bet it was the Russians. They were fucking pissed when I told them Cruz didn't want to let them in on Helios yet. Those fucking commie bastards!" Stone yelled.

Jäger held the phone away from his ear as Stone's panicked tone nearly ruptured his ear drum.

"Are you still there?" Stone demanded.

"Yes, sir," Jäger replied.

"I want you to find out who did it," Stone said. "If the Russians were behind this, there will be hell to pay. I don't care if we have to delay the whole operation. They don't fuck with us. Got it?"

"Yes, sir, I understand. I will look into it."

"No, you will find out exactly what the fuck happened," Stone barked.

"Yes, sir, but what if he really did die of a heart attack?" Jäger asked.

"Bullshit! He was healthier than I am!"

"I understand, sir. I am just looking at all possible contingencies," Jäger replied.

"Well, if that's the case, then our plan may have to be altered slightly," Stone said.

"How so?"

"Those fucking Russians are getting too grabby. When they realize it's just me, they may get ballsy. We'll bring the Chinese back in to keep them at bay," Stone said.

"Very well, sir."

"Call me when you figure it out," Stone said as the line went dead.

Jäger smiled as he stuffed his phone into his coat pocket. Despite a few minor complications, the plan was starting to come together nicely.

CHAPTER FIFTY

Under a moonlit sky, the operators of two rigid-hull inflatable boats killed the outboard engines and coasted to the edge of the rocky cliff. Each boat contained four men dressed in all black, wearing body armor and night vision goggles. They tethered the boats to the narrow shore and started up the jagged rocks.

Upon reaching the top of the cliff, the man leading the first team unsheathed his knife. Sneaking up behind an oblivious guard, he grabbed the man's mouth with his left hand and sliced the guard's throat with the knife in his right. He slowly lowered the guard to the ground and then signaled to the rest of his team to continue as the man bled out.

The two teams split up, systematically and silently taking out the meager security presence as they moved through the courtyard. As they reached the mansion, the lead man dispatched a member of the security detail with two rounds from his suppressed AKS-74U while the second team cut power to the estate.

After entering and clearing the downstairs area, they moved upstairs. At the top of the stairs, a lone guard had drawn his handgun and had it crossed over his flashlight as he investigated the disturbance. Through the monochrome green image of his night vision goggles, the leader of the tactical team watched as the guard turned toward the master bedroom. A single suppressed shot to the back of the head dropped him and the team moved quietly toward the bedroom.

Reaching the double doors to the large master bedroom, the lead operator slowly tried the doorknob and found that it was unlocked. He motioned to his teammates to stack up behind him as he readied his rifle. After a silent countdown using hand signals, he opened the door and shot in, quickly clearing left.

The team's entry woke the occupant of the king size bed at the far end of the room. He groggily sat up in the bed as he tried to make sense of what was going on. His eyes widened as he saw the four armed men moving quickly toward him. He tried to reach for his handgun on the nightstand, but the lead operator was instantly on top of him, pinning the man's arms as the second operator jabbed a needle into his neck.

The sedative quickly took effect. When the man in the bed stopped struggling, the leader pulled out two sets of Flexcuffs and secured the man's hands and feet together. The leader stepped out of the way and the third operator hoisted the small man over his shoulder to fireman-carry him out of the room.

The leader radioed to the second team that the package was secure and the two teams rendezvoused outside of the mansion. They took an alternate route to egress the objective, following a winding dirt path down the side of the cliff as they carried their high value target toward the water.

Reaching the shore, they doubled back in single file down the narrow path toward their waiting boats. The man carrying the target dumped him into one of the boats as the others disconnected the tethers. Seconds later, their high horsepower outboard motors were started and the two boats sped out into the bay.

Once clear of the shore, the boat operators went full throttle as they jetted out into the Tyrrhenian Sea. They followed their GPS, riding for twenty minutes before decelerating to a stop in the middle of the dark ocean.

Ten minutes after they came to a stop, they saw the infrared lights of a submarine surfacing through their night vision goggles. Once it settled on the surface, they throttled up once more and quickly approached the waiting vessel.

The two boats approached the submarine from the rear. The first stopped at the stern of the submarine where four men from the sub were waiting to help secure the boat and offload the men and equipment.

The operator carrying the prisoner carefully walked up the slippery deck and helped lower him through the hatch into the submarine. The other men deflated and sank the boats and joined him. Once all the men were safely aboard, the submarine killed its infrared running lights and began its dive below the surface.

The Akula-class submarine K-335 *Gepard* set its course for Bizerte, Tunisia, where Nicholas Stone would be transferred to the Russian GRU, and flown to Moscow.

CHAPTER FIFTY-ONE

After sleeping just over four hours, Kruger got up and ordered Cowboy and Shepherd to bed. They had planned to break the watch up into six hour shifts, but Kruger had too many things on his mind. There was no point in making the others stay up when he was wide-awake.

Kruger brewed a pot of coffee and found a mug in one of the kitchen cabinets. He cleaned it out and then poured a cup before heading to the third floor of the three-story townhouse. The first floor contained weapons, electronics and communications equipment, while the second and third floor contained bunks that MI-6 agents operating in D.C. used.

The third floor was a single room with windows overlooking all four sides of the townhouse. The rear of the townhouse was nothing more than an alleyway that led to a garage. On each side were two-story townhouses, giving them a superior tactical vantage point. The front overlooked the street and other townhouses.

Kruger took a sip from his mug as he sat down next to a suppressed M40A5 sniper rifle Shepherd had been using. He took a look at his watch as he gently placed the mug on the ledge next to the window. It was five a.m. and all was quiet.

He picked up the pair of thermal binoculars next to his coffee mug and surveyed the street. Tanner's Tahoe, with its broken windows, was still parked across the street. As Kruger scanned the street, a lone jogger passed the Tahoe.

Switching the binoculars to night vision mode, Kruger saw a woman in her twenties wearing yoga pants and a sports bra jogging down the street. He watched her as she reached the end of the block and then noticed an occupied car parked near the stop sign.

He flipped the binocular imaging mode switch back to thermal and saw two occupants. The hood of the car still showed a white hotspot indicating that the engine was either still running or hadn't yet cooled down. The two occupants seemed to be watching the townhouse, or something in the general proximity.

"You're up early," Tuna said from behind Kruger, who was considering who might be watching them.

"You should be sleeping," Kruger said, still watching the men through his binoculars.

"Smelled coffee and couldn't sleep. What are you looking for with those?"

"Look at this," Kruger said, handing the binoculars to Tuna and then pointing to the car at the end of the street.

"Who are they?" Tuna asked.

"Good question," Kruger said. "With the system we're up against, it could be anyone, including our own government."

"Do you want me to grab the boys and have a chat with them?" Tuna asked, still watching the men through the binoculars.

Kruger thought about Tuna's proposition for a moment. If they were working for Cruz or Stone or Jäger, it would be nice to know what they were planning. It would be a step in the right direction.

But on the other hand, if they were CIA, FBI, or some law enforcement agency acting on forged documents created by the supercomputer, Kruger didn't want to go off on friendlies. Helios had blurred the line between friend and foe, and Kruger didn't want any good guys getting hurt or killed just for doing their job.

"No," Kruger said finally. "Could be friendlies. I don't want to risk it."

"Friendlies?" Tuna asked as he placed the optic back on the window ledge.

"We don't know who we're up against with this computer system forging orders."

"So let's go talk to them and find out," Tuna replied.

"Not yet," Kruger said. "Spectre and his wife are taking the FBI agent to meet with POTUS and Cruz in a little under two hours. Let's see what they do."

Tuna shrugged. "You're the boss."

"No," Kruger said as he stood and turned to face Tuna. "There is no organization as far as I'm concerned. We're in this as brothers, nothing more."

"Lyons is still alive," Tuna argued. "We'll get through this and so will Odin."

Kruger shook his head as he exhaled softly. "I was done before this happened, bub."

"What does that mean?" Tuna asked. "Are you talking about Iraq?"

"No, not Iraq. I'm talking about my involvement."

"You quit?" Tuna asked.

"I cleaned out my desk and handed Lyons my resignation the day the office went down," Kruger said, avoiding eye contact.

Tuna's eyes widened. "What the fuck, Kruger? And you didn't talk to me about it first?"

"There wasn't anything to talk about," Kruger said as he looked Tuna in the eye again. "You had it covered. My time with the team was done. It was time to move on and let you take it from there."

"What were you going to do? Where would you go?"

"Nursing school."

Tuna laughed derisively. "Nursing school? *You?*"

"You got a problem with that, bub?"

Tuna held up his hands defensively. "No, sir. I just never pegged you for the type to wear a white skirt and fishnets."

"Halloween party nurses aren't real nurses, dumbass."

"Whatever floats your boat, Krug. *Not that there's anything wrong with that,*" Tuna said with a hearty laugh.

"Whatever, bub. Bottom line is, when this thing works itself out, I'm out," Kruger said. "So, no, I'm not the boss anymore."

"But for the time being?"

"We stop the threat," Kruger said flatly.

"Fair enough," Tuna said.

They took turns watching the car while also keeping watch for secondary surveillance teams. The two men in the car had stayed put, watching the house the entire time. At six a.m., the rest of the team started to wake up. Decker and Spectre joined Kruger as Tuna went downstairs to check their gear.

"We've got company," Kruger said as he pointed to the car down the street.

"You didn't pull them out of the car at gunpoint?" Decker asked with a wry smile.

"No, honey, they didn't pay for the full experience," Spectre said.

"Funny," Kruger said. "But no, we're not going to jack them up just yet."

"Why not?" Spectre asked.

"I want to see if they're just here for the voyeur experience or if they want to get in on the action."

"So you're using us as bait?" Decker asked.

"Precisely."

"What else is new?" Spectre said as he rolled his eyes. "Standard."

"You wouldn't want me to get rough with your G-men buddies, would you?" Kruger asked, looking at Decker.

"They're not my buddies," Decker replied. "I'm not with the bureau anymore, remember? Have at it."

"What about the bureau?" Tanner asked, as she held a mug of coffee with both hands while entering the room.

"We've got company," Spectre said.

"I can find out if the FBI has a surveillance order on this place," Tanner offered.

"No," Kruger said. "You folks go get ready for your meeting. I'll take care of it."

"I'll make breakfast," Spectre said as he turned with Decker to walk out.

As they reached the door, they came face to face with a frantic Tuna who stopped them in their tracks. "We've got a problem."

"What's going on?" Spectre asked as he stepped out of Tuna's way.

"The news is on downstairs. Cruz is dead," Tuna said.

"No way!" Tanner yelped.

"This is on the news?" Kruger asked.

Tuna nodded. "They're running a memorial story on him right now. His bodyguards found him dead in his bed about an hour ago. Autopsy will be done, but they're saying it appears he had a heart attack in his sleep and died."

"Bullshit," Kruger said.

"Well, your buddy Lyons is still alive," Spectre offered. "Do you think this guy might be faking his death too?"

"Lyons isn't my buddy," Kruger replied. "I have no idea."

"I don't think so," Decker interjected. "Unless he was completely bullshitting us, he was very serious about meeting with President Clifton and stopping Helios. He didn't appear to be lying."

"And why would he have gone to all this trouble to find us and tell us just to fake his own death and skip the meeting?" Tanner added. "Not that any of their plan makes sense to me so far, but that *especially* makes no sense."

"So if he really is dead, now what?" Tuna asked.

"Well, we can't get the Helios device from him now, so we'll have to find Stone to make that happen," Kruger said. "And that might explain the people watching us across the street."

"*Now* can we grab them?" Tuna asked.

Kruger shook his head. "Stick to the plan. We still don't know who they are or what their intentions are."

"Should we brief President Clifton, then?" Decker asked.

"There's nothing to brief her on now," Spectre said. "If Cruz is dead, we have no proof."

"Unless we bring Lyons back from the dead," Decker said, looking to Kruger.

"Not yet," Kruger replied. "It's better that no one knows that he's alive."

"I thought you weren't working for him anymore?" Tuna asked.

"I'm not, but Coolio is with him. And if these assholes find out that Lyons is still alive, they'll go gunning for him. We need to keep our footprint as small as possible for the time being. I don't want to split up forces trying to protect them with the limited manpower we have."

"So, you want me to cancel?" Decker asked.

Kruger nodded. "Yes, but not yet. I want to see how the surveillance team outside handles you leaving."

"Great," Spectre said. "*Still bait.*"

CHAPTER FIFTY-TWO

D o we follow?" Sergei Romanov asked as he watched the man and two women walk across the street to their Chevy Tahoe.

"The boss said to keep an eye on them and report back," Alexander Agron replied from the passenger seat. He scratched the Spetznaz tattoo on his neck as he fished his phone out of his pocket with his right hand. "We call, yes?"

"Da," Sergei replied as he watched the three people get into the Tahoe.

"Boss, they are leaving the house. Do we follow?" Alexander asked when the phone connected. He received a short series of instructions and then said, "Da," as he hung up.

"We follow," Alexander told Sergei. "And kill them."

"Da," Sergei said.

The Tahoe pulled onto the street and made a left at the first stop sign. Sergei put the Ford Fusion in gear and followed. As he reached the stop sign, he kept his distance, allowing the Tahoe to turn right before he made his turn to follow.

He turned left as the Tahoe went out of view. There was no reason to follow closely. If they lost sight, Alexander's phone was capable of tracking the Tahoe's GPS. Alexander stopped at the stop sign and then leisurely turned right onto the one-way street, seeing the Tahoe in the distance as he slowly accelerated.

Sergei watched an SUV skid to a stop at a stop sign on a perpendicular street ahead of them. He took his foot off the accelerator as it started moving forward. It turned left onto the one-way street they were on, barreling toward them as Sergei slammed on the brake.

Sergei let out a string of expletives in Russian as he pushed the brake pedal to the floor and braced for impact. With cars lining both sides of the street, there was nowhere for him to go to avoid hitting the massive SUV. They stopped just feet of hitting head on, and four men wearing body armor and carrying rifles emerged from the vehicle.

Alexander reacted immediately, drawing his CZ P10C handgun and exiting. The four armed men approaching were much faster, firing three shots that struck Alexander in the throat and face. He fell forward, dropping his handgun as his body crumpled to the ground into a pool of blood.

Sergei struggled to get out of the car and draw his weapon. He didn't have the training Alexander had and by the time he was out, one of the attackers was already within striking distance. The bearded man disarmed Sergei. Before Sergei could fight back, the attacker struck him in the temple with the butt of his rifle causing Sergei's knees to buckle as he lost consciousness.

Kruger and his team bound Sergei's hands and dragged him to the rear of the SUV. Tuna and Cowboy helped lift him into the back and Kruger closed the rear hatch.

"What about the car and this body?" Shepherd asked as he stood over the lifeless passenger's body.

"Arlington PD can deal with it," Kruger said. "Let's go."

Shepherd nodded as he hopped into the driver's seat. With everyone on board, he threw the Tahoe into reverse and backed into a nearby driveway, turning around to join the one-way street. They headed back to the townhouse where Tanner's Tahoe was now parked in the back alley with their other SUV.

They unloaded their peeping tom and dragged him into the townhouse. Decker and Tanner were waiting downstairs when they came in, while Spectre was upstairs changing out of the suit he had borrowed from the MI-6 "go" closet for their visit to the White House.

"Did you cancel?" Kruger asked as he started to take off his body armor. Their custom carbon nanotube jackets were in the basement armory of the Odin building in Falls Church, so they were relegated to traditional ceramic plates and plate carriers provided by MI-6.

"I rescheduled," Decker said. "I asked the Attorney General to pass to the President that we needed more time to gather information in light of Cruz's death."

"Good job," Kruger said as he turned back to help Tuna and Cowboy with their prisoner.

He was starting to come to as they dragged him into the kitchen. He mumbled something in Russian as they sat him down in a metal chair and bound his hands to his feet behind him, arching his back into a stress position.

Kruger motioned for everyone to leave the area as he pulled a chair from the table and placed it in the open space across from his prisoner. "Let's talk, bub."

"Fuck you."

"Is that really the road you want to go down?" Kruger asked ominously. "Do I look like I am new to this?"

"Fuck. You."

Kruger dodged an attempt to spit on him and shot toward the Russian, punching him in the throat. Although he wasn't as fast as he used to be, he was still more than a step ahead of the defiant moron in front of him.

The Russian gasped for air. Kruger had punched him just hard enough to restrict his breathing, but not hard enough to crush his windpipe. As the Russian wheezed, Kruger pulled out his Benchmade Infidel knife and flicked it open, holding the double-edged blade up for the Russian to see.

"I can fix it if it gets too bad. I watched a video on tracheostomies last night," Kruger said, still holding up the blade.

"Fuck you. I am Bratva. We will kill you and your family!"

"Now we're getting somewhere," Kruger said as he sat back down and crossed his leg. "Tell me more."

"Fuck you!"

Kruger frowned as he played with the knife's spring-assist button, flicking it open and closed in front of the Russian.

"You don't scare me."

"Really?" Kruger asked gruffly. "Are you sure?"

"The Bratva do not know pain. Is trial by fire. You cannot do anything worse to me. You Americans are too weak. No balls," he replied defiantly.

"I see," Kruger said, still playing with the knife. "What's your name?"

The Russian stared at the blade as it extended and retracted. Kruger could tell his feeble mind was trying to decide if withholding his name was worth whatever torture Kruger had planned with the knife.

"C'mon, it's just a name," Kruger said. "I'll go first. My name is Fred Mack. Have you heard of me?"

"No," the Russian replied softly.

"Of course not," Kruger replied. "So obviously I'm not that important. It's just a name."

Kruger could see the hamster wheel spinning at full speed. The Russian's eyes betrayed him. Despite his big talk, he was terrified and out his element. He obviously had no real training in interrogation resistance.

"I promise I won't hurt you if you tell me your name," Kruger added.

"You cannot hurt me," the Russian replied defiantly. "This is America. I have rights."

Kruger laughed. "You know, everyone says that. Do you know what the funny thing about that is?"

"What?"

Kruger suddenly turned serious. "I don't care about your rights," he replied menacingly.

The Russian stared at Kruger, straining against the stress position he was in.

"Look, I'm a nice guy. Tell me your name and I'll get you out of the stress position," Kruger said.

"My name is Sergei Romanov."

Kruger stood and walked toward the Russian. Sergei eyed the blade in Kruger's hand until Kruger was out of view behind him. Kruger cut the ziptie that had been binding the Flexcuffs on Sergei's hands to his feet, causing Sergei's body to unwind like a spring as the pressure was released.

Sergei let out a sigh of relief as he righted himself and Kruger returned to his seat. "See? I'm a man of my word," Kruger said.

"Let me go and I promise not to kill your family," Sergei said as he regained his confidence. "I too am a man of my word."

"You've already met my family, bub," Kruger replied. "Molon Labe."

"Molon Labe? What is this?"

"It means come and take them, you dumbshit," Tuna answered as he walked in.

"What is it?" Kruger asked, slightly annoyed that Tuna was interrupting the interrogation.

"Cowboy's sister is on the phone for you," Tuna said, avoiding the use of names in front of the prisoner. "Says she has some intel you will want to hear."

"Tell her I'll call her back. But in the meantime, have her run the name Sergei Romanov for me," Kruger said as he looked at Sergei.

"Will do," Tuna said as he disappeared out of the kitchen.

"Now, where were we?" Kruger asked rhetorically. "Oh, right. You're going to kill my family. By the way, how did that work out for your buddy?"

"Fuck you."

"Spetznaz, right? That's what the tattoo was, wasn't it?"

"I grow tired of your games," Sergei said.

"Fine, then we'll do it your way," Kruger said as he stood and walked back to Sergei.

Kruger extended the blade of his knife. "Since you're tired of my games, here's how this is going to work. I'm going to ask you very direct questions. Questions that I know you will have the answer to."

Squatting down beside Sergei, Kruger tapped the Russian's knee with his blade. "If you lie to me or fail to answer the question, I'll start with this knee first. Do you know what it feels like to have the tendons in your knee sliced? I'll give you a hint – not good."

Sergei said nothing as his eyes nervously darted between Kruger and the blade.

"You see, Sergei, I've been doing this for a long time – mostly with terrorists, but I've dealt with a few Russians as well. Have you ever tried to talk to a Chechen? Now those are some tough motherfuckers," Kruger said. "Anyway, you're a lightweight, and I'm going to show you how unprepared your brotherhood made you if you don't start talking. That's what Bratva means, right? Brotherhood?"

"Da," Sergei replied.

"See, that wasn't so hard was it?"

Kruger moved the blade from Sergei's knee and stood. "My beef isn't with you. As far as I'm concerned, you're a victim of circumstance."

"You killed Bratva."

"That's a good place to start," Kruger said. "What *was* your colleague's name?"

Sergei started to speak, but stopped as Kruger raised an eyebrow and waved the knife in the air.

"Alexander."

"Alexander…?"

"Alexander Agnon," Sergei replied.

"Bratva?"

"Da."

"Very good," Kruger said as he retracted the blade. "You're not as dumb as you look."

"I want water," Sergei said hoarsely.

"You'll get water," Kruger said. "Why were you following that Tahoe?"

"We were not—"

Kruger extended the blade as Sergei caught himself. "Were not?"

"We were told to watch the house and follow the two women and the man."

"And then what?"

"We were to kill them."

"Why?"

"Do you question orders?" Sergei asked.

"I don't kill people that don't deserve to die," Kruger replied.

"I do what I am told."

"Who told you to kill them?"

"Bratva."

"Give me a name," Kruger growled.

"Semien Ivankov."

"Where did he get the order?" Kruger asked.

Sergei shrugged. "I am merely foot soldier. I do not question."

"And Ivankov? Who is he?"

"*Pakhan.*"

"What is *Pakhan?*"

"He is boss. He ordered us."

"From where?"

"New York."

Kruger sat and crossed his legs once more. "You're doing great, by the way. So tell me, what do you know of a man they call Jäger?"

As soon as he asked the question, Kruger saw the tell in Sergei's face. It was a microexpression, barely perceptible, but enough to tell Kruger that the man in front of him knew something.

"He'll kill my family," Sergei said in a defeated voice. "Please don't."

Kruger uncrossed his legs and leaned forward, putting both elbows on his knees. "I'm the one you need to be worried about right now, bub."

"No," Sergei said, shaking his head vigorously. "No, he is much worse. They call him *Abaddon.*"

"What does that mean?" Kruger asked.

"He is the destroyer. *The angel of death,*" Sergei replied nervously.

CHAPTER FIFTY-THREE

K ruger sat down at one of the computers near the foyer of the townhouse and dialed into the secure videoteleconference. Moments later, Sierra Carter appeared on the screen and smiled.

"Good morning, Kruger," she said in her British accent.

"Sorry I couldn't answer earlier. I was having a sit down with my new Russian friend."

"Yes, about that, did you receive the information we have on him?" Sierra asked.

Kruger nodded. "I didn't find anything he didn't already tell me – mid-level Bratva from New York. He said the Bratva ordered him there."

"What are you going to do with him?"

"I noticed he had a few outstanding warrants in the file you sent, so Cowboy and Tuna are on their way to drop him off on Arlington PD's doorstep. So what did you need to talk about?"

Sierra frowned. "We have a high level asset within the Russian government that we tasked with locating Jäger in Moscow. I won't get into specifics, but we were able to determine that the flight from Minsk to Moscow did not go as scheduled. In fact, another flight originating from Minsk headed to the United States at the same time on a diplomatic clearance."

"Let me guess, D.C.?"

"Right," Sierra said. "We believe with a reasonably high confidence that Jäger may be operating near you. Please be careful."

"That explains the hit team. Did you know Jäger worked with the Bratva in Israel when he was Mossad? Apparently he gained quite a reputation. They called him 'The Destroyer.'"

"Jäger's files have been almost completely erased. Other than a small service record with Mossad, he doesn't exist. He's a ghost. Meeks and our team have been working to try to reconstruct some of the archives to figure out who he is."

"Wait, Coolio has been talking with you?" Kruger asked.

"Yes, he has been conversing with my analyst using a secure communications system they set up during our last operation together."

"When?"

"When what?"

"When is the last time they sent these messages? How long ago?"

"Perhaps an hour or two ago, why?"

"Christ," Kruger said as he stood. "I have to get going."

"What? Why?"

"Because they have a supercomputer that can hack or trace anything. Coolio is a sitting duck if they intercept him," Kruger said. "It was stupid of him to do that again. I told him not to."

"Wait, Kruger, there's one more thing," Sierra said.

"What?" Kruger snapped.

"Our person on the inside also told us about chatter about a billionaire that was grabbed by a Spetznaz team early this morning from a villa in Rome. He didn't have a name, but we think it may be related somehow. We're still trying to gather information."

"Nicholas Stone," Kruger replied. "Goddammit!"

"Is it something I should know? What is his significance?"

"Last night, Walter Cruz was found dead in his apartment in D.C. The news says it was natural causes, but he was set to meet with the U.S. Attorney General and President to confess to their plot. Stone was the other person involved. If a billionaire was abducted in Rome within the last twenty-four hours, I guarantee it was him," Kruger said angrily. "This is bad."

"What do the Russians want with him?"

"Cruz and Stone created a supercomputer called Helios. It can gather intel and manipulate data streams. Supposedly neither of them was told where it was physically for security purposes, but I doubt the Russians know that. If the Russians have him, that means they're trying to find it for themselves. That explains the Bratva trying to kill Michelle and Spectre. Shit!"

"How capable is this system?"

"Capable enough to take down the United States and drag down the rest of the Western world with it."

"So full alert, then," Sierra replied. "Got it."

"Not yet," Kruger said. "And even if you did, it wouldn't matter anyway. Helios can manipulate your systems."

"Not if we put everything on lockdown."

"You need to pull your asset from the inside," Kruger said. "If he's not compromised already, he will be when the Russians get control."

"How will they get control?"

"Cruz and Stone both had handheld devices with access. If the Russians have Stone, they'll have the device. It's only a matter of time before they hack it and find the location of the server."

"So what do we do, Kruger?" Sierra asked.

"Sit tight," he replied. "Right now, I need to get to Coolio and Lyons. I'll be in touch."

"Godspeed, Kruger," Sierra said as the video chat ended.

CHAPTER FIFTY-FOUR

It was almost too easy. The Helios device he had obtained from Cruz had been a game changer. It was only a matter of time before all of the pieces of his plan were in place.

Jäger had been skeptical about how the device worked. Cruz and Stone had been feeding him information as he requested it, but refused to give him unfettered access. He often wondered if they were gathering data from other sources.

But as he tried it for himself, he saw its incredible capability firsthand. With a few swipes of the system's graphical user interface, Jäger was able to access and unlock secure communications between Lyons's cyber analyst and MI-6. From there he had discovered that they were both still alive, but their location was unknown.

Jäger had thought he had reached a dead end, but Helios pulled through for him yet again. Within minutes, it had pinpointed the location of Lyons and Meeks. Despite the various proxy servers and forms of encryption the young hacker had used, Helios was able to quickly solve the problem and produce a reliable result.

In the meantime, the Russian Bratva foot soldiers he had employed were keeping Kruger and his team busy. Jäger had no doubt that Kruger would dispatch them promptly, but the head start would be enough to ensure he reached Lyons first. He could take care of the team later.

Once Lyons was dead, taking care of Kruger and his team would simply be a personal endeavor. Lyons was the last piece of the puzzle. With him dead for real this time, no one would be alive to give firsthand testimony as to the true nature of Odin and their Helios project. Once the Russians were in full control of it, America would finally fall as the world's only remaining superpower.

Jäger had been dropped off by Cruz's private helicopter into an open field a few miles from Lyons's secluded compound. He hiked through the rising and rugged terrain for two hours until he reached the base of the ledge he had picked out.

From there, he effortlessly scaled the wall with nearly fifty pounds of gear on his back. When he reached the perch, he started to unpack his gear, first removing and unrolling the shooter's mat and then removing the Barrett M107A1 rifle from its rifle bag.

Jäger extended the rifle's titanium bipod and gently placed the rifle in front of the mat. He retrieved a magazine that had ten rounds of .50 BMG and placed it next to the rifle's receiver. He then pulled out a pair of Newcon Optik LRB 12K Laser Rangefinder Binoculars and measured the distance to the target: just under 1300 meters.

Satisfied that his shooting position was still optimal, Jäger dropped to a prone position and powered on the Barrett Optical

Ranging System (BORS) computer attached to the Leupold Mark 4.5 scope. Using the buttons on top, Jäger clicked through the menu on the BORS screen, calculating the range information once more and then entering the wind information.

Once the information was entered, Jäger turned the elevation knob until the BORS screen matched the distance. Internal sensors automatically calculated the ballistic solution and compensated for temperature and barometric pressure. All he had left to do was wait.

The target house was mostly covered by trees, but the position he had picked had a small line of sight to the living area and front door. Jäger suspected that the glass would be bullet proof, and although the .50 BMG round would likely slice right through most ballistic glass at that range, he didn't want to leave such a shot to chance. He would simply wait them out. He had done it many times before in his career.

After an hour of lying perfectly still, Jäger saw two vehicles approaching from the east. Picking up the binoculars, he zoomed in and saw that Kruger was sitting in the front passenger seat of the lead vehicle. He had been expecting them, but they had arrived sooner than he had calculated.

He followed the vehicles through the trees as they made their way up the winding road to the house. As they neared, Jäger dropped the binoculars and placed his cheek on the rifle's thermal cheek rest. He adjusted his aim for the front door and reentered the wind information.

As he fixed his scope on the front door, the door suddenly opened. Lyons stepped out to greet Kruger and his team. Jäger recalculated the range using the BOR: 1287 yds.

Jäger steadied his shooting position and slowed his breathing. Kruger came into the edge of his view as Jäger fixed the crosshairs on Lyons's center of mass. With a smooth press of the trigger, Jäger sent the big fifty caliber round downrange as the rifle jerked violently.

The register of the rifle echoed throughout the valley. Jäger kept the crosshairs on Lyons as the round entered the upper right side of his chest and exploded out his left side. Kruger and company ducked as Lyons fell to the ground.

Jäger considered taking another shot, following up on Kruger to end it once and for all, but thought better of it. Kruger had already taken cover out of Jäger's narrow line of fire. Any further attempts risked giving away Jäger's position.

Not that it mattered anyway. With Lyons dead, his mission was complete. There would be no way to stop them now. Besides, Jäger reasoned, it would be more sporting to meet Kruger on even ground at close range than to kill him at such an extreme distance. It was far too easy and impersonal.

There would be plenty of time for that later, Jäger thought. He collected his gear and summoned his helicopter pilot to meet him at the preplanned extraction location.

CHAPTER FIFTY-FIVE

The two-vehicle convoy sped through mid-day traffic. Shepherd was at the wheel in the lead vehicle, with Kruger riding shotgun urging him to go faster as they sprinted to the West Virginia compound.

"This ain't my first rodeo," Shepherd said as he passed cars on the shoulder and pushed the Tahoe's speedometer past one hundred miles per hour. As a deputy sheriff, Shepherd had raced to calls in the same model vehicle many times before. The last time he had sped to a call, however, he had nearly lost his life, and his wife and daughter had been murdered in front of him.

In the vehicle with them were Spectre and Decker. Behind them, Cowboy had trouble keeping up as Tuna rode shotgun, with Tanner in the backseat. Kruger had tried calling Coolio's emergency satellite phone three times, but received no answer. There was no chance to warn them or get a situation update. They were rolling in blind.

"Don't get yourself killed, mate," Cowboy warned over the radio. "Smooth is fast."

It took them two and a half hours to reach the dirt road leading to Lyons's mountainside estate. They had somehow managed to avoid attention from law enforcement, despite their high-speed blitz through traffic. Some vehicles even pulled over to the shoulder to let them by, most likely assuming that they were some three letter federal agency en route to a hot call out of D.C.

Shepherd veered onto the dirt road and raced up the winding road. The Tahoe fishtailed as he negotiated the narrow mountain path. As they reached the top, Shepherd slammed on the brakes and the Tahoe slid to a stop, nearly hitting the iron gate. He pressed the red call button. Seconds later, Coolio appeared on camera.

"Wolf? Is that you?" Coolio asked.

"Coolio, this place has been compromised! Lock it down and get ready to move!" Kruger yelled from the passenger seat.

"What? You're coming in garbled. I can see you, but the audio isn't working. I'll let you in," Coolio said as the gate opened.

"Shit!" Kruger yelled. "Gun it! Go!"

Shepherd floored it, spraying Cowboy's vehicle with rocks and dirt as he continued up the mountain. It was another eighth of a mile before the cabin came into view. As they stopped, Lyons walked out to greet them.

"Stay inside!" Kruger yelled as he jumped out of the vehicle.

They heard the shot before they could react. The round hit Lyons at an angle through his chest and exploded out his left side, splattering blood and guts everywhere as he fell to the ground. The teams in both vehicles exited and went for cover as Kruger ran to Lyons.

He dragged Lyons out of the line of fire and behind cover, as Shepherd and the others tried to locate the shooter and return fire. As he started to assess Lyons's injuries, he realized there was no hope. A large caliber bullet had entered through his chest and gone straight through his heart on its way out his side. Jeffrey Lyons had been killed instantly.

"Wolf, status?" Kruger yelled as he turned back to reenter the fight. Shepherd had been a counter-sniper in his previous life on the sheriff's office SWAT team.

"Searching!" Shepherd replied.

Kruger peeked out from behind the metal construction dumpster he was using for cover. Based on where Lyons had been standing and the path of the bullet, he deduced that the bullet had been fired through a narrow clearing in the trees just to the left of the vehicles.

"Everyone stay down!" Kruger ordered. "The bullet came from that clearing over there!"

Shepherd low-crawled to the back of the lead Tahoe, retrieving his M40A1 sniper rifle. He then crawled back to his cover position behind the Tahoe and crouched. Peering around the front fender, Shepherd used the scope to scan the clearing.

He used his knee as support as he rested the gun over his left arm. Scanning the side of the mountain across from their position, he noticed movement. As he readjusted his scope and zoomed in, he saw a man carrying gear climbing down the face of the cliff.

Shepherd guessed that the shot was over a thousand yards away. It was well outside the effective range of the 7.62 mm round of the M40A1, but Shepherd refused to let the asshole that had just shot Lyons get away. He used his best guess for windage, range, and bullet drop and took aim at the man moving down the cliff face.

With his sights set, Shepherd exhaled slowly as he squeezed the trigger. The rifle recoiled and Shepherd cycled the bolt for a follow up shot. The round hit low against the rocks, just left of the sniper's back.

As Shepherd adjusted for a second shot, the sniper let go of the rock face and jumped the remaining five feet. He hit the ground and rolled before picking himself up and jogging off into the woods, obscured by the treeline.

"Motherfucker!" Shepherd yelled.

"Status?" Kruger yelled back.

"He's gone," Shepherd replied as he stood. "We're clear."

"Are you sure it's just one shooter?" Kruger asked.

"I'm sure," Shepherd said as he walked to Kruger's position and saw the lifeless Lyons. "Goddammit!"

"Did you get a good look at him?" Kruger asked.

"His back was turned to me. I missed the shot by less than a foot. Goddammit. I'm sorry, man," Shepherd said. "I won't miss again."

"Help me get him inside," Kruger said, indicating Lyons's lifeless body.

Tuna and Cowboy emerged from cover to help. "Did you get him?" Cowboy asked.

"Fucking missed," Shepherd said dejectedly.

"Oh no!" Decker cried as she and Spectre arrived with Tanner to help and saw Lyons. "Dammit!"

Coolio opened the door and rolled his wheelchair back out of the way as the men brought Lyons in and placed his body on the floor. Jenny joined him and put a hand on his shoulder as she started to cry. A tear rolled down the young analyst's face as he stared at Lyons.

"This is my fault," Coolio mumbled. "I shouldn't have been talking to Rebecca. Oh God, I'm so sorry."

Kruger turned and grabbed Coolio by the shoulders. "This is not your fault, kid. You didn't pull that trigger. That asshole out there did."

"I know, but—"

"But nothing," Kruger interrupted. "You didn't do this. But you're going to find the son of a bitch that did. Where's your sat phone?"

"On the kitchen counter," Coolio said. "Why?"

Kruger ignored his question and walked to the nearby kitchen. He found the satellite phone sitting on the counter and picked it up. The front screen indicated that it had no connection and could not make or receive calls. It was clear that Jäger had jammed it, preventing them from communicating a warning in time to save Lyons.

"Shit!" Kruger hissed.

"What is it?" Decker asked.

"He must have used Helios to block this phone. That's why we couldn't warn anyone," Kruger said before turning to the group. "Alright, get whatever supplies you can and pack up. We're rolling out in ten."

"Where are we going?" Decker asked.

"Can you get us a meeting with the President?" Kruger asked.

"I can try."

"Can you set it up in person when we get there?" Kruger asked.

"You mean last minute?" Decker asked. "Kruger, it's the President. I don't think she takes walk-ins."

Kruger turned to Jenny. "Can you fly?"

"Of course I can fly," Jenny said with a sniffle.

"No," Kruger said, shaking his head. "I know you *can*, but is your head in it? Are you good to go?"

"I'll be fine," Jenny said.

"Good," Kruger said. "I want you to take Spectre, Decker, and Tanner to D.C. to work on getting an appointment. We'll drive and meet you guys there. Hopefully that's enough lead time."

Jenny shook her head. "It's not that easy, Krug. We're not flying into New York. D.C. has very strict airspace requirements.

By the time I get a clearance and we land and get a car, it would be faster to drive."

Kruger considered it for a moment. They needed an audience that also provided some level of security while they planned their next move.

"I don't think we'll be able to just walk-in with the President unless we have solid proof of something," Decker said.

"What about Chapman?" Tuna asked.

"What about him?" Kruger answered.

"He's the Director of the CIA. This whole thing is in his wheelhouse. He's in the best position to help, and he still owes you for saving his life," Tuna replied.

"Umm...excuse me, but the CIA tried to kill us," Coolio interjected.

"Yeah, but wasn't the order a forgery using that Helios system?" Tanner asked as she stood in the doorway.

"I like it," Kruger said. "Alright, folks, new plan. Grab your stuff and load up the Tahoes. We're heading to Langley. It's time to blow the lid off this thing."

CHAPTER FIFTY-SIX

No one said a word as they made the three hour drive to the headquarters of the Central Intelligence Agency. There was simply nothing left to say. In Kruger's mind, he had once again failed.

They made it as far as the main gate before they were detained and forced to explain themselves. Kruger's vehicle had been selected for a random vehicle inspection, where the security team discovered enough weapons, explosives, and tactical gear to start a small war. Special Agent Tanner tried to intervene from the trail vehicle, but it wasn't until Kruger politely told the guard to let DCI Chapman's assistant know they were there that they made any headway.

Within minutes of the phone call, Chapman's executive assistant came speeding out to the guard shack on a white golf cart. He apologized to the guards and then instructed Kruger and his team to follow. He led them to the DCI's private parking area in the garage and then escorted them to Chapman's private elevator.

"I wish I could say I was surprised to see you," Chapman said as he greeted them in his office. "But after I heard that one of my off-the-books teams had tried to take out Ms. Martin, I figured we'd be chatting sooner or later."

Chapman ushered them all in and instructed his assistant to retrieve more chairs so that everyone could have a seat. Shepherd wheeled Coolio in at the tail end of the conga-line, and when everyone was seated, Chapman's assistant excused himself and closed the door behind him.

"This office is regularly swept for bugs, so please, feel free to speak openly," Chapman began. "What's up?"

They took turns briefing Chapman on the events of the last few months, starting with their operation in Iraq to capture a high-ranking ISIS propagandist named al-Baghdadi. They each recapped their role since the failed mission, and what they had learned since returning to the states.

Chapman sat behind his desk and listened intently to the story, interrupting only with questions or requests for further clarification. He made no notes, promising that any information obtained from the meeting would receive the highest levels of classification.

"So Lyons is truly dead this time," Chapman repeated as Kruger finished telling the story of the sniper in West Virginia.

"He couldn't fake what happened to him," Kruger replied.

"I'm sorry to hear that," Chapman said and then let out a deep breath. "Boy, this is a lot to digest."

"Do you know anything about Helios?" Decker asked.

Chapman shook his head. "I've heard rumblings about a super computer, but I'm afraid MI-6 is ahead of us on this one. I'm not aware of any current or pending threat."

"We need to get my sister involved," Cowboy said from the back of the room. "They have a man on the inside that can help with the Russian angle."

Chapman frowned. "Run that part by me one more time. How do the Russians play into this?"

"We don't know," Kruger answered. "We think they grabbed Nicholas Stone yesterday and this morning we had Russian Bratva doing surveillance on us."

"I'll see what I can dig up on it. Obviously we also have assets operating in that region that may be able to shed some light on it," Chapman said. "And I'll see what they know about Jäger."

"Don't bother," Coolio said. "It's already been wiped clean. The man doesn't exist beyond a few service records with Mossad."

"Son, we have ways to—"

"Won't work, already tried it," Coolio said.

"I'd trust him, bub," Kruger said. "He's better than anyone you have."

"Fair enough," Chapman said. "So, if I'm understanding correctly, we have a computer that can access any network and invent, modify, delete, or otherwise alter information to create any narrative it wants. It can also flawlessly replicate and synthesize voices without leaving a trace."

"If you're skeptical, I'd like to remind you that you apparently ordered a hit on me," Decker said.

"Oh, I'm not skeptical. I'm trying to get my head wrapped around how big a threat this is," Chapman replied. "And it's a nightmare. It can presumably shut down our entire infrastructure, create any narrative it wants, and start a civil war. Am I right so far?"

"And it could potentially be in the hands of the Russians," Decker added. "Lyons told us that only three devices were ever made to access it. Lyons destroyed his and stayed away from the project. Cruz is dead, and Stone is presumably in the custody of the Russians."

"Do we know what happened to Cruz's device?" Chapman asked.

"Either his security detail has it, or it was taken by whoever killed him," Kruger said.

"But you don't know for sure?"

"No, we don't know for sure."

"I'll send a team to look for it," Chapman said. "Verbal orders only. I don't want anything getting out if our systems are compromised."

"If you can find it, I may be able to use it to locate Helios," Coolio said.

Chapman nodded and then turned to Kruger. "Would you be willing to talk to the President about this?"

"I don't do dog and pony shows, bub."

"This isn't a dog and pony show," Chapman said. "A threat like this will require Presidential authorization, especially if it involves a nuclear power like Russia."

"Michelle and Spectre can go," Kruger offered.

"Are you kidding? I've already said my piece," Spectre shot back. "It's your turn, *bub*."

Kruger glared at Spectre, who shrugged and nodded back to Chapman.

"She needs to hear it from you, Mr. Mack," Chapman said. "You've been involved with this Odin organization longer than anyone. You and Mr. Turner both."

"We don't need another meeting," Kruger said. "You need to find and recover Stone, and we need to find and destroy that computer."

"You're absolutely right," Chapman said. "But I can't do any of that without authorization. For that, I will need your help."

"I'll go with you," Decker said, touching Kruger's arm. "It'll be OK."

"What about the others?" Kruger asked.

"I've got an off-the-books safe house near the farm. It's old school, no digital footprint or record – paper only. There's no way Helios will know about it," Chapman replied. "I'll put you all up there."

"You're the Director of the CIA. Can't *you* talk to the President and get her to do this?" Kruger asked, circling back to the meeting.

"She'll want to hear it from you," Chapman replied.

"Fine," Kruger grumbled. "But I'm not wearing a tie."

CHAPTER FIFTY-SEVEN

Nicholas Stone woke up in the fetal position on a cold concrete floor. His hands were bound behind him and a burlap sack covered his head. As he came to, he suddenly felt sick and vomited on himself and the inside of the burlap sack.

He rolled onto his knees. He felt weak and could barely keep himself upright. Whatever they had given him was making him sick. The stench of fresh vomit only made him feel worse.

Stone tried to stand, but his legs were too weak and he fell over onto his side. He screamed out for help, but no one came. He was finally able to sit upright on the floor and leaned against the wall. He didn't know who had taken him, but he had a few guesses.

The most obvious culprit seemed to be the Russians. After the meeting in Lajes, they seemed to be pushing harder to get more hands-on with Helios and have a say in its operation. They had offered money, positions of power, and even oversight of their use in exchange for direct access.

Stone had talked to Cruz about bringing them in as partners. After all, he argued, they had provided material support in the development of Helios. Cruz's reaction, however, had been unexpected.

Instead of listening to the argument, Cruz suddenly became angry and paranoid, accusing Stone of trying to negotiate his own side deal. The old geezer had started to go senile, and paranoia came with it. It wasn't the first time Cruz had lashed out like that, but it was by far the most extreme.

But perhaps he had been right. It's not paranoia if they really are out to get you. Stone was convinced the Russians had killed Cruz. After Stone had told them that Cruz wouldn't agree to a partnership, they seemed disappointed. Had that been enough to kill him? To remove him from the board altogether?

The only other possibility was Kruger. In hindsight, it had been a mistake to let him live. He was on the loose and working with MI-6, having somehow escaped from their interrogation site in Poland. The reward had seemed to outweigh the risk if they could get him on board with their plan. He and his team could have surgically removed any resistance quickly and quietly, and if they faltered, they could be used as a scapegoat, highlighting the failed government's use of mercenaries without Congressional oversight. In hindsight, that plan seemed ill advised. They had underestimated his sheer willpower.

Stone hoped that MI-6 and Kruger had taken him, but deep down he knew it was a pipedream. His captors hadn't said anything as they had taken him from his bed, but he thought he had heard someone speak in Russian before the sedative took effect. If that was the case, he was royally fucked. They would torture him to get whatever information they thought he had. He had no rights. There would be no mercy.

Stone was left to contemplate his life choices for what seemed like hours after he awoke from sedation. As he drifted in and out of sleep, he suddenly heard a door open and the sound of boots approaching on the concrete floor.

Two men each grabbed one of his arms and dragged him out of the room. They took him to another area where they removed his restraints and then strapped him to a wooden chair. They took the burlap sack off and then left the room.

He found himself face to face with a mirror. His gray hair was disheveled and his silk pajama shirt was covered with dried vomit. Moments later, a man entered the room and stood behind him, staring at their reflection in the mirror.

"You look terrible," he said with a thick Russian accent.

"Borya? Please. What is the meaning of this? We had a deal! Let me go," Stone pleaded as he recognized the Russian intelligence agent standing over him. "I will tell you anything you want to know. Just don't hurt me."

"Of course you will," Borya Medvev replied, as he walked around the chair and stood in front of Stone. "That is my specialty."

"Please," Stone repeated. "Don't hurt me. I will tell you anything you want to know. Give you anything you want. We'll make you partners if you want!"

"It is too late for that, Mr. Stone. Your partnership no longer interests us," Medvev said with a smile. "That time has passed."

"What do you want? Are you going to kill me?"

"That is up to you," Medvev replied. "It depends on your level of cooperation."

"I'll tell you anything!"

"Where is Helios?"

"It was on my nightstand!" Stone shouted frantically. "It's probably still there! You can have it!"

Medvev laughed. "Of course we have that, Mr. Stone. In fact, my hackers are working on it as we speak. That is not my question."

"I don't understand," Stone replied sheepishly.

"Where is Helios located? The server, the hardware. Where did you hide it?"

Stone shifted nervously in his chair. He knew there was no way to answer that question in spite of the threat of being subjected to enormous amounts of pain. The truth was, he had no idea.

"Well?" Medvev asked as he watched Stone squirm.

"I don't know," Stone said softly.

"You don't know?"

Stone shook his head. "It wasn't set up that way! I swear! It was developed in a laboratory in Silicon Valley under the guise of a medical computer. Once it was complete, we knew it would be too dangerous for any of us to know where it was. There was just too much of a risk that one person would try to take over. Absolute power corrupts absolutely and all that. You understand, right?"

Medvev said nothing as Stone continued. "So we used it to find a place for itself. It used a random algorithm to find a government building that was unused and secluded. It then created its own work order and assembled as if it were just a run of the mill server at some government office. I have no way of knowing where it is. I swear!"

Medvev walked to a nearby table and unrolled a set of tools. He removed a pair of pliers and walked back to Stone. "I don't believe you."

"I swear!" Stone cried out.

Medvev ignored him, grabbing Stone's left hand as he struggled against the restraints. He dug the pliers deep under the nailbed of Stone's pointer finger before twisting and ripping the fingernail off.

Stone screamed and writhed in pain. Medvev calmly repeated the question. Once again, Stone responded that he did not know.

They repeated the process until only the fingernail on Stone's pinky remained. As Medvev wiped the blood off his hand, someone opened the door and asked to speak to Medvev outside.

He placed the pliers back on the table and walked out of the room, closing the door behind him.

"What is it?" Medvev asked in Russian.

"We have successfully hacked the device and located the server," Dmitry said proudly.

"Where is it?"

"It's in a Government Services Administration building in Baltimore, Maryland," Dmitry replied.

"Are you sure?"

"Based on the power consumption of the building that is empty, we are completely certain," Dmitry said.

"Good," Medvev replied. "Very good."

"What will you do with him?" Dmitry asked, nodding toward the interrogation room.

"He doesn't know anything," Medvev replied before going back into the room.

"Please!" Stone yelled as he saw the door open. "I'm sorry!"

Stone watched his interrogator reenter the room through the mirror. Medvev walked up behind him and stopped, staring at Stone for what seemed like an eternity.

"Please! We can still be partners!! I can help you find it! I have many friends and plenty of money!"

Medvev pulled out a CZ P-10C handgun from the small of his back and placed it against the Stone's temple.

"*Nyet,*" he said, as he pulled the trigger.

CHAPTER FIFTY-EIGHT

Kruger had never been to the White House. It was a streak he had hoped to keep alive, but unfortunately mission accomplishment trumped his desires. Chapman was convinced that Kruger could make the case better than anyone.

Chapman kept the meeting small. Only Kruger and Decker went with him while the rest of the team set up shop at the blacksite in northern Virginia. Between the two of them, they had enough firsthand knowledge to paint the clearest picture of what was going on. And Decker's personal relationships with the President and Attorney General didn't hurt either.

President Clifton had just finished dinner when she joined them in the Oval Office. Kruger gave her a firm handshake as

Chapman introduced him. She seemed slightly intimidated by him as she immediately turned to Decker and greeted her with a hug.

"So what have you learned?" she asked, getting right to business as they sat on the couches across from her desk.

Chapman looked at Kruger. "I'll let them brief you. Mr. Mack?"

Kruger cleared his throat. "Are you familiar with Helios, ma'am?"

"Vaguely," Clifton replied.

"Well, I'm not a computer guy, but the bottom line is that it's a really high-speed supercomputer that can infiltrate every system connected to a network. It's a major threat to our infrastructure, and we think the Russians may have, or will soon have, control of it," Kruger said.

"*The Russians?*" Clifton asked incredulously.

"Yes, ma'am," Kruger replied. "You see, Odin is the group that came up with this. That's who I used to work for. They were four billionaires who concocted this plan to take America down a notch, and in the process they brought in the Russians to play cleanup in the aftermath."

"They aftermath of what?"

"A total collapse of our government and civil war, ma'am," Kruger replied.

"Jesus Christ."

"Well, the Russians being who they are, they wanted a bigger piece of the pie. I believe they killed Walter Cruz and kidnapped Nicholas Stone and are currently working to find Helios."

"Wait, Walter Cruz? The billionaire that was found dead in the city this morning?" Clifton asked.

"Yes, ma'am. He and Nicholas Stone were part of Odin with Lyons. And as of this afternoon, Lyons is also dead."

"This afternoon? I thought he died in the building collapse?"

"We found him in the basement," Decker said.

"Why didn't you tell me?" Clifton asked, glaring at Decker.

"We wanted to keep the knowledge of his survival a secret to keep him safe."

"How did he die?" Clifton asked.

"Shot by a sniper, ma'am," Kruger replied.

"Well, obviously the secret got out," Clifton said.

"That's how bad this system is, ma'am. Our computer guy used highly encrypted communications to talk to his friend at MI-6, and it was intercepted and decoded by Helios," Kruger said.

"So where is this Helios system?"

"They set it up so none of them would know," Decker answered. "That's the problem. We can't find it to turn it off."

"Can the Russians?" Clifton asked.

"If they grabbed Stone and the device he used to connect to the system, then yes, they can," Kruger replied. "That's what we were trying to accomplish."

"How long before they can locate it?" Clifton asked Chapman.

"They'll put their best hackers on it, so it could be a matter of days or even hours," Chapman replied.

"And the Brits know about this?" Clifton asked.

"They know some of it," Kruger replied.

"So what are you asking for?" Clifton asked.

"Obviously our systems may be compromised," Chapman answered. "So, what I'd like to get is an off-the-books mission authorization from you, to find and recover Helios."

"You could have authorized that yourself," Clifton said.

"Not to go into Russia, ma'am," Chapman replied. "We're going to have to go get Stone. If it goes south, it could start a world war."

Clifton sat back on the couch. "We're just now getting over nearly going to war with China, and now you want to risk picking a fight with Russia?"

"If they get Helios, there won't be a fight, ma'am," Kruger answered. "They'll destroy us from within."

"Let me think about it. When do you need to know by?" Clifton asked.

"Yesterday," Kruger answered. "We're already behind the eight ball on this."

"And if you're wrong?" Clifton asked. "If the Russians aren't trying to get Helios?"

"We're not wrong," Kruger replied flatly.

"What Mr. Mack is trying to say is that the intelligence is solid," Decker interjected. "We think there's a high probability that the situation is as we briefed it. Which means we must act quickly to stop the threat."

"No," Kruger growled. "What I'm saying is that we don't have time to be indecisive. If we don't grab Stone and find Helios, innocent people will die. We don't have time to wait around and hope it gets better. This is as good as it gets, bub."

"Excuse me?" Clifton asked, shocked that anyone would talk to her in such a manner.

Chapman sat forward on the couch. "Ma'am, I'd like to propose reinstating a group that your former Vice President disbanded as his last act as Secretary of Defense."

"What group is that?" Clifton said, still eyeballing Kruger.

"It was called Project Archangel."

"Never heard of it."

Chapman smiled. "That's because it was off-the-books. They reported directly to the Secretary of Defense and were ideally suited to handle situations like these, giving you plausible deniability in the event that things didn't go as planned."

Kruger's eyes widened as he sat up and turned his body toward Chapman. Decker intervened, grabbing his arm before he could say anything.

"Go on," Clifton said.

"Give me authorization to stand up the group. I can get creative with the budget and fund it. I even have someone in mind to run it for me," he said as he looked over at Kruger with a knowing grin.

"Fat chance, bub," Kruger mumbled.

"Can you stand the group up that quickly?" Clifton asked.

"I think so, ma'am," Chapman said. "The pieces are already in place. They just need new equipment and a little direction."

"And none of this gets tied to the White House?" Clifton asked.

"Just a piece of paper with your signature that reauthorizes Project Archangel and puts it under my authority. No digital footprint whatsoever," Chapman said.

Clifton thought about it for a moment.

"Do it."

CHAPTER FIFTY-NINE

"Well, gents, it's been fun working with you all, but I am obviously out," Cowboy said. The team had assembled around a dinner table in the CIA safe house as Kruger and Director Chapman recapped their meeting with President Clifton. Kruger had just finished explaining Project Archangel when Cowboy was the first to speak up.

"Why do you say that?" Chapman asked. He was sitting next to Kruger near the head of the table and had changed out of his suit and into a polo shirt with tactical pants.

"Because I'm obviously not from here, mate," Cowboy replied.

Chapman smiled knowingly. "Hold that thought. I have a new vision for Archangel."

"What kind of vision?"

"It's a little soon, but I promise you'll have your answer in the coming days," Chapman said. "For now, just know that you're welcome to be a part of this team and we'd be glad to have you aboard."

"Besides that, do you have any issues?" Kruger asked.

"None," Cowboy said.

"What do you think about all of this?" Tuna asked from the back of the dining area.

"That's something we can talk about when the mission is complete," Kruger replied. "For now, Director Chapman is giving us the assets we need to put an end to this."

"So you're in?"

"Yes," Kruger said flatly.

"Then so am I," Tuna said as he folded his arms and leaned back.

"Me too," Jenny added.

Spectre and Decker exchanged a look. "We'll help," Spectre said, "but when this is over, we're going back home."

Decker looked at Director Chapman. "I think you should bring Agent Tanner in," she said. They had made Special Agent Tanner walk outside and wait while they discussed the way ahead.

"You do?" Chapman asked.

"Project Archangel always had an FBI liaison, and in the past they were pretty bad," Decker said, referring to her kidnapping at the hands of the crooked FBI liaison two years earlier. "Maddie is young but she's a sharp agent. She'll do a good job."

"Kruger?" Chapman asked, looking to the new Project Archangel leader for a verdict.

"If Michelle trusts her, so do I," Kruger said before nodding to Cowboy to go get her.

"What about you, Mr. Shepherd?" Chapman asked Alex Shepherd who was sitting next to Tuna staring at the table with his arms folded.

Shepherd looked up and unfolded his arms, placing his hands on the table. "My family is dead because of inept government," he said grimly. "I appreciate everything Kruger and this team have done for me, but I think when this is over, I'm moving on."

"The whole point of Project Archangel is to bypass some of the bureaucracy and get things done," Chapman replied.

Shepherd shook his head. "This operator shit just isn't for me," he replied. "But I will see this through."

"Fair enough," Kruger replied before Chapman could argue any further.

Cowboy returned with Tanner who walked over to where Decker and Spectre were sitting and stood behind them.

"You've been reassigned," Chapman said to the young agent. "Effective immediately, you are now the liaison to the FBI for this team."

"Team?" Tanner asked.

"I'll fill you in later," Decker whispered to her. "You can say no if you want, but I recommended you for this position. I think you'll do great."

"I'm in!" Tanner said enthusiastically. "Whatever *this* is."

"Good," Kruger said. "With that out of the way, let's get down to business. Coolio is working with his friend at MI-6 to locate the server. Once he gets the location, we've got air assets on standby to infil and secure it."

"By the way, where is Coolio?" Decker asked.

"Working," Kruger said. "I asked him to join us but he said he wanted to work instead. Didn't even want me to explain what we were offering. Just said he would do it."

"He's such a good guy," Tanner said.

"Speaking of," Spectre said as they all turned to see Coolio wheel himself into the room.

"What?" Coolio asked as everyone seemed to be staring at him. "What did I do?"

"We were just talking about you," Decker said. "Your ears must have been burning."

Coolio tilted his head. "I am not sure what that means, but I wanted to tell you I think we found something."

"Send it," Kruger said.

"Rebecca at MI-6 has been doing a search for government buildings that are listed as vacant and cross referencing them against power usage since a system of that size would use incredible amounts of power," Coolio explained.

"And you found it?" Chapman asked eagerly.

"We've narrowed it down to five possible locations," Coolio replied, producing a piece of paper where he had scribbled five different addresses and handing it to Kruger.

"Detroit, Baltimore, Seattle, Phoenix, and Dallas," Kruger said as he read the list. "Pretty spread out."

"Sorry, boss," Coolio said. "We're still trying to narrow it down, but I wanted to give you what we have so far. It's really hard without being able to traceroute IP addresses."

"Those are all near major FBI offices," Tanner said. "I can ask the Bureau to get warrants and go in."

"Warrants," Shepherd grumbled. "Good luck."

"Wolf is right," Kruger said. "And even if we did manage to get approval, these guys could probably alter them with Helios. We'd be tipping our hand."

"Can I see the list?" Chapman asked.

Kruger handed Chapman the list. He studied it and then said, "A warrant might be a stretch, but Agent Tanner has the right idea. Surveillance teams thinking that they're watching suspected drug storage locations might work. The DEA is always chomping at the bit for stuff like this."

"I'll work it," Tanner said. "I have a connection at the DEA."

"In the meantime," Chapman continued, "I can get satellites looking at these addresses."

"Won't work," Coolio said. "The Jäger guy managed to cover his tracks when he left Poland. They can edit footage."

"Keep working it," Kruger said. "I have faith in you, Coolio."

"Will do, boss," Coolio said as he turned his chair around and wheeled himself out.

CHAPTER SIXTY

The target building looked like another example of government excess. It appeared to have been built within the last five years, but was completely vacant. The lights were on in the offices on each floor, despite the empty parking lot. It appeared to be fleecing the American taxpayer, but it certainly didn't look like a major storage facility for heroin.

Special Agent Joe Webb took a sip of coffee from his YETI tumbler as his partner scanned the building with their FLIR thermal binoculars. They were hiding in a closed used car lot across the street. It was going to be a long night, watching an empty building on direct orders from Washington.

They had been called out just as they were going home and told to watch the building and report any activity whatsoever. The only other details they were given were that it was a possible storage location for a major heroin trafficker. Hardly constituted an emergency, but Webb wasn't in charge.

"Building is empty," Special Agent Don Hyatt reported from the passenger seat. "But there's a lot of heat coming from the basement. It might actually be something."

"In Baltimore?" Webb replied skeptically. "Give me those."

Hyatt handed him the binoculars. Webb scanned the building, confirming that it was empty before moving his attention to the surface area. The yellow and red among the backdrop of pink and purple indicated that the ground floor just inside the glass front doors was hotter than the surrounding area.

It wasn't uncommon for drug labs or storage facilities to use excess energy and radiate large amounts of heat, but it still didn't explain why a government building would be used for such a place. Was it the perfect crime? The last place anyone would look? How did they even get into it?

"Huh," Webb said as he handed the FLIR binoculars back to Hyatt. "Interesting."

"Maybe there's more to it than we thought," Hyatt said as he went back to surveilling the building.

"But no people, right?"

"Nope," Hyatt replied without looking away.

"So some drug cartel managed to hide drugs in the basement of a government building and there's no one here to guard it? Bullshit."

"Well, we're in a pretty underdeveloped area. Maybe they discovered it, broke in, and knew that no one would bother it since the building has sat unused for a few years. I mean that would be the perfect crime. What cop would sniff around a government building looking for drugs?"

"I guess," Webb replied as he took another sip of coffee. "Still going to be a long night."

"Maybe not," Hyatt said, pointing to the empty parking lot.

Webb looked up to see two SUVs turn into the parking lot followed by a large white cargo truck. They continued around to the back of the building and out of view.

"That's suspicious," Webb said.

"Ya think?" Hyatt replied. "Want me to call it in?"

"Let's go see what's going on first," Webb said as he started the car and put it in gear. "Could be nothing."

"*Nothing?*" Hyatt asked skeptically as Webb drove to the edge of the car lot. "The building we're watching just happens to have a big ass cargo truck escorted by two vehicles roll up, and you think it might be nothing?"

"I'm just saying, it would be nice to have more info before we cry wolf," Webb said.

"I'm calling it in," Hyatt said as he pulled his phone out of his pocket.

Webb pulled out onto the four lane highway and turned left into the parking lot. Hyatt dialed the Special Agent in Charge. It rang once, but as they neared the building, the call suddenly dropped and Hyatt's phone reported that it had no service.

"What the fuck," Hyatt said as he tried the call again.

"What's up?" Webb asked as he put the car in park.

"No service."

Webb pulled out his phone. It also showed that it could not connect to the network. "Same here."

"We should get out of here," Hyatt said. "If they're using cell phone jammers…"

"And let them walk away?" Webb asked. "Do you want to end up with a shitty assignment in south Texas?"

"No."

"Then let's go," Webb said as he exited the car.

They went to the trunk and grabbed their body armor with DEA on the back in yellow. Webb drew his issued Glock 17 and headed for the side of the building. Hyatt followed in trail as he adjusted his plate carrier and drew his weapon.

They moved down the side of the building toward the back lot. Webb stopped at the corner of the building and held his hand up for Hyatt to wait. He peered around the corner to see what had become of the cargo truck and its escorts.

He saw armed men standing in front of the truck as others moved in and out of the building. The armed men were dressed in all black and carrying suppressed rifles. At that distance, Webb couldn't make out what kind but he could see the suppressors on the end. They definitely weren't run of the mill drug dealers. Cartel?

Webb turned back to Hyatt and holstered his weapon. "I'm going to get video," he said as he pulled out his cell phone.

"What do you see?" Hyatt whispered.

"Armed men, about a dozen or so. Looks like they're moving product," Webb said as he turned back to the corner of the building.

Webb unlocked his phone and opened the camera app. He zoomed in on the armed guards and then turned the camera toward the men walking in and out of the building. They appeared to be loading the truck.

As the camera focused under the dim parking lot lamps, Webb realized that they weren't carrying drugs but what appeared to be computer equipment. Were they hiding the drugs in computers?

Webb continued filming until he heard a shuffle and then a gurgle behind him. He turned back to see a wide-eyed Hyatt fall to the ground as he dropped his gun. His throat had been cut.

As Hyatt's lifeless body fell, Webb saw a man wearing a suit standing behind him. Webb dropped the phone and tried to draw his weapon, but his attacker was too fast. The man was instantly on top of him, slashing Webb's jugular and then stabbing him in the throat with the knife in his right hand as he grabbed the back of Webb's head with his left.

Jäger pulled down on Webb's head, driving the blade through the DEA agent's neck. When Jäger was satisfied that he was dead, he wiped the serrated blade on the agent's shirt and then retracted the blade and put the knife back into his pocket.

He picked up the phone and stopped the recording as he walked toward his men. He put the phone into his pocket as he reached the leader of the Spetsnaz team.

"We must hurry. As expected, the agents came to investigate. They are dead now," Jäger said in flawless Russian.

"The system will be completely loaded in five minutes."

"Good," Jäger replied. "Backup will surely be sent when they fail to check in."

CHAPTER SIXTY-ONE

The body of Nicholas Stone was placed in a bodybag along with the weapon Borya Medvev had used to kill him. He was taken to an incinerator on the other side of the Russian airbase in Libya under the supervision of Vladimir Sokolov.

Sokolov watched as the men hoisted the body bag up and into the incinerator. The bag instantly erupted in a bright flame before one of the men closed the steel door. Sokolov nodded his approval and then told them to go get lunch. He would join them later.

As the men climbed back into their five-ton transport, Sokolov walked to a secluded area of the base. He made sure no one could hear or see him and then pulled out an encrypted satellite phone from his bag. He dialed the number he had been given and waited.

"Eli Blackman," he said in English as the line connected.

"One moment please," came the reply.

Seconds later, a female voice came on the line. "Eli, what do you have?" Sierra Carter asked.

"Medvev killed Stone," Blackman replied. The son of a Russian immigrant who moved to London after World War II, Blackman had been working deep cover in the Russian FSB for MI-6 for the last six months.

"What?" Carter responded. "It can't be."

"We just incinerated his body. Medvev was done with him."

"Did he say why?"

"He doesn't talk to me directly," Blackman said. "But I overheard talks that he had some kind of device that they hacked. They found whatever it was they were looking for and got rid of him."

"Do you know where they found it?"

"Somewhere in the States. That's all I know."

"Good job, Eli. Let me know if you find out anything else."

"Wait!" Blackman said in a hushed tone.

"What is it?"

"You have to get me out of here."

"Have you been compromised?" Carter asked.

"I don't know. I have a bad feeling about this. They know *everything*."

"Everything?"

"I also overheard them talking about you and your computer analyst. It almost seems like Medvev knows things before they happen. It's not safe here."

There was a brief pause as Carter seemed to consider it. "All right. I'll make arrangements."

"Thank you," Blackman replied, feeling a sense of relief.

"You're quite welcome. Was there anything else?"

"Please be careful as well," Blackman warned. "I believe they are tracking you personally."

"Don't worry about me," Carter said. "Let's just get you home. Well done, Blackman."

"Thanks, ma'am," he said as he hung up the phone.

He powered the phone down and put it back into his bag. Walking out of the alley he had been hiding in, he turned left back toward the operations building they had been using. He walked the half mile back to the building.

As he started to enter, he suddenly came face to face with Medvev and three other men.

"Where have you been?" Medvev asked in Russian.

"I walked back from the incinerator to get some fresh air."

"What's in the bag?"

"Just some tools and food," Blackman replied.

"I see," Medvev said.

Blackman could feel the other men closing in on the side and behind him.

"Tell me, Eli, how was Miss Carter?" Medvev asked, switching to English.

Blackman's eyes widened. His fight or flight instinct suddenly kicked in as his adrenaline surged. Getting captured by the Russians was not an option.

Blackman shrugged as if he didn't speak English. "I don't know what you said," he replied nervously in Russian.

Medvev nodded. Suddenly one of the men behind him kicked Blackman's knee, causing it to buckle as the man wrapped piano wire around Blackman's neck.

Blackman struggled and fought against his attacker, but the man proved too strong. As blood started to pour from his neck, Blackman started to lose consciousness. Medvev smiled, seemingly enjoying the sight of the British spy taking his last breaths.

The last thing Eli Blackman saw before he died was a grinning Borya Medvev.

CHAPTER SIXTY-TWO

S hepherd squatted down and peeled back the white sheet that had been placed over the slain DEA agent's body. He shined his flashlight on the body, cringing as he observed the fatal slash wounds that had killed the husband and father of three. It was obviously the work of a professional.

Shepherd gently placed the sheet back over the victim and then turned to Kruger. He was discussing the crime scene with a local detective, Agent Tanner and Decker. Kruger had selected them based on their experience in law enforcement while the rest of the team stayed at the CIA safe house.

"Looks like Agent Hyatt didn't see it coming," Shepherd said, pointing to the body closest to them. "Agent Webb, on the other hand, appears to have been face to face with the killer."

"We found tire marks of a large vehicle of some kind near the rear entrance," the detective said. "There was a security camera system, but it was deactivated."

"Not surprising," Decker said. "Any witnesses?"

"None alive," the detective replied.

"Did you find any casings?" Shepherd asked.

"We found nothing but these bodies," the detective replied. "Even the rear entrance has no sign of forced entry, and the alarm never went off."

"Was there anything in the basement?" Agent Tanner asked.

"Completely empty, like the rest of the building."

"Thank you for your help, detective. Do you mind if we take a look around?" Tanner asked.

The detective looked at Tanner. "Special Agent Tanner, as long as you escort them, I don't have a problem with it. Just remember it's an active crime scene."

"Got it," Tanner said as they turned and walked toward the rear entrance.

"I think that pretty much confirms where the server was located," Decker said as she walked next to Kruger.

"That means the Russians already have it," Kruger said.

They walked up to the rear door. Kruger opened it and walked in as the others followed. To his right was the stairwell. He opened it and walked down to the basement where he found an empty room. Dust outlines were all that was left of the computer equipment that had once been there.

Kruger shook his head and then turned to walk back upstairs. As he reached the exit, the phone Chapman had given him rang.

"What do you have for us, Coolio?" Kruger answered.

"The satellite imagery just came in. I ran it back to the time Baltimore PD found the bodies and then backtracked from there. Three vehicles – two SUVs and one moving truck were in the rear of the building," Coolio said.

"Can you track it?"

"All of the surveillance footage from the building has been erased. Same with the traffic cameras. Rebecca at MI-6 said she might have a way to get it. Is it OK if I work with her again? I know I screwed up last time…"

"Do what you have to do to find it, Coolio."

"Yes, boss. Miss Carter also wanted me to pass along that their asset within the FSB may have been compromised. They haven't heard from him in several hours. The last thing he reported was that Nicholas Stone is dead."

"I'm not surprised," Kruger said. "They wanted Helios all along, and now they have it."

"I'll keep working on it."

"Good job, Coolio," Kruger said as he hung up the phone.

"Did Coolio find anything?" Decker asked as Kruger rejoined the group outside.

"Stone is dead and MI-6 thinks their man on the inside was found," Kruger said. "Otherwise, everything has been erased. We're still no closer."

"Coolio said the surveillance cameras were erased?" Shepherd asked.

"Yeah," Kruger replied. "They covered their tracks."

"What about those cameras?" Shepherd asked, pointing at an adult video store across the service road from where they were standing.

"It's a little far, don't you think?" Tanner asked.

"A lot of these places have switched to high definition surveillance systems," Shepherd replied. "I'd have Coolio try to pull the footage and see what he can find. But that's just me."

Kruger pulled out his phone and dialed Coolio. "We'll take any leads we can find at this point," he said as he waited for Coolio to answer.

CHAPTER SIXTY-THREE

Port of Baltimore

Shepherd had been right. With the help of Rebecca, Coolio had been able to use the surveillance footage from the adult video store across the street to identify the cargo truck. Although the nearby traffic cameras had been disabled, the surrounding license plate readers had not. Coolio and Rebecca had managed to reconfigure these cameras to identify specific vehicles and were able to match the images from the video store to the cargo truck on the cameras.

From there, they tracked the cargo truck to the Port of Baltimore where the Russian merchant ship *S.S. Minsk* was waiting to take Helios to Russia. After a quick mission brief, the team was ready to roll, and hopefully put an end to Jäger and the impending Russian threat.

It was just after 2 a.m. when Kruger and his team reached their positions. They were all running on caffeine and adrenaline, pushing through the fatigue as they focused on completing the mission.

"Punisher One-One is in position," Kruger announced over the secure tactical frequency as he and his team reached the shipping yard.

"Overwatch is ready," Shepherd said. He was perched atop a nearby crane, providing sniper cover for the team. He could see armed men loading boxes from a cargo truck into a shipping container. "I have eyes on."

"Punisher copies," Kruger replied. "Chariot, status?"

"Tally target, visual friendlies," Spectre replied, indicating he saw the IR strobes on the top of their helmets with the FLIR pod, and was also seeing the objective. Spectre and Jenny were in orbit high above in a Pilatus PC-12 specially configured for surveillance operations. Director Chapman had managed to acquire it on short notice. It was much like the one they had used previously with Project Archangel.

"Punisher is a green light," Kruger said as he stood and moved toward the fence. Tuna, Cowboy, and Decker followed. They were all wearing plate carriers with level IV ceramic plates, and carrying Sig MPX suppressed rifles chambered in 9MM.

"Oracle copies," Coolio replied. He and Tanner were watching the mission feed in real time back at the safe house. He was watching their body cameras, FLIR datalink, and had tapped into the surveillance cameras of the shipping yard. He was also monitoring local emergency and law enforcement radio frequencies.

As the team reached the fence, Tuna pulled out a pair of cutters and cut the chainlink. He held it open enough for the others to pass through, and then Decker turned around to hold it open for Tuna. She had been a last minute addition to the mission, insisting that she was more than capable of holding her own.

Despite the fact that she lacked the training that the others had, Kruger agreed. Decker had training from the FBI and had proven herself time and again in tactical scenarios. She had saved the President on Midway Island and would be a welcome addition to the team. Tanner had tried to make the same argument, but because she had yet to prove herself and she was still injured, they decided it was best to leave her back home with Coolio. A four-person team was plenty to get the job done.

"One tango at the end of that container," Spectre announced as the team regrouped and moved forward. "Appears to be facing away from you."

"Contact," Kruger replied. He let his rifle fall against its sling and then drew his fixed blade knife from his vest. He snuck up behind the guard, grabbing his mouth with his left hand as he drove the blade down into the guard's neck with his right.

Tuna helped him drag the guard's body out of the way as Spectre called "Clear."

"Punisher, this is Oracle, looks like they're almost finished loading the container," Coolio reported.

"Roger," Kruger replied. "Weapons free."

The team picked up their pace as they moved through the rows of shipping containers. Spectre called out another set of guards patrolling the area. Running next to Kruger, Tuna fired three shots at the guard on the left while Kruger dropped the other one. They reached the last row of shipping containers just as the men were closing the target container.

"I see five tangos," Shepherd called out.

"Take 'em out," Kruger replied.

Shepherd went to work with his suppressed M40A1 rifle as the team moved from cover and into the open. He took out two guards before they even knew what was going on. The other three turned to react, but Kruger and his team easily dropped them.

"Area clear," Spectre called out as they reached the container.

Cowboy used a pair of bolt cutters to break the lock and Tuna opened it, revealing computer equipment stacked to the ceiling. "Looks like we found it," Cowboy said.

"Blow it," Kruger ordered.

Tuna turned to Kruger. "I thought we were supposed to recover it," he said in a low tone so the others couldn't hear him.

"You've seen what this thing can do," Kruger said. "Blow it."

Cowboy pulled three C4 bricks from his pack and placed it on the equipment. He then removed a remote detonator from the pack and handed it to Kruger. "Would you like to do the honors?"

The team moved away from the container and then Kruger detonated it, bringing an end to the destructive nightmare that was Helios. The container erupted into a brilliant fireball that lit up the night sky. The team took off in a jog back toward the opening in the fence where they would load up in the SUV and drive back to the safe house.

"All players, this is Punisher, we are Milltertime," Kruger announced on the tactical frequency, indicating that they were mission complete and heading back to base.

"Krug...help!" they heard over the radio.

"Oracle?" Kruger said, pressing his earbud into his ear hoping to hear better. "Oracle, do you copy?"

There was a pregnant pause before a heavily accented voice said, "Hello, Mr. Mack. It's good to hear from you again. It appears you are well."

"Who is this?" Kruger said as his heart started to race.

"You have forgotten me already?"

"Jäger, you son of a bitch!" Kruger yelled.

"Very good, Mr. Mack," Jäger replied. "It seems you are one step behind as usual."

"Helios is down," Kruger growled. "I'm coming for you next."

Jäger laughed. "Such a simpleton. You really think I'd make it that easy for you? No, Helios is well on its way to the motherland. But you shouldn't worry about that right now since I have your friend. Coolio, is it?"

"If you fucking hurt him, I'll—"

"Do nothing," Jäger replied. "Just as you did nothing in Poland."

"What do you want?" Kruger snapped.

"You, Mr. Mack," Jäger said. "I will leave instructions for you here. I will see you soon, *Kruger.*"

"Jäger? Jäger!" Kruger said.

There was no reply. "Wolf, get your ass down here. Let's go," Kruger ordered.

"Do you want me to cover your exfil?" Shepherd asked.

"No, we need to get to the safe house. Spectre?"

"We're already on it," Spectre said. "We'll be on station in ten mikes."

"Goddammit!" Kruger yelled out.

* * *

Jenny and Spectre were over the scene in the modified Pilatus PC-12 within ten minutes. Spectre started a scan of the area, looking for vehicles or aircraft within the vicinity but came up with nothing. He saw the bodies of the security detail Chapman had provided littered about the outer perimeter of the property.

They called back to Langley and had a quick reaction force dispatched. The QRF arrived prior to Kruger and company and cleared the area. They reported that they found six dead and one critically injured female. Spectre assumed it was Tanner as he watched them load her into an ambulance and race to the hospital.

Spectre and Jenny stayed on station in the air until Kruger arrived on the scene nearly an hour later. Kruger told them to land

and return to the safe house, as he walked in and pushed his way past the CIA operators that had secured the scene.

Decker and Shepherd took one of the vehicles to meet Tanner at the hospital and check on her condition. One of the QRF operators mentioned that she had been shot twice in the abdomen and had lost a lot of blood when they arrived. Her pulse was weak and thready, but she was still alive.

Kruger walked into the computer room where Coolio and Tanner had been working. He found Coolio's empty wheelchair. It was stained with blood and a note had been taped to the back. Kruger picked it up and read it.

Meet me at these coordinates and I will free your dear friend. Come alone and face me like a man. It is time to put an end to the legend of Frederick "Kruger" Mack.

"What's it say?" Tuna asked as he and Cowboy entered the room behind Kruger.

Kruger handed him the letter. His hands were shaking with rage. He had no idea who Jäger was or what he wanted, but a quick death was too good for him. Kruger wanted to slowly kill the former Mossad operative and watch him die in the most gruesome and painful way imaginable.

"Bollocks!" Cowboy yelled as he read the note over Tuna's shoulder. "What a bloody mess!"

"What are you going to do, Krug?" Tuna asked.

"I'm going to fucking kill him," Kruger growled.

"This is a trap, mate," Cowboy warned. "He's just trying to goad you. Do you two have a history or something?"

"We do now," Kruger said as he balled up the letter. "It's time to end this."

CHAPTER SIXTY-FOUR

I t was just after 5 a.m. when Kruger walked past the empty police car and into Thomas Jefferson Memorial park. He was unarmed and alone, still walking with a slight limp as he made his way to the memorial.

He walked along the path next to the Tidal Basin. Across it, he could see the red lights atop the Washington Monument and he could just barely make out the side of the Lincoln Memorial. They were a testament to the rich history of the nation he had spent his life defending.

Kruger walked to the steps of the Jefferson Memorial and stopped. He wasn't in communications with anyone. The restricted airspace above the White House prevented any air support, and he had made it clear to the team that he would do this alone, despite their objections. It was his fault that this had happened to Coolio, he argued, and it was time for him to personally end it.

He started up the steps to the location of the coordinates in the note. As he made it to the top, he found a man in a suit standing next to the statue of Thomas Jefferson.

"Where is he?" Kruger barked.

"Safe," Jäger replied, taking off his coat and hanging it on one of the posts supporting the chain barrier surrounding the statue. "For now."

"Wrong answer, bub," Kruger said as he approached menacingly.

Jäger calmly pulled out his smartphone and started a Facetime session. When it connected, Jäger turned the phone toward Kruger so he could see it. On the screen, Coolio was bound and gagged on the floor with a man pointing a gun to his head.

"If you or your men kill me, my subordinates have instructions to execute young Mr. Meeks," Jäger said.

"What the fuck is your deal, bub?" Kruger asked as he froze in place.

Jäger laughed as he closed the Facetime connection and put the phone back into his pocket. "You don't remember, do you, *bub?*"

"I remember your bullshit mind games in the Polish prison, *fucking amateur.*"

"Much before that, Mr. Mack," Jäger said as he closed the distance between them, "Iraq 2012. Ring any bells?"

Kruger thought back. He had been recruited for Project Archangel in early 2012. One of his first missions was to Iraq to help dismantle an *Al-Qaeda in Iraq* cell. Their mission was cut short when they learned that a Russian Spetsnaz team was working a hostage rescue in the same area. They were told to stand down to avoid an international incident.

"No idea, bub," Kruger said finally.

"Alexi Androkov," Jäger said. "Beheaded by Al-Qaeda on August 22nd, 2012."

"And?" Kruger asked. "What does an Israeli Mossad operative like you care about some commie?"

"That *commie* was my brother, you fool!" Jäger yelled. It was the first time Kruger had seen any emotion from the former Mossad operative. The man had seemed ice cold up to this point.

"What?" Kruger asked.

"I grew up as Haim Jäger, but before my father changed our family name and moved to Israel, his name was Ivan Androkov. He remained with the KGB, despite moving to Israel. He had another son, Alexi, who stayed in St. Petersburg. Alexi worked for the FSB and was captured while on a security mission with Russian bankers looking to invest in Iraq's oil reserves," Jäger explained.

"Great family history, but just what the fuck does that have to do with me?"

"The Imam you killed while on your mission in Iraq that year was the cousin of the man holding my brother hostage," Jäger said angrily. "Because of your American arrogance, the hostage takers executed my brother, but not before cutting off his testicles and feeding them to him, as revenge for the Imam's death."

"So you've had a crush on me ever since? That's why you kidnapped me and whispered sweet nothings to me for all that time?"

"No," Jäger said. "Had I known that you were involved, I would have killed you in Poland. It was Cruz and Stone who wanted you alive due to their misguided notion that you were some sort of hero that could help them. I only allowed you to escape in hopes that you would save me the trouble of killing them, but of course you failed and I had to handle it myself."

Jäger drew a blade and held it loosely in his hand for Kruger to see. "It wasn't until I gained full access to Helios that I learned of your mission in Iraq."

"So your beef is with me. Let Coolio go and we can settle this like men. And when I'm done with you, we can have a little chat about where Helios is now."

Jäger smiled. "I still don't see what they saw in you. Always one step behind. Of course I knew you would try to track us. Do you really think I would risk it? Of course not!"

"So where is it?"

"On a plane to Moscow as we speak," Jäger said as he spun the blade around in his hand. "Now, let's end the myth of Fred Mack."

"Do you really need a knife to do that, bub?" Kruger asked. "Are you that big of a pussy?"

"Oh, I believe you're mistaken, Mr. Mack," Jäger said. "I'm not here to prove anything to you. I'm here to watch you bleed."

"Bring it," Kruger said as he took a step back and assumed a fighting stance. He stared at the knife, knowing his chances of survival were slim. He was still recovering from his injuries and even on his best day, Kruger wasn't sure he could defeat the expert assassin in front of him.

Jäger moved toward Kruger as Kruger shuffled back. Without warning, Jäger suddenly lunged toward him in a slashing attack.

Before Kruger could avoid the blade, he heard something zip by him. Jäger suddenly stopped in his tracks as his white shirt began to stain with blood. Jäger dropped to his knees as the blade fell from his hand.

Kruger instinctively ducked for cover until he realized that Jäger was lying face down in a pool of his own blood. He hobbled over to him, rolling him onto his back to find lifeless eyes staring back at him.

As he walked back toward the steps of the entry of the memorial to see where the shot had come from, he felt his phone vibrating in his pocket.

"Kruger," he answered gruffly.

"I told you I wouldn't miss him a second time. You OK?"

* * *

Shepherd would have preferred an elevated position, but given the time constraints and the limited field of fire, it was the best he could do. He was lying prone in the park four hundred meters across the Tidal Basin from the Thomas Jefferson Memorial.

On the south side of the memorial, Cowboy was in a more elevated position sitting on the railroad bridge crossing the Potomac River. It was a direct crossfire, but given the limited openings into the memorial and the lack of cooperation from the man they were providing overwatch for, it was the best they could do.

Shepherd settled into position just as Kruger reached the base of the steps into the memorial. They were operating without his knowledge or permission. He had been clear in his instructions to stay back. It was a suicide mission and everyone knew it.

But they were a team. None of them wanted to let Kruger walk into a trap, especially since he was only operating at 60% because of his injuries. So they decided to take matters into their own hands.

"Angry Ginger has reached the objective," Shepherd announced over the tactical frequency.

"I've almost finished triangulating the position from the last call," Rebecca replied over the satellite communications relay. She had been working overtime to help find Coolio, and shortly before the meeting, Jäger had made a call that they were able to intercept and use to figure out that Coolio was elsewhere.

"Let us know," Tuna said over the frequency. He and Spectre were standing by in an SUV in the general area Rebecca had last narrowed Coolio's location down to, hoping for confirmation of the specific building.

Shepherd watched Kruger enter the memorial. He saw Jäger appear, but any hope he had of a shot was blocked by Kruger. "Donut One-One has no shot," he announced. "What about you, Cowboy?"

"Nothing," Cowboy replied. "No visual on either from this vantage."

"Shit," Shepherd hissed under his breath.

The two men appeared to be talking. Shepherd saw Jäger pull something out of his pocket and show it to Kruger.

"He's making another call," Rebecca announced. "I'm narrowing it down. Ten more seconds."

"He put the phone away," Shepherd announced. "And now he has a knife."

"Wolf, do you have a shot?" Cowboy asked.

"Negative," Shepherd replied, still trying to adjust his aim. He had a fleeting headshot, but it was too risky with Kruger standing there. If Kruger moved a step to the right as Shepherd pulled the trigger, the bullet would hit him instead. Shepherd couldn't risk it.

They seemed to talk some more. Jäger appeared visibly angry as Kruger took a step back. Shepherd did his best calculation of the wind and adjusted his scope. It was a four hundred meter shot. A headshot wasn't impossible at that range, but he really didn't want to risk it.

Shepherd watched as Kruger assumed a fighting stance. Whatever discussion they were having had come to an end. "Move out of the way, dammit," Shepherd said under his breath.

Kruger took a step back and slightly to his left as Jäger lunged toward him. It was the only opening he needed. Shepherd squeezed the trigger of his suppressed M40A1 and sent the round downrange.

The bullet hit Jäger directly in the chest, ripping straight through his heart. Shepherd set up for a follow up shot as he watched Jäger collapse to the ground. He watched Kruger reorient and move to Jäger's body.

"I've found Coolio!" Rebecca announced over the radio. "Sending the location to you now."

"Jäger is down," Shepherd announced.

Shepherd pulled out the phone he had been given and dialed Kruger's number to make sure Jäger was dead.

* * *

Spectre and Tuna sped to the building Rebecca had sent them. She had been able to pinpoint the exact location Jäger had been calling. They were going in blind, but having heard that Jäger was down, they knew they didn't have much time.

They checked their body armor and suppressed Sig short barrel MPX rifles a final time and then headed for the front door. It was a single story warehouse located next to the District Wharf near the Washington Channel.

After exchanging a thumbs-up, Spectre opened the door and Tuna entered. Spectre followed closely on his heels. Tuna fired three rounds, dropping a startled hostage-taker in the entryway. They continued toward the offices in the southwest corner of the building where Rebecca said he was most likely being kept.

Sweeping high and low, Spectre moved with Tuna. A second guard walked out to investigate, but Spectre shot him in the throat and face using the Trijicon MRO optic. Reaching the office, Tuna opened the door and Spectre moved in quickly, coming face to face with one of Coolio's captors.

He fired three rounds, all center of mass and then followed up with a kick to push the guard out of the way. Tuna entered behind him and button-hooked right, killing the final guard as he attempted to pick Coolio up off the floor to be used as a human shield.

"Clear," Spectre announced.

"Clear," Tuna repeated as he rushed to Coolio and removed his gag and blindfold. "You OK buddy?"

"I'm fine," Coolio said weakly. "How's Kruger? Is he OK? They said they would kill him."

"He's fine, man," Tuna said. "Let's get you home."

CHAPTER SIXTY-FIVE

Langley, VA

Despite Jäger being dead and Coolio safe, Kruger still didn't get any sleep after leaving the Jefferson Memorial. After confirming the scene was secure, Kruger had called Chapman who sent out teams to clean up the warehouse and recover Jäger's body. He also requested a meeting at Langley as soon as Chapman got to the office at 0630.

Kruger sent Coolio back to the safe house with Cowboy and Shepherd, while Spectre went to the hospital to join Decker and Jenny as they awaited word on Tanner. The last anyone had heard, she was in surgery and just barely hanging on. She was facing a long recovery if she made it through the morning.

Kruger asked Tuna to join him as his de facto second in command during their meeting with their new boss. "New boss" was a tentative title. Kruger still wasn't sold on bringing Project Archangel back from the dead, much less assuming command.

He wasn't sure if it was the lack of sleep or just the events of the last few months, but he was conflicted. On one hand, he wanted nothing more than to go back to killing people and breaking their things in the name of Lady Liberty.

On the other hand, he was battle-weary and ready to move on. The idea of nursing school still made sense. He still wanted to make a difference, and after a career of killing, he thought it might be time to start helping people survive.

But still, there was something lingering inside him. Killing was what he was good at. It was what he thrived at doing. He had the unique ability to channel and control his rage, using it to accomplish the mission at all costs. Neither failure nor quitting was an option, ever.

That was the biggest part of the decision. Was moving on from the operator life quitting, or a personal failure? Was he letting down his country when it needed him most? These were questions he'd have to sit down and answer for himself after it was all over. For the time being, he had a mission to accomplish and would stop at nothing to accomplish it.

Kruger and Tuna arrived at the main gate at 0620 and were directed to park near Director Chapman's private elevator. They were given visitor badges that allowed them access to the appropriate secure areas of Langley. Chapman's assistant had promised that they would all be given permanent badges and access codes once there was time to get them processed through the system.

When they arrived at Chapman's office, he was already sitting at his desk reading his morning briefing on his computer. His assistant ushered them in and then excused himself as they sat down in two chairs across from Chapman's desk.

"Good job this morning," Chapman said as he stood to shake their hands. "I'm glad Coolio is doing OK."

"We need to find Helios," Kruger said, cutting straight to business as they all sat.

Chapman looked at his watch. "We have a VTC on that in fifteen minutes. You're a little early."

"VTC with…?"

"Nigel Williams and Sierra Carter," Chapman replied.

"Who is Williams?" Tuna asked.

"He's the British Minister of Defence," Chapman replied.

"Do they have a lead on Helios?" Kruger asked.

"You can ask during the video chat," Chapman answered.

Kruger shifted in his chair. "Look, bub, I hope you're not making big plans already. I think we're all here to see this mission through, but long term, nothing is set in stone. We have a lot of talking to do once this is all over."

Chapman held up his hands. "I completely understand and agree one hundred percent. I appreciate what you've done so far, and we will definitely sit down and work everything out as soon as it makes sense."

"Good," Kruger said gruffly.

"Well, let's get down to the video teleconference room and see if our friends across the pond are ready to chat," Chapman said as he stood.

As if on cue, Chapman's assistant appeared as they walked out of the office. He escorted them through a long series of vault doors and hallways into the secure video teleconferencing center at the heart of the building.

They sat down at the conference table where three large screens were mounted on the far wall next to a high definition camera facing the table. Director Chapman sat at the head of the table while Tuna and Kruger each took a side. At the center of the table was a speakerphone. The assistant moved it closer to

Director Chapman and then went to the computer beneath the displays to connect the chat.

Moments later, an older gentleman appeared on the middle screen and Sierra Carter on the screen to his left.

"Good morning, Director Chapman," Nigel Williams said.

"Good afternoon, Minister," Chapman said, before going around the room and introducing everyone.

With the introductions out of the way, Chapman began the meeting. "As we discussed briefly on the phone yesterday, I am here to make a proposal of sorts. Our countries have worked together for many years, and today we share a common threat in the form of a significant cyber threat, as I'm sure you're all well aware."

"We are," Williams replied.

"At the direction of President Clifton, I have reconvened a covert organization codenamed Project Archangel to directly address this threat, as well as future threats. Ms. Carter has been working with us unofficially through MI-6 and has been a great help. Today, Minister, I'd like to formally invite your country to join this initiative, and make Project Archangel a joint program," Chapman said.

"And how would that work, exactly?" Williams asked.

"As it was before, Project Archangel will remain an unacknowledged organization under the cover of a defense contractor. It will report directly to you and me, giving our governments plausible deniability. No operations will be sanctioned by my president or your Prime Minister directly. It will all be off the books to address the looming threats we face, and will therefore allow us increased flexibility to address these threats.

"The team will initially be led by Mr. Fred Mack, but ideally tactical leadership of this organization will be on a rotational basis with both American and British leadership. You and I will have sole control, and no other government entities will be involved.

I'm sure you have ways to fund black ops off the books, is that correct?"

"I can neither confirm nor deny," Williams replied.

Chapman smiled. "Of course, Minister. Project Archangel is the best chance we have in dealing with a multitude of threats, especially the Russian issue that we are now facing. As you know, any missions directly tied to either of our governments could be construed as an act of war, something that's unpalatable with an unstable nuclear power like Russia. Neither our citizens nor our leadership have the stomach for such a war, but the threat must be stopped even so. We must work together, both now and in the future, to ensure the safety of our countries."

"Agent Carter, what are your thoughts?" Williams asked.

"Minister, I have worked with the men at that table before, and I am eager to be a part of this," Carter replied.

"Good, then you will be our attaché to this project," Williams said. "Director Chapman, what will you need from us?"

"Kruger?" Chapman asked, looking to his right.

"Right now, Captain Smith and at least two men that he hand picks," Kruger said. "And later we'll need helicopter and fixed winged pilots, but we can discuss that later."

"Consider it done," Williams replied.

"And just so we're on the same page, sir, it is imperative that this program not be divulged to anyone," Tuna said, speaking up for the first time. "That was the biggest challenge with Project Archangel the first time. We spent a lot of time screening people before letting them anywhere near it. Discretion is the only way something like this works."

"I will make sure of it," Sierra answered. "No worries, Minister."

"Great," Chapman said. "Now that the formal stuff is out of the way, let's get down to business. Kruger, can you catch our partners up on the last twenty four hours?"

Kruger briefed them on the operations they had undertaken since he and Sierra had last spoken. He explained the background Jäger had given him, as well as the bait and switch that had been pulled while moving Helios to Russia.

When he finished, Sierra said, "Jäger being a Russian operative makes sense. Our contact on the inside mentioned something about activating an asset, but had no further information."

"Can your contact find anything more?" Chapman asked.

"I'm afraid not," Sierra said with a pained look. "I'm sorry to report that Eli Blackman was found dead only a few hours ago. He was working directly for Borya Medvev from the Russian GRU."

"Shit," Kruger said under his breath. "OK. Well, we need to find Helios, and if it requires grabbing this Medvev guy, we'll do that too."

"I will have my analyst start looking at flights out of the U.S. in the last twelve hours bound for Europe," Sierra said.

"Tell Rebecca good job for finding Coolio," Tuna added. "That was really clutch."

"I'll pass it along," Sierra replied.

"Speaking of Coolio," Kruger said, "those two seemed to work well together. Perhaps we need to bring him along when we go to Europe and put them in the same room."

"That can be arranged," Sierra said. "I'll read Rebecca in."

"We're going to Europe?" Tuna asked.

"Pack your bags," Kruger said. "It's time to end this, and you know they're taking Helios straight to Russia."

CHAPTER SIXTY-SIX

Before heading back to the safe house to gather the rest of the team and head to the airport, Kruger and Tuna stopped at the hospital. Tanner was still in surgery when they found Spectre and Decker leaning on each other asleep and alone in the surgery waiting area.

Spectre heard them walk in and woke up, gently moving Decker from his shoulder as he stood to greet them. Decker yawned and stretched as she stood and hugged Kruger.

"How is she?" Kruger asked softly.

Decker frowned. "Second surgery. She lost a few feet of intestine and they're trying to remove fragments near her spine. She may never walk again."

"She's a tough kid," Kruger said.

"The toughest," Decker replied. "I completely underestimated her."

"She's going to pull through. We'll do whatever we can to help," Tuna added.

"So what's the plan? You doing OK?" Spectre asked.

"Dynamic Aviation Consulting Group is back, and now it's a joint venture with a British company," Kruger said, using the name for the defense contractor that once served as a cover operation for Project Archangel.

"Makes sense," Spectre said. "Sounds like you guys worked well with the Brits before."

"It's going to be interesting," Tuna said. "So are you coming with us to Europe?"

Spectre exchanged a look with Decker and then turned to Kruger. "You found it?"

"Not yet," Kruger said. "Coolio and their cyber analyst are working it. We're heading there to rendezvous and come up with a plan when they find it."

"You think it's going to Russia?" Decker asked, careful to ensure no unauthorized listeners were in earshot.

"It's our best bet, and we'll have to get to it before they have a chance to reassemble it and get it online," Kruger replied.

"Wheels up in two hours," Tuna added. "You in?"

Spectre looked at Decker. Kruger could tell they were fatigued and ready to go back to their family life. He could see it in Spectre's face in particular. Part of him was envious that they had taken the time to start a family. He knew it must be killing them to be away from their son.

"Go home," Kruger said before Spectre could answer. "We have it covered."

Spectre looked confused. "Are you sure? You don't have a full team and you're down to one pilot."

"The Brits are providing assets. We've got it. Go home and be with your family," Kruger said. "Thank you for all that you did."

Spectre looked to Michelle who put her arm around him and said, "It's time to put this behind us."

"Don't worry, we'll save a job for you when we get back...*if you want it*," Kruger said.

Spectre chuckled. "I may need it. I don't remember much, but it sounds like I walked off a flight mid-sequence at the airline. Being on probation, I doubt I'll be working for them for much longer."

"You'll find something better," Decker said reassuringly.

"Well, we'd better get to work," Kruger said.

Decker hugged Kruger again. "Thank you," she said.

"I didn't do anything."

"More than you know," Decker said as she let go and wrapped her arm around Spectre's waist.

Spectre shook Tuna's hand and then Kruger's. "Be safe. Both of you."

"Always," Kruger said. "Let me know how Tanner's doing."

"We will," Decker said. "We're going to stay here with her until her family gets here."

"Make sure she knows we'll be back for her," Kruger said.

"Will do."

Kruger nodded and then walked out with Tuna. They drove back to the safe house where they found Coolio engaged in a video teleconference with Rebecca, while Cowboy and Shepherd slept.

The bodies of the men guarding the safe house had been removed and Tanner's blood cleaned up. The place smelled of bleach and cleaning chemicals, but looked as clean as the day they moved in.

"Glad you're back, boss," Coolio said as he downed the last of his Rip-It energy drink, a special gift from Director Chapman. "We think we have a lead on Helios."

"Hi Rebecca," Kruger said, seeing the young British cyber analyst staring at him on the video chat.

"Mr. Kruger," she replied with her heavy Irish accent.

"They used two cargo trucks," Coolio explained. "Both with the same plates, markings, and features. They knew we'd rework the ALPR cameras and find them. It was pretty brilliant actually, but Rebecca was able to find another hit at the Baltimore airport. I guess they swapped trucks somewhere during the drive to the Port of Baltimore."

"I pulled the airport security footage, and found them loading the computer equipment into a Gulfstream G-650ER. It is registered to a shell company owned by Nicholas Stone," Rebecca added.

"The dead billionaire?" Tuna asked.

"Sounds like they're still using him as top cover, even as a dead man," Kruger said. "Any ideas where they're heading?"

"Looks like they're on a diplomatic clearance into Poland," Coolio answered.

"Any specific city?" Kruger asked.

"Doesn't say," Coolio said. "Just has the expected time into Polish airspace."

"Shit," Kruger said under his breath. "Ok, start packing up. We're wheels up in an hour."

"You want me to go too?" Coolio asked, seemingly surprised by the order.

"Are you up for it?"

"Well, I'm not staying at this death trap alone!"

"Then why are you asking? Pack your stuff. Let's roll," Kruger said.

"Just wanted to make sure I wasn't getting left again," Coolio said as he said goodbye to Rebecca and started closing out his programs to shut down his computer.

CHAPTER SIXTY-SEVEN

K ruger slept from the time the Gulfstream's engines started turning until Tuna woke him up in London. He was exhausted and his body ached. The adrenaline had finally worn off and the events of the last few days had caught up with him.

He grabbed the green c-bag filled with his gear and hobbled out of the aircraft behind the rest of his team. Shepherd helped Coolio down the stairs and into a wheelchair at the base of the stairs where Sierra Carter and Captain Smith were waiting to greet them.

"Are you OK, Kruger?" Sierra asked as she took off her sunglasses and approached Kruger. "You look like you've been hit by a bus."

"I'll be fine," Kruger said as he tossed his bag to the ground. "Do you have anything?"

"We think the aircraft may have landed in Warsaw," Sierra said. "But you're not going to like the rest of it."

"What is it?"

"We believe they've loaded the hardware into several trucks to drive the parts into Russia," Sierra replied.

"I'm new at this spy stuff, but what's the point of that? Why not just fly directly there and not risk a truck being intercepted?" Shepherd asked. He had been standing behind Tuna listening intently to Sierra's update.

"Multiple vehicles would be much harder to track," Sierra answered. "And more difficult to pinpoint the exact destination. We will be completely blind once they reach Russia."

"Well that just sounds awesome," Shepherd said as he stepped back behind Tuna.

"Right," Sierra said. "Shall we get you to our headquarters? I'm sure you're all very hungry. I've arranged for your dinners to be delivered while we plan the next mission."

"Brilliant," Cowboy said as he hugged his little sister. "I knew you were good for something."

"You're such a pillock," Sierra replied, as she playfully pushed him away.

As they turned to get in the waiting line of SUVs, Kruger pulled Shepherd aside. "Got a second, bub?"

"Sure," Shepherd said as he stopped and allowed the others to continue to the SUVs. "What's up?"

"We didn't get a chance to talk about what happened earlier in D.C.," Kruger said.

Shepherd nervously took a step back, fearing he was about to face the wrath of the famous angry bearded ginger for disobeying orders. "Look, I'm sorry we went against you, but—"

"Relax," Kruger said holding up a hand. "Don't be sorry."

Shepherd gave him a confused look while still maintaining a defensive posture.

"I just wanted to thank you," Kruger said. "That's all."

"Thank me? Are you sure you're feeling OK?"

"That shot took balls," Kruger said. "You did a good job."

"Thanks, boss," Shepherd replied sheepishly. "It was the least I could do for you saving me in Syria…and giving me a second chance to make a difference."

Kruger extended his hand. Shepherd shook it as Kruger leaned in, holding the handshake a little longer and firmer than Shepherd had expected.

"That was a freebie," he said in a low growl. "Don't ever ignore my orders again, bub."

* * *

After they were given a chance to eat and get a shower, the team piled into a briefing room with theater seating. Kruger stood at the front of the room next to Sierra Carter and Captain Smith as the rest of the operators took their seats. Coolio sat in his wheelchair next to Rebecca in the front row while the rest of the team spread out in various rows behind them.

"As most of you know, I'm not one for speeches, so I'll make this quick," Kruger said as he addressed the team. "For those of you that don't know me, my name is Freddie Mack. You can call me Kruger if you like. As of yesterday, I am in charge of the group you've all been invited to join – Project Archangel."

"This is Captain Jacob Smith, he was a tactical team leader with MI-6 and will be joining us along with two of his best men, Sullivan Churchill and Phillip Taylor," Kruger said, nodding to Captain Smith. "Sierra Carter will be the MI-6 liaison to our group."

Kruger paused before continuing. "Folks, this organization is off-the-books, and unacknowledged by both governments. Our funding is indirect and as far as the world is concerned, we're just mercenaries doing our own thing. If you are captured, the people in this room will be the only ones coming to get you. If you are killed, we'll be the ones sending you off to Valhalla. Discretion is of the utmost importance. We survive by keeping this organization a secret, classified at the highest levels."

Kruger looked around the room, gaging the reactions of those new to the team. Except for Tuna, Coolio, and Jenny, that was nearly everyone in the room.

"Quidquid victor ero," Kruger continued. "Come what may, I shall be victorious. That is our motto. We live and die by it. Any questions?"

"Good," Kruger said when he was satisfied that everyone understood. "As far as chain of command goes, Captain Smith will be my second in command. Come to either of us if you have any issues. Jacob, do you have anything for the group?"

Smith stepped forward. "It's a pleasure to be serving with you all. And indeed, we shall be victorious."

"Thanks," Kruger said. "Sierra, what do you have for the briefing?"

Kruger and Smith took their seats at the front next to Rebecca and Coolio. Sierra nodded to Rebecca and the lights dimmed. The projector at the rear of the room lit up the screen behind her, showing the classification of the briefing.

"Thanks, Kruger," Sierra said. "I'm afraid the news is not good. We have confirmed that the aircraft carrying Helios landed in Warsaw, Poland, earlier today."

A satellite image of the airport appeared, showing a Gulfstream business jet parked next to five cargo trucks. "As you can see here, the aircraft was unloaded into trucks. We are not sure whether the equipment was separated into each truck, or if they intend to use decoys."

The image behind her then changed to a map of Eastern Europe showing highlighted routes into Russia. "Each truck appears to have taken a separate route. We have only been able to successfully track two out of the five trucks."

A picture of a white cargo truck at a border checkpoint appeared on screen. "This is a picture of one of the trucks at the Ukrainian border two hours ago. Its cargo manifest declared computer equipment en route to Russia. Due to tensions in Ukraine, we have continuous satellite coverage in this area and are currently tracking it in real time."

"It is our belief that this vehicle represents our best chance at intercepting Helios. Your mission will be to intercept the cargo and detain the occupants for interrogation. That will hopefully lead us to the final location," Sierra concluded as the lights came back on. "Any questions?"

"Couldn't these just be decoys? And the driver was just told to drive a truck from Warsaw to Russia using this route?" Shepherd asked from the back row.

"Excellent question," Sierra replied. "There is a reasonably high probability that this vehicle is a decoy, but given its projected path through Russian-occupied territory in the Ukraine, we do not believe this to be the case. It is likely that they are using this route to provide cover from air attack or surveillance using the surface to air missile batteries already in place along the route. They also have infantry support should they come under attack in these areas."

"So what you're saying is, it's going to suck worse if we're right?" Shepherd asked.

"In a manner of speaking, yes," Sierra replied.

"Oh. OK then, no further questions," Shepherd said.

"This obviously won't be an easy mission," Sierra said, "but it has never been more important that we succeed. If the Russians gain full control of this technology, it could cause the collapse of the West as we know it."

CHAPTER SIXTY-EIGHT

The team touched down in Kiev just after 9 p.m. Sierra Carter had coordinated two armored Land Rovers to be waiting for them at the airport. She had stayed behind with Coolio and Rebecca to provide tactical control and support, while Kruger led a team to intercept the cargo truck.

Kruger established encrypted satellite communications with Coolio as Tuna drove the lead vehicle. Cowboy and Shepherd rode in the back seat while Captain Smith and his men followed in the rear vehicle.

"We need to come up with better names for those guys," Shepherd said as they headed toward the intercept point.

"Huh?" Cowboy asked.

"Captain Smith, Sullivan Churchill and Phillip whatever-his-name is," Shepherd explained. "When I first showed up, everyone had cool call-signs. *Tuna. Kruger. Cowboy.* Hell, you guys started calling me Wolf and that was badass, but what about these guys?"

"So come up with a name, mate," Cowboy said.

"I don't know," Shepherd said. "That's your thing. Smitty? Blackbeard?"

"They called him Ringo," Kruger said as he turned back. "At least back when I worked with him."

"You knew him?" Shepherd asked.

"We worked together when I was in Delta," Kruger replied. "He used to be SAS."

"You two didn't know each other?" Shepherd asked Cowboy.

"Must've been before my time," Cowboy replied.

"He wasn't there very long," Kruger said. "They pulled him to work MI-6 when he was fairly junior."

"Did you say you worked with Sierra Carter with Odin?" Shepherd asked. "Did you work with him then?"

"No, just Sierra. That's how we found the wanker next to you," Kruger said.

"Good use of the term, mate," Cowboy said.

"So what about the other two?" Shepherd asked. "Do you know them too?"

"Never met either of them before this," Kruger answered. "But if Ringo trusts them, so do I."

"The big one—Sullivan— kind of looks like Shrek," Shepherd said. "Maybe we'll call him that."

"Good luck with that," Tuna interjected, looking up at them in the rear view mirror. "But, *please*, I want to be there when you call him that."

Before Shepherd could reply, their tactical radios crackled to life. "Punisher Actual, this is Oracle."

"Send it," Kruger replied.

"The target appears to have stopped for the night," Coolio replied. "It's a brothel in Korosten. But that's not the worst part."

"Sounds pretty good to me," Cowboy said with a chuckle.

"It's a known FSB safe house," Coolio continued. "Sierra is trying to get more info, but from what we've found so far, there could be at least a dozen or more agents there. They're part of the Russian operation against the Ukraine."

"Get me all the intel you can, Coolio, and send it to my tablet," Kruger ordered.

"Yes, sir," Coolio replied. "We also think the truck may have an armed team with it."

"How could you tell?" Kruger asked.

"Director Chapman was able to get a U-2 overflight. Looks like six heat signatures in the back," Coolio said.

"Ringo, are you getting this?" Kruger asked over the tactical frequency.

"Wow, I haven't heard that name in years. Yeah, I copy," Smith replied.

"Ringo it is," Shepherd whispered to Cowboy.

"Oracle, get us what you can. We're about two hours from Korosten. We'll stop as soon as we get everything and then plan the op. We'll take it down tonight," Kruger said.

"Roger that," Coolio replied.

"Good job, Oracle," Kruger said.

CHAPTER SIXTY-NINE

They parked their Land Cruisers a few blocks from the target building. Tuna hand-launched a micro-UAV and confirmed that Coolio was receiving the satellite datalink back in London. He reported that there were sixteen occupants in the building based on thermal imagery from the drone.

"Two guards out front, two in the back alley with the truck, one on the roof, and five armed men inside," Tuna confirmed as he viewed the footage from the drone on his tablet. "The cargo truck is parked in the back alley."

Shepherd and Cowboy went to an apartment building and set up a sniper position in an empty apartment on the fourth floor. It was a block away from the objective, separated by a soccer field. They found the apartment overlooking the brothel and picked the lock to get in. Coolio had selected it because he confirmed that it was empty.

They set up a table away from the window to mask their position. Cowboy opened the window, giving Shepherd an unobstructed view of the brothel and the men standing out front as well as the man smoking a cigarette on the roof.

"Overwatch is in position," Cowboy called out on the tactical frequency.

"Copy," Kruger replied. He and Ringo were set up with Taylor a few blocks from the brothel in full tactical gear. He looked over at Tuna and nodded for him to start walking that direction. Tuna and Churchill were wearing civilian clothes and carrying concealed handguns.

Churchill was fluent in Russian. The plan was for them to pose as customers and locate the driver of the cargo truck. Although facial recognition had failed, Coolio had been able to get a clear picture of the truck driver and passenger using traffic cameras. Shepherd and Cowboy would provide sniper support while Kruger and company would be on standby.

Tuna let Churchill take the lead as they casually approached the two-story brothel. He was nearly half a foot taller than Tuna and outweighed him by nearly one hundred pounds. When combined with his shaved head and beard, it created an intimidating presence.

"We are here for girls," Churchill said in Russian as the closest guard took an interest in him as they approached.

"You have money?"

Tuna pulled out a wad of cash, part of the care package Sierra had arranged along with the vehicles in Kiev.

The guard held out his hand. Recognizing the culture of bribery, Tuna pulled two large bills from the wad and handed them over. The guard gestured for another and Tuna gave him two more just to be safe.

Satisfied, the guard nodded for Tuna and Churchill to enter the brothel and then walked over to the other guard to brag about his bribe. Tuna motioned for Churchill to lead the way, using the big Brit as a plow to get through the line of potential suitors at the entrance of the brothel.

"We're in," Tuna announced over the tactical frequency. "Now where is this guy?"

Churchill was stopped by a man standing just inside the entrance. He said something to Churchill in Russian and then two other men patted Churchill down. Satisfied that he was unarmed, the man moved on to Tuna.

Tuna stared straight ahead. The man asked him something in Russian, but Tuna said nothing. He didn't speak the language, but also didn't want to give away that he was American.

Frustrated that Tuna wasn't responding, the man repeated his question.

"Just say '*Da*,'" Coolio said over the tactical frequency.

"*Da*," Tuna said finally and nodded. Satisfied, the man went back to Churchill and motioned for him to follow.

"What the fuck did I just say yes to?" Tuna said under his breath over the tactical frequency.

"He wanted to make sure you were into women," Coolio replied. "He had men to offer as well."

"I think you meant to say *nyet*," Cowboy interjected over the freq.

"Shut the fuck up," Kruger barked back. "Keep this channel clear."

The pimp they were following took them to a private room. Five women dressed in lingerie sat on a black couch waiting for their next customer. The pimp closed the door behind them and then pointed as he said something in Russian.

"He wants to know which one you'd like," Coolio translated for Tuna as he listened in.

Churchill pointed to the brunette at the end of the couch and said, "I'll take that one."

The woman stood as Churchill handed the pimp money.

The pimp asked another question. "He wants to know if you two are together," Coolio translated.

"*Da*," Tuna said.

The pimp extended his hand for more money. "He said that will be extra," Coolio once again translated.

Tuna handed him a wad of cash. The girl took Churchill's hand and led them upstairs. There appeared to be five rooms, one of which had a guard posted outside.

"That's the one," Tuna whispered to Churchill as they passed the guarded room.

The woman led them into the room at the end of the hall. As she turned to kiss Churchill, he spun her around and bound her hands behind her back with a pair of Flexcuffs he had in his pocket. He sat her down and showed her a fistful of money, telling her to be quiet in Russian.

"Oracle, this is Trojan, we have eyes on the room. Second floor, second room on the western side," Tuna said.

"Oracle copies," Coolio said. "Standby."

Coolio maneuvered the drone into position, using its thermal imaging to decipher how many occupants were in the room.

"Oracle sees three in the bed. Looks like one male and two females. One asleep on the bed next to it. No other contacts," Coolio replied.

"We're moving," Kruger announced over the tactical frequency.

Kruger led Ringo and Taylor through a back alley out of sight of the two guards out front as Shepherd kept watch. They maneuvered to the narrow side alley on the south side of the building, and Kruger and Ringo posted on either side of Taylor.

Slinging his rifle across his back, Taylor climbed up the side of the building using a drainage pipe as footholds. He reached the window of the target room and stopped. "Punisher One-Three is in position," he announced.

Hearing that Taylor was in position, Tuna nodded to Churchill who reminded the girl to remain quiet. Tuna walked out of the room first. The guard standing out front was holding an AK-74U rifle. He looked at Tuna as he pretended to stumble out toward him.

"Hey buddy, you got a light?" Tuna asked in English, still putting on the drunken act.

The guard shouted something at Tuna in Russian as he gripped his rifle and brought it to a low-ready position.

"I don't speak Spanish," Tuna said, still stumbling toward him.

The guard raised the rifle and pointed it at Tuna's face. Churchill walked out of the room, causing the guard to divert his attention to the much bigger target.

Tuna seized the opportunity, twisting the weapon away as he followed up with a strike to the guard's forehead with the butt of the rifle. Churchill lunged forward, following up Tuna's attack with a hammer fist of his own. The guard crumpled to the ground. Churchill removed the guard's handgun and checked it, nodding to Tuna that he was ready.

"We're clear," Tuna said as he checked the weapon. "On your mark."

"3...2...1...Mark!" Taylor called.

Tuna kicked in the door and moved straight for the bed with the three occupants, while Churchill moved in behind him and headed for the other bed. Startled, the girls jumped back, knocking the man they had been having sex with onto the floor.

The man in the other bed woke and pointed his gun at Churchill who fired two rounds, killing the man as the blood soaked the white sheets. "Goddammit!" he hissed.

"Help me," Tuna said as he fought off the women and restrained the remaining driver.

Taylor climbed in through the window and unpacked a harness and rope. "I heard shots, you guys OK?"

"We're fine," Tuna replied. "Oracle, status?"

"Looks like the front guards are alert and talking on radios," Oracle said.

"Copy that," Tuna replied.

The hookers ran out of the room. Tuna and Churchill put the harness on the driver and found an anchor point for the rope. They knocked the man unconscious and then carried him to the window.

Tuna covered the door as Churchill and Taylor lowered him to the alley. Once he was down, Taylor descended using the rope and Churchill followed.

"Two hostiles heading to you," Coolio said, watching the thermal drone feed.

As Tuna went to climb out of the window, he heard footsteps on the wooden floorboards. He turned and aimed at the door. He shot the first man that entered three times, causing him to collapse in the doorway. The second man tripped over the body, but managed to get a shot off, narrowly missing Tuna.

Tuna returned fire, hitting him in the throat and face before he turned back to climb out of the window.

"Punisher, this is Overwatch, I've got a Tango headed to you," Shepherd announced over the tactical frequency as he watched one of the guards out front head toward the alley.

"We have the package," Kruger said. "Take them out."

"Copy," Shepherd replied.

Shepherd went to work with his suppressed M40A1. He took down the guard approaching the alley and then aimed at the man on the roof who was heading for the door.

Churchill carried the unconscious prisoner as the team in the alley regrouped. Ringo took point with Tuna behind him and they headed for the side alley where the cargo truck was parked.

"Wolf, status?" Kruger asked.

"All clear out front. Unknown inside," Shepherd replied as he took down the remaining guard he could see.

"Copy," Kruger said.

Ringo made his way around the corner, dropping the lone man guarding the cargo truck and then sprinting to it. They set up a defensive perimeter as Taylor pulled out bolt cutters and broke the lock on the truck.

Climbing into the back of the truck, Taylor found it was mostly empty, but there were boxes with computer equipment. It was impossible to tell whether they were generic computers or part of Helios.

Churchill tossed the driver in the back and hopped in with him. Tuna and Kruger climbed into the cab and fired up the truck's diesel engine.

"We're moving to extract," Kruger announced. "Cover our escape and then move to the rally point."

"Copy that," Shepherd replied.

CHAPTER SEVENTY

Once the truck was clear, Cowboy and Shepherd moved to where they had parked the Land Cruisers and then drove them to the rally point outside of town. It was an abandoned farmhouse that they had identified in their pre-mission planning.

Kruger and company had parked the truck in the barn and were prepping the driver for interrogation, while Taylor took pictures of the serial numbers on the equipment to send back to Coolio. Ringo directed Cowboy and Shepherd to pick up an overwatch position and cover the dirt road leading to their position.

There were no chairs in the empty barn, so Kruger made the driver kneel completely naked in the straw and dirt. His hands and feet were bound together behind him, creating a stress position.

"Alright, bub, we don't have all day, what's your name?" Kruger asked as Churchill translated.

"He says, 'Fuck you,'" Churchill said as the driver finished speaking and tried to spit at Kruger.

Kruger calmly drew his Glock 21 and screwed in the suppressor. "Suit yourself," he said with a sigh as he walked behind the man.

He aimed the gun at the man's feet and pulled the trigger. The round went through the driver's left foot, causing him to scream out in agony and fall over to his side with his back arched.

Churchill picked him up and put him back on his knees as Kruger walked back in front of him. "I've got plenty of ammo," Kruger said.

Churchill translated as the man groaned in pain.

"Yuri Pachinko," the driver said finally. "You will die for this."

"You speak English! Good!" Kruger said as he squatted down in front of him. "That will make this much faster."

"Bratva will kill you," Yuri said defiantly. "You are dead man."

"So you're not FSB," Kruger said. "Good to know."

"Fuck you," Yuri said.

"Do you know what you were carrying?" Kruger asked.

"Computers and shit," Yuri said. "Are you blind? Look for yourself."

Kruger nodded to Churchill who walked behind the defiant Bratva thug. Churchill smashed his boot down on Yuri's foot, causing him to fall over once more as he screamed in pain.

"I can't breathe!" Yuri cried as he lay on his side.

"Of course you can. You wouldn't be screaming if you couldn't," Kruger said, crouching down next to him.

"They'll kill me!" Yuri yelled as he coughed and grunted.

"You'd better worry about me first, bub," Kruger growled.

"What do you want from me?"

Kruger nodded to Churchill who helped Yuri back to his knees.

"Where were you taking the equipment?" Kruger asked.

"Russia," Yuri replied.

Kruger held up the weapon. "Just Russia?"

"Moscow!"

"What part?"

"They told me they'd tell me when I crossed the border, I swear!"

"Who sent you?"

"I don't…"

"You don't know?" Kruger asked, holding up the suppressed handgun.

"No! His name is Suvarova. Please! He'll kill me!"

"Who is he?"

"He is *Pakhan*," Yuri replied nervously.

"What about the other trucks?"

"We were all given routes. Told to watch for American CIA."

"What do you know about the equipment you have?" Kruger asked.

"I don't know anything! I swear!"

"Yuri…"

"All I know is that we each took trucks. It's something big, and when Pakhan gets it all, Bratva will take over the world."

Kruger stepped away. "Coolio, are you getting this?" he asked over their satellite communications.

"I'm researching Suvarova now, boss," Coolio said. "Looks like he is the head of the Podolsk Bratva."

"Kruger, it's Sierra," Sierra interrupted.

"What's up?"

"Suvarova is known to have heavy influence within the Russian government and their intelligence agencies. It would make sense that he would use the GRU or FSB to acquire Helios. It's unimaginable what they will do when they get all of it together," Sierra said.

"Hey boss, not to pile on, but these serial numbers are just normal desktop computers. Nothing meeting the specs of what would be needed for what Mr. Lyons described. So unless they're fake, I don't think this is our truck," Coolio said over the frequency.

"Copy that," Kruger said as he turned back to Yuri.

"Have you been to Suvarova's mansion?" Kruger asked.

"Twice," Yuri replied nervously.

"Tell me everything you know about it, and I just may let you live," Kruger said ominously.

CHAPTER SEVENTY-ONE

Kruger cut Yuri loose and destroyed the cargo truck with the computers after getting the low down on the Suvarova mansion. They drove back to Kiev and took the Gulfstream to Moscow.

This time Director Chapman was able to arrange housing and vehicles for their stay at a CIA safe house just outside of Moscow. They spent three days doing surveillance on the mansion, learning the patterns of the guards, the movements of Suvarova and his habits.

During their surveillance, they saw a cargo truck enter the estate. It was offloaded out of sight and sent on its way. Based on the information Lyons had given before he died, Coolio believed Helios would take two to three days to assemble and get up and running once delivered. They decided to plan an assault to take down Helios once and for all.

It wouldn't be easy. Suvarova was one of the most powerful and well-defended men in Russia, if not the world. He was a paranoid man who took security very seriously. Any hint of trouble would send him to his panic room while his former FSB and Spetsnaz security detail defended his estate.

The obvious answer was a flight of F-35s to level the mansion and end the threat. But President Clifton wouldn't authorize it. The risk of detection by the SA-20 and SA-22 surface to air missile systems was too great. A shootdown of an F-35 over Russia would be catastrophic and could start a third world war. Besides, she argued, what if the computer system wasn't even there?

Shepherd set up in an empty warehouse on the north side of the mansion. It was facing the entrance and had a decent view of the left and right sides of the mansion. Because of their limited numbers, he was alone to allow Cowboy to be a part of the entry team.

On the south side, Kruger set up a sniper perch on the fifth floor of an empty office building. Because of his injuries, he was still a step slower than the rest of the team – a risk they couldn't take given the complexity of the mission. He had been a sniper with Delta before becoming an interrogator. So after a special request to the CIA for a suppressed SOCOM Mk-13 chambered in .300 WIN, Kruger became the team's second sniper. It also gave him a better vantage for command and control.

He had an unobstructed view of the pool and pool house, as well as the master bedroom and its double doors leading out into the courtyard. "Snake One-One is in position," he called over the tactical frequency.

"Snake One-Two is ready," Shepherd echoed.

"Bucket Two-Zero is set," Ringo called. He was leading the tactical team of Cowboy, Churchill, and Taylor, that would infiltrate the mansion to locate and destroy the equipment.

"Oracle copies," Coolio replied. "Say the word."

"Send it," Kruger said.

"Done," Coolio said. He had hacked into the mansion's fire alarm and suppression system, creating a false fire indication in the kitchen and guest bedrooms to activate the house's alarm and sprinkler systems and send an alert to the local fire department.

Kruger could hear the fire alarms in the distance as he watched the guards start to react through his night vision scope. As he waited with his sights fixed on the bedroom doors, he heard sirens approaching in the distance.

"We're rolling," Ringo announced. They were dressed as firefighters and driving a fire and rescue support vehicle. They waited for the fire trucks to pass and then joined the end of the convoy, speeding through the open gate as the fire trucks rushed to the main residence.

"Snake copies," Kruger replied.

Kruger waited patiently as he watched through his scope. He had moved a desk away from the window and cleared it off, sitting on a chair and stabilizing the rifle on its bipod. As the scene grew more chaotic, Kruger finally saw the master bedroom door open.

A man emerged, escorted by two half-naked women and a couple of bodyguards. Kruger adjusted his aim for the wind and exhaled slowly. He squeezed the trigger, sending the .300WIN round downrange.

He cycled the bolt as he watched the round hit Suvarova in the chest, piercing through his heart and causing him to collapse to the ground.

"Bucket is in," Ringo announced as they arrived at the mansion. The kept their suppressed MP-7 submachine guns hidden under their fire jackets as they entered the mansion. Chaos among the staff grew as people woke to fire alarms and sprinklers.

"Lots of chaos, but still quiet out front," Shepherd announced over the tactical frequency.

Ringo and company made their way through the kitchen to the basement entrance. The layout of the mansion so far matched the blueprints they had received for their mission planning. Reaching the door, the found that it was secured by a keypad.

"Oracle, we need a code," Ringo said over the tactical frequency.

"Standby," Coolio said.

"Hurry if you can, please," Ringo said, hearing shouting and people approaching.

"I can't get into the system and there's nothing in the building schematics," Coolio said.

"Can you cut power to the building?" Ringo asked.

"This grid is old. It's not connected to a network," Coolio replied frantically. "I'll keep trying."

"Snake One-Two, I have eyes on a transformer on the west side," Shepherd reported, after listening to their exchange. "I can take it out."

"Do it," Kruger ordered.

Seconds after Kruger ordered the hit, the power flickered and then went out in the mansion. Ringo pulled out his flashlight, but found that the keypad was still illuminated on a battery backup. Before he could say something to Coolio, he heard the lock click and the door started to swing open.

He stepped back, aiming his MP-7 as an armed man emerged. Ringo fired three suppressed shots, dropping the man. Ringo nodded to the rest of the team. He mounted his flashlight to the MP-7 and they proceeded down the stairs single-file.

"That woke them up out front," Shepherd reported. "They're starting to harass the emergency workers."

"Same on this side. Weapons tight until the team gets out," Kruger ordered.

"Copy that," Shepherd replied. "Standing by."

Ringo and company moved down the stairs. They encountered two more armed men but summarily dispatched them as they made it to the ground level. Using their lights, they identified the computer equipment and went to work setting up the charges to destroy it.

When they were finished, Ringo reported, "Bucket Two-Zero is set, we're moving to exfil."

"Shit! They just shot one of the firefighters!" Shepherd yelled over frequency.

Without waiting for Kruger's permission, Shepherd picked off the Russian thug that had just executed the unarmed firefighter. The other guards ran for cover as they realized they were dealing with a sniper and attempted to locate him.

"One down," Shepherd reported.

"Goddammit, Wolf!" Kruger yelled.

Ringo and his team made their way out of the basement. When they reached the kitchen, Cowboy shot a guard that had been hiding and looking out the window for the sniper. Churchill and Taylor pulled out more C4 from their packs and tossed it into the living area and kitchen.

"Bucket is coming out," Ringo announced.

"Roger," Kruger said. "Wolf, cover them."

They ran out into the circle drive and jumped into one of the waiting firetrucks, as Shepherd picked off fighters around them. As soon as they were in the truck, Taylor pulled out the remote detonator and detonated the C4.

A fireball blew out the first floor windows and the floor above the basement collapsed. Cowboy drove the big firetruck, speeding out as the Russian fighters tried to stop them in vain. Taylor and Churchill returned fire, killing the fighters behind them while Ringo, sitting next to Cowboy, focused on the ones out front.

They made it out of the gate and turned right, nearly rolling the big firetruck onto two wheels as they cleared the mansion property. "Bucket is clear," Ringo announced. Kruger watched as the second floor of the mansion partially collapsed and the house went up in flames.

"Copy that," Kruger said. "Snake One and Two moving to the rally point."

Kruger picked up his rifle and collapsed the bipod. Suvarova was dead and Helios was down. There was only one target left to take down to end the nightmare that had destroyed Odin.

CHAPTER SEVENTY-TWO

Borya Medvev sat down on the leather chair in the living room of his small apartment. He was holding a bottle of vodka that he had grabbed straight from the shelf as soon as he had walked in the door. It had been that kind of day.

It had started before dawn. Sasha Kalesnikov had called him to tell him that his boss and leader of the Podolsk Bratva had been assassinated and his house burned to the ground. It all seemed like a bad dream.

But it wasn't a bad dream. Medvev was dressed and on scene within an hour of the phone call. The house had been reduced to rubble and smoldering ash. Suvarova and nearly twenty of his men were dead. The Podolsk Bratva, the second most powerful organization within the Russian Mafia, had just been decapitated.

Of course, that wasn't the worst of it. The delivery of the Helios equipment had gone flawlessly. Having so many trucks at the airport all loaded with computer equipment had caused the Americans to chase after the wrong one, allowing the actual truck to arrive unscathed. Everything was unloaded and ready to be assembled. It was only a matter of days before Helios went live once more.

But now, just like Suvarova, Helios had been assassinated. There was nothing left. Everything he had worked for during his twenty year career would be lost. When the Kremlin found out that he had brokered the deal under the guise of a state operation, he would be executed as a traitor.

It would have been worth it, had it worked. Suvarova had offered him a seat at the high table in exchange for delivering Helios. He never told his superiors about Helios or his meeting in Lajes. They only knew that he was running a counter-intelligence operation against the Americans. He knew they wouldn't appreciate the significance of Helios or its capabilities. They were slow to embrace technology in that way.

Part owner of a Russian tech firm, Suvarova was the only man who could truly understand its capabilities. The Russian Bratva was deeply embedded in the operations of the Russian Federation anyway, how was it wrong to take a piece of the pie for himself?

Medvev leaned back and closed his eyes. He thought about what he would do next. He had no intentions of spending the rest of his life in a Russian prison or being executed as a traitor. He had accumulated over a million U.S. dollars in bribes and kickbacks over his career and kept it in a Swiss bank account for just this purpose. Maybe it was time to retire.

Retirement was starting to sound like his best option. He had a go-bag full of cash and fake passports standing by. He could easily make his way into Europe and then access his account. He would pick an island somewhere far away, living on a warm, sun drenched beach surrounded by scantily clad women.

As Medvev started to drift off to sleep, he felt something cold and firm press against the back of his head. He didn't have to open his eyes. He immediately recognized it as the cold steel of a suppressed barrel.

"I didn't think you'd come so soon," Medvev said in Russian. His voice was calm and steady. He knew if the Russians didn't get to him, the people who killed Suvarova would. He just didn't think it would happen on the same day.

"This is for Eli Blackman," the man replied in Russian.

"They'll come for you, you know," Medvev said, his eyes still closed as he awaited his end. "Everyone involved. They'll kill all of you."

"Quidquid victor ero," the man said as he pulled the trigger and sent Medvev into the abyss.

CHAPTER SEVENTY-THREE

Spectre and Decker landed in New Orleans just after 10 a.m. and headed for Bear's house outside of Baton Rouge. A little over two hours after deplaning, they reached the familiar path leading through the woods to Bear's secluded home.

They were both exhausted. They had spent the last two nights at Tanner's bedside while waiting for her parents to drive up from Florida. A weather event in Orlando and the Southeast had cancelled all flights, forcing them to forego the fastest option.

Tanner's condition was better, but still critical. After lengthy surgeries, the doctors were now more optimistic about her chances for walking and functioning again, but the risk of infection was high. It would be a long road for her.

Spectre pulled his truck up to the metal gate as he crossed the cattle guard and pressed the call button. "You're late," came the gruff reply as the gate swung open.

"It's good to be home," Spectre said as he continued through the gate and it closed behind them.

As they pulled up to Bear's large cabin, they saw Bear standing out front waiting for them. A few seconds later, an attractive, middle-aged woman appeared holding their son.

"Umm…Who's that?" Decker asked.

"Good question," Spectre said as he killed his truck's diesel engine and exited.

"Welcome home," Bear said as he walked to Spectre and shook his hand. "There's someone I'd like you two to meet."

After Spectre stepped aside and turned toward the woman holding his son, Decker hugged Bear. "It's good to see you again," she said.

"Cal, Michelle, this is Lynn," Bear said as he walked with them to the woman standing on the porch.

She had light brown hair and was taller than Bear and Decker. Spectre guessed that she was 5'10" or so. She handed Calvin to Decker as she smiled and extended her hand to Spectre. "It's nice to finally meet you. I've heard so much about you."

Spectre awkwardly shook her hand. "It's nice to meet you," he said as he turned and exchanged a look with Decker.

"Lunch is ready," Bear said. "C'mon inside. We have something to tell you."

Bear and Lynn walked in hand-in-hand. Spectre turned and kissed Calvin on the forehead before they followed them into the cabin.

As they sat down at the table, Bear placed a bowl of gumbo in front of each of them. Decker held Calvin in her left arm as she started to eat.

"Can I get you anything to drink?" Bear asked.

"Water is fine, thanks," Spectre said.

"Tea please," Decker replied.

After serving their drinks, Bear sat down next to Lynn. "I want to hear all about what happened while you were gone, but first, we have an announcement. Lynn and I are getting married."

Spectre choked on the water he had just sipped and started coughing. "What?" he asked incredulously as he tried to recover.

"Bear, that's great, congratulations," Decker said. "When did this happen?"

"He proposed yesterday," Lynn replied. "It was very sweet."

Spectre looked at Decker. "Am I still drugged? Is that what's going on here?"

"No, you weren't drugged," Lynn answered. "We're sorry we didn't tell you sooner."

"Lynn and I have been best friends for almost twenty years," Bear explained.

"*Twenty years?*" Spectre exclaimed. "Holy hell!"

"We've only been dating for about six months," Lynn explained. "We were friends, but I was married."

"We didn't want to tell anyone until her divorce was final," Bear said. "And you've been so busy with changing jobs and all the spy shit you've been doing, I didn't want to bother you with it."

"Jesus," Spectre said, staring into his gumbo, not sure how to respond.

Decker handed Calvin to Spectre and then walked around to hug them both. "Well I'm happy for you. Welcome to the family, Lynn," Decker said as she kissed Bear on the cheek and hugged Lynn.

"I'm happy for you too," Spectre said. "It's just…holy shit, I had no idea."

"I really wanted to tell you, Cal," Bear said. "But I wanted to tell you when the time was right. Things just kept getting in the way."

"Well, I'm thrilled for you, Bear. You both seem very happy," Decker said as she went back to her seat.

"We are," Lynn said, stroking Bear's hand. "We've been best friends for so long. Something always seemed like it was missing, until I finally left Daniel. Now things just...*click*."

"Daniel is a pussy," Bear grumbled.

"Sweetheart!" Lynn yelped.

"Sorry, but he is," Bear said unapologetically.

"That's awesome," Decker said. "You should always marry your best friend. I did."

Spectre was still sitting there, staring with a dumbfounded look at the new couple. "What else are you two hiding? Kids? More dogs? Are you secretly Russian spies?"

"Well, I have two kids," Lynn said. "They're with their dad this weekend. And a dog named Ralph. I don't know anything about Russia."

"Speaking of spies," Bear said. "Why don't you tell us about your adventures?"

Spectre was still speechless so Decker started the story, explaining everything that had happened after she arrived in D.C. and why she hadn't been able to check in. Spectre eventually joined the story, telling the parts of what he remembered of his captivity and meeting with President Clifton.

"Glad she'll be out of office soon," Bear grumbled. "Good riddance."

"So what's going to happened to Odin?" Bear asked.

"Jeff Lyons was killed," Spectre said. "I think it's over."

"What about the people responsible?" Lynn asked. They had intentionally left out the part about Kruger leading the new Project Archangel due to its highly classified nature.

"Dead," Spectre said. "Stone was killed by the Russians. Helios was destroyed by Kruger and what was left of Odin. It's over."

"What do you think your company will say about you wandering off after a flight?" Bear asked.

Spectre frowned. "That's probably over too. I had a voicemail when we landed. I have a meeting with the chief pilot on Monday morning. I have a feeling they will be fixing the glitch and sending me on my way."

"You hated that job anyway," Bear said.

Spectre nodded. "Getting fired still sucks though."

"So what will you do for work?" Lynn asked.

"I don't know," Spectre said as he shrugged. "I got an offer to do a contracting job similar to one I had a few years ago."

Spectre saw the recognition in Bear's face. He was talking about Project Archangel and the offer Kruger and Chapman had extended.

"The boys are back in town!" Bear said with a chuckle.

"I haven't given them an answer yet, but I don't think it's for me," Spectre said as he looked at his wife and son. "It's time to move on and be with my family."

"Are you sure?" Bear asked. "You're still young!"

"I want to watch my son grow up," Spectre said. "We've been through a lot in the last five years. I think it's time to hang it up for good."

"I'll support anything you do," Bear said. "You know that."

"I think it's great," Lynn added. "Family is important."

"Cal will find something," Decker said reassuringly. "We're not worried."

"Well, I'm glad that chapter of your life is finally over," Bear said. "There's something to be said for the quiet life. I hope it stays that way for you."

"Me too," Spectre said.

EPILOGUE

D irector Chapman was waiting for them at the FBO at Dulles when they landed. He greeted each member of the team as they descended the stairs onto the ramp and thanked each of them for their service.

After the mission in Russia, they had returned to London and debriefed the mission. They spent the next two days recuperating before flying back to D.C., leaving behind Sierra, Cowboy, Ringo and his men. They would regroup later once proper protocols were in place for where and how Project Archangel would train and operate permanently.

Kruger was the last one off the plane after Shepherd and Tuna helped Coolio down. Coolio was doing much better, walking to the door of the aircraft under his own power before they helped him down the stairs and into a waiting wheelchair. He still had a long road of recovery ahead, but for someone who had nearly died in a building collapse a week earlier, he was doing extremely well.

"Welcome back, Kruger," Director Chapman said as Kruger reached the bottom of the stairs. "You did an outstanding job."

"It was all them," Kruger said, nodding to his teammates who were waiting near the vehicles lined up to take them home.

"And our friends across the pond as well, I know," Chapman said excitedly. "It was a great field run. This unit can do great things."

"Not now, bub," Kruger said. "Everyone needs some downtime."

"Right...of course!" Chapman replied. "Take as much time as you need. I'll have my assistant start working on finding applicants for you and a base of operations. We might even be able to get your old place in Tampa back."

Kruger held his hand up. "Not now," he said. "We'll talk about the way ahead later."

"Still on the fence?"

"Later," Kruger said as he turned to meet his team.

Kruger joined the rest of his team. "You each have your own vehicle and driver. They'll take you wherever you want to go. Someone will be in contact with you to let you know the way ahead, but expect a couple of weeks off at the very least. You've all earned it."

"What about you?" Tuna asked. "Are you going to come back?"

"I don't know," Kruger said. "But if I do, you'll be the first to know."

"Kruger, can I talk with you for a second?" Shepherd asked. "Privately?"

Kruger nodded and the two stepped out of earshot from the others on the ramp. "What's up?"

"You haven't mentioned what happened in Russia. I know you were pissed and said not to go against you again, but those people were dying and—"

"You did what you had to do," Kruger said, cutting him off. "That's just who you are."

"Well, that's the other part," Shepherd said. "I know you're not sure whether you'll come back, but I am. I think I'm done."

"I understand," Kruger said.

"You do?"

"You're *The Wolf* for a reason," Kruger said. "You work better alone and don't do well with orders. I get that. This life isn't for everyone."

"I just want a second chance. I want to try having a real life again. I think I'm ready now," Shepherd said.

Kruger held out his hand. "Then go get it, bub."

"Thank you," Shepherd said as he shook Kruger's hand.

The two returned to the group. Before anyone could ask, Shepherd spoke up. "I just wanted you all to know it's been a pleasure serving with you. But it's time for me to move on. Thank you for saving my life, and for giving me a second chance."

"We're sorry to see you go," Tuna said, shaking Shepherd's hand.

"I'll make sure your name is clear as soon as I get to a computer," Coolio said. "There will be no record of anything that happened in Syria, or the warrants in Mississippi. I promise."

"Thanks, bud," Shepherd said as he turned and shook Coolio's hand. "I really appreciate it."

"Looks like it's just you and me left," Coolio said, looking up at Tuna. "You *are* staying, right?"

"For now," Tuna said with a grin. "Somebody's got to hold this place down until Nurse Kruger makes up his mind."

* * *

Kruger had the driver drop him off at his apartment in Falls Church. He hadn't spent much time there since joining Odin. He still hadn't unpacked most of his boxes, but it had been a place he called home in between operations.

Tossing his keys on top of one of the boxes, Kruger went straight to the fridge and grabbed a cold beer. He popped open the top and collapsed onto the sofa. His body was still aching and he was jet lagged.

"I'm getting too old for this shit," Kruger grumbled as he took a long pull from the bottle.

Less than five minutes after sitting down, Kruger heard a knock at his door. He instantly jumped to his feet, drawing the Glock 19 from its appendix-carry concealed holster. Sierra had warned them that the Bratva would try to seek revenge should they find their identities, but Kruger couldn't imagine that it would happen so soon. Still, he was on full alert.

As Kruger quietly approached the door, he heard more knocking. "Mr. Mack, it's Kevin," a voice said. It was his apartment building manager.

Kruger checked the peephole in the door. Kevin was standing there holding a package. There was no one else around.

Tucking the Glock back into its holster, Kruger covered it with his untucked shirt and opened the door.

"I'm so sorry to bother you," Kevin said. "But I saw you come in and I wanted to deliver this before I went home. I know you travel a lot, so when they tried delivering it a third time, I went ahead and signed for it for you."

"What is it?" Kruger asked gruffly.

"It's from some law firm," Kevin said, handing the package to Kruger. "I didn't open it."

"Thanks, bub," Kruger said as he took the package and closed the door.

"You're welcome!" Kevin yelled through the door.

Kruger opened the package as he walked back to the small living area. It was a DVD with Kruger's name written on it with a Sharpie.

With no DVD player or even a TV to speak of, Kruger walked into the bedroom and fished out his laptop. He plugged it in and powered it on as he sat on the bed and took the DVD out of its case.

When the laptop was ready to go, Kruger inserted the DVD and hit play. Jeff Lyons appeared on screen, sitting at his desk.

"Hello, Kruger," he began. "I know it's probably a cliché, but if you're seeing this, I'm dead...for real this time. That sucks."

Lyons paused for effect before continuing. "Hopefully I explained to you how Odin works before I died. If I have, skip to the next chapter. If not, sit down and grab some popcorn because it'll take a few minutes."

Kruger skipped to the next chapter. He didn't need or want to hear the story of Odin again. In fact, he was ready to have that part of his life behind him.

"Now that you know about Odin," Lyons continued, "let's talk about the way ahead. I'll keep it short and sweet because I know you're not a fan of bullshit. As part of the charter of Odin, each member sitting at the table was eligible to designate an heir. This heir would be given the passing member's seat at the high table and inherit some or all of his estate. The option also existed to designate no one and have the shares of Odin roll back to the remaining members. That was the case with Stevens. He had no immediate family and chose no one to assume his position.

"Now, traditionally, the heir would be family. I inherited my stake from my father and he from his father, but as you may have guessed, I don't have any family. You and your team are my family. Which is why I'm offering my stake to you," Lyons said.

Kruger sat speechless listening to Lyons. He didn't know what to think of the billionaire's offer.

"That is, if you want it, of course," Lyons continued. "You have thirty days from the date of receipt of this message to contact my lawyers. If you agree, they have been instructed to give you everything as my sole heir, with a modest donation to charity of course. But the important thing is that Odin will live on through you."

"I know it's a lot to process. It was a lot for me to process as well, but I urge you to carefully consider my offer. Yes, you'll probably have to deal with Cruz and Stone, and they can be assholes, but the good you can do will be immeasurable. You can make Odin even better than I ever could. I know it in my heart.

"So in closing, please consider my offer. There's obviously nothing I can do if you don't, except maybe haunt you and possess your TV or something," Lyons said with a chuckle. "But seriously, think about it. Thank you for everything you've done for Odin. Thank you for your service. See you in Valhalla."

"Stamus Contra Malum," Lyons said before the video quit playing.

Kruger closed the laptop and set it aside. He went back to his kitchen, bypassing the fridge and going straight for the Crown Royal in the cabinet. He took a long swig and just stood there, considering his options.

It was a lot to process. On one hand, he was ready to leave the operator life and go on to help people in different ways. Nursing school might not be the best option, but it seemed like a good idea at least. It was still very much on the table.

On the other hand, he firmly believed that those who had the capability to stand up against the bullies and psychopaths of the world should do it. He was a sheepdog and like the rest of the team, his nature was to stand against the evil of the world.

But even that left him with two options. Director Chapman had offered him the reins of an elite fighting force. One that was legitimate, reporting to his government and fighting for his country. It wasn't nebulous. There was no convoluted history of billionaires trying to play puppet master. It was simply doing what needed to be done to promote his nation's interests and ensure national security. It was something a soldier could understand.

And now Lyons had left him a parting gift from the afterlife. Not only was he offering full control of Odin, but all of his assets. Kruger would become a billionaire overnight, or whatever Lyons's net worth was after the government and charity got their share. It was still enough to never want for money or have to beg a bureaucrat for funding for his team. It was incredibly tempting.

He suspected, however, that the same pitch was possibly being given to two other people. There was no way to know who Stone and Cruz had picked to succeed them. Would they be worse? Would they be better? How would they use their newfound positions? Would he end up fighting them again with Project Archangel anyway?

There were more questions than answers. As Kruger took another swig from the bottle of Crown, he decided that it was best to step back and give himself some time to think. He needed to go home to Florida and spend some time with nature to get his head right before he rolled into another quagmire.

It was time to go fishing.

Thanks for reading! Stay tuned for *I AM THE SHEEPDOG* (Alex Shepherd Series Book Two) coming in 2018!

If you enjoyed this book, please leave a review!

VISIT WWW.CWLEMOINE.COM FOR MORE INFORMATION ON NEW BOOK RELEASE DATES, BOOK SIGNINGS, AND EXCLUSIVE SPECIAL OFFERS.

ACKNOWLEDGMENTS

To all my readers, thank you for continuing on this journey with me. I appreciate the comments, feedback, and reviews. It has been an honr.

To **Mrs. Beverly Foster**, thank you for everything you do. You're an awesome editor, even when I am hard-headed. I appreciate your hard work.

To **Dr. Doug Narby**, as always, thank you for your help in content-editing. I appreciate having your wisdom and feedback. Your notes are always on point and help me to be a better writer.

Michael Hayes, you rock, man! I can't tell you how great it is to have you as a beta reader. It is awesome to get instant feedback and to have someone pushing me along to write more. Thank you!

Pat Byrnes, you've been there since the beginning. Thank you for being my first fan and beta reader. I appreciate your comments and reviews.

Thanks again to everyone that has supported me. Hopefully it is only just beginning. I can't wait to see what the future will hold.

Thanks for reading!

C.W. Lemoine is the author of *SPECTRE RISING*, *AVOID. NEGOTIATE. KILL.*, *ARCHANGEL FALLEN*, *EXECUTIVE REACTION*, *BRICK BY BRICK*, *STAND AGAINST EVIL*, *ABSOLUTE VENGEANCE*, and *THE HELIOS CONSPIRACY*. He graduated from the A.B. Freeman School of Business at Tulane University in 2005 and Air Force Officer Training School in 2006. He is a former military pilot that has flown the F-16 and F/A-18. He currently flies for a Legacy U.S. Airline. He is also a certified Survival Krav Maga Instructor and sheriff's deputy.

www.cwlemoine.com

Facebook
http://www.facebook.com/cwlemoine/
Twitter:
@CWLemoine

Made in the USA
Coppell, TX
04 October 2021